CAPE *of* STORMS

a novel

BIANCA BOWERS

CAPE OF STORMS

A catalogue record for this book is available from the National Library of Australia

Print ISBN-13: 978-0-6484426-4-6
EPub ISBN-13: 978-0-6484426-5-3

Second Edition Printed and Bound in Australia by Ingramspark.

Typeset in Adobe Jenson Pro by Bianca Bowers.

ENVIRONMENTAL RESPONSIBILITY
This book is printed using the print-on-demand-model i.e. it is only printed when an order has been received. This type of manufacturing reduces supply chain waste, greenhouse emissions, and conserves valuable natural resources.

For my motherland

GLOSSARY

A LIST OF AFRIKAANS, ZULU, COLLOQUIAL WORDS, AND TERMINOLOGY USED IN THE NARRATIVE. IN ORDER OF APPEARANCE.

COOLIE a derogatory term for a person of Indian origin

AFRIKAANS a language derived from dutch settlers

NGA a clicking sound made with the tongue

NET BLANKES whites only

KNOBKERRIE a wooden club with a large knob at one end

JA afrikaans origin, and slang for 'yes'

CABO DAS TORMENTAS cape of storms

MEVROU Mrs

NOOIT never

JY IS DIE MOEILIKHEID, EK SÊ you are trouble, I tell you

UITKOM get out

LAAT MY KLASKAMER get out of my class

EK SAL MY ONDERWYSER GEHOORSAAM I will obey my teacher

OUMA/OUPA Afrikaans words for grandmother/grandfather

DORP small town

GRENADILLA passionfruit

KOEKSUSTER a dutch/afrikaans syruppy sweet

SANGOMA African witchdoctor

MUTI medicine

MY MEISIE IS SO GROOT! HOE OUD IS JY? My girl is so big. How old are you?

EK KAN DIT NIE GLO NIE I can't believe it

COZZIE swimsuit

MOSSIEPOP sparrow's fart

NOG A DAG, ASSEBLIEF One more day, please

ÊK SAL PRAAT MET I will speak to…

BAIE GOED very good

GOEIE MÔRE good morning

OPPENHEIMERS one of the richest families in the world, and involved in Anglo American Corporation and De Beers Consolidated Mines

BAAS boss

YEBO yes

KAYA servant's quarters

ROBOT traffic light

DANKIE thank you

WELKOM ALMAL welcome everyone

MÂ mother

TOKOLOSH an evil spirit, the size of a leprechaun

NEE no

KOPPIE a granite ridge

DROIT DE SEIGNEUR 'lord's right'

DASSIES from old Dutch dasje, meaning 'badger'

MATRICULATION final year of high school

REFERENDUM a 1992 referendum on ending apartheid

TOYI TOYI a dance used in political protests

IFP inkatha freedom party

ANC african national congress

COSATU congress of south african trade unions

CODESA convention for a democratic south africa

SADF south african defence force

RECORD OF UNDERSTANDING 1992 agreement between government & ANC, dealing with constitutional assembly/interim government/political prisoners

BUNNY CHOW a half loaf of hollowed-out bread filled with curry

TULA zulu word for 'hush'

COLOURED a person of mixed race

MPNF MultiParty Negotiating Forum

COSAG Concerned South African's Group

SHEBEEN an illicit bar where alcohol is sold without a licence

SAMP an African food consisting of dried corn kernels that have been stamped and chopped until broken

LOBOLA amount paid (usually cows) for a prospective bride

ASSAGEI a zulu throwing spear

SAWUBONA zulu greeting for hello

EISH colloquial exclamation in zulu

CREMORA a sachet of evaporated milk, used in coffee and tea

AIKONA zulu exclamation for 'no way!' or similar

KIKUYU the largest ethnic group in Kenya

MAU MAU the mau mau revolt was a war in the British Kenya Colony

BRAAI south african word for barbecue

BOEREWORS south african spicy sausage

CURFEW/PASS law an apartheid law limiting the movements of black citizens in white urban areas between 9pm and 4am

EUGENE TERRE'BLANCHE afrikaner nationalist, white suprema-cist, founder of the AWB, major figure in right-wing backlash against apartheid

AWB afrikaner weerstandsbeweging (afrikaner resistance movement)

GAAN KAK piss off in afrikaans

PANGA a broad-bladed African knife used as a weapon or an implement for cutting sugar cane

VOETSAK afrikaans for 'get lost' or 'fuck off'

TSOTSI a young urban criminal from a township area

MELK TERT milk tart, south african dessert made with sweet pastry crust and milk custard filling

YISLAAIK YONG afrikaans exclamation (similar to bloody hell)

AMARULA COFFEE similar to Irish Coffee, but made with a creamy liqueur made from the fruit of the African Marula tree

FLOSSIE Afrikaans slang for mistress

LAW ARTICLES law articles a law student is required to work with a practicing attorney for a period of time (up to 2 years) before they sit the board exam

BLUE BOTTLES portuguese man o' war with stinging tentacles

AG oh in afrikaaans

BAKKIE a pickup truck

BARBEL catfish

SAPS south african police services (south african police force in apartheid era)

NINETEEN VOETSAK/19VOETSAK a humorous afrikaans/colloquial expression for a very long time

WONDERBOOM afrikaans — directly translated as wonder tree

MADIBA nelson mandela's clan name — a xhosa term colloquially meaning 'troublemaker'

KIST a wooden chest

O Cape of Storms!
After all I've seen and suffered here,
there are strong links that bind me to thee still

~ Thomas Pringle

PART I

1982 - 1988

CHAPTER 1

The infrastructure of my world began to decay when I collided with apartheid during the summer of 1982. The warmth of my mother's petite hand guided me along Hill Street, where crimson streaks formed in the dusky African sky. We paused on the pavement, splattered with mottled bird droppings, and waited for a break in the rush hour traffic.

'Those coolie mynas make such a racket,' said my mother.

'What's a coolie?' I said.

'Nga,' she made a clicking sound with her tongue, which usually signalled her annoyance. 'It means loud.'

I nodded and looked up to see hordes of Indian myna birds returning to their nests in the Natal mahogany trees that separated the dual carriageway. My mother clutched my hand before crossing the road and we hugged the inner sidewalk, like a Formula 1 racing car would hug the inside lane. Her anxiety pulsed like an electric current amidst the streams of pedestrians who raced past us, destination downtown, to join the congested taxi rank queues.

When we reached the shopping arcade she ushered me

toward the concrete ramp and we followed the smell of cheeseburgers to the Wimpy Bar entrance. I stopped to let a black-suited myna strut territorially across our path. In those nanoseconds, something other than the bird's orange crown and yellow beak caught my attention — a black and white sign, nailed above the door. It read:

NET BLANKES

Having been forced to learn Afrikaans from Grade One, I translated the words — only whites — in my head. It didn't make sense. I asked my mother to explain.

She released my hand and sighed loudly. 'That is something you don't need to know.'

I studied her furrowed brow and pursed lips and felt my curiosity tug at me, like the myna tugged at a Wimpy wrapper stuffed into the mouth of a discarded coke bottle.

'Please mom, I want to know.'

She shook her head and muttered, 'Nga, it means that only whites are allowed in the Wimpy.'

'What's a white?' I shrugged

Her hazel eyes searched the empty arcade and rested on an African man, who used a gnarled wooden knobkerrie as a walking stick. He had the type of weathered skin you'd see on an elephant's trunk, and a crooked back that curved into a question mark. She waited for him to shuffle past before she spoke.

'That man is a black man', she whispered, 'and we are white'.

I frowned and said, 'I still don't understand.'

She sighed loudly and rubbed her forehead. 'The colour of our skin is white.' She touched the skin on her arm to illustrate her point. 'The colour of that man's skin is black.'

I nodded my understanding so far.

'Ja,' she said. Her voice dangled like a hooked fish poised for release.

I looked at my mother, and then through the Wimpy windows. 'But, there are black people in the Wimpy,' I said.

Her shoulders drooped forward as if they too were sighing.

'Black people can work in there, Ros, but only white people are allowed to eat.'

I stared at her, open-mouthed. Awareness engulfed my mind like a fire spreading through the veld and the injustice of her revelation burned wildly. 'But, why? That's not fair.'

'It's a rule,' she said.

'I thought that rules were supposed to help people?'

'Ag, honestly, Ros, why are you so difficult?'

'What is Mohini?' I said.

'What?' she said, caught off guard.

'If we are white, and that man is black, then what is Mohini?'

She narrowed her eyes and scrutinised me like an explosive device. 'Mohini is Indian,' she said, 'and before you ask me any more questions, no, Mohini is not allowed in there either.'

'At Sunday School they say that God is love. I don't think that God would be happy with this rule.'

'I told you. You're too young to understand.'

'I do understand,' I said. 'Jesus loves white people more than blacks and Indians.'

Her cheeks flushed and she slapped my face. 'Sometimes you have to do things you don't like. Now, take my hand, your father's waiting for us.'

When I didn't move, she placed her hand behind the small of my back and pushed me across the threshold of the black and white sign, and into the home of the hamburger, where the upbeat sounds of Michael Jackson marched out of the speakers.

'What about Michael Jackson?' I said.

'Speak to your daughter,' she said, pushing me toward my father.

'Finally,' said my father, 'I was about to call a search party.' He looked at my mother, then at me, then back at my mother.

My mother shot him one of her notorious dirty looks, then sat down next to him without saying a word.

'Hmmm. Well, I went ahead and ordered everyone's favourite,' he said, as if the universe had not tilted.

I sat opposite my parents and scrutinised them like strangers. I wondered why I saw things so differently. Rules were supposed to be good, but this colour rule seemed bad. The clatter of a tray jolted me out of my thoughts. Our jolly, black waitress didn't seem to mind that she could work, but not dine, in the Wimpy. I entwined my arms like a straitjacket across my chest, and thought of all the years I had been oblivious to the colour rule. I felt foolish. Deceived. My mind reeled like a fishing line in deep waters.

CHAPTER 2

Layers of discrimination were stripped in the four years following that Wimpy Bar episode — right down to the word coolie. And each year, the anger, shame, and disappointment continued to burn inside of me like one of those candles that are designed to never go out. I may have been a child, but I knew right from wrong.

I grew up in a house called *Sea Breeze*, with my parents, my Uncle Jericho, Mohini (our housekeeper) and Gunther (our blue-eyed Weimaraner). The Sea Breeze Estate, a throwback to Palladian architecture, stood in the Durban suburb of Umhlanga Rocks, and overlooked the Indian Ocean and lighthouse. Once through the decorative wrought iron gates and up the winding driveway to the fountain statue, you entered through double wooden doors that led into a grand circular entrance hall with polished, yellowwood floors, that had been constructed from Sea Breeze's own yellowwood plantation — a plantation that Uncle Jericho forbade me to enter for reasons unbeknown to me at that stage of my life. Of the multiple rooms that stretched over four levels, via a spiral staircase running through the centre of the house, I mostly sought refuge in three: the library, my bedroom, and Mohini's room.

The Sea Breeze Library, lit with green banker's lamps and furnished with aged leather armchairs, was my father's greatest passion. Its wood-panelled bookshelves extended to a mezzanine level, and were stocked with books that he had collected since childhood. Be it reference, entertainment, or my eternal thirst for knowledge, the Sea Breeze library had it all.

My bedroom, located in the third storey, was shaded by an umbrella thorn tree that attracted a family of vervet monkeys to my windowsill each morning. Beyond the tree, were views of the outdoor pool — edged with marine tiles, and embedded with a jade and turquoise dragonfly mosaic that paid homage to the dragonflies that nested in the nearby water garden — and the lighthouse — an immutable guardian with its ivory suit, vermilion top hat and compound eyes — which guarded one of South Africa's most treacherous coastlines, and, I liked to think, me. At night, I would stand at my bedroom window and count the twenty seconds it took for the lighthouse beam to illuminate—saying the word lighthouse out loud. The word *light*, so featherweight on my tongue, and *house*, as heavy as the anchor on Uncle Jericho's yacht.

When Mohini wasn't cooking, cleaning and waiting on us, you could usually find her tucked away in her room above the garages. Sandalwood incense tinged the air, and posters of Hindu deities adorned the marigold walls. A Ganesh figurine took pride of place in the centre of an altar that fit snugly in the far right corner of the room. More often than not, Mohini sat poised, on a crimson velvet cushion, in front of her prized possession; a cast iron treadle fiddle base Singer sewing machine. My head brimmed with memories of Mohini's brown, weathered fingers, gripping and guiding colourful threads into shape, and her petite foot, pressing rhythmically against the pedal; the comforting sound of the needle whirring and clicking as it zigzagged through fabric.

Mohini and my ouma were the only two people in the world who called me Lindy. As if they knew and recognised a different part of me. As if I belonged to them in a different way. In retrospect, Mohini knew me better than my own mother did. My mother excelled at being pleasant to Mohini's face, but sang a different tune behind her back. She loathed the scent of incense that burned daily in Mohini's room, referred to her food rituals as uncivilised, and vehemently discouraged me from partaking in Mohini's *funny* traditions and *evil* religion. Considering my mother and I clashed in every possible sense, I complied for the most part to keep the peace, but, when Mohini and I were alone, I eagerly partook in her funny traditions.

Cooking vegetable curry and eating it with our hands was one such funny pastime. I would watch as Mohini peeled and chopped the brown onions, and help her measure out the vibrant, pungent spices — saffron threads, ground orange turmeric, cumin seeds, fresh green chillies, chunky cinnamon sticks, and curry powder the colour of tabasco chillies. When the onions turned translucent in the battered silver pot, Mohini would add the garlic and spices to make the curry sauce, and within seconds the fragrance of India would fill the kitchen. Minutes later she would add the carrots, cauliflower, and potatoes and allow the ingredients to simmer while she cooked the rice. That was my cue to prepare our eating spot in Mohini's room. Kneeling down on the handwoven rug, I would gently unroll the rectangular turquoise straw mat, and lay it with two white ceramic bowls and turquoise linen napkins. Just before the pot came off the stove, Mohini would tip the frozen peas in, secure the lid, and let them cook in the steam. In Mohini's room, we kneeled and gave thanks before plunging our hands into the fragrant food. I'll never forget the first time I watched Mohini eat. A knife and fork had been my customary utensils, but Mohini used all five fingers of her right hand to scoop up the rice and curry into her mouth. Like so many of Mohini's rituals, it was completely foreign and yet so comforting.

Mohini's funny religion was another mystery that captivated me like a tree I wanted to climb. I visited her one morning before Sunday School, and found her cleaning the altar.

I pointed to the little statue in the centre of the altar that looked like an elephant with four arms. 'Can you tell me more about your God?'

'Your mother wouldn't like that, Lindy.'

'I know,' I said, remembering that my mother referred to the statue and colourful posters on Mohini's walls as idols, 'but I'm curious.'

'Okay, Lindy. Let's start with this picture. Brahma is the Creator,' she said. 'Like the Christians, the Hindus have a Trinity known as Brahma, Vishnu, and Shiva.'

I nodded.

'Christians believe that one God created the universe, the Hindus think of God and the Universe as one and the same.'

'I prefer that idea,' I said.

She smiled and continued. 'Hindus also believe that the universe undergoes three different cycles.' She used her fingers to count. 'The first is creation, the second is maintenance, and the third is destruction and renewal.'

'Destruction?' I said, having second thoughts about Hindu-ism. 'Is that like the Book of Revelations?'

'No,' she laughed. 'Not at all.' She pointed to the second poster. 'This is Vishnu, the Preserver. Vishnu maintains order and harmony of the universe.'

'This must be Shiva,' I said, pointing to the third poster.

'Yes,' said Mohini. 'Shiva is the Destroyer, but it is not a negative destruction. Shiva destroys the universe in order to prepare for its renewal at the end of each cycle.'

'Oh,' I said, sighing with relief.

'And it's not necessarily the physical world, Lindy. It's also a metaphor for a person's spiritual life and growth.'

'Why does your religion scare my mother?' I said.

'It's what she's been taught, Lindy.'

'Do you ever think about going to India,' I said, 'to get away from apartheid?'

'I would like to visit someday, Lindy, but India has its own form of apartheid.'

'It does?'

'There are people in India called the *Untouchables*. They are seen as the lowest of all classes. Doomed to be inferior forever. Untouchables would not be allowed to enter a Hindu temple, for example, and they would only be allowed to do menial jobs. It's called the Caste System.'

I shook my head in disbelief. 'I don't understand how people can be so mean to one another.'

She kissed me on the forehead and approached the altar. 'This is Ganesha, Shiva's first son, and the remover of obstacles. Most Hindu altars will have a statue of Ganesha.'

'What is the bell for?'

'I use it for worship,' she said, 'as well as these.' She pointed out a bell, an incense holder, a lamp, a water container with spoon, and a small pot of red kumkum powder. 'Each relate to one of the five senses, and they help to focus the mind when meditating.'

'What is meditation, Mo?'

'It's quiet time for the mind, Lindy. You sit or lie in a quiet place, focus on your breathing, and encourage your mind to be quiet. You can meditate for relaxation, or religious reasons, or to ponder a question. You should try it some time.'

I nodded. 'How does it work? I mean, if you have a question, or if you're worried about something. How does meditating help?'

'It connects you with your deeper self; your intuition. All the answers are deep within you, Lindy.' She tapped her fingers lightly against the centre of my chest. 'You can learn to tap into it.'

Mohini fed my mind and soul in a way that nobody else did. She always seemed to be teaching me something. Unlike my school teachers, who force-fed information, Mohini guided with a gentle hand and heart.

'Why is there food here, Mo?' I pointed to the banana leaf dotted with samples of fruit and rice.

'Every morning I give an offering to Ganesha.'

'Is this yesterday's offering?'

'Yes, and you're just in time to help me replace it.'

I helped Mohini replace the burnt sandalwood incense sticks and withered flowers. We threw the browning banana leaf away and dressed a fresh green leaf with pomegranate, pineapple, cooked basmati rice, a chicken drumstick (taken from a fresh chicken curry), and sliced bananas in coconut milk.

An angry hoot-hoot-hoot interrupted us like rolling thunder. I hugged and thanked Mohini before I rushed out of her room and down the stairs toward the garage. On the drive to Sunday School I thought about how I hated being a child at the mercy of my parents and Uncle Jericho. Mohini, it seemed, was my only ally.

CHAPTER 3

Jericho Morris, my maternal great uncle, inherited Sea Breeze after my grandfather's accident. The brothers had been traveling in convoy with their spouses one Christmas when a flash flood and hailstorm resulted in a collision with an oversized truck. My grandparents' Jaguar crashed first, head-on, and became wedged underneath the lorry. Uncle Jericho, in the car behind, had swerved, but skidded, and clipped the side of the truck before rolling and crashing into a barrier. My grandparents, Uncle Jericho's wife, and his newborn son had died on impact. Jericho, my mother and her sister, Maeve, survived. After the accident, the sisters had gone to live with Jericho at Sea Breeze. Mohini was hired soon after to look after the house and the girls. The male bloodline dried up after that. My Aunty Maeve had married young, but never had children, while my mother only had me. So, unless my mother had another baby, or Jericho discovered an illegitimate love-child, the likelihood of a male heir to inherit Sea Breeze and the construction empire remained slim.

Before Morris Construction, my great-great grandfather had partnered with Henry Malvern, a fellow entrepreneur, during the gold boom in 1886. By anticipating and catering to the mining and building boom, they became the modern day equivalent of property developers. While Malvern managed the building materials, my great-great grandfather managed the building and construction. Both made a fortune by riding the wave of the gold boom, but at the height of their success they had a fallout and split the company. Morris Malvern became Morris Construction and the Malverns returned to their roots and became a building supply company. Before the split, the Morris family had lived in the wealthiest suburb of Joburg, Upper Houghton, but afterwards, Morris Senior had moved the family business to Durban and built Sea Breeze. He went on to grow the company into one of South Africa's top construction giants. Jericho had carried the torch and singlehandedly grown the business into an empire.

I only knew Jericho post his traumatic life event, and my time living under his roof would best be described as walking through a forest in a thunderstorm; dodging lightning bolts between trees. I imagined that the death of his wife and son had resulted in the death of Jericho himself, or at least a part of himself. Despite the tragedy being twenty years in the past, Jericho's anger lived on his face like it had happened yesterday.

Other than ruling Morris Construction and taking the family yacht, Cabo das Tormentas, out on cruises and fishing expeditions, Jericho's favourite pastime was mowing the lawn. Despite having the money to pay for a gardener, he chose to tame the rebellious grass himself. He referred to it as his hobby, but treated it like an obsession. Jericho maintained his flawless green grass by rigging the garden with sprinklers that snaked through the flower beds, and watched obsessively for the first blade to breach 1.5mm. Then he would unsheathe his polished Fox lawnmower and unleash its power on the offending lawn.

Nothing deterred him from mowing. Even when the heat could be seen hovering like an apparition above pavements and streets.

Like Jericho had his obsession, I had my imagination. On the days when I watched him manhandle the lawn I would imagine a family of subversive moles rising up to overtake Jericho's picture-perfect garden. In reality, I didn't wish what I imagined into existence, because the consequences for an un-suspecting mole popping its head out of its mountain of earth would be dire. The thought entertained me nonetheless, and helped to take the sting out of Jericho's harsh attitude toward me.

The most vivid and antagonistic memory I had of Jericho took place one Sunday lunchtime on a warm November day.

'Ros, come and sit down. Lunch is ready,' said my mother.

'Can't I sit outside today?' I said.

'Nga. Fine,' she said. 'Come and dish up.'

'What's with the long face?' said Jericho.

I shot him one of my mother's looks and said nothing.

'Rosalinde, Uncle Jericho is talking to you,' said my father.

I glimpsed tinges of red spreading across Jericho's cheeks, while I filled my lunch plate, and knew that I was balancing recklessly on a tightrope of tension.

'Don't give any food to Gunther,' said Jericho.

I ignored him for a second time, as you would a spoilt child, and headed toward the kitchen. Gunther was technically Jericho's dog, but everyone knew that he belonged to Mohini. She had once told me quietly that Jericho had bought Gunther for his wife and son before the accident. She said that Gunther served as a constant reminder of all that Jericho had held dear and lost. She had taken Gunther under her wing and Jericho had only been too happy, but it didn't stop him from asserting his power and projecting his pain now and again.

I paused in the kitchen to thank Mohini for the lunch and then joined Gunther outside in the shade of a blooming jacaranda tree. The sea breeze ruffled the jacaranda's lilac petals and I collected each one as it fell — on a curl of my hair, on my shoulder, my plate, my bare feet — and placed them in a neat pile in my lap, so that Mohini and I could thread the petals into bracelets and chains in the afternoon. I finished my lunch, but for a meaty bone. Gunther, who had been eyeing my roast beef, jumped up and wagged his bushy tail when I held the bone in the air and considered what to do with it. He cocked his head this way and that, punctuating his doggy smile with whines. I couldn't help but jump up and hug the glorious creature before I tossed the bone on the grass for him.

I saw the shadow before I turned my face into an oncoming slap. The force of the blow caught me unawares, and I fell backwards, landing on Gunther's hind leg. He yelped and took his bone with him, tail between his legs, around the side of the house.

'I told you NOT to feed Gunther!' Jericho said, looking down at me, red-faced, eyes alight.

Shock kept me on the ground, but emotional flames leapt from my eyes to his, fuelling the fire between us. Mohini ran to my side, but my parents stood passively and watched. Anger and humiliation welled inside of me as the shock of Jericho's outburst took root. A prickly silence descended as I purposefully stood up and collected my plate, knife, fork and serviette, before I stood opposite Jericho and said, 'I am not scared of you.'

He lifted his hand again. 'How dare you backchat me you

little shit!'

Mohini quickly stepped in and ushered me to her room. Once inside she pried the plate out of my hands and sat me down on her bed.

'Lindy, are you alright?'

My lip quivered, and my eyes blurred as they filled up like a lake in the rain. The sound of tears filled Mohini's little room and she held me close and smoothed my hair until the emotional waterfall became a trickle.

'Rosalinde.' The door burst open, and my father glared at me. 'Your mother and I are going for a drive. No thanks to you.'

'But...'

'Don't you dare say a word,' he said, raising his index finger and holding my gaze. 'You have no respect.'

CHAPTER 4

My father worked as a Labour Lawyer in a top tier
Durban law firm called Spencer & Mason, but he had
started from humbler beginnings. Not that he talked about it.
The only knowledge I could glean, during my school years, was
that he grew up in Kenya but left suddenly, at the age of ten,
due to some traumatic event that changed the trajectory of his
life. While my mother knew no other reality, my father never
forgot his working class roots, and instilled a deep sense of
gratitude in me for what I could easily have taken for granted.
My father remained impressed, and embarrassed, by his own
fortune, as if he had received permission to rub shoulders with
the rich, but felt like an imposter at heart. In many ways I identified with his sense of not belonging.

It would be easy for an outsider to think that my mother
had married into the Morris family versus my father. Jericho
treated my father like the son he never had, and my father
reciprocated his reverence. Morris Construction was Spencer
& Mason's biggest accounts, and the story goes that Jericho
introduced my parents to each other at a cocktail party. My

mother remained as much a mystery to me as my father's past. She seemed perfectly happy to keep her reading intelligence at a level no more taxing, stimulating, or subversive than Mills and Boon novels, and uniformly succumbed to the male opinion as if it were some sort of superior default position. Her sister, Maeve, seemed equally as pliable under her husband Léon's thumb. As husbands went, my mother and aunt shared much in common. Both seemed to have swallowed the myth that women should only aspire to be secretaries, wives or mothers, and that men claimed ownership to everything beyond that scope.

As I worked my way through school, I stopped trying to understand my role models and turned to dreaming about my eighteenth birthday and the day I could leave in protest. Hollywood birthed my love affair with America, and the fact that my parents, Uncle Jericho, and South Africans in general, harboured anti-American sentiment only served to reinforce my bond and remind me that I'd been born in the wrong country. The day that I bid farewell to South Africa and said hello to America propelled me as a future milestone.

Only one tiny detail bothered me about America. Why hadn't she intervened in apartheid? She held the title of most powerful nation in the world. Why hadn't she rescued us? Sanctions were not enough. As long as South Africa held the trump card of self-sufficiency, an American cold-shoulder was wasted. After school and on weekends I would lose hours in the Sea Breeze library, reading the aged pages of world history books. America didn't have a great track record either. Civil rights and African Americans. Slaves and slaveowners. Stories of inequality and injustice weren't buried that deep in the history books to know that America could easily be labelled *hypocrite.* Still, I dreamed of an American rescue from the evil Afrikaners who forced us to live in isolation from each other and speak Afrikaans.

Afrikaans was a story in itself. My father referred to it as the oppressor's language. After all, the Afrikaans were ultimately responsible for apartheid, and it was the Afrikaans who fortified their hierarchy with language. It wasn't enough to be white. The white Afrikaner reserved the title of supreme white. At school, Afrikaans was compulsory from Grade 1 to Matric, as well as being a failing subject. Like apartheid, I saw Afrikaans as the enemy, and, like I refused to eat that Wimpy burger in protest, I applied the same theory to my Afrikaans studies, making minimal effort and scraping through with thirty-three and a third percent year after year. My Afrikaans teachers declared me defiant, with the worst school incident occurring in my last year of primary school, under Mevrou Van Dyk, who had assigned me an oral assignment to talk about an admirable person. The assignment was open-ended; not limited to a politician or celebrity. 'Anyone,' she had clearly stated.

I chose Stompie Moeketsi; a black teenager and political activist from Soweto. When I announced the name of my admirable subject, Mevrou Van Dyk's olive complexion turned scarlet and she flung the chalkboard duster directly at my head. I ducked, and it hit a boy named Edward slap bang in the forehead. The class burst into laughter, and Edward, who would pass me love notes in class, smiled as if another one of cupid's arrows had hit him. But Mevrou van Dyk was not impressed. She stood up and shook her finger at me.

'Nooit, young lady, nooit. Jy is die moeilikheid, ek sê!'

'Why?' I said. 'Why is it unacceptable to talk about a young political activist? We should all be ashamed of ourselves for sitting here and doing nothing about apartheid. Lazing on our lilos in the pool, and sipping lemonade while our black brothers and sisters don't have the right to vote in their own country.'

Shock registered on everyone's faces and some gasped.

'Uitkom.' She pointed toward the door. 'Laat my klaskamer.'

'Fine,' I said. 'Where would you like me to go?'

She picked up her cane and thrashed the air with it. 'To the principal's office,' she yelled in English.

I gave her one of my mother's looks and went to the girl's toilet. I knew that trouble would swallow me whole for speaking my mind and disrespecting the teacher, but I didn't care. Stompie Moeketsi knew right from wrong and was not afraid to stand up and fight against injustice. What was I doing? Nothing. What had happened after that Wimpy episode? Why wasn't I fighting harder? Why wasn't I louder? Why was I afraid of being expelled from school, or being thrown in jail, like Stompie? These questions kept me up at night. Questions that I didn't want to meditate on lest I received answers I couldn't live up to.

Mevrou Van Dyk punished me with a month's detention, and thousands of lines. Every day after school I had to stay back for an hour and write her abominable lines in cursive:

Ek sal my onderwyser gehoorsaam.

Ek sal my onderwyser gehoorsaam.

Ek sal my onderwyser gehoorsaam.

Ek sal my onderwyser gehoorsaam.

Ek sal my onderwyser gehoorsaam.

Ek sal my onderwyser gehoorsaam.

Ek sal my onderwyser gehoorsaam.

Ek sal my onderwyser gehoorsaam.

Ek sal my onderwyser gehoorsaam.

Ek sal my onderwyser gehoorsaam.
Ek sal my onderwyser gehoorsaam.
Ek sal my onderwyser gehoorsaam.

It didn't deter me. I wrote the lines in the back of my English composition book, for the joy of irony, and felt further vindicated when she failed to make the connection.

CHAPTER 5

The annual visit to my ouma, who lived in a far flung Karoo dorpie called Coetzeesdorp, remained the highlight of my year. So, when my parents confirmed that we would be spending a week of the '88 Christmas holidays with Ouma, I bristled with anticipation. I say confirmed, because it was by no means definite. I learned that little fact in 1985, at age 11, when my mother cancelled our trip at the last minute. At that stage I hadn't worked out the reason behind my mother's general resistance to spending time with her mother-in-law, but my diary entries thereafter, coupled with memories from previous years, soon revealed a pattern. Every year, a month before we were due to visit Ouma, my mother would go to war with everyone around her; me, my father, Jericho, Mohini, random people in shopping centres. She would lock herself in her bedroom, permanently attach her ear to the telephone, and literally spend hours whispering to her sister, Maeve, in Joburg. I could safely say that if our annual trips were not followed by a trip to my Aunt Maeve and Uncle Léon in Joburg, then my mother might never have agreed to visit Ouma.

Coetzeesdorp made its home in the Karoo; a nine-hour drive from Sea Breeze. Geographically, it sat inside the Eastern Cape and outside the Orange Free State border. The word karoo had its origins in a khoi word meaning Land of Thirst, which aptly described the dry, dusty veld with its tufts of coarse, hay-coloured grassy mounds that pained the naked soles of your feet when you stepped on them. If you looked into the distance you would see the flat veld meet the clear blue sky on the horizon. My father called it God's country, because if you walked far enough you were sure to reach heaven.

Johannes Coetzee had developed and marketed the grid-shaped dorp to retirees who needed their money to go further, and who wanted a peaceful retirement in an isolated part of the country. My ouma had allegedly bought her house for nine thousand rand, a low price by any standard, along with thirty other retired couples and widows. My uncle William, who owned a farm near Pietermaritzburg in Natal, had offered my ouma a room, but she turned him down on the grounds that she still had plenty of years left in her.

The dorp felt like another planet; an accidental seed that never received enough water or sunlight to reach its full potential. With an Anglican church at its heart, it boasted a single-pump petrol station, a convenience store, and one coffee shop that peddled my ouma's baked treats. That was the extent of it. The dorp streets had never been tarred, so people walked instead of drove. You always knew when a visitor arrived, because the car tyres would loosen dirt and create a cloud of red dust behind it. The Dutch-style houses were whitewashed, trimmed with green gables, and surrounded by verandahs. While most of the gardens were paved and decorated with hardy potted plants, that conserved water like camels, my ouma's garden defied its surrounds and gleamed like an oasis in a sea of sand. She had insisted on having a bore hole so that she could rig sprinklers around her garden and grow vines of ruby grapes, beds of strawberries, trellises of grenadillas, and rows of lettuce, herbs, tomatoes, potatoes, and carrots. Her garden attracted bees, butterflies, birds, and chameleons. I loved finding chameleons, putting them on my arm, and watching them wobble uncertainly; their oversized eyes swivelling around and their elastic-like tongues catapulting toward unsuspecting flies.

Days, like the clouds, moved slowly in Coetzeesdorp, and our visits usually involved the same routine. Ouma and my father would sit outside on the verandah overlooking the above-ground pool, where I would spend much of my time. They would debate every subject under the infinite karoo sky, from the time the chameleons stalked the sun, to when the crickets began their nocturnal orchestra. I imagined my ouma imbibing the contents of every book, magazine, and newspaper article in the months between our visits; storing the information, questions, and opinions, like raindrops in a rural water tank, until my father arrived. My mother never took part in those discussions, nor did she swim in my ouma's pool. She insisted that I accompany her on a fifteen-minute drive to a public pool.

'Why?' I would always whine in reply. 'There's a pool right here.'

My mother would answer with a dirty look and tell my father to speak to his daughter.

While my ouma and father debated outside, Eunice, my ouma's maid, would slave away in the sweltering kitchen, baking syrupy koeksusters and sausage rolls for my father's eating pleasure. Every now and then my ouma would go inside to check on Eunice. I could hear her from the pool giving orders in Afrikaans, and Eunice answering her back in the oppressor's language. I could not get used to the sound of an African voice speaking Afrikaans. The mechanism of apartheid personified by the thing it fought to oppress. If Mohini and I were on the lowest rungs of the ladder, then Eunice surely lived at the bottom. I would listen to my ouma's commands, wince at her dismissive tone and eventually speak up for the silent woman whom society happily oppressed. My ouma's long, cold stares told me she didn't like my irreverence, but should my father reprimand me, she would hush him halfway through and send him out of the kitchen. I couldn't quite work out why, but it fascinated me enough to roll it over in my mind, like a dice, when I went out for my walks around the dusty dorp.

Coetzeesdorp may have been small and isolated, but it was safe enough for me to walk the streets alone. Outside of the dorp, my parents were anxious about all kinds of misfortune. My mother warned me about the Chinese who allegedly kidnapped girls and whisked them out of Africa to become child sex slaves. My father warned me about the African Sangomas who kidnapped children and babies to harvest their body parts and organs for muti. Both warned me about the ANC blacks who planted bombs in restaurants and hotels. Both assured me that there were plenty of things to fear, which made it more odd that they didn't visit Coetzeesdorp more often.

When we arrived in December '88, my ouma stood outside waiting as if she had radar. I imagined her beforehand, watching from her kitchen window for the telltale cloud of red dust.

'My meisie is so groot! Hoe oud is jy?'

'I'm fourteen, Ouma.'

'Ek kan dit nie glo nie.'

She embraced me in a bear hug and held onto me for so long

and tight that I got dizzy. My mother seized the opportunity
to brush past and steal inside. When Ouma finally released me,
she promised to bake rusks with me in the morning, and then
led my father by his elbow to discuss the numerous bombings
that the ANC had perpetrated during the year. My mother
rolled her eyes and told me to put on my cozzie because she
wanted to swim in the public pool. I asked why we couldn't
swim in Ouma's pool and she answered me with a dirty look,
followed by a quiet 'Nga, not now, Ros,' through gritted teeth. I
pulled a face and went to my room to dress.

The public pool was in close proximity to the Hendrik
Verwoerd Dam. It had three diving boards of varying height
and met the olympic standard of fifty metres. Four silver
ladders, with curved handles, were fastened at each corner
and submerged into sparkling water. The pool had the loving
fingerprints of a loyal groundskeeper, but we never saw anyone on our occasional visits. We never saw locals either, which
suited me perfectly, because I had the whole pool to myself. I
favoured the deep end; that underwater world where I could
make-believe I had superpowers and push my lungs to capacity
by touching the bottom. My mother inched herself into the water like a gazelle anticipating danger, but only got as far as her
knees. While I swam, she laid out a towel on a bathing lounger,
closed her eyes and offered herself to the suntan gods. Each
time we visited, I had pondered the origins of the pool, but
never followed up. I made a mental note to ask Ouma when we
baked rusks in the morning.

Ouma always woke up before the birds did. She called it waking up at 'mossiepop' — Afrikaans for sparrow's fart. She liked
to potter in the garden, to clip browning leaves and withered

31

flowers. She said that people's lives would be vastly improved if they consistently pruned their thoughts and habits every day. It reminded me of something Mohini would say. I asked her if she pruned her thoughts every day. She nodded and said that she had a backlog of pruning to do. Then she laughed and asked me to help her pile the clippings into the wheelbarrow and dump them in the compost heap in the garden's corner.

On the morning that we set aside to bake rusks, I found her pruning the strawberry patch. She gave me a pair of black gloves, imprinted with red ladybirds, and invited me to help. I knelt alongside her and dug in the dirt, carefully lifting the strawberry vines from the earth to remove any decaying leaves. We worked in silence for a little while before I asked her about the public pool and who tended to it.

'An old man named Piet Senior built it many moons ago for his daughter, Opheila,' she said. 'From the day Ophelia could talk, she told her father that she remembered being a mermaid in another life. Her mother dismissed her as silly, but it sparked her father's imagination. Unfortunately, they were too poor to build a pool, so her father collected other people's bric-a-brac to make her an assortment of splash pools. He used everything from worn car tyres, to the frames of discarded lounge suites.'

Ouma stood up and stretched her back.

'That's not the end of the story, is it?' I said.

She shook her head. 'Not even close. Come, let's put our feet in the pool while I tell you the rest.'

We removed our gloves and sat on the edge of the wide silver ladder with our feet in the cool water.

'Fate intervened the year she turned eight,' said Ouma. 'She fell ill, and her muscles rapidly wasted away until she couldn't walk. Piet took her to dozens of doctors, but none had a concrete diagnosis. As water was the only environment where her legs were not stressed, the doctors suggested water therapy. Her father took drastic measures and proposed that the local municipality build a public pool. He must have stated his case convincingly, because they approved the funding. It took a year to build, and each day Ophelia's condition worsened. On completion, the council held a special ceremony and dedicated the pool to Ophelia. From her wheelchair, she cut the opening day ribbon, and, with assistance, christened the pool. The pool was magnificent from what I'm told, sparkling as though polished by God himself. But a terrible thing happened a week after opening day.'

'What happened?' I said, frowning.

'Ophelia accompanied her father to check on the pool in the evening. While he busied himself in the pump house to retrieve chemicals, Ophelia must have wheeled herself over to the edge of the pool.'

'Oh no,' I said.

'Nobody can say for sure what happened, but it's likely the little girl bent over to touch the water and fell in. Whatever happened, her father found her too late.'

'She drowned?'

Ouma nodded. 'Ja, she was at the bottom of the pool and no amount of CPR, begging, pleading, or praying did any good. Devastated, the poor man resolved to maintain the pool for the rest of his days in honour of Ophelia. He and his wife went on to have a son, Piet Junior, who took it upon himself to carry on his father's tradition.'

'Wow,' I said. 'Is that why the pool is always deserted?'

'Ja,' said Ouma. 'Sometimes he says he sees the blur of Ophelia's ghost hovering above the water where she drowned.'

'Are you friends with Piet Junior?' I said.

Ouma nodded. 'Ja, he has a sweet tooth. I bake and deliver koeksusters to his home every week. Maybe you can come with me before you leave?'

'Yes, please,' I said.

'What do you say we go and bake those rusks now,' she said.

'Ja,' I said enthusiastically. 'I'm hungry after all that gardening.'

The day before our departure, Ouma tried to persuade my father to stay one more day, but my mother said no and an argument broke out. The tension had been building from the moment my mother brushed past without saying hello, but emotions had been placed on the back burner of the aga and set to simmer. I sat at the kitchen table, dunking my rusk into coffee, while Ouma and my father spoke in Afrikaans. It annoyed my mother when they spoke Afrikaans, because she spoke broken Afrikaans and she assumed that they were talking about her.

'Nog a dag, Wilstan, asseblief,' said Ouma.

'Êk sal praat met Marilyn,' said my father.

'It need not concern Marilyn. You're the man, make a decision.'

'Maeve and Léon are expecting us, Mâ. It's their eighteenth wedding anniversary, and they're planning something special.'

'We won't be staying an extra day,' my mother said on entering the kitchen.

'Marilyn, please,' said my father, 'we can discuss this later.'

My mother crossed her arms. 'No, there's nothing to discuss. Maeve has plans for us the day after we arrive. You won't want to miss it.'

'We'll discuss it later,' my father repeated.

'You come here once a year, Marilyn, what's the harm in letting me see my son and grandchild one extra day?' Ouma chimed in.

'Oh, I bet you've been waiting to say that since the day we arrived,' said my mother.

'Please, Marilyn, Mâ, can we not do this in front of Ros?' said my father.

'Fine,' said my mother. 'Ros, go to your room, or go for a walk.'

'I'm drinking my coffee,' I said.

'Ros, this is not the time,' said my father, his voice deepening a notch.

I gave him a look, left my cup of half-drunk coffee, took another rusk and left. I snuck out of the back garden gate and sat on the dusty road underneath the open kitchen window. By the time I'd reached my listening spot the argument raged and voices were raised. My mother told Ouma to make an effort and visit the family in Durban every now and then, and that it wasn't her fault that Ouma never made an effort to see her own grandchild and son.

'If we didn't visit you once a year, would you make the effort to visit us?' My mother demanded in a way that suggested she already knew the answer.

'It's different for me, Marilyn. I'm retired. I have people who rely on me here.'

My mother laughed. 'Oh, please, the dorp is not going to fall apart if you decide to go on holiday for a month.'

Ouma switched back to Afrikaans and addressed my father, saying something along the lines of, 'are you really going to let her talk to me like that?'

'That's it,' said my mother. 'I'm going to pack.'

With that she obviously left the room, because the argument stopped and a long silence followed.

I heard my father's voice after several moments. 'Did you have to antagonise her, Mâ?'

'She has no respect, Wilstan. You and Lindy are the only reason she is welcome in my house.'

'Ja, Mâ, you make that perfectly clear each time we visit.'

I heard the chair scrape across the floor and assumed that my father had left the room. I absentmindedly gnawed at my rusk. I didn't want to take my mother's side. We did only visit once a year. I blamed my father too. He domineered my mother in so many respects, but succumbed to her in others. I couldn't understand why. She certainly made sure that she regularly visited Maeve, so why not my ouma?

We left the dorp that evening instead of the next morning. I begged my father to let me stay with Ouma while he and my mother went to Maeve and Léon, but he refused and my mother assumed her family-fallback-position; *your absence will be noticed...my family will be disappointed...blah blah blah.*

Ouma almost squeezed the life out of me she hugged me so hard. 'Write to me, Lindy,' she whispered in my ear, 'and I'll write back.'

I knelt on the back car seat and watched the red dust dance around her silhouette until the motion sensor light above her went out. Every time we said goodbye to her I worried that it would be our last. I thought about what I would tell her if I wrote her a letter, and what she would tell me.

Minutes later the dorp was behind us. I could feel the change in texture by the sound of the tyres moving from dirt road to tar. No street lights lit the way, only cat's eyes that lit up small sections of the road ahead. I watched the black sky until I grew sleepy and then lay down on the back seat and fell asleep, thinking about what tidbits I could share with Ouma in order to coax her secrets out of her.

CHAPTER 6

I woke to discover that I had, thankfully, slept five of the six hours of travel between the Orange Free State and Joburg. I only cared about the latter end of the trip, where the magical Oppenheimer Estate could be glimpsed along the ridge. When it appeared, I hurled myself across the backseat of the car and pressed my hands against the window, straining my neck to peer upwards at the majestic eucalyptus trees that soared towards the cumulonimbus clouds and cast a shadow over the freeway. Many people were oblivious to it, unaware that a splendid, secret garden lay tucked away above the M1. Much like Ouma's oasis — a splash of green on an earthy canvas — at odds with the surrounding indigenous Transvaal landscape of dry veld. My father, the keen historian, had educated me about the Oppenheimer home on a previous trip. The estate spread across a massive tract that had been landscaped into beautiful gardens, and the house featured frequently in House & Leisure magazines. I held it in my gaze until we exited the freeway and it disappeared.

Within minutes we entered Parktown, home to the Oppenheimer's, and most affluent suburb of Joburg (if not the whole of South Africa). Parktown neighboured the suburb of Upper Houghton, where my Aunty Maeve and Uncle Léon lived. Uncle Léon's house did not nearly match the scale of Brenthurst, or Sea Breeze for that matter, but it certainly made a healthy statement about his personal wealth. My father once commented to my mother that Léon had done well for himself considering he imported and exported antiques for a living and didn't have any formal qualifications. My Aunty Maeve didn't work either. For one, she didn't need to, but mostly because Léon forbade her. When they weren't eating out at new restaurants and going to the cinema, Aunty Maeve busied herself by waiting hand and foot on Uncle Léon. And while it was acceptable for the maid to wash, clean, iron, vacuum, and dust, it was unacceptable for her to touch or prepare my Uncle's food.

Every year, when we visited Uncle Léon and Aunty Maeve, my mother would tell me the story about how they met. Aunty Maeve had travelled to Paris for her eighteenth birthday and met Uncle Léon at the opening night of Don Giovanni. He had spotted her sitting on the balcony with his opera glasses and approached her during intermission. He must have done a grand job of charming her, because she returned to South Africa with an engagement ring and they married on Christmas Eve — hence our annual Christmas visit to Joburg. The only thing we knew about Uncle Léon's family is that he had grown up without a father, and his mother had died before his twenty-first birthday.

The Merc slowed down, and we turned right into the driveway. My father pressed the intercom button and waited.

'Goeie môre.'

'Goeie môre, Philemon. It's Wilstan.'

'Yes, baas. Come in, baas.'

The wrought iron gates opened like a yawning hippo. Invisible from the road, the house slowly revealed itself around the bend of a long driveway.

Philemon and Gladys were an inherited feature of the house when Léon purchased it in 1960. They lived with their twelve-year old daughter, Promise, in the kaya, located beneath the main house. I had never seen the kaya, because it was strictly out of bounds. Philemon worked as a full-time gardener and doubled as a gatekeeper and general dogsbody. Thanks to him, the five acre property was a sight to behold. Several statuesque jacarandas populated the property and fuchsia bougainvilleas cascaded over the courtyard archway. Edged between the lawns and eight-foot white stucco wall flowered an assortment of white arum lilies, violet and yellow birds of paradise, rose hibiscus, and lilac agapanthus. Not to mention the themed garden spaces — the Japanese garden with its ornate bridge, sculptures, water features and koi pond; the traditional English garden which attracted bumble bees and butterflies; and the indigenous garden with proteas and kikuyu grass.

The house sat in the centre of a sloping five-acre plot. The 1930s era estate started life with original art deco features, including a flat roof, white stucco exterior, turquoise panels and geometric balconies. Fifty years later, it had undergone several additions and changes at Uncle Léon's behest. The white stucco exterior now stood beneath a slanted slate roof. The guest suite, overlooking the front garden, had french doors and a wrought iron juliette balcony. Brown awnings arched over the downstairs windows and the vibrant turquoise panels could only be recalled from memory and photographs. The few remaining art deco features were the two bronze female statues at the top of the driveway — holding a globe-shaped light, and situated at the feet of two flamboyant trees.

We heard Léon shouting at Gladys before we parked in front of the garage. I gritted my teeth and willed him to stop. My father got out of the car and saved Gladys by asking Léon to come and help him with the bags. My mother didn't wait for anyone and made a beeline for the house to see Maeve. Once my bags were in my room, and the adults were settled in the lounge drinking tea, I went in search of Philemon. I greeted Gladys as I passed through the kitchen and met with a pair of white butterflies as I opened the bottom of the stable door. I followed their enchanting spiralling dance down the stairs, that ran alongside the house, until I found myself near the kaya. My curiosity drowned my fear of consequences, and I inched down the stairs to investigate. If spaces were represented by seasons, then summer ruled the main house, and winter ruled the kaya. I walked straight into a kitchenette-cum-diner-cum-sitting room with its concrete floors and unpainted walls and I shivered. A short corridor led to three doors that contained a bathroom and two bedrooms. The toilet had no seat cover, and the shower had no curtain. The first bedroom likely belonged to Gladys and Philemon, because it had a double bed that was elevated by concrete breeze blocks. An African superstition known as the *tokolosh* called for extra elevation. The tokolosh was an evil spirit, the size of a leprechaun, that targeted females in particular, and visited at night. Similar to the bogeyman, it was generally ridiculed by the white population. When I saw Promise's sparsely furnished, cold, room, I felt like I'd won the karma lottery and come face to face with the person who'd lost. I closed the door quietly, and snuck back outside. The clean air and warm sunshine felt so sweet and foreign compared to the kaya dungeon. My spine tingled and my body shuddered at the thought of being subjected to a life of modern-day slavery. I wandered around the grounds, picking flowers, until I had enough to fill a vase, then went in search of Philemon.

He bowed his head and smiled when he saw me.

'I picked these for Promise's room,' I said. 'Do you know where she is?'

Philemon shook his head and frowned. 'Baas would not like that, Miss Rosalinde.'

'Baas doesn't need to know,' I said.

'Nee, Miss Rosalinde. Baas knows everything.'

I frowned, feeling deflated, and then nodded, not wanting to cause trouble for Philemon and his family. 'Philemon?' I said.

'Yes, Miss Rosalinde.'

'You don't need to call me Miss.'

He smiled and nodded. 'I do, Miss Rosalinde.'

I sighed and took the flowers to my room with a heavy heart.

CHAPTER 7

Uncle Léon organised a tour of Brenthurst Gardens, the day before Christmas, as a special anniversary gift to Aunty Maeve. My mother oohed and aahed as if he deserved Husband of the Year Award.

'Welkom almal. I am Johan and I will be guiding you through these beautiful gardens and magnificent estate.'

Everyone said hello and thanks.

'You are most privileged to be here today. Not too many people have caught a glimpse of this magical place, never mind an entire tour. So, without further ado, let's begin.'

We formed a line of sorts — my father at the front (so that he could ask questions), my mother and Maeve behind him, Léon and I at the back — and followed Johan's lead while he walked and talked.

'This magnificent estate you see today began as open veld,' he said. 'Edouard Lippert planted the first trees here in 1890 to meet demand from the mining and building boom. At one time there were two million trees in his plantation.'

We paused in front of the elegant house with its statuesque Cape Gables to learn about its history.

'Consolidated Goldfields of South Africa bought Brenthurst, and commissioned Sir Herbert Baker to design this house for their directors. It dates back to 1906,' he said, 'and as you will see in a little while, Baker designed it to perch majestically on the bare rock of the koppie.'

'When did the Oppenheimers move here?' said my father.

'Ernest Oppenheimer brought his family to live at Brenthurst in 1922,' said Johan, 'and the Oppenheimers have occupied it ever since.'

My father nodded and we continued our walk to the next attraction known as Little Brenthurst.

'The Oppenheimers moved into 'Little Brenthurst' during World War II,' continued Johan, 'and allowed the Red Cross to use Brenthurst as a fifty bed hospital, called Brenthurst Auxiliary Hospital. The hospital treated hundreds of patients from the Mediterranean and the Middle East. Dr Jack Penn pioneered new methods of treatment at the hospital and established Africa's first centre for plastic surgery.'

Uncle Léon didn't seem to be listening to Johan's speech, because he repeatedly stopped without warning, causing me to walk into the back of him. Then he would laugh, as if I was in on the joke. When it happened a fourth time, I decided to employ a safe walking distance.

Johan stopped walking and switched to his next topic. 'In 1959 Harry and Bridget Oppenheimer commissioned Joane Pim to redesign the garden. As you can see here, she redesigned the terracing and made the garden easily accessible for the first time in its history.'

Everyone admired the terracing and wandered around on their own to appreciate the garden before Johan continued.

'Dick Scott took over fourteen years ago, in 1974, when Joane Pim died, and he is still here today. One of his projects is to develop the wild garden. One of his favourite quotes is as follows:

Encouraging and matching indigenous plants for their temperament and ability to live together.

Dick Scott's quote caught my imagination. If one could match and encourage indigenous plants to live together and thrive in each other's company in a wild garden, why couldn't the whites do the same? Was colour that much of a divider? A cocky Indian myna interrupted my maudlin thoughts, and I couldn't help but smile.

'Bloody coolie mynas!' Johan shouted, flapping his hands wildly as he ran toward the myna.

We all stared at Johan. Indian mynas (or coolie mynas as they were commonly known) were one of the most commonly found birds. It didn't matter where you went or where you were in the country, you were sure to see Indian mynas. Like pigeons in London, mynas were ubiquitous.

'Ha-em. My apologies, everyone,' said Johan. 'He may look like a harmless little guy, but the fact is that these mynas are one of the biggest pests and threats to our indigenous birds.'

'Why?' said my father.

'Let me explain,' said Johan throwing both hands up in the air dramatically. 'Indian mynas are noisy, territorial, and not afraid of humans. They use superior numbers to aggressively seize and defend territory. They kill the chicks of other birds or destroy their eggs, or build their own nests on top and smother them. They have been seen to block the entries to hollows, causing the inhabitants to die of starvation, after which they lay their eggs in the hollow. Mynas build and defend several nests during the breeding season, although they only lay in one.'

'Which excludes native birds and animals from those nesting sites,' said my father.

'Exactly,' said Johan.

'So, they're like the South African government and apartheid,' I blurted out.

My mother's cheeks blended with the pink hydrangeas behind her, and everyone else assailed me with thorny stares. My father grabbed my elbow and ushered me across the lawn to the shade of an enormous plane tree.

'Your defiance has run its course, girlie. You're still young and naïve and you have no bloody idea what those kaffirs are really like.'

I flinched. 'Don't say that word.'

'It's true. I've seen it firsthand.'

'I don't know what happened to you. All I know is that Philemon, Gladys, Promise, and Mohini are all kind people.'

'Nothing is perfect, I agree. Philemon, Gladys and many more blacks are good people. But make no mistake. If a situation arose between us and them, we wouldn't stand a chance. War is messy.'

'What war?' I interjected.

'It is something you will come to understand one day,' he said. 'As for Mohini, it's a shame that she has to pay a price for the colour of her skin, but such is life.'

I frowned.

'Don't worry about Mohini,' he continued, 'she has a good life and she's well looked after. As for this apartheid business, I don't want to hear anymore outbursts from you, understand?'

'Apartheid is bigger than race,' I said. 'It's a regime. It's propaganda. It's...'

'Rosalinde,' my father interrupted me, 'this is the situation that we live in and there's nothing that you or I can do to change it.'

'Why not?' I said. 'A few people have tried, but it will only work if we all try.'

'Make things easy on yourself, Ros, and go with the flow on this. Please. If you don't, you'll be in for a tough time.'

'I saw Promise's room yesterday,' I said.

'What?'

'I will never be able to go with the flow.'

My father stared at me as if he was defending his record in a staring contest, and then said, 'You owe everyone an apology.' When I didn't respond, he led me back to the group, which was moving up the hill on stone pathways and up steps toward the rose garden.

'Joane Pim created the rose garden as a spiral circle, shaped like a snail's shell, and positioned within a sunken square,' said Johan as my father and I joined them.

My mother gave me a filthy look.

My father nudged me and said, 'Rosalinde has something to say.'

'I apologise,' I paused, 'for having an opinion.'

My father looked at me as if I'd blasphemed. 'Rosalinde!'

'Next time I'll keep it to myself,' I said.

Johan shook his head and said, 'Let's continue, shall we?'

With the exception of Uncle Léon, everyone nodded and turned away from me in disgust. Léon seemed half bemused and half seething. While Johan brought the conversation back to the garden, I took refuge amidst the tall roses growing around the edges of the spiral garden. I breathed in the individual scents of the fragrant red, yellow, pink, and white petals, and focused on the butterflies wafting in and out. But it was no use. My emotions bubbled and tears slid down my cheeks.

I kept quiet for the rest of the tour, past flowering jacarandas and gigantic eucalyptuses, while my thoughts trailed behind me like butterflies in distress. Johan stopped at the water fountain and two bronze statues of a boy and a girl. The boy stood naked on his toes, arms outstretched to the blue sky and glowing sun while the girl looked at him from the middle of a pond.

'And now for the *piece de resistance*,' said Johan with an unconvincing French accent. He stepped aside and swished his arms sideways as if to unveil the treasure that stood behind him, smiling like Alice's cheshire cat. 'Allow me to introduce *Venus Victorieuse*; sculpted by none other than Pierre-Auguste Renoir, and completed in 1914.'

'Renoir,' my father echoed.

'Yes, Harry Oppenheimer brought it to Brenthurst in the early 1970s and renamed it Eve and the apple. She stands facing the house and is the jewel in the crown that is Brenthurst,' he finished triumphantly.

Everyone, except me, cooed with delight and finished with a round of applause. I had finally seen the garden of Eden that I had so often glimpsed from the backseat of the car. A garden that had captured my imagination, and been immune to apartheid. But, as I followed my family out of the garden gates and toward the parked cars, I realised that immunity did not exist. Apartheid touched everything

CHAPTER 8

Christmas with Uncle Léon and Aunty Maeve was as predictable as my mother's Mills and Boons books. Breakfast, church service, traditional roast lunch, followed by afternoon tea and adult conversation. I usually spent my afternoon in the garden or listening to music in my room, but the Christmas of '88 took an unexpected turn for the worst, and, unlike my mother's romance novels, there was no happy ending.

While Gladys cleared the dining room table, the adults retired to the lounge for tea and conversation. I itched to go outside, but my mother warned me off and insisted that I stay and talk for ten minutes. Uncle Léon sat in his habitual spot; a cream leather lazy-boy in arm's reach of the remote control, that lived on the table alongside him.

'Maeve, turn on the TV,' he said.

She obeyed and headed back to the kitchen.

The end credits of a show rolled across the screen. I pinched my mother's knee and pointed to the garden when Uncle Léon bellowed.

'Maeve, turn off the goddamn TV!'

The room fell silent.

'There's a fucking kaffir on TV, Maeve.' The decibels in-creased between words, and his usual anaemic skin turned the colour of bird's eye chilli, giving his liver spots a sunburnt look. 'Turn it off,' he shouted.

Maeve's footsteps echoed off the wooden floorboards as she ran from the kitchen, her face as flushed as Léon's, as she fumbled for the off button on the remote control. I stood up; unable to fathom his hatred. My mother tried to pull me back down, like one would hoist a flag down a pole.

'What is wrong with you?'

'Ros!' said my mother, tugging my arm harder.

'No, Marilyn. Let the child speak,' said Léon.

'I'm a child, but I know right from wrong. You're refusing to watch a TV show because the actor has black skin.'

'You have no idea what these kaffirs are like, but one day you'll find out for yourself.'

I shook my head in disgust and left the room. I took the stairs two at a time, slammed my bedroom door and slid my favourite Michael Jackson cassette into the tape deck.

I leaned out of the window and sang along to the end of *Beat It*. My bedroom, tucked away at the back of the house on the top floor, had the best views of the largest and oldest of all the jacarandas. A gust of wind blew the lace curtains and thunder reverberated overhead. The jacaranda's grey trunk change to sil-ver as a lightning bolt lit up the sky. As *Beat It* finished and the creaking sounds of *Thriller* began, I spotted Uncle Léon skulk-ing alongside the house, below my window, at basement level. One minute he was hugging the wall, the next he disappeared — as if the wall had opened its mouth and swallowed him.

I snuck downstairs and out the back door to investigate.

In all the years that I had visited the house and explored the grounds, I had never seen an entrance or window near the spot where Léon disappeared. On closer inspection, I noticed that the brick walls on the basement level were different to the white render of the main house, and, hidden in plain sight, was a brown door handle. My heart rate elevated as my imagination conjured up what could be waiting on the other side, and I hesitated as to the consequences of following Léon into a secret place and getting caught red-handed.

I gently eased the door open, in case it creaked or squeaked, but it opened silently — as if recently oiled. In the several seconds it took for my eyes to adjust to the dark, I wondered what I'd find. What I didn't expect was a basement of prison cells. The room smelled of damp, and the low temperature made me wish I had brought a jersey. A single bulb lit the middle of the room, offering enough light to make out an old, wooden table with a large key ring filled with long rusted keys.

I heard a grunting sound, but could see very little, so I tiptoed forward and strained my eyes in the direction of the sounds. It got louder and louder as I neared the cell at the end of the room. A candle burned in the corner of the cell, illuminating my Uncle Léon, who stood behind Promise, pants around his ankles, thrusting himself against her and grunting like an animal. Léon's right hand covered her mouth, and his left hand cupped her breast.

'Get away from her,' I said, horrified.

Promise's eyes widened. Uncle Léon looked surprised, but not perturbed.

'I said, get away from her.'

'What are you going to do about it?'

I scanned the room, unsure of my next move. 'I won't let you out unless you let Promise go,' I said, slamming the cell door shut.

He studied me for a moment and then pulled away from Promise and pulled up his trousers. Promise sunk to the floor and wrapped her arms around her knees.

'I tell you what,' he said, smiling, 'why don't we make a swap?'

'What do you mean?' I said.

'You for her,' he said.

'I'm the one with the keys,' I said, gesturing to the table.

'Yes, and I'm the one with the gun.' He pulled a small hand-gun from his sock and forced it into Promise's mouth. 'What's it gonna be?' he said. 'How much do you really love these kaffirs?'

I frowned and swallowed.

He cocked the hammer. 'Well?'

'What do you want from me?' I said.

'I want you,' he said. 'I'll let the kaffir go if you agree to take her place and swear to never speak a word of this to anyone.'

I stared at him. Take her place…was God testing me? I kept voicing my disgust for racism, but was I willing to put myself in Promise's shoes, literally?

With the gun still in her mouth, he moved her toward the prison door and said: 'Open the door and I'll let her go.'

'Fine,' I said. I fetched the key and unlocked the cell door. Léon kicked Promise out of the cell and she fled.

Léon closed the cell door behind him and took my chin in his hand.

'Droit de seigneur,' he said, looking into my eyes.

I pulled my chin away in disgust.

'Until next time,' he said, then turned his back on me and left.

CHAPTER 9

We left Léon's house the day after Boxing Day, knowing that we would see him and Maeve in Durban a week later for New Year's Eve. I quietly hoped that my courage, or stupidity, depending on how you looked at it, had given him pause, but his parting words, combined with the knot in my gut, told me otherwise. I thought about telling my parents, but my mother's bond with her sister outranked her bond with me, and my father had instructed me at Brenthurst to 'go with the flow' and stop causing an uproar. So, I concealed my discovery and dilemma, hoping that it would never amount to anything, but worried the entire seven hour drive that it marked the beginning of a story that would not end happily.

A sense of relief flooded me when the lighthouse illuminated the backseat of the car, and we pulled into the driveway at Sea Breeze. Gunther was the first to welcome me — jumping up on his hind legs and whining happily. I flung my arms out and let him rest his paws on my shoulders. 'I missed you, boy,' I said, hugging him tightly.

While my father took the suitcases out of the boot and carried them up the stairs into the house, I lay on my back on the front lawn, with Gunther at my side, and allowed the sound of crashing waves to soothe my fears.

'Lindy, I've missed you,' said Mohini, standing over me.

'Mo,' I said, jumping up and throwing my arms around her neck.

She laughed. 'Did you enjoy your holiday?'

While I found it easy to lie to my parents, I found it impossible to lie to Mohini. 'Coetzeesdorp was the best part,' I said.

'Tell me all about it tomorrow?' she said.

I nodded. She said goodnight and retired to her room. I stayed outside for a long time. Lying on the cool grass and searching the starry sky for answers. Listening to the sound of the waves rushing toward shore and crashing against the weathered rocks of the tidal wall. Counting seconds between light rotations. Making futile attempts to banish the images of Léon violating Promise. Shuddering at the thought of Léon touching my naked skin.

The following night, my parents celebrated their fifteenth anniversary at The Oyster Box — the restaurant responsible for manning the lighthouse. Jericho locked himself in his air conditioned office to escape the humidity, and Mohini started a new sewing project for her niece, Lolly. I lay in bed reading until I heard the phone ring. I instantly regretted answering it when I heard Léon's voice.

'Sorry, my parents are out, can I take a message?'

'No,' he said. 'I didn't phone to speak to your parents. I want to speak to you.'

I held my breath.

'I've been thinking about you,' he said. 'When I'm fucking my wife. I'm thinking about you.'

My stomach knotted, and I clenched the phone.

'Can't wait for New Year,' he said, and hung up.

I stood for a long time with the phone in my hand, as one fear after the next raced through my head like relay runners.

I stole out of the kitchen door, walked past Gunther, who slept in his kennel, and down the twelve steps into the garden. The black sky was cloudless and starry, but the claustrophobic air clung to my skin like cling wrap. The familiar sound of crashing waves, chirruping crickets, and chuckling geckos brought the night to life. Light spilled out of Mohini's room and drew me toward it like the sun beckons an African daisy. While I spent many hours in her room during the day watching her sew up a storm, or talking to her, I had never spent time with her after hours, when she prepared for bed.

I tapped quietly on her door, anxious about disturbing her.

'Yes, mum' she called out, mistaking me for my mother.

I pursed my lips. My mother didn't deserve the reverence Mohini gave her. I turned the doorknob, smelt the familiar aroma of burning incense, and heard the exotic sounds of Indian music coming from her bedside radio. She sat at her dressing table, hands poised to remove the black bobby pins that secured her bun.

'Lindy,' she said and motioned me to sit on her bed.

I made myself comfortable on her handmade taffeta patchwork quilt and watched her dismantle her bun as if she was alone again. From the radio, the female vocals faded and the ancient sound of the sitar filled the room. As the bobby pins grew in a pile on her dresser, the bun began unravelling. Her

57

shiny, black hair tumbled down past her shoulders and along her spine. In all the years that I had spent time in her company, and shared meals with her, I never knew that she had long hair. A blush travelled along my cheek. I looked away for a moment — as if she had disrobed and stood naked before me — as if I was seeing her properly for the first time. In that moment, she ceased to be Mohini the cook, Mohini the cleaner, Mohini the babysitter. As I watched her comb sections of her hair with a tortoiseshell brush, I saw Mohini, the woman. A beautiful woman in her own right. A woman who, once upon a time, had possessed her own aspirations and dreams. What had happened to her dreams? What had brought her to Sea Breeze to be someone's domestic servant, when it was usually the place of an African woman to be a maid? Was she happy with the way her life had turned out, or deeply sad?

I didn't ask my questions out loud. Instead, I let them float on the silent sea within me, along with secret of Léon and Promise, in the hopes that the tides would eventually reveal the answers I sought.

CHAPTER 10

December 29, 1988

Two days before New Year's Eve, I was playing chess with my father while Uncle Jericho and my mother watched TV. My father had taken one of my black rooks in a move that I didn't see coming when a breaking news bulletin interrupted the show.

'Fourteen-year old Stompie Moeketsi's body has been found in Soweto,' said the male reporter.

I stopped mid-move.

'Moeketsi was the youngest political detainee and was alleged to have been a police informant. Police say that Moeketsi was kidnapped by Winnie Mandela's football team along with two other boys, and tortured for days. Moeketsi was badly beaten with his throat slit, but the other two boys managed to escape with their lives.'

The image on the screen flicked from the reporter to a township scene, and the report continued with voiceover.

'Winnie Mandela is believed to be involved in township

necklacing.'

As he spoke the cameraman zoomed in on a township mob who shouted and cheered as a black woman was imprisoned inside a stack of car tyres. 'A vicious and barbaric custom that burns a person alive using a tower of burning tyres.'

He continued speaking, but the sound of the woman screaming and pleading drowned him out. If agony had a voice, it was surely the torturous sounds that emanated from the burning woman. I had to look away. I blinked. I swallowed. I inhaled sharply. I did everything I could to stop the tears, to keep the bile down. I had never witnessed nor heard anything more excruciating and barbaric. And worse than the burning, dying, woman, was the crowd who jeered and cheered. A crowd of people, watching as a woman's flesh literally burnt to a crisp.

'It's horrific, isn't it?' said my father.

I nodded. 'It's unforgivable,' I said, swallowing the bile that had come up my throat.

'Now you know why your father and I are so cynical,' said Jericho.

'That Winnie Mandela is a murderous bitch,' said my mother.

'How can they do that to their own?' I said. 'Aren't they supposed to be uniting and fighting against apartheid?'

'It's not as simple as apartheid, or black and white, Ros,' said Jericho. 'The blacks themselves are divided by tribes. There are the Xhosas, the Zulus, the Tswanas, the Sothos…the list goes on,' he said. 'This is what they're like. They're savage. They don't want to be civilised.' He shook his head and sipped his drink.

'I don't know what to say,' I said. 'That is the most horrendous thing I've ever seen. I will never get the sound of that woman's screams out of my head.'

'God help us when apartheid ends,' said my father.

I told my father that I no longer wanted to play chess, and went to my room to lie down. When I failed to take my mind off the horrific images by focusing on the lighthouse flashes, I put the pillow over my head and sobbed.

That night I had nightmares of burning flesh and unimaginable pain. I lay in bed for hours, unable to return to sleep, and thought about what my father and Jericho had said. I thought about Léon and Promise. I thought about the Wimpy Bar. How naïve I had been in thinking that the situation was as simple as black and white. It wasn't at all. I had spent my whole life admonishing my father and Jericho in particular for their callous attitude towards the black population, for their unwillingness to fight against apartheid. Now I saw another side of the coin. A side I had neither considered nor believed possible. I had always painted the blacks as victims in the canvas of my head. But now I had seen proof of the opposite, and that realisation made my head spin, hurtling my whole belief system into a black hole, from which I had to start over and seriously consider a post-apartheid future; the inevitable decay of a world turned against itself.

CHAPTER 11

Sea Breeze heaved with people on New Year's Eve, and my parents looked to be in their element. My mother, comfortable with a glass of champagne in her hand, flirted with men who found her irresistible. Meanwhile, my father, who claimed to hate parties, willingly commanded the room with his oratory skills and intellect when the clock struck party time. Maeve busied herself in the kitchen, even though catering was provided, and Léon moved like a hunter between trees. Every now and then I would glimpse him staring at me with a look that made me avert my eyes and move in the opposite direction. I did my best to avoid him, but with Mohini visiting her niece, Lolly, in Chatsworth, for a few days, I had nowhere to hide and nobody to protect me.

After much surreptitious movement and darting between tuxedoes and dresses, I decided that it would be safer to leave the party. I considered my room, but struck a line through the idea because Léon clearly had no respect for boundaries. The lighthouse flashed an answer. I snuck outside into the crisp sea breeze blowing off the ocean. In my sleeveless dress, I considered returning inside to fetch a jersey, but I didn't want to risk running into Léon again, so I ignored the rising goosebumps on my arms and legs and ran in the direction of the lighthouse. By the time I reached the white sentinel the run had warmed me up and my Léon-induced anxiety had worn off. I sat, cross-legged, on the edge of the concrete base and watched the ocean as the light traced its circular path. The lighthouse may have been designed to warn and protect ships at sea, but in the absence of Mohini, the act of sitting in its presence, while it actively saved lives, provided a sense of protection in itself.

'Duran Duran.'

I jumped when I heard Léon's voice behind me.

'Happy New Year's Eve,' he said, holding out a cassette tape.

'Thank you,' I said, taking the tape, not wanting to antagonise him.

Before I could pull my hand away, he grabbed my wrist, pulled me toward him and tried to kiss me. I shook my head aggressively and pushed him as hard as I could.

'I'm going to enjoy this,' he said, throwing his head back and laughing.

'What if I tell someone?' I said.

'Two things,' he said. 'First, nobody will believe you. Second, remember your promise. If you breathe a word of this to anybody, I will force my gun into Promise's mouth and pull the trigger. Her blood will be on your kaffir-loving hands.'

'How do I know you're not going to do that anyway?' I said.

'Because this,' he said, 'is much more fun.'

'I won't let you do to me what you did to Promise,' I said.

He laughed as if I'd told the joke of the year. 'And what makes you think you have a choice?' He turned and walked away from me. 'Enjoy your tape.'

CHAPTER 12

In the days, weeks, months, and years that followed that New Year's incident, Léon's pursuit of me became increasingly aggressive, and my inner light dimmed. The seven-hour drive remained a godsend, but it didn't prevent him from routinely harassing me with phone calls and talking to me as if we were lovers entangled in a consensual affair. When he and Maeve visited, he would grope me every chance he got — cornering me alone in my bedroom, or in the car when my mother let him pick me up from school. The visits to Joburg were only made bearable by the fact that I had a lock on the bedroom door. Given the state of things, and how I had allowed them to spiral out of control, I couldn't imagine telling anyone what had happened. The sum of Léon's phone calls and visits had resulted in my sense of overwhelming guilt and shame. I blamed myself. I convinced myself that the fault lay with me. That I emitted some sinful sexual signal. And although I withdrew into myself, I hid it well enough for nobody to take any real notice. From the outside, any behavioural and mood excesses that I underwent were neatly squared away with the excuse of teenage hormones and female changes.

I pursued creative outlets that allowed me to channel, express and release the anger, shame, guilt, hatred, confusion and all of the other indescribable emotions and stages that I went through. I wrote imaginative stories in which Léon would meet his end, and spent hours at the piano playing Beethoven's Moonlight Sonata — a perfect accompaniment to my dark fantasies in which I would take Jericho's yacht beyond the shark nets, into open water, tie the anchor around my ankle and fall overboard, sinking into the murky depths of the Indian Ocean. Hair floating above me, like a fallen angel descending to her watery grave.

My mother was less enthralled with my choice of piano pieces. Every time I played, she would yell from whatever room she was in and say, 'For God's sake, Ros, stop playing that depressing music.' Of course I would ignore her and play louder and longer, to be greeted with a slam of the door.

I also developed an obsessive-compulsive approach to everything I did. My bedroom was the primary subject of my obsession. Every single book, pen, hair on my hairbrush, speck of dust, placement of furniture — you name it — was accounted for and etched into my memory like a brand. In hindsight, my bedroom should have been my safe haven, but Léon's threats had turned that space into a crime scene. My bedroom had become a vulnerable battleship out at sea, surrounded by enemy submarines with nowhere to hide. My only power was knowing every minute detail; an inventory of safety to protect me from unseen dangers and lurking peril.

My relationship with my mother deteriorated. The trip to Coetzeesdorp, in 1988, turned out to be our last. Days after the New Year's party, I overheard my parents argue. My mother declared it her last trip on the grounds that my ouma lived to insult her. My father tried to mollify her, but she only reminded him what a bad mother Ouma had been to him. And then nothing but silence. My relationship with my mother was like a terminal illness. Each time she revealed another piece of herself to me the disease claimed another organ, and our relationship moved closer to its own mortality. But I refused to cut Ouma out of my life like my parents did. I wrote to her, like she asked, and organised for Mohini to mail my letters during her monthly shopping trips to the Indian Plaza in Durban. I also wrote a letter detailing what had happened with Léon, but never mailed it. I thought that she'd blame me, like I blamed myself. Instead, I tried to drop clues that might arouse her suspicions. I told her that other girls my age were obsessed with boys but that I would rather eat slime than kiss a member of the opposite sex. I told her that I had no friends, and that everyone at school labelled me a lesbian, because I dry-retched at the thought of parties and boys. I told her these things in the hopes that she would see them as symptoms as opposed to traits, but like my mother, father, and Jericho, she lumped them into the basket of hormonal changes.

The political situation went a long way to hiding my personal turmoil. In February 1990, FW de Klerk released Nelson Mandela from prison and unbanned the ANC. Many whites began to emigrate like flocks of migratory birds, ruffling the feathers of those left behind. My father was one such bird who was deeply unsettled about the future of South Africa, but I'd dare say that I was the only one to notice. He tried to hide his true feelings by drinking more, cracking more jokes, and becoming a workaholic, but I was playing the same game and he didn't fool me for a second. The only thing I didn't know was why?

And, like I suspected deeper misgivings within my father, it was Mohini who suspected foul play regarding my behavioural changes. I longed to tell her, confess my secrets, but my shame kept me on the back foot. Instead, I answered her questions monosyllabically and stopped spending time with her in the kitchen and her room. And, as I witnessed pieces of myself wither and die, so too did I watch my own hands killing off pieces of Mohini.

PART II

1991
3 YEARS LATER

CHAPTER 13

In early March Jericho announced plans to take me and my parents on a cruise to Cape Town during the mid-year school holidays. He had commissioned a Cape boat builder to renovate the Morris family luxury yacht — Cabo das Tormentas — and planned to accept delivery at the end of June. As it was the first major renovation since her maiden voyage to the Cape of Good Hope, he thought it fitting to christen the re-vamped yacht by sailing her original route; starting in Durban, and stopping in East London, Port Elizabeth and Mossell Bay, before the final leg past Cape Agulhas through to Cape Town. The date coincided with the annual sardine run, which would make for excellent fishing, as well as whale sightings around Hermanus.

My mother suggested that Maeve and Léon join us.

'This is a trip I want to take with you, Wilstan and Ros,' said Jericho, 'but if you'd rather spend your time with Maeve and what's-his-face just say the word.'

'It was only a suggestion,' said my mother backing down.

Jericho's comment surprised me as much as a plot twist in a

movie.

'Wilstan, do you need me to square the time away with Spencer & Mason?' said Jericho.

'That won't be necessary, Jericho. I'll sort it out.'

'Try and stay out of trouble, young lady,' Jericho said to me, with a wink. Thankfully, it wasn't a Léon-wink.

'Is Uncle Jericho okay?' I said to my father. 'He's acting strange today.'

'Maybe he's finally mellowing,' said my father.

'Fat chance,' I said. 'He's definitely up to something.'

Mohini never went missing in action, so when twelve thirty came and went on the Sunday before our trip, her absence did not go unnoticed.

'Ros?' my mother knocked on my door.

'Ja, come in.'

'Can you do me a favour?'

'Depends what it is,' I said.

She tutted and shook her head.

'Take a joke, mother,' I said. 'What is it?'

'I need you to remind Mohini that it's lunch time.'

'She's probably in her room. Just call her.'

'She is in her room,' said my mother, 'with her niece.'

'You don't know her name, do you?'

'Don't be ridiculous,' she said.

'Her name is Lolly, mother.'

'Ja, whatever.'

I sighed.

'For God's sake, Rosalinde, for once in your life can you not argue with me and just do what I ask?'

'Sure,' I said, and laughed, 'I'll go and tell Mohini that the royal family is hungry.'

She rolled her eyes.

I couldn't help but eavesdrop outside of Mohini's room. The door was ajar and Lolly had such a loud voice.

'I'm going to varsity next year to do a BCom. That's a Bachelor of Commerce in case you didn't know,' said Lolly.

'How wonderful Lolly, I am so proud of you,' said Mohini.

'What about you, Hini? What are your plans?'

'What plans are you talking about, Lolly?'

'Well, you know. Do you really want to be a maid your whole life?'

She didn't wait for Mohini to answer.

'Honestly Hini, I don't know what's wrong with you. Everyone knows that it's a black woman's place to be a maid. You're the only Indian woman I know who has ever agreed to be some white woman's bloody help.'

Mohini didn't anger, like I would have done. She replied calmly. 'When you say things like that you sound no different to one of those white women.'

'Maybe, but you know it's true. Indians are better than that.' Things were different when I was your age. I didn't have the same opportunities…' her voice trailed off as if travelling to a distant memory.

'It's not about opportunities, Hini. We make our own opportunity in life. It's about choices.'

I peeked through the crack in the door.

'Yes, you're right Lolly. It is about choices. I had a choice and I made it — for better or worse.'

Lolly fell back on the bed in a huff of frustration. 'And what were your choices?'

'Hasn't anyone ever told you why I left?'

'No. You're the black sheep that everyone admonishes but nobody talks about.'

A long silence ensued before Mo spoke. 'When I was your age, daughters were not educated, they were married to a suitable partner — usually the son of an established, wealthy, and respected family, which in turn raised the bride's family profile. It had nothing to do with love and feelings, and there was no choice.'

'Oh my goodness', Lolly interjected.

'My parents thought they were doing the right thing,' said Mohini, 'after all, the same tradition had a hand in their marriage.'

'Did you meet the boy they picked?'

'Yes, they decided on a boy named Sunil. He was training to be a doctor. I only met him once, and he seemed nice enough, but I didn't love him. I didn't choose him. I did not want to marry him.'

'What did you do?'

'Well, I tried to talk to my mother, but she lacked the courage to stand up to my father. She said that marriage would be difficult and awkward in the beginning, but after a few years I would grow accustomed to it.'

'But you didn't want to grow accustomed to it.'

'No, Lolly, I didn't. And although I had never rebelled in my life, I couldn't accept an arranged marriage.'

'Did you tell them?'

'No, Lolly, they wouldn't have listened.'

Lolly raised herself up on her knees, her anticipation as palpable as mine. 'So,' she said, 'how did you get out of it?'

'I planned my departure, scratched some money together, and escaped. I left my mother a note to reassure her of my safety and promised to contact her at a later date. I knew that she and my father would be furious because I had embarrassed both families, but I had to put myself first and do the right thing for me.'

'So how did you end up working for Jericho?'

'Well, I got a job cleaning an office building that happened to be Mr Jericho's head office.'

'Mr Jericho, pfft,' Lolly interjected.

Mohini ignored her and continued. 'I cleaned the office late at night, after everyone went home, but Mr Jericho always worked late. He obviously appreciated the job I did because he offered me a full-time job working for him at his home.'

'I don't doubt that you did a good job, Hini, but I think Jericho prefers coolies to kaffirs.'

'Oh, please Lolly, don't say those words.'

'Okay, okay,' Lolly said, 'but you know that's how they refer to us.'

'Not everyone, Lolly. That much I do know. Now, can I please continue my story?'

'Sorry, I Iini.'

'The job paid well, provided meals and accommodation, so I accepted. Marilyn and Maeve lived with him, but they were almost grown, so I spent most of my time maintaining the house, cooking meals, and walking Gunther.'

'And then Marilyn got married and Ros came along.'

'Yes,' said Mohini, 'then sweet little Lindy arrived and everything changed.'

'Don't you get lonely, Hini? Don't you wish you'd had a

chance to fall in love, or start a business, or do something you've always dreamed about?'

'I have always been content with my own company, Lolly, so my solitary life has not bothered me until recently.'

'Until recently?' said Lolly. 'Does that mean that you're growing restless?'

'Yes, Lolly, now that Lindy is getting older, I'm beginning to crave companionship and regretting not having a family of my own. I love Lindy like she's my own daughter, and she is the reason I have stayed for so long…'

Mohini's words stung like an onion mid-peel, and tears threatened to spill. I swallowed hard and blinked them away.

'I don't know what to say Hini. I'm so sorry. I always assumed you were weak and submissive because you never fought for your rights. But you did fight; you fought for yourself when nobody else would, and there is no fight more noble than that.'

She stopped talking for a minute and embraced Mohini. 'As for Rosalinde,' she continued, 'you're like a second mother to her, but she is growing up. At some stage, you need to go out into the world and fight one more fight for yourself. Find out what's waiting for you.'

Mohini nodded in agreement.

'Mohini?' Jericho's voice reverberated across the garden, and Gunther started barking and chasing his tail in excitement. 'The lunch isn't going to serve itself!'

Mohini rushed out of her bedroom and ran down the stairs without seeing me. Lolly swore and slammed the door.

I slunk into the garden and kneeled on a shaded patch of lawn with my disgrace. Mohini was an integral part of our lives, and yet we knew so little about her life before Sea Breeze. As long as she cooked the meals, took care of everyone, and kept her funny religion to herself, nobody treated Mohini like a person in her own right.

CHAPTER 14

The morning we arrived at the Royal Natal Yacht Club, the sky was clear and the water calm. Jericho called it 'perfect sailing conditions' and looked to be the happiest I had ever seen him. He handed me a bottle of Dom Perignon and asked me to christen the yacht.

'Cabo das Tormentas,' I said, swinging the base of the bottle into the bow. Everyone, including the crew, clapped and cheered.

Before we set sail at nine am, Jericho introduced his right hand seaman, Matt, and delivered a brief speech about the major factors that governed the route we were taking from Durban to Cape Town.

'This coastline is notoriously hair-raising for sailors,' said Jericho, 'partly because the continental shelf lies very close to shore for large stretches, and partly due to the Agulhas current that runs down the coast from Mozambique on a southwesterly course at a speed of up to 6 knots. The area has been compared to the Bermuda triangle because ships have disappeared after reporting monster waves that materialised from nowhere.'

'But, it's not all doom and gloom.' Matt laughed. 'This coast-line is as dramatic as it is dangerous, and we are guaranteed to see whales in Hermanus, great white sharks in Mossell Bay, Cape fur seals, penguin colonies, and dolphin pods along the way.'

'The key to success on this route is to constantly monitor the weather reports,' said Jericho.

'That's right,' said Matt, 'and Cabo has all the latest tools to do just that.'

'Will we be stopping in all the ports?' said my father.

'Unlikely,' said Matt, 'as Jericho mentioned, the success of this route boils down to weather, so if we've got good weather ahead, it's best to keep going.'

'We've got perfect weather today,' said Jericho, 'so we best get going.'

Dinner that evening was a formal affair. My mother wore a dress fit for a royal gala, while my father and Jericho both wore tuxedoes. I wore a simple, knitted long-sleeve black dress, which my mother insisted on dressing up with her late moth-er's pearl necklace.

'Honestly, Ros, would it kill you to wear some make-up?' she said.

'Um, yes, I think it would,' I said.

She rolled her eyes. 'You'll have to make an effort if you ever hope to marry.'

'Maybe I should save myself the trouble and become a lesbi-an.'

She straightened her spine and crossed her arms over her chest. 'Why do you always resort to shock tactics, Ros?'

'Shock tactics? Seriously, mother, there is nothing wrong

with being a lesbian.'

'Not according to the bible,' she said.

'The bible. Uggh.'

'I'm not talking to you anymore, Ros. It's impossible to have a normal conversation with you.'

'You mean it's impossible to have an intelligent conversation.'

She crossed her arms. 'Why couldn't God give me a normal daughter who likes make-up and clothes and does what she's told?'

'Um, maybe because He or She wanted to teach you something different.'

'There you go with your shock tactics again.'

'It's not shock tactics, mother. It's called thinking for yourself.'

She shook her head and left me with a dirty look. I shook my head in despair and finished getting ready for dinner. We might as well have been Saturn and Mars. One made of gas, the other made of rock.

Fairy lights hung like strands of gossamer threads from the dining ceiling, and Brahms' Symphony No. 3 created a relaxed atmosphere. The yacht's French chef cooked a seven course dinner that included escargots in a Roquefort sauce, lemon sorbet palate cleansers, fillet mignon served with a creamy pepper sauce and pommes frites. The table buzzed with conversation between crew members, and Uncle Jericho commanded the room with his charismatic storytelling.

After our crème brulée dessert, Jericho asked me to accompany him outside on the deck. An icy wind blew off the water and I shivered. Jericho took off his jacket and placed it around my shoulders.

'Thank you,' I said.

We both leaned over the railing. The water slapped the hull on each downturn of the yacht as it moved in and out of the swells.

'Isn't the ocean magnificent,' he said, in more of a statement than a question.

'It is,' I said. 'We are fortunate to have the added luxury of sailing across it in our own yacht, don't you think?'

He looked at me and nodded. 'Yes, Ros. We are most fortunate. And we need not feel guilty about it. After all, we have worked hard for this.'

I frowned. 'It has less to do with guilt, and more to do with unfairness,' I said. 'Apartheid creates a massive gap between the haves and the have-nots, and I don't think that I will ever learn to accept that.'

'Ros, the blacks in this country don't want to be civilised. You've seen it yourself with the necklacing.'

I pulled a face in remembrance.

'We build them schools and they burn them down. They will always have a tribal mentality, and no amount of money, opportunity, or equality is going to change that,' he said.

'All I want is fairness. Is that so naïve?'

'Fairness is swinging around again, Ros. These negotiations between de Klerk and the ANC have already led to a number of apartheid laws being dismantled. One being land ownership restrictions.'

'Land ownership will remain the right of a privileged person. Be that person white or black. I have no doubt Mandela will come out on top when all of these negotiations are over. But what about the rest of the black population that are stuck in townships? I doubt much will change for them.'

'No, probably not, Ros, but everyone has a choice at the end of the day.'

'Would you agree that those with privilege have more choices than those in poverty?'

'Yes, Ros, I would agree with that.'

And would you agree that white South Africans chose to upheld apartheid because it afforded them privilege?'

'I would agree with that, Ros, but I also have an age-old conundrum for you.'

'I'm listening.'

'If you can get any mass of people to rise up against injustice you will have accomplished something not even Jesus managed to do.'

'Nazi Germany. Case in point,' I said.

'Three things, Ros: government; propaganda; and the masses. Take the NP's Referendum Yes-Vote-Ad-campaign running at the moment.'

I nodded. 'De Klerk is trying to persuade the whites to end apartheid.'

'Exactly, he's persuading us by tapping into our deepest fears.'

'You mean the threats of a civil war and continued international sanctions?'

'Precisely, my dear. All of which is true. But when you think about the majority of white South Africans, you'll know that they don't need encouragement to end apartheid. With the exception of Eugene Terre'blanche and the rest of those in the Afrikaner heartland, most want to end apartheid, if for no other reason than to save face with the rest of the world. Why then, does de Klerk need to resort to scare tactics? That is the question you should be asking.'

'There is no way that the ANC will share power with the NP,' I said.

He leaned in close and tapped my nose with his index finger. 'Your conviction will be an asset so long as it doesn't blind you to what's right in front of you.'

I nodded and said, 'Why are you being so nice to me all of a sudden?'

His laugh echoed off the water. 'Let's just say that I've been too hard on you, and I'd like to change that.'

'Why now?'

He leaned in closer and whispered. 'I've discovered some disturbing things about your Uncle Léon, and I know that I have let you down.'

His statement caught me completely off guard and I cleared my throat a few times before I said, 'disturbing things?'

'Disturbing enough to revise my will and take serious action.'

I nodded and swallowed.

'But I need you to tell me everything he has done and threatened to do to you.'

I nodded again, unable to find my voice.

'You're shaking, Ros.' He wrapped his arm around my shoulder. 'You weren't expecting this, I'm sorry. We can talk about it before we get back to Durban. Okay?'

'Okay,' I whispered.

He patted me on the back. 'It'll all be okay, Ros. I give you my word.'

My father joined us on the deck. 'Jericho, there's a Macallan on the rocks with your name on it.'

'Splendid,' said Jericho, 'I'll catch up with you in a second.'

My father went back inside and I returned Jericho's jacket.

'Are you coming in?' he said.

'No, I want to watch the water for a while longer,' I said.

'Then keep it,' he said with a wink.

Jericho's words whirred in my head, like the engine in the yacht's belly. I had neither anticipated a truce with Jericho, nor considered how empowering it would be to have him in my corner. The mere idea of telling him the truth about Léon thrilled and terrified me. Would he believe me? And, if he did, what would he do to Léon? I rolled the fantasies of Léon's demise around in my head like a lucky eight ball.

'Time for bed, Ros,' said my father.

'Just a few more minutes,' I said.

He nodded and joined me. 'Being out here reminds me of my childhood when my father took me out fishing on his boat,' he said, inhaling the salt air.'

'You don't talk about him much,' I said.

'He chose to stay behind in Kenya and face certain death when I was ten years old, Ros.'

'Why?'

'Indeed, why? When I figure it out, you'll be the first to know.'

'I'm sorry, Dad. Maybe that's why you're so close to Jericho.'

'Yes, you're probably right,' he said. 'Now, how about we go inside? It's freezing out here.'

When I woke the following morning the weather was the antithesis of the previous day. The ocean hue matched the battleship sky, both mirroring my inner turmoil. The night had not brought any resolution on what information I would relay to Jericho about Léon. My mother unburdened me for a while, at least, when I found her in the kitchen eating scrambled eggs on toast.

'Jericho has been up most of the night with the crew steering us away from an approaching storm,' she said.

I breathed a quiet sigh of relief, like a Catholic after confession. 'What are you reading?' I said.

She held up the Mills and Boon book.

'I don't know how you read those books.'

'And I don't know why you insist on making me look so stupid all the time,' she said.

'I don't think you're stupid, mom,' I said.

'I'm not in the mood for arguing this morning, Ros.'

I poured myself a cup of tea and offered her a refill. She nodded and went back to her book.

The storm postured and kept us on edge, but the day passed without drama, and we eventually sailed through the uncertainty unscathed. By evening, everyone was hungry for food and conversation. Jericho set the tone with his story about Cabo das Tormentas, the Morris family vessel.

'While on an expedition in the 1400s, the Portuguese explorer, Bartolemeu Dias, discovered our fair maiden the Cape of Storms,' said Jericho. 'He named it such for the violent, wild, and unpredictable seas that hurled him into the Southern tip of Africa. Many men lost their lives and ships were wrecked and sunk on that coastline, leaving behind stories of tragedy and woe, danger and narrow escapes. Stories that captured the imagination of my Morris ancestors, who had their own stories of passage and pilgrimage from their birth countries to this wild and savage place that is Africa. In retrospect, one could say that they not only appropriated the Cape of Storms' spirit as their own emblem of triumph, they incorporated it into their personal philosophy and made it their own coat of arms — a reminder that no matter how insurmountable a problem seemed, and no matter how treacherous a situation appeared to be, the human spirit would endure and conquer if it retained the will to do so.'

Jericho sipped his Macallan and gazed around the table.

'Never lose hope. Never take no for an answer,' he said. 'This is what my ancestors believed. This is what made them indomitable and triumphant. They came to this great land with nothing, but viewed everything as an opportunity. Much like this old maiden, Cabo das Tormentas, who started life as a frigate, but has now been transformed from caterpillar to butterfly. The lesson that we can take is that any problem can be overcome, and that we only have to endure as long as we choose to endure.'

He looked at me when he emphasised the word choose, and his story infused me with enough courage to decide that the Léon situation had run its course. No matter the consequences, I had to speak up.

CHAPTER 15

On the day we visited Cape Point, the slate grey sky matched the cold, rocky, cliff, that housed the historic lighthouse, and a cold sprint of wind whipped and blew us up the mountain of stairs. The lighthouse resembled a volcanic rock that had been grown at oceanic depth, amongst seaweed and darkness, and then birthed atop a mountainous outcrop of rocks. Its white body and blue band identical to the cold grey boulders, etched with rain stains, that surrounded and protected it. Positioned high above ocean cliffs, the historic lighthouse only stood half the size of a standard lighthouse, but, like a king preceded by his retinue, or a man on the shoulder of giants, its own stature mattered little. The plaque read:

Historic Lighthouse
1860 -1919
This prefabricated cast iron tower was erected on Cape Point
Peak 249 metres above sea level. The white flashing light of 2 000
candlepower could be seen by ships 67 kilometres out to sea. The
lighthouse proved to be ineffective as it was often covered by cloud

and mist. After the wreck of the Portuguese liner 'Lusitania' in 1911, it was decided to erect the present lighthouse on Dias Point below, 87m above sea level.

We spent half an hour at the historic lighthouse taking photos. On the walk down, my father and Jericho took turns giving their own history lessons about the Cape of Good Hope. Bartolomeu Dias, the first European to reach the cape, named the rocky headland Cabo das Tormentas due to the rough seas, bad visibility, and perilous conditions. It was later renamed by John II of Portugal as the Cape of Good Hope, because of the possibilities it promised as a sea route to India and the East. Uncle Jericho and my father insisted on calling it the Cape of Storms, because they believed it was a more accurate description of Southern Africa's rugged, wild nature. In their minds, South Africa was stormy in every sense of the word, and it was destined to remain that way.

The actual point where the Atlantic and Indian Oceans converged was a sight to behold. From the clifftop viewing platform you could see a clearly demarcated line between the darker, colder water of the Atlantic, and the lighter, warmer water of the Indian. It seemed to defy the laws of science and evoked a visual of apartheid — two oceans colliding, but neither allowed to amalgamate.

Table Mountain was next on our sightseeing list. My anticipation had been building from the moment I woke up and saw the mist-shrouded mountain through my porthole window. Apart from the ocean, it was the most beautiful thing I'd ever seen — a mystical, faraway land. Though I'd experienced the cable car on previous trips, this particular ride was as hair-raising as an Atlantic storm. My mother shared my queasiness, and sat with her face tucked under my father's arm. The final ascent was the worst. As we neared the top, the cable moved from a horizontal to vertical position and the car swayed from side to side as it collided with the infamous Cape wind. I shut my eyes until the car made it safely into its bay. We clambered out in single file, and delayed the terror of the descent by enjoying the unique sights for a few hours. The bluish rocks and wild proteas that grew up the mountain face, were also present at the top. While Jericho and my parents chatted, I went in search of a quieter spot (away from tourists) where I could see Robben Island and watch dassies dart between rocky outcrops. I thought about Mandela, who had been imprisoned on that island for fighting fire with fire. I thought about his impassioned speech, given ten years before my birth:

I have fought against white domination, and I have fought against black domination. I have cherished the ideal of a democratic and free society in which all people will live together in harmony and with equal opportunities...But, my Lord, if it needs to be, it is an ideal for which I am prepared to die.

My mother spent the following day shopping while I joined Jericho, my father, and some of the crew, to see the annual sardine run. Every year, from May through July, as long as the water temperature remained within fourteen to twenty degrees Celsius, billions of sardines (pilchards as they were better known) would spawn in the cool waters of the Agulhas Bank and then move northward along the East coast. Their sheer numbers created a feeding frenzy along the coastline, making it a fertile time for fishermen, dolphins, and sharks alike.

We set out across choppy waters, with Jericho and Matt navigating the yacht in proximity to the Agulhas Bank — said to be a natural boundary between ocean currents from the Atlantic, Indian, and Southern Ocean. By the time we'd reached our destination my hair resembled a bird's nest and my cheeks stung from the wind's slap. But those were minor dissonances relative to the symphonic triumph at play in the water. A pod of dolphins frolicked around a large patch of ocean that looked like a mass of black ink on the surface. On closer inspection, the dolphins danced at the edges, like a natural fish net, herding the packed pilchards like a shepherd boy would herd mountain goats. I watched for at least thirty minutes, mesmerised, until a great white appeared on the scene and the dolphins dispersed. Despite its size, the shark was no less graceful to watch.

I asked Uncle Jericho to forfeit his fishing plans and teach me how to sail Cabo das Tormentas.

'Nothing would make me happier,' he said.

I smiled and told him I'd be right back with my notebook.

'If you can handle the waters of our fair Cape, you can handle anything,' he said when I returned. He started the lesson with a walk around the yacht, pointing out the sailing terms for each different part and its associated equipment.

'This is the boom,' he said tapping the horizontal bar with his hand, 'It's what you need to watch out for when you change direction. It can give you one hell of a wallop on your head if you're not paying attention. Ask me, I learned the hard way when I was a boy.'

I nodded. 'How old were you when you learned to sail?'

'About eight or nine,' he said. 'If I had known you were interested, I would have taught you sooner.'

'Don't worry about that,' I said, 'I'm a fast learner.'

'That I know, Ros, that I know.'

The conversation between Jericho and I finally took place on the first night of our return trip to Durban. When everyone had gone to bed, we took our mugs of tea to the upper level viewing platform, and sat in large, floor-bolted swivel armchairs. I ignored the butterflies in my stomach, took a deep breath, and looked my uncle directly in the eye as I told him everything that had happened with me and Léon. I didn't hold back, and left out nothing. I don't remember taking a breath, or looking away, but I will never forget Jericho's darkening expression as I told my story. As emotions flickered across his face, I couldn't help but think about the afternoon at Léon's house when I watched the electric storm approach, and then discovered his dungeon of perversion. And I can't say when it started, but sometime during my waterfall of words, a real storm made its approach across the ocean toward Cabo. One of those unexpected, but quick and violent, squalls that struck from nowhere and left wreckage in its wake.

Matt burst in on us and pointed to the sky. It looked as if a lion had torn the sky open with its claw. As the three of us stood and stared, lightning bolts lit the darkness, the heavens opened, and torrential rain pelted the yacht. Jericho gave me the loud-hailer and Matt returned to the helm to steer the yacht through the waves that were rapidly gathering size and momentum.

'Tell everyone to get life jackets and assemble at the emergency evacuation point,' said Jericho.

The first wave hit before I reached the evacuation spot. The impact knocked me headfirst into a wooden pillar and the yacht rocked back and forth as waves began to pound it. I kneeled down and crawled along the floor, figuring it would be less dangerous to roll, as opposed to smash, should another wave knock me flying. I didn't have to crawl far, because my father and a crew member came to find me. They gave me a life jacket and we made our way to the evacuation area where there were seats with seat belts. The wind wailed like a banshee and the waves hammered against the frame of the yacht. My father went to check on Jericho and my mother held onto me so tightly that I had nail marks in my arm.

My father returned minutes later, his face as grey as the water.

'Jericho and Matt are missing,' he said.

A group of crew members jumped up and headed toward the control room. I unbuckled my belt. My mother grabbed my arm.

'Stay in your seat,' she said.

'No, mother, I cannot lose Jericho.'

A breaking wave knocked me down as I reached the deck. I didn't care. I got up and searched and searched, until I'd exhausted every nook and cranny. Alas, Jericho and Matt already seemed to be ghosts at sea.

When the squall passed and the waters calmed, we all searched the yacht again. Empty handed, we called the coastguard and declared that there were two men overboard. The coastguard ordered us to stop the yacht and drop anchor until they arrived. When we finally reached the safety of Durban Port, Jericho and Matt were still missing, and we all thought the worst. Back at Sea Breeze, I went to my room, got down on my knees and prayed like my life depended on it. In a short time, my feelings for, and opinion of, Jericho had made a one-eighty degree turn, and the thought of losing him at the beginning of our new relationship rocked my foundations like that squall had rocked the ocean hours before.

CHAPTER 16

The search and rescue expeditions promised possibilities but delivered a dead end. After four weeks of searching, Jericho and Matt were presumed dead. The days following the announcement were tumultuous. From the snippets of argument I overheard between my parents, my mother wanted to relocate to Joburg and be close to her sister, whereas my father wanted to stay in Durban where he could continue to court his partnership at Spencer & Mason. My mother argued that his partnership meant more than she did, and my father didn't necessarily protest. As soon as the dates for the funeral and will-reading were confirmed, my mother invited Maeve and Léon to stay.

The funeral took place on a cold, wet Friday in the West Street Cemetery; the resting place of all the Morris ancestors. The historic cemetery, situated in the heart of Durban, had changed greatly since the first Morris had been laid to rest. What was previously a quiet spot now bustled with a noisy intersection of people, cultures, races, and religion. It lay on the perimeter of the CBD, and was crisscrossed and surrounded by a motorway flyover, the crowded Indian Plaza, and Grey Street Mosque.

Due to the weather, a white tent, the size of a dance hall, was erected over the grave site. Folding chairs, dressed with white cotton covers, were placed in a semi-circle, with the Minister's pulpit front and centre. My father and I greeted people at the entrance of the tent. He held a jumbo umbrella that had the blue and white Morris Construction logo on it. The cemetery was populated with Natal mahogany trees, and the noisy chatter of Indian mynas could be heard above the sound of rain and midday mosque prayers.

When the service began, I sat in the front row, making sure to wedge myself between my father and Mohini. My mother sat next to my father and Maeve, with Léon on the end. I did my best to avoid eye contact with him, but I could feel his gaze burning my skin. My mother cried more often than not and the relentless rain did not help the situation.

I listened to the first five minutes of the sermon, but lost concentration when Léon's persistent gaze could no longer be ignored. I slunk into my chair to avoid his view and then switched off and disappeared into my thoughts. I had to try and convince my father to stay in Durban. The prospect of Joburg and Léon overwhelmed. I thought about talking to Mohini, but immediately decided against it. She had sacrificed enough of herself for one lifetime. The problem belonged to me. Besides, I had already successfully managed it for three years, and only had another twelve months before my eighteenth birthday. If worst came to worst and we had to move to Joburg until I finished school, at least I could move back to Durban to study.

The congregation stood up to sing *Amazing Grace* and offer

a final prayer. Mohini, my father, and I left the cemetery early
to lay out the food that Mohini had prepared for the wake —
mutton biryani, chicken curry and rice, vegetable samosas, and
chilli bites. My mother caught a lift with Maeve and Léon. Oh
to be a fly on that window. I could imagine her telling them her
plans to move back to Joburg. Léon would think Christmas had
come early. The hunter would no longer have to track and chase
his prey. It was coming to him. It would be in close proximity.
It would be unprotected. All he would need to do is aim and
shoot.

CHAPTER 17

Alistair Steadman, a lawyer from Spencer & Mason, conducted the will-reading at Sea Breeze, on a Monday evening, in Jericho's study. He informed us beforehand that my parents, Maeve, Mohini and I needed to be present. My mother sighed her irritation when Mohini arrived, which annoyed me to no end. After all of the years that Mohini had cooked, cleaned, and cared for us, my mother still only saw her as the hired help.

Alistair sipped his scotch on the rocks and cleared his throat. 'Are we ready to begin?'

Everybody nodded.

Mohini's name was first. Alistair expressed Jericho's sincere thanks to Mohini for her twenty-two years of service and then dropped the quarter of a million rand inheritance bomb. The room quietened enough to hear the ocean through the open window, and Jericho's generosity made me sit up and wonder what to expect next.

'In addition,' said Alistair, 'Sea Breeze is to remain in the family, and Mohini can stay as long as she likes.'

Mohini thanked Alistair and excused herself.

Alistair opened a separate letter, written by Jericho and addressed to my mother and Maeve. He sipped his scotch before reading the letter out loud.

Dear Marilyn and Maeve,

If you are reading this letter then you have neither managed to bear a Morris male nor taken an interest in your family's business. I have dedicated my life to Morris Construction and built it into the vibrant, cash-rich, highly respected business that it is today. I hoped that I would one day pass it on to one, or both, of you. Alas, your only ambition has been to marry and collect my fortune when I die.

Alistair looked up to scan our faces for a second and then continued reading.

For this, and other reasons, I am leaving the business to Rosalinde.

Everybody eyed me with mouths agape, and Alistair cleared his throat.

Wilstan, you have proven to be a hard worker and intelligent man whom I respect and regard as a son. Which is why I ask you to run and manage the business, along with a board of trustees, until Rosalinde comes of age.

I tried to make eye contact with my father, but his head was down.

In addition to a large sum of money (to be disclosed to Rosalinde privately) I bequeath her Sea Breeze, the family home in Umhlanga Rocks, and Cabo das Tormentas, the family yacht. Both assets will remain in a trust until her twenty-first birthday, when she comes of age. The house will continue to be maintained by Mohini, who will be allowed to stay as long as she likes.

Alistair cleared his throat, and I shifted in my seat.

Marilyn and Maeve, before you go off the deep-end, I bequeath a sum of money to each of you. Enough to ensure that you never have to work another day in your lives, should you so choose.

When Alistair finished reading the letter, faces were pale, and lips pursed. The atmosphere in the room was akin to that moment before a tsunami, when the ocean sucks in its breath and the water retreats before the moment of impact. I ducked my eyes to avoid the tidal wave of looks and excused myself.

I knocked on Mohini's door and sighed with relief when she welcomed me inside.

'I'm making a cup of tea, Lindy, would you like one?'

'No, thanks, Mo, I can barely keep still never mind eat or drink anything.'

She put the tea cup down. 'What happened, Lindy?'

'Uncle Jericho dropped a bomb. That's what happened.'

'What could be worse than giving me all that money?'

'He has left the business to me and asked my father to run it until I turn twenty one.'

'What?'

'Ja, I can't believe it either, and neither can anyone else. I formed such a negative opinion of Jericho for most of my life, until recently when he started to reveal an altogether different side of himself.'

'Maybe he was hard on you because he saw potential, Lindy.'

I nodded as I pondered her suggestion.

'How do you feel about your inheritance?' said Mohini.

'I'm not sure. On the one hand I've won the lottery, and on the other hand, this is going to change relationships — especially the one between my mother and I.'

'How can she not be happy for you?'

'Have you met my mother?' I said and laughed.

'I'm sure that your mother will come around.'

'Mo, you always see the best in people, but I know my mother. Plus, you never heard what Jericho said about her in the letter. In his brutal style, he basically said that her and Maeve were useless women who had no ambition beyond marriage.'

'Oh, dear.'

'What about you, Mo? What are you going to do with your inheritance?'

'I have not had time to think about that, Lindy, but you'll be the first to know.'

She opened the door. 'You better get back to the others. I don't want them to think that we're conspiring.'

'Okay,' I said. 'Mo?'

'Yes, Lindy.'

'I know I don't show it, but I love you.' I ran down the stairs before she could answer and disappeared into the garden.

The full moon lit a path down to the rocky retaining wall, where I perched on the edge and took counsel from the ocean. The tide was high and the sea spray sprinkled my face each time a wave broke. The night sky seemed brighter than usual and I spotted a shooting star. After all the stormy years playing cat and mouse with Léon, wallowing in the past, and raging about the unfairness of apartheid, the sky relented and revealed its magic. Jericho's revelatory will had given me the validation I didn't realise I'd been seeking, and while I wasn't sure if I wanted to run the Morris construction business, I didn't want to pass up the opportunity to find out.

I shimmied off the wall when I heard a car door slam and sprinted across the lawn. Alistair's car was pulling away, and my father sat in the passenger seat. He opened his window and turned the interior light on.

'Rosalinde, you left before I could speak to you,' said my father. 'This must have come as a surprise.'

'Surprise. Ja, you can say that again.'

'Your mother is not happy with either of us,' he said, 'so I'm going out with Alistair for a drink.'

Alistair leaned forward to speak. 'Ros, we still have a number of things to discuss in private, so why don't we set up an appointment during the week?'

'After school?' I said.

'Yes, or I could come here again one evening. I'll get my secretary to call and set up a time.'

'Okay,' I said.

'Goodnight, Rosalinde,' he said.

'Goodnight, sweetheart,' said my father.

'Goodnight,' I said.

I stood in the driveway until the tail lights disappeared. A shiver electrified my spine. My ouma referred to that sensation as someone walking over her grave. I hoped it was merely an aftershock from the will-reading.

I tiptoed as I approached the house, keen to avoid my mother, but when I got inside I heard raised voices coming from the lounge and couldn't resist eavesdropping.

'How could he leave the business to Rosalinde?' said my mother. 'He must have been out of his mind. It's the most ridiculous thing I've ever heard.'

'You and Maeve are next in line,' said Léon, 'you can't let him get away with this.'

'How am I going to face Mohini?' said my mother. 'This morning she was the hired help, but after tonight she might as well have more rights than I do.'

'If I was in your position and Léon had left money to Glad-ys, I would have to let her go. If for no other reason than pride,' said Maeve.

'Exactly,' said my mother.

'You two will have to fight this,' said Léon, 'and I'm going to help you do that.'

'What would I do without you?' said my mother.

I didn't wait to hear anymore. When I reached my bedroom, I headed straight into the ensuite, turned on the hot water in the shower, turned the lights off, locked the door, and then lit a candle. For years this ritual in the steamy darkness had proven to comfort and drown out the static. I stood face-first under the pounding hot water and rested my hands against the tiles. I would not let my mother destroy what turned out to be the best news and most hope that I'd had for as long as I could re-member. I would phone Alistair first thing in the morning and make an appointment. I needed to know if Jericho's will would hold up in court, and if not, then plan a course of action.

When I got out of the shower and opened the inter-leading door to my bedroom, Léon was sitting on my bed.

'What the hell do you think you're doing?' I said, clutching my towel.

'Waiting for you, of course,' he said, smiling.

'Get out,' I said.

'Jericho's will was quite a surprise,' he said. 'Seems you worked your magic on him too.'

'In what sense?' I said.

His smile dissolved into a grimace. 'Makes me wonder what you've been up to.'

The thin shell of hope cracked, and my thoughts, emotions,

and fears scrambled.

'I thought you only had eyes for me, but you're obviously quite the little slut.'

His words hit me like an assagei. 'My eighteenth birthday is months away,' I said, fighting to stay composed, 'and when that day arrives, I will do everything in my power to get as far away from you as possible. Now, get out of my room before I scream the house down.'

'You seem to have forgotten one little detail,' he said. 'Remember Promise. Remember your promise to me.'

'You know what, Léon,' I said purposefully omitting the word Uncle. 'I don't give a continental fuck about my promise. I've spent the last three years worrying about everyone else and doing what's obviously worse for me. Go fuck yourself, Léon, because I'm certainly never going to.'

He sprang from the bed and grabbed my hair with one hand and gagged my mouth with the other. I stamped my heel on his toe, but he slammed me into the desk and wedged me with the bulk of his body weight. He let go of my hair and ripped the towel off. I struggled and wriggled frantically until he cocked his gun and pressed the cold metal against my breast. I heard the sound of a zip, and then felt a sharp sensation as something hard rammed into me. I couldn't move. Couldn't fight back. Couldn't scream. I was Promise in the prison cell. I could hear him grunting, like I'd heard all those years ago. I could see the silver, twin bell, alarm clock on my desk. The whole thing lasted four minutes, though it felt like hours.

In those minutes of grunting and thrusting I wished that I had kept my mouth shut, that I had never ventured into the kaya, that I had never followed him that day into the prison cells underneath the house. If I had never done those things, then I wouldn't have been bent over my desk, naked, with my uncle raping me. I could smell the scotch on his breath as he breathed against my face and stuck his tongue in my ear. I wanted to die. I wanted to kill him. I wanted to yell. I wanted to howl. I wanted to scream at my mother, and kick Maeve down the steps. I wanted to punch my father in his face, and cry into Mohini's lap. I wanted my ouma to hug me, and tell me that it wasn't my fault. I wanted to do all of those things, but knew that I would not and could not. I was useless and powerless and full of blame. I had brought it on myself and I had no idea how I was going to extricate myself from the mess I'd made.

I knew he had finished when he pulled out of me, and I felt hot liquid run down the inside of my leg. When his hand dropped from my mouth, I didn't turn around. I didn't move at all. I stayed frozen in that position until I heard his zip close. He grabbed my chin and pulled my face toward his, but I shut my eyes tightly so I didn't have to look at his face.

'Droit de seigneur,' he said, as he had done in the dungeon with Promise.

With my eyes still shut I spat in his face and he slapped me hard in return. I grabbed the towel the minute I heard the door open and click shut, then locked it and began moving furniture to secure myself. When the door was jammed tight, I went back to the shower, locked the door behind me and climbed into the scolding water for the second time that night.

I slept fitfully, and then not at all. I couldn't scrub Léon from my mind, like I had from my body. I couldn't forgive myself for being so stupid and for letting my guard down when I knew that he lurked under my roof. I stupidly thought that Jericho's will was distraction enough. How wrong I was. It had delivered the perfect opportunity. That night I had a dream about a super spider, with a metallic body and unbreakable shell. The spider grew twice my size, and trapped me. I tried to kill it, but it only strengthened and grew bigger. My terror paralysed me in my dream, and I couldn't scream or move or fight back.

The next morning, I found Léon sitting at the breakfast table. He smiled and said, 'good morning, Ros,' as if he hadn't snuck into my room the night before and raped me. I ignored him and walked back out toward the kitchen. Mohini wasn't there, but my mother was; drinking a cup of tea and staring out of the window at the ocean.

'I want to go to school early today,' I said.

'Your father's already left for work, so you'll have to wait. Or maybe you can get Léon to take you.'

'No,' I said loudly, causing her look at me.

'Why not?' she said studying me. 'Is everything alright?'

'I had a lot of nightmares and kept thinking about Jericho,' I said.

Mentioning the word Jericho seemed to flick a switch, and her initial concern quickly turned to annoyance.

'Look, Ros, forget that ridiculous will. Your father is talking to Alistair today and hopefully this whole fiasco will be sorted out so that things can return to normal.'

'Things can never return to normal,' I said. My voice, decibels higher than it should have been.

'What is that supposed to mean? Are you sure you're alright?'

She moved toward me and touched my forehead. I pulled back, as if her touch repulsed me, and she stared at me for several seconds.

'I'm going to wait for you in the car,' I said.

'Oh, fine,' she said. 'I'll go and get the keys.'

I made my way across the lawn to the garage, but the over-cast sky made the garage darker than usual. I thought better of sitting in the car alone in the dark — opening myself to another unwanted visit from Léon. I stood for a moment and thought about my situation. I couldn't avoid him indefinitely, but I could protect myself. I turned the garage light on and scanned Jericho's workshop. He had organised it perfectly; his tools nailed to the wall in order of size and functionality. I studied the screwdrivers and chose one as long as my forearm. It wasn't much, but better than nothing, and it would certainly deter Léon in the event of another attack. Though I had resist-ed and avoided him, I hadn't stood up to him because he had wielded my promise against me, but now it didn't matter. All bets were off.

I remembered the phone in Mohini's room and snuck up the stairs to see if she was there. Fortunately, the room was empty. After my ordeal the night before, Alistair's business card was burning a hole in my pocket. His secretary said he wasn't in yet, so I left an urgent message for a follow-up appointment that evening. She said that she would put it in his diary and confirm later in the day. I thanked her and hung up.

My mother hooted in annoyance and I snuck back down the stairs unnoticed and slunk into the passenger seat.

'When is Maeve going home?' I said.

My mother slammed her foot on the break and corrected me. 'Aunty Maeve to you.'

'Ja,' I said, ignoring her, 'when is she going home?'

'Today,' she said.

'Good.'

'You know you're extremely rude. You didn't say goodbye.'

She shook her head and clicked her tongue.

'I'm sure they'll survive, mother. I'm sure they'll survive.'

We drove the rest of the way without another word, and I said a silent thank-you-prayer that Maeve and her arsehole husband would be gone by the time I arrived home from school.

CHAPTER 18

I met with Alistair that evening in the safety of Jericho's study. 'Before we begin, I want you to know that I am acting for Jericho, not your parents.'

'That's a relief,' I said, sitting on the edge of my chair.

'Do you have any questions for me, Ros?'

'Yes, my mother and her sister think it's ludicrous that I've inherited the business and Sea Breeze, and they are questioning the validity of the will.'

'You don't need to worry about that. Jericho wrote his will with my legal advice and I can assure you that it's watertight.'

'I know my Uncle Léon. He will stop at nothing.'

'Ros, believe me when I tell you that you needn't worry. Jericho anticipated your Uncle Léon.'

I met his eyes.

'Speaking of which,' he said. 'Jericho left a video for your eyes only.'

He picked up the remote control and pressed play. I watched Uncle Jericho flick into life on the screen, and Alistair left the room.

Hello Ros. If you're watching this video, then I am addressing you from beyond the grave, and I apologise that I have not lived long enough to take action.

After years of suspicion, my investigator has finally confirmed what I thought to be true — your Uncle Léon is a predator — and provided damning information that you can use to put him away or get rid of him (whichever you choose) for good.

I hit pause on the remote control and stared at the screen. Talk about a wheelbarrow full of surprises. For years, I had viewed Uncle Jericho as my nemesis, and now, in one fell swoop, the past unravelled as he hit me with one surprise after the next. I inhaled and exhaled, thinking about his comment — put him away or get rid of him. What did he mean? I pressed play to find out.

It's taken time and money to delve into Léon's history in France. Turns out all the stories he told us were lies. He never came from a wealthy family. On the contrary. He never knew his father and his prostitute mother was homeless more often than not. From what I can gather, our Léon did not have an ideal childhood and had a strange relationship with his mother. The evidence and first accounts suggest that Léon murdered his mother and then married a wealthy French widow. They were married for less than a year when the widow died of unknown causes. The medical examiner ruled it as 'death by natural causes', because no evidence of foul play could be found. Léon inherited everything, because the widow had no children or next of kin. That's the real source of his money. He met Maeve soon thereafter.

I'm telling you this because I've noticed some changes in you, and I've seen how he looks at you. But, you've never had a problem standing up for yourself. Hell, if you can stand up to me you can stand up to anyone.

He laughed, as if remembering a specific incident. I paused the tape and thought about what he had said. He was right. I wasn't easily manipulated or controlled, which was why I shouldered so much blame for what had happened with Léon. I sighed and pressed play.

However, if he has done something to you, then I want you to confide in Alistair. Alistair knows everything, and he is YOUR lawyer now. He can arrange for my investigator to assist you going forward. You'll need external help if you're ever going to make it to twenty-one.

I smiled.

Take care, Ros, I have great expectations for you and great faith in your ability. Whatever you do, always seek counsel first. Don't be impulsive and make decisions when you're emotional. Trust your gut. Most people have hidden agendas — don't ever let your-self become a casualty of someone else's agenda.

Last, but not least. I bet you never saw any of this coming, did you? Don't over think it. I did what I thought best.

Goodbye, Ros.

Static replaced Jericho's image. I pressed eject and called Alistair back into the study.

'This must be a lot for you to take in,' he said. 'I questioned whether or not to tell you the information about Léon, but Jericho insisted. He believed that you knew, be it via instinct or experience.'

I met his eyes and tried to slow the racing thoughts in my head before I spoke.

'Was Jericho right?' he said.

'Yes.'

'I want to make this easy for you, Ros, so I'll ask you questions that only require short answers. Is that okay?'

I nodded.

'Instinct or experience?'

'Both,' I said.

'Okay. Recent experience?'

'Yes.'

'Can you tell me when?'

'Last night.'

He swallowed and studied me for a moment. 'At home?'

'Yes, in my bedroom.'

He paused again.

'I know this is a sensitive question, Ros, but did he use protection?'

I shook my head and frowned.

'Don't panic, Ros. I know a discreet doctor who supplies emergency contraceptives.'

I nodded, because my words had evaporated.

Alistair picked up the phone, dialled a number, and spoke to someone called Raj. At which point I cut off. I had spent the entire day trying to herd my emotions to safety, and hadn't given a second thought to the fact that I could be pregnant. The possibility made my stomach swell like ten foot waves.

'Ros?' he said.

'Yes,' I said, returning from my thoughts.

'You'll have the pills before I leave tonight. The doctor is on his way.'

I nodded again. 'Thank you, Alistair.'

'Ros, again, I'm sorry to be insensitive, but I strongly recommend that you lay a charge against Léon.'

I shook my head and swallowed. 'This is my fault.'

Alistair stood up as if in protest. 'No, it's not.'

'Yes,' I nodded as if in a trance. 'It really is.'

'Ros,' he said sitting back down.

'Alistair,' I interrupted, 'I've watched the Courtroom TV shows about girls who get raped. They are not seen as victims. And on a practical level, I have washed off all of the evidence. I have no proof.'

Alistair looked at me like an opponent who had stumped him in court. 'Would you be willing to tell me what happened so that I might make a legal affidavit and use it as evidence?'

'What evidence?'

'Well, Jericho had a number of ideas — conventional and unconventional.'

'For example?'

'He has a private investigator who could take care of this quietly. Or, we can present the evidence to the police and do everything by the book.'

'When you say quietly, do you mean pay him off and send him back to France, or do you mean a shallow grave?'

Alistair studied me before the hint of a smile crept into his eyes. 'I can see what Jericho recognised in you,' he said. 'As your lawyer, I would never advise the latter.'

'I know,' I said, laughing, 'wishful thinking on my part.'

'Considering what's happened,' he said, 'I understand, but if you were to bring a case against him he might find himself in a lot of trouble. However, I must warn you that if you pursue that avenue, you will undoubtedly come up against a vicious backlash from your family. They may believe you, but they will not want this to become public. It will be an embarrassment to all of them. I don't want to dissuade you either way. I want you to know exactly what you're getting yourself into, and consider your options carefully. What would be the best outcome for you personally? What avenue could you live with in terms of conscience?'

'Can I think about it?' I said.

'Of course. I would have insisted regardless.'

'How do I handle Léon in the meantime?' I said.

'Léon is back in Joburg, yes?'

'Yes.'

'As long as he's there, he can't hurt you. If there's any news or rumour of his visiting Durban within the next week then call me and I will make arrangements. In the meantime, you need to pay careful attention to what you want to do. I am ready to act as soon as you decide.' He stood up and looked at his watch. 'The doc should be waiting outside. Care to walk me to my car?'

'Thank you, Alistair, words cannot convey my gratitude.'

'Don't mention it, Ros.'

We walked out into the hall and straight into my mother, who fired off a round of twenty questions. Alistair winked at me to meet him outside, and I reassured my mother that it was a bunch of boring legal stuff. She bought it and walked off down the hall, muttering to herself.

I waited at Alistair's car while he walked to the end of the driveway to meet the doctor. When he returned, he slipped a strip of pills into my hand. 'The doc says to take two tonight and one a day for seven days thereafter.'

'What's going to happen?' I said.

He slipped a folded sheet of paper into my other hand and said, 'this is a fact sheet, but it's my understanding that it should cause no more than a little vomiting.'

'Okay,' I said.

'Ros?'

'Yes.'

'I'm sorry about all this.'

'It helps to have someone in my corner,' I said.

He nodded and opened his car door. 'Ros, I'm curious. Have you considered studying law?'

'It's the only career I'm interested in pursuing.'

'Well, you'll be matriculating before you know it. I could organise for you to spend some time at Spencer & Mason if you're interested?'

'I would love that so much,' I said.

'Have you thought about a specialty?'

'Criminal law has always fascinated me.'

'I think criminal law is a lot more interesting in places like America, because they have the jury system. Here, we only have a judge, and it can be rather tedious.'

'Would I be able to sit in on some cases?'

'Absolutely, Ros.'

My mother opened the front door and called me to come in.

Alistair reached into his car for his diary. 'Are you free next Friday after school for a follow-up meeting?'

'Yes.' I nodded and smiled.

'Great, I'll get my secretary to confirm tomorrow.'

'Thanks, Alistair. I look forward to it.'

'Me too, Ros.'

I'd been in my room a couple of minutes when my father knocked on the door. Instead of telling him to come in, like I usually did, I opened it a fraction.'

'Ros? Everything alright?'

'Ja,' I nodded.

'Can I come in?'

'I'm a bit tired, Dad.'

'It'll only take a few minutes, Ros.'

'Okay,' I said, opening the door.'

I sat at my desk with my journal pinned beneath my elbow. He sat in the armchair next to my desk.

'How was the meeting with Alistair?'

I let out a huge sigh. 'He put my mind at ease,' I said.

'You seem a bit on edge, Ros, did something happen?'

I scrutinised him for a long time, wanting to tell him about Léon.

He frowned. 'Ros?'

'Something did happen, but Alistair fixed it.'

'You can talk to me, Ros. I hope you know that.'

I nodded and said, 'What did you want to talk about, Dad?'

'We haven't had a chance to talk about Jericho's will,' he said. How do you feel about inheriting Morris Construction?'

'I'm grateful that Jericho saw so much potential in me, and it's prompted me to think seriously about my future. How do you feel?'

'Honestly, Ros, Jericho has put me in an awkward position. I am a lawyer first, and I don't have any desire to run Morris Construction. Add to that, your mother is furious enough to have moved to one of the guest bedrooms indefinitely.'

'I overheard her talking to Léon and Maeve last night. He's telling her to fight it in court. Do you think she will?' I said.

'Not a chance,' he said. 'Knowing your mother as I do, I can guarantee you that she won't fight for anything. If Jericho hadn't given her a sum of money, then maybe, but as it stands, no way.'

'Well, what are you going to do?' I said.

'I don't know yet, Ros. I'm talking to Alistair just like you. There must be some way around it. I'm concerned about you.'

'Why me?' I said.

'This is a huge responsibility for you, Ros. Is it something you want?'

'I don't know, but I'd like to get the chance to find out.'

He nodded and patted my knee. 'I'll keep that in mind. Whatever I decide, I will try to ensure that it impacts you minimally.'

'Thanks, Dad.'

We stood up and hugged.

'Dad?'

'Yes.'

'Alistair has offered me a three-week law experience at Spencer & Mason during the holidays. He's going to speak to you tomorrow. Will you please say yes?'

'Of course,' he nodded. 'I had no idea you were interested in law?'

'I didn't either until recently.'

'You'll be great. Whatever you decide.'

He closed the door behind him and I locked it for my own sanity. I had spent the entire day trying to occupy my mind and not think about Léon. Every time I let my guard down, my head replayed the night's events and I had to use every ounce of strength to blink the darkness away.

I took the pill before I went to bed. Recurring nightmares of the spider and mutant pregnancies plagued my sleep. I got up several times during the night to vomit. I wasn't sure if it was the pill or the vile dreams that refused to relent. The only thing that kept me halfway sane was the knowledge that I had flushed any seed before it took root inside my body.

CHAPTER 19

Mohini broke her news a week later. With Jericho gone
and a lump sum of money, she thought it time to leave
Sea Breeze. My mother stood up and clapped. My father
expressed his regret but wished her well. As for me. After
overhearing Mohini's conversation with Lolly, my rational brain
had already started planning her exit, but not nearly so soon. I
processed it for a few days before I trusted myself to speak to
her without crying.

I knocked on Mohini's door on a Saturday morning, and
opened it when she said, 'come in, mum'. Her whole face smiled
when she saw me. Sitting behind her sewing machine, her bare
foot continued to tap rhythmically after I entered.

'Is that a new incense?' I said, easing into the conversation,
and not entirely sure of what I wanted to say.

She nodded. 'It's frankincense. We burn it in memory of the
dead.'

'It smells divine,' I said, watching the smoke waft and curl.
'What are you making, Mo?'

'I'm sewing my last ribbon for Mr Jericho's ceremony.'

'I didn't know there was a ceremony?'

'Oh, it's not official, Lindy. It's a Hindu tradition. I was going to do it on my own before I left Sea Breeze. Do you want to join me?'

'Yes, please,' I said. 'How does it work?'

'First, a story,' she said. 'When I first came to Sea Breeze for an interview, Mr Jericho took me on a tour of the grounds. Apart from it being the most beautiful place I'd ever seen, it had an omen that convinced me to take the job.'

'An omen?'

'Yes, a Pippal tree,' she said, smiling at the memory. 'Bring and come.'

She gathered a handful of ribbons for us to hold and then led me down the stairs and towards the back garden. We walked up the sloping lawn toward the pool, past the umbrella thorn tree where the vervet monkeys congregated, through the banana plantation, and up and over a couple of mini hills. We stopped at the edge of the lawn — where the landscaped gardens ended and the yellowwood forest began.

'Where is the Pippal tree, Mo?' I said.

'It's through the forest,' she said.

'Uncle Jericho always warned me against going into the forest,' I said.

She laughed. 'And you listened? That's not like you at all.' She patted me on the shoulder. 'Come on, follow me.'

The forest was darker than I expected. I had associated yellowwood trees with a yellowish trunk, like the yellow hue of the floors and timber finishes inside Sea Breeze. But the bark was almost blackish in colour. The deeper we walked, the more melodious the birds grew, and I wanted to kick myself for obeying Jericho when I shouldn't have.

'It's amazing, Mo,' I said. 'I can't believe I've lived at Sea Breeze all of these years and have never ventured in here.'

'I have been coming here every Saturday since the day I moved to Sea Breeze,' she said.

'Only Saturdays?'

'Yes, the Pippal tree is said to be extra special on Saturday, because Lakshmi visits on that day.'

'Is Lakshmi a Hindu deity?'

'Yes, she is the goddess of wealth, prosperity, and fortune — both material and spiritual,' she added.

'Is that why you come to visit the tree? To be near Lakshmi?'

'Yes and no,' she said. 'I'll explain when we get there.'

We walked until the tree line thinned and the sunshine dilated. When we reached the clearing, the Pippal tree came into view. Rooted as strong as an oak, with branches reaching out like long, elegant piano fingers in every direction, the most amazing aspect was its heart-shaped leaves.

'Wow,' I said. I ran past Mohini toward the tree to take a closer look. 'How come you never brought me with you?'

'I always wanted to, Lindy. I planned to bring you when you got a bit older, but then you grew distant from me...'

Her voice trailed off, like a butterfly, while mine remained cocooned; a caterpillar still feeding on leaves of regret.

With my head down, I said, 'I'm sorry, Mo. I...' I stopped mid-sentence to think about whether or not I should tell her about Léon.

'Lindy, I feel that there is something you need to tell me, but I don't want to pry.'

I looked into her eyes for a long time, biting my lip and agonising over my secret. But then I thought about how selfish that would make me. She was finally putting herself first, and

I owed her the debt of entering her new chapter with a clean slate. My burden would only become her burden, and I loved her too much to do that.

'Something happened to me, Mo,' I said. 'One day I promise to tell you, but not today. Today, just accept my apology for pushing you away when I didn't want to.'

'You can tell me, Lindy. It's not a burden.'

'Mo, I promise to tell you another day. Right now, everything is under control and I'm getting help.'

'Does it have something to do with your Uncle Léon?'

'What makes you say that?' I said.

'A hunch,' she said.

'I'm going to miss you, Mo.' I hugged her tightly, like my ouma used to hug me, and then changed the subject. 'So,' I said, waving the ribbons, 'what do we do with these?'

She sat under the tree and told me to sit next to her. 'The reason I visit this tree every Saturday is for Mr Jericho,' she said.

I cocked my head for her to explain.

'As you know, your uncle lost his only son. And, ever since that day he has mourned that loss and prayed for another son. Alas.' She sighed and closed her eyes as if in prayer.

'I think he wished I was a boy,' I said.

'Perhaps,' she nodded. 'One Saturday afternoon I found Mr Jericho sitting under this tree. Right where you're sitting now. He looked the most upset I'd ever seen him. He wasn't one to show his emotion, you know, but that afternoon was different. I think he needed to talk, because he waved me over and told me to sit with him for a while. He spoke of how much he missed his son and his wife. He said that there were days when the pain of missing them was unbearable. Days when he wanted to

126

take the yacht out and never return.'

I thought about my own fantasy about the yacht — sinking into the blue oblivion of the ocean. I had never seen that side of Jericho, nor suspected its existence. Clearly I wasn't the only one hiding secret emotions.

'I never saw him like that, Mo. It was only toward the end that he started to thaw towards me.'

'I know.' she patted my knee. 'He had a hard time showing his love. I think he was scared of having his heart broken again.'

'So what happened that day?'

'I felt so very bad for him, Lindy, so I told him the story about the Pippal tree. I told him that the Hindus believed that if a man did not have a son, the Pippal should be regarded as one. And, as long as the tree lived, the family name would continue.'

'Is that true?' I said.

'Yes, all true, Lindy. I went on to tell him that it was customary for a woman to ask the tree to bless her with a son by tying red ribbons around the tree branches and trunk.'

'What did he say?'

'I think it caught his imagination and warmed his heart a little, because he asked me to start that same custom on his behalf.'

'And you agreed,' I said.

'Yes, I promised that I would perform the ritual every Saturday, and ask for Jericho to be blessed with a son.'

'Wow,' I said. 'I feel like I've missed out on a lifetime of memories.'

'Don't worry, Lindy. There is still time. It is never too late to start over, is it?'

'I hope not, Mo. I hope not.'

She squeezed my hand and stood up. 'Come, Lindy, let's tie some ribbons for Mr Jericho.'

'Are you still asking for a son?'

'No,' she laughed. 'I am asking the tree to bless him in the afterlife, and thanking it for looking after me all of these years.'

I watched her tie a red ribbon around a low-lying branch and listened to her chanting and speaking in Hindi. I did the same; tying each ribbon slowly and purposely while saying thanks in my mind.

'Perhaps you can continue this weekly tradition after I leave?' she said.

'Oh, yes,' I nodded enthusiastically, 'I would be honoured.'

We spent a few hours at the Pippal tree. Mohini talked about the tradition of building a wooden platform around the tree trunk when it turned twelve years old. Jericho had built such a platform for Mohini to store her basket of incense, ribbons, and the figurine of Lakshmi. The Pippal tree was also known as the Sacred Fig Tree, and part of her weekly ritual involved collecting dead leaves and figs from the ground to maintain the immaculate tree.

On our walk back to the house we talked about Mohini's future plans. She yearned to work with her hands and create. Her cousin had a shop at the Indian Plaza. Perhaps she would sell her wares via his shop. She promised to stay in touch and let me know.

I woke up before sunrise on Mohini's leaving day. A thick mist concealed the ocean but for the sound of waves. With coffee in hand, I sat on the verandah with Gunther at my feet. The lawn swarmed with flying ants; a phenomenon that occurred fairly regularly in summer, due to a combination of humidity and the Queen Ant's mating period. I thought about the cycles of nature and how similar they were to human cycles. Just like the Queen Ant knew to mate, so Mohini knew to leave the nest, and so I knew that it was time to let her go. It didn't change the fact that I was gagging to knock on her door and spend every last second with her, but it did give me a sense of peace about her leaving.

Half an hour later her door opened, and I ran to meet her in the garden.

'Morning, Mo,' I hugged her, and Gunther barked and jumped excitedly. 'Need any help packing?'

'I'm all packed.' She bent down and ruffled Gunther's bushy neck. 'But you can walk with me one last time along the beach.'

We walked in the opposite direction to the lighthouse, silent for the first five minutes. Each time a wave crashed on the shore it covered us in sea spray and Gunther barked like an excited puppy.

Mohini was the first to speak. 'I'm going to miss you, Lindy.'

'I'm going to miss you too, Mo. More than you will ever know.'

'Maybe you can write your story and post it to me,' she said. 'It's often harder to talk about something painful than it is to write about it.'

'You're always so wise, Mo.'

Lolly fetched Mohini a few hours later. Gunther went with her, which was even more heart-wrenching. I struggled to say goodbye without crying. But after she left, I cried for three days solid, continuously and without control. I wept as if my mother and my best friend had died. My eyes hurt when I blinked. As if all the grief in my heart had been transferred to a stinging, burning, throbbing pain in my eyes. I didn't know when, or if, I would see Mohini again, and that uncertainty only exacerbated my grief.

CHAPTER 20

I tapped on Alistair's door, armed with my decision about Léon, and opened it when he said, 'Come in, Ros'.

'How have you been?' said Alistair.

'Mohini left,' I said and sighed.

'You were close?'

I nodded. 'She was like a mother.'

'I take it Léon hasn't made contact?'

'Thankfully, no,' I said. 'Speaking of which, I've made a decision.'

'Before you say anything, Ros, I've got one more surprise.'

I raised my eyebrows.

Alistair walked over to the TV and turned on the video. 'Jericho made a second video tape in which he addresses Léon directly.'

He pressed play, and I leaned back in my chair to watch.

Jericho's stern appearance reminded me of the Jericho I'd grown up with. He told Léon exactly what he had told me. The only deviation being the end, where he gave Léon a threat, or ultimatum, depending on your perspective.

'What do you think?' said Alistair.

'I was going to suggest that the investigator confront him with the evidence that Jericho mentioned. But this tape is way better.'

'We could certainly do that, but we need to weigh up the risks of confronting him before we actually do confront him.'

'You mean worst case scenarios?'

'Precisely.'

'Well, Léon doesn't like to be told what to do, so if he feels cornered he might do something unpredictable. On the other hand, he prides himself on the fact that he puts one face forward but hides another, so the threat might be enough to give him pause.   What are your thoughts?'

'I think Léon probably has a warped sense of entitlement when it comes to his perversions, and if confronted —yes, I agree — he might do something rash.'

'So we agree,' I said. 'The investigator shows Léon the videotape and then keep tabs on him until we can ascertain his next move.'

'Sounds like a plan,' he said.

'Will I meet the investigator?'

'I think it would be better if his identity remained unknown to you. He is skilled at what he does, but he's also ex-military and not exactly what you would call an upstanding citizen.'

'I trust your judgement, Alistair.'

'Your holidays start in two weeks' time. Would you be comfortable if we synchronised the Léon item with your work here? That way you'll be with me during the day.'

'Genius,' I said. 'Thank you, Alistair.'

We shook hands and he walked me to my father's office on the floor below.

'Everything's arranged for the first Monday of the school holidays, Wilstan. She's all yours until then.'

My father and I spoke at the same time — 'Thanks, Alistair.'

'My pleasure,' he said and left.

'So, you're serious about studying law, eh?' my father said.

'The more I think about it, the more it makes sense,' I said.

'Good. You can tell me about it on the way home. I need to finish up a few things.'

He handed me a twenty rand note and said, 'I'll meet you in the cafeteria in an hour.'

I bought a grenadilla yogi sip from the canteen and then wrote in my journal as if I'd parachuted from a plane and had limited time before I hit the ground.

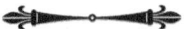

My last two weeks at school were supposed to be ticked off the calendar without incident, but my defiance had reached new heights with Léon's impending exorcism. Of my six school subjects and teachers, only Mr Lawrence, my English teacher, appreciated me. A self-proclaimed atheist (unheard of in my little corner of the world), and the exception to most rules, he possessed his own brand of radical defiance and shamelessly tread his own path. Even his physical appearance defied convention and set him apart from his colleagues. From his unkempt beard, to his creased shirt and tie, he always looked scruffy. No matter how many times he tucked his shirt in, it somehow found its way out in the course of a few steps —as if his clothes knew that they were being forced onto an imposter's body and were determined to escape. I loved his classes, because he encouraged independent thought and welcomed debate.

Mr Darwin, my biology teacher, was the antithesis of Mr Lawrence, and the irony did not end with his name. Neanderthal in proportion, he did in fact resemble a creature from Darwin's theory of evolution. At six foot four he towered above his colleagues during Monday assembly, and appeared more formidable in class with his hirsute body, bear-like hands, clod-hopping feet, and dark narrow-set eyes. Mr Darwin used his intimidating assets to his advantage in the classroom, which kept the majority in line, the majority of the time. Until, that is, one sunny Monday afternoon, when he told me to dissect a frog. I flatly refused on the grounds that I fundamentally disagreed with it. Unimpressed, Mr Darwin switched effortlessly from carrot to stick, and threatened to fail me if I didn't participate. It undeterred my resolve and I told him to go right ahead in a Dirty Harry kind of way. I sat quietly, staring back at him with narrowed eyes as he digested my retort. As his face reddened, he eventually reached the realisation that his negotiation skills were seriously undermined and his grim expression darkened. He stared back at me with a bruised ego and said, 'Consider yourself failed, Miss Wright!'

My father was furious and my mother rolled her eyes as if my morality had exhausted her power of speech. They decided in their infinite wisdom that punishment was the best way forward. I said that I didn't care, but when they unveiled their plans, I instantly regretted my defiance. My punishment did not fit the crime; they postponed my first week with Spencer & Mason and organised a flight alongside my mother, to spend time with Léon and Maeve in Joburg.

The phone rang long enough for me to consider hanging up when Alistair's secretary answered.

'Hi Mariette, can I please speak to Alistair?'

'Hi Rosalinde, he's been called away on urgent business. Can I take a message?'

'Is everything okay?'

'Ja, of course. He had to fly to Joburg to attend an emergency hearing with a client.'

'Oh, right,' I said, feeling relieved and annoyed at once.

'He usually phones me at the end of the day to get his messages. Do you want to leave one?'

'Yes, please. Tell him that there's been a change of plans and I have to go to Joburg with my mother during the first week of the holidays.'

'Oh, weren't you supposed to come here?' she said.

'Yes. That's why I need to talk to him.'

'Okay, Rosalinde, I'll be sure to tell him if he calls me today. Bye for now.'

'Bye,' I said, hanging up the phone and feeling like a puppet in a Punch and Judy show.

CHAPTER 21

My mother put me on a plane to Joburg a day ahead of her, due to a client dinner with my father, and before Alistair returned my call. I arrived at the airport, expecting to be picked up by Aunty Maeve, only to find Léon standing at the mouth of the airport lounge. His eyes looked like open mouths preparing to feast. My heart began its palpitations and my stomach turned into a sailing knot. I wanted to run. Instead, I stood like a defenceless victim, quietly cursing my mother and her wretched family ties. He kissed my cheek and used my elbow as a rudder to lead me toward his metallic blue BMW in the parking lot. He opened the passenger door as if I was his date, and attempted to take my bag, which I clasped tightly and refused to relinquish.

The thirty-minute drive felt like thirty hours as he repeatedly attempted to grope my breasts, and stick his hand between my legs. He talked to me like a long distance lover, against the audio backdrop of Julio Iglesias. Worse still, he made a detour to Eastgate, an upmarket Shopping Centre in a suburb of Joburg. He walked around to open my door, but I locked it and refused to get out, which only angered him. After sixty seconds of him unlocking and me locking the door, he climbed into his seat and grabbed me by my chin. I told him calmly that if he laid a hand on me I would tell Maeve everything – no matter the repercussions. He let go after staring me down for several seconds and we drove to the house without incident and without Julio. I felt empowered for a brief moment, hopeful even, that my stand had triggered a shift in the power dynamic, but my defiance only strengthened his resolve to conquer me. That night, after Maeve had gone to sleep, I could see the shadow of his feet outside my bedroom, hovering like an incubus, waiting to pounce. While he went about the business of rattling the handle and whispering threats through the keyhole, I quietly thanked God for door locks.

The next morning brought its own challenges. Feeling safe in the assumption that Maeve was pottering around the house, I stood in the kitchen, still wearing my dressing gown, waiting for the toast to pop when Léon grabbed me from behind and thrust his hand between my legs. I swirled around and charged him like a bull, then ran to the safety of my room. He stood outside the door and laughed.

'You can run, but you can't hide,' he said.

I cursed my mother for offering me up to the monster on a silver platter.

We went out for dinner on the evening of my mother's arrival. I didn't say much, but I did note an interesting bit of dinner conversation that I thought might come in useful for the private investigator and our plans to confront Léon in a territory other than his own.

'It's our twenty first wedding anniversary in December,' Maeve told my mother.

'I know,' she said, clapping her hands in triumph.

'We're planning to come to Durban,' said Léon, looking at me.

'Oh, how wonderful,' my mother said. 'What are you planning?'

'I'm glad you asked,' said Léon, taking Maeve's hand in his. 'We've booked a number of rooms at the Edward so that you, Wilstan, and Ros can have dinner with us in the Mandarin room and avoid the hassle of driving home afterwards.'

'Oh, I can't wait,' said my mother. 'I adore the Edward.'

'Great,' I said, hoping that Léon would drop dead and save me the trouble of having to deal with him at all.

The rest of the trip passed without further incident from Léon, because I made nice with my mother and stayed by her side. I didn't want to piss her off and alienate her with Léon inches away, and I needed to stay in her good graces so that I could attend my law experience with Alistair. Before Jericho's death I had resisted my father's advice to *go with the flow*, but I finally held a hand of cards, and I needed to play them like a pro. With the poker face perfected, I had to learn to wheel and deal, because, like it or not, the house was calling the shots until I came of age. That small knowledge awarded me a slice of control, and control was important. Control kept me from sinking into that blue oblivion. We returned to Durban at the end of the week, and I set up an appointment with Alistair, hopeful that the Edward could be the perfect stage for Léon's demise.

I persuaded my mother to meet me at the *Workshop* — a railway workshop, dating back to 1860, that had been transformed into a shopping centre — after my meeting with Alistair. I changed into causal clothes en-route in the car, not wanting to show up in my school uniform.

'Ros,' said Alistair pulling a chair out for me. 'I'm sorry about the trip.'

His characteristic serene face clouded, as if a storm had swept over the escarpment without warning, leaving me with an uncharacteristic urge to touch his face and kiss him. The rogue thought triggered a blush and I lowered my head in fear of his reading my thoughts.

'Ros, are you disappointed in me?'

'No, not at all,' I said, standing up unexpectedly. 'I better get going.'

'But you just arrived.'

'Ja, I know, but I'm sure you've got better things to do, right?'

'I can assure you, Ros, you are the best part of my day.'

Our eyes met and I felt the heat of a flush return to my cheeks.

'Please, sit down and stay a little longer. We have yet to organise the law experience. That is, if you're still keen?'

'Of course I'm keen. It's all I've been thinking about.'

'Really?' he said, looking bemused.

I couldn't read the signals. Was he flirting, or did he think of me as a silly schoolgirl? I couldn't tell. I didn't know his exact age, but he was much older than me, so it was probably the latter.

'I can arrange it for the December school holidays.'

'Alistair?'

'Yes, Ros.'

'Léon and Maeve are having an anniversary dinner and sleepover at the Edward in December. Léon has organised rooms for everyone, including a separate room for me. I don't think I can handle anymore.'

'Right,' he nodded. His eyes flared like a stick of dynamite. 'I'll get my investigator friend to guard you from a distance. Would you be comfortable with that?'

'It would certainly make me feel better,' I said, exhaling loudly.

'Leave it to me,' he said, placing his hand on the small of my back. I felt the hum of a cicada travel up my spine and a squadron of dragonflies hover in my stomach.

'I wish you could be there,' I said spontaneously.

Our eyes locked. I blushed again and covered my burning ears with my hair in a useless attempt to hide my embarrassment.

'It could be arranged,' he said.

I nodded. 'I'd like that.'

We said goodbye, and I made my way on love-struck knees to the elevator.

I fantasised about Alistair on my walk to the Workshop and as I browsed for clothes at Edgars and Truworths. I imagined what it would feel like to kiss him. Ever since I had discovered Léon and Promise in the basement, I had seen men as enemy number one, but the thought of Alistair gave me butterflies. Not to mention the fact that it would remove me from Léon's menu. I picked an outfit that flattered my curvy figure, in the event that Alistair did show up, but didn't show too much skin in the event that I'd be alone with Léon.

I met my mother at five o'clock near the Wimpy Bar and

grilled her about The Edward celebration on the way home. I itched to ask her if Alistair could attend, but refrained. She would think it weird and question why I wanted to invite him to my aunt and uncle's anniversary dinner. So, I left it alone and hoped that Alistair had a plan up his sleeve. He was the last thing I thought about when I closed my eyes that night and the first thing I thought about when I woke up the next morning. Like the lighthouse, thoughts of him filled my head every twenty seconds and I felt like a child again; a child who had nothing better to do than daydream.

CHAPTER 22

My first week at Spencer & Mason was like sipping the air of adult freedom. Alistair stacked manila folders in front of me with instruction to read through and offer my opinion. I attended client meetings, work lunches, hearings, court proceedings, and everything in between. Six days in, Alistair called me on a Sunday night with instructions to meet him at Virginia Airport at 4.30am the next day.

My father waved goodbye from behind the floor to ceiling glass windows, and Alistair waved me to the airstrip. We boarded a six-seater plane, which only served to put me in closer proximity to my romantic feelings. I had no idea if Alistair was my type, because I hadn't given much thought to types. Alistair wasn't blonde or dark, and while his toned physique was obvious beneath his tailored suit, it was his long, slender fingers that weakened my knees. The fingers of a classical pianist combined with a brain to stimulate my own. Maybe that was my type.

I managed to get Alistair talking about himself for the duration of our sixty-minute flight. It was only fair, considering how much he knew about me, and how little I knew about him. Alistair Steadman differed to his colleagues at Spencer & Mason, who were sons of the white elite. While they had attended private schools and gained their post-graduate degrees in America and Britain, Alistair had schooled at Glenwood Boys, where his father taught English, and completed his tertiary studies at Natal University.

In his two-year compulsory army service, he had forged an unlikely relationship with a guy called Mark, who came from a dysfunctional family and troubled childhood. At the end of their service Mark had been recruited by an elite force that operated during the Angolan Border War, followed by private security roles and a stint in the SADF.

Once Alistair had finished his articles, with a suburban law firm, he had set his sights high and targeted Spencer & Mason as the law firm of his future career. But, with hiring based on nepotism versus meritocracy, Alistair joined forces with his old pal Mark and tackled employment from another angle. Mark uncovered a valuable piece of information about one of Jericho's executives and Alistair had been bold enough to set up an appointment with Jericho and present it to him. His plan worked and he won Jericho's trust. Jericho had carried out his own investigation and fired the executive shortly thereafter. Spencer & Mason welcomed Alistair to the flock at Jericho's behest and entrusted him with the Morris Construction Account.

Alistair was an only child, like me, and didn't have a girlfriend because his work was his life. I did an imaginary Mexican wave when I heard that.

The hearing played like a gladiator battle, except their arguments replaced physical weapons. Alistair, on behalf of Morris

Construction, remained cool and calm, while Ciko, the Union Leader, made a performance of it. He paced back and forth, and threw his hands in the air for dramatic effect. It thrilled me to watch Alistair in action — in the zone and oblivious to all but Ciko. The more I witnessed the law in action, the more I wanted to pursue a Law Degree.

On the flight back, Alistair and I discussed my future as a lawyer. He remarked on my memory for conversations and details that most people lost through the sieve of their daily life. I confided that I had an insatiable sense of competition with men. I wanted to beat them. For no other reason than I was a woman and they were men, raised to believe they were superior beings by birth.

He laughed. 'You're going to make a formidable lawyer, Ros.'

When he laughed, his eyes crinkled, and when he looked at me, his gaze penetrated my armour.

CHAPTER 23

Léon's and Maeve's anniversary celebration took place on a Saturday night at the Edward Hotel. Unlike the modern, flashy Maharani down the street, heaving with its nouveau riche clientele, the Edward was a colonial beauty with high service standards, understated elegance, and a professional Indian waiting staff reminiscent of the Raj. Similar to London's Savoy, Dorchester, and Grosvenor, the Edward was the original grand old dame of Durban beachfront. It had a strict dress code and boasted a range of eateries, including the Mandarin Room and Seafood Buffet.

My father took us on an extended drive through Durban CBD to enjoy the Christmas decorations. Littered city streets were transformed into Christmas wonderlands, complete with giant wreaths, garlands, flashing lights, and snowmen. We got as far as West Street before my mother told my father to put his foot down and drive her to the Edward already.

Signs of Christmas were evident when we pulled into the semi-circular drive of the Edward too. Hundreds of fairy lights lit the hotel exterior and a giant Christmas tree decorated with silver tinsel and lights stood proudly to the right of the revolving door. The valet opened the doors and ushered us into the festive atmosphere of the hotel, where the bellboy handled our luggage and the receptionist introduced us to Dev, our Indian waiter.

Dev led us toward the bar lounge, where a man in a red velvet dinner jacket played Elton John's *Candle in the Wind*. Maeve and Léon were sitting on an oversized sofa with drinks in hand. After I ordered a ginger ale and my parents ordered a bottle of wine, several minutes of congratulatory hand-shakes and cheek-kissing began. When Léon tried to kiss me on the cheek, I pulled my head away and glared at him. Maeve frowned at me and my mother told me not to ruin the night. My father said nothing. I counted down the months to my eighteenth birthday; an oasis in my desert.

Forty-five minutes later, I had all but given up on Alistair, my mother had drunk a whole bottle of Chardonnay, and I had run out of reasons to visit the ladies room again. My flickering eyes must have caught Léon's attention, because he followed my gaze across the room as Alistair entered the lounge and made his approach.

In previous encounters, my mother had projected her ill feelings about Jericho's will onto Alistair and treated him like enemy number one, so it surprised everyone when she stood up and threw her arms around his neck.

Alistair laughed nervously and swiftly tried to extricate himself. 'Fancy seeing you here,' he said to nobody in particular.

'Yes, fancy that,' said Léon eyeing him closely.

'Is this a special occasion?' said Alistair.

'Yes, it's Maeve's and Léon's anniversary next week,' said my mother, pronouncing s as sh.

'Congratulations,' he said holding out his glass of beer to clink with Léon and Maeve. Maeve clinked happily, but Léon was noncommittal and only went so far as to raise his glass.

'Why don't you join us, Alistair?' said my mother, slurring her s for the second time.

'I'm sure Alistair has other plans,' said Léon.

'Actually, I've been stood up,' said Alistair, raising his eyebrows and cocking his head to one side in a poor me gesture.

'Oh, that's awful,' said my mother grabbing his arm and pulling him down into the seat next to her. 'Join us for dinner. I insist.'

'If it's not an inconvenience,' said Alistair, treading carefully. 'I don't want to gatecrash your party.'

'Oh, don't be silly,' said my mother. 'Tell him Léon, he is welcome to join us for dinner.'

Léon cleared his throat as if struggling to release the word yes from his throat.

'Yes, of course. Who was this girl you were supposed to be meeting?'

'A blind date. Set up by my mother,' said Alistair laughing. 'She thinks that I work too hard and takes it upon herself to set me up with suitable women every chance she gets.'

'Well, you never know,' said Léon winking and raising his glass. 'La nuit est jeune.'

I rolled my eyes. Every time Léon uttered a French phrase, he ruined the romantic language for me. I raised my glass of ginger ale and forced a smile.

Léon wanted to stay in the lounge bar for as long as possible — most likely holding out for Alistair's blind date to appear — but conceded an hour later. We moved to the *Mandarin Room* and seated ourselves around a large round table. The Mandarin

Room was a Chinese restaurant with an open grill, burgundy table cloths, and a lazy susan in the middle of each table. It had a variety of set menus to choose from, but the highlights were the sweet and sour fish and chicken, beef in oyster sauce, vegetable fried rice, and prawn fu yong. Alistair and I waited for everyone to take their seats and strategically placed ourselves away from Léon, who was sandwiched between my father and Maeve.

Mid way through dinner Alistair visited Reception to try and book a room. I used it as an excuse to go to the bathroom. The bathroom at the Edward was a treat in itself. Christmas music played softly in the background, and it smelled more like a perfumery than a bathroom. A long Edwardian bench with blue velvet trim sat opposite a gilded mirror lit by the lights you see in an actress's dressing room. A bathroom attendant was on standby to ensure that fresh warm towels were regularly replenished. Alistair was waiting for me when I exited.

'I've organised for my investigator friend to take over watch when I leave after dinner.'

'You couldn't get a room?' I said, revealing my disappointment.

'The hotel is full tonight, Ros. I can't exactly stay in your room, now can I?'

'Is that a rhetorical question?' I said with a wry smile.

'You're going to get me into trouble young lady.'

'What's all this?' said Léon from behind.

'I was telling Ros that the hotel is booked for the night, so I'll be leaving after dinner,' said Alistair.

'Oh, that's too bad. Never mind,' he said, walking into the gents' with a smile on his face.

'Arsehole,' I muttered.

Alistair smiled and nudged me with his elbow. 'If he tries anything tonight my investigator will deal with him.'

'Ooh, can I watch?' I said.

'Are you sure you haven't had any alcohol, Ros?'

'Not a drop,' I said. 'When I'm not being chased down by that fat pervert, I actually have a wicked sense of humour.'

He smiled and hooked his arm through mine. 'Try to avoid him as best you can and keep your door locked. If he gets any clever ideas there's no need to panic. There will be eyes on you, I promise.'

'Alistair,' I said taking his hand and kissing it, 'thank you.'

Léon came out of the gents' before Alistair could answer. 'The night is young, Alistair, are you sticking around for tea and dessert or are you hitting the clubs?'

Léon looked directly at me when he said hitting the clubs, as if he could smell my affection for Alistair in the air like a perfume left behind by a passing female.

'No clubbing for me, Léon. Besides, I'm having a great time.'

They shot each other knowing glances and I broke the tension by walking back into the restaurant. They each tried to pull out my chair before I sat back down. My mother took no notice, but Maeve's eyes flickered with a hint of annoyance. She stared at me longer than expected and I tried to disarm her with a smile. When that didn't work I asked my father what dessert he'd chosen.

The dessert and fortune cookies arrived along with the jasmine tea. I opened my fortune and read:

A stranger will turn your life upside down.

It intrigued me. What stranger? Would it be tonight, or a month, or year from now? Total nonsense? I held onto the belief that things happened for a reason, even if the reason eluded me at the time. I had to have some kind of belief given what had transpired. I was less sure about karma. But perhaps that was en-route to change. Alistair had certainly ushered the sun into my life; his mere presence and willingness to listen had certainly changed my perspective in ways I had previously thought impossible. Maybe Alistair was the stranger? After all, I didn't know much about him until the reading of Jericho's will. Yes, maybe Alistair was the stranger.

'What does your fortune say, Ros?' said Léon.

'I'll read mine if you read yours,' I said.

'Ha ha, I've already read mine,' he said. 'We've been going round the table reading them out. Where have you been, missy?'

'Lost in thought,' I said redundantly.

'Penny for your thoughts,' said Maeve from across the table.

'My thoughts are worth far more than a penny,' I said.

Everybody looked at me and Alistair nudged me under the table.

'Kidding,' I said.

I read my fortune out loud and laughed, which set everybody at ease. Léon stared at me and I stared back with a smirk on my face. I felt cocky and protected with Alistair by my side.

When Alistair stood up to leave, my mother practically fell over herself trying to convince him to join the adults for a nightcap.

'Thank you, but I really have to go,' he said. 'Happy anniversary, Léon and Maeve.'

'I'll walk you out,' I said, using it as an excuse to leave. Léon eyed me as Alistair ushered me to walk in front of him.

'We'll see you at breakfast, Ros,' said my father. 'Sleep tight.'

'Thanks, Dad,' I said, hoping that I would in fact be able to sleep tight and not be harassed by Léon.

I walked with Alistair through the rotating door and into the warm December air. I took advantage of the few drinks he'd consumed, reading his professional barriers as down, and huddled against his body while we waited outside for the valet to fetch his car.

'What did your fortune cookie say?' I said.

'You really weren't listening?' he said.

'No, I was lost in thought,' I smiled.

He narrowed his eyes and offered me the wryness of a half-smile. 'It said,' he leaned closer to whisper the rest in my ear. My stomach fluttered and he felt close enough to hear me swallow. The beams of his Mercedes broke our moment. He pulled away and looked at me apologetically. 'You need to get yourself to your room.'

I nodded and started to turn, but he grabbed my hand and kissed me on the cheek. 'I'll speak to you tomorrow.'

I couldn't help but smile like a schoolgirl.

'Go,' he said, urging me back inside. He gestured two fingers to his eyes, to assure me that I would not be alone.

Once in my room, I locked the door behind me, switched on the light, and dragged the heavy curtains shut. The phone rang.

'Hello,' I said, expecting to hear the receptionist or my father reminding me about breakfast times.

'I keep thinking about our night together,' said Léon, breathing heavily down the phone line.

My body stiffened at the thought of our night together. I had made a concerted effort not to think about that night. I had tried to cast it out of my mind. I had tried to change the story — told myself that I had fought him off, like I had in the past, that he had grown tired and left me alone.

'Ros, are you there?'

'Ja,' I muttered.

'I didn't book *you* a room at the Edward, I booked *us* a room,' he said, as if his statement was perfectly reasonable and rational.

My head swam in fearful memory and my stomach flipped like a gymnast.

'Ros, will you stop with the silent treatment?'

'Are you joking?' I said, after a long pause.

'No, I am not joking. I have been patient with you long enough. I finally got a taste after waiting for so many years and I can't think about anything else. You drive me insane with your games and your teasing. I thought the chase thrilled me, but it's not, it's you. Marriage is the only thing for it. I want to marry you…'

I dropped the phone. My hands shook. A wave of nausea coursed my body. I ran to the bathroom and flung up the toilet lid to vomit. Things had escalated beyond control. Confronting him with a videotape would never be enough. He spoke as if we'd been having a consensual affair for years, as if we'd made plans and our final step would be marriage!

I went back into the room and placed the phone back on the hook. It rang instantaneously. I picked it up hesitantly, and brought it to my ear.'

'Rosalinde, are you okay? What happened? Shall I come and get you?' he spluttered.

'Over my dead body,' I said, feeling the surge of anger, fear, and adrenaline.

'Now listen here,' he shouted.

'That's enough!' I said, on the verge of losing control. 'I don't know what planet you're on, but this romantic notion of you and me is psychotic. There is no you and me! You're a fucking perv and now you've gone too far!'

'Don't you dare speak to me like that you fucking cunt. Who do you think you are? I've paid a lot of money for this room and I've bought you lingerie….'

'I'm hanging up now!'

'Don't you dare hang up on me you fucking bitch! I'll fucking kill you. If I can't have you, no-one will!'

I took the phone off the hook and barricaded the door with every piece of furniture I could move — writing desk, armchair, coffee table. I paced the room all night, expecting him to bash on the door or lie to the receptionist and open the door with a spare key. But he didn't.

When I saw the hint of sunshine peeping through the slit in the curtains, I thanked God for sparing me another struggle. My head spun and my emotions were spent. I forfeited the shower and opted for the busy breakfast dining room instead. My father was already there. Alone.

'Are you the only one without a hangover?' I joked.

'Ros, I've got a bit of bad news.'

'What?' I sat down opposite him.

'Your Uncle Léon had a heart attack last night and he's in the hospital.'

'What?'

'Your mother and Maeve are at the hospital with him.'

'What time did that happen?' I interjected.

'What time? Um, I'm not sure exactly. The receptionist found him in the phone box in the lobby. I have no idea who he was calling, but stranger things have happened, haven't they?'

My father's voice trailed off along with my thoughts. Could it be? Could he have had a heart attack after our repulsive conversation? My scepticism about God softened as I absorbed what could only be called a miracle. I had prayed for him to die of natural causes, and now, when he had raised the stakes beyond my capacity, a heart attack had struck him down. Of course, he wasn't dead yet.

'Ros, are you okay?'

'Ja, fine. Deep in thought. Um, is he going to pull through?'

'I'm not sure. I won't know anything until we go to the hospital.'

'Well, what are we waiting for?' I said, standing up.

'You sure you're okay?' he said, a confused look on his face.

'Ja, fine. Let's go.'

My father settled the bill and the valet brought the car around. Once the suitcases were packed into the boot we accelerated away from the Edward and headed toward St Augustine's Hospital. The Christmas tree, in the corner of the reception room, did little to disguise the hospital atmosphere. The receptionist gave us directions to Léon's ward and we took the elevator to the Cardiac Unit. The ward nurse looked at us as if she knew something we didn't and then directed us to Léon's room at the end of the corridor on the right. Both the room and the bed were empty.

'Can I help you?' said another nurse.

'Ja, I'm looking for Léon Valmont. The ambulance rushed him from the Edward Hotel this morning.'

'And you are?' she said.

'I'm Léon's brother-in-law. My wife was with Léon when they brought him in.'

'Okay, look I'm sorry to be the one to tell you this, but Mr Valmont passed away about an hour ago. He was taken to surgery for a heart...'

'Where is his wife?' my father interjected.

'I think they went to the chapel,' she said. 'I'm terribly sorry.'

'Thank you,' said my father. 'Where is the chapel?'

'Take the lift to the ground floor and follow the signs.'

'Thank you,' he said.

I followed him out of the ward and waited for the lift to arrive. 'Are you okay, Ros?' he said again.

'Ja, fine,' I said, trying to conceal my joy. Little did he know that I wanted to run to the rooftop and shout, sing, clap my hands, and yell to the world, or Durban at least, that my perverted Uncle had pegged. That I had experienced a miracle. That the saddest day of Maeve's life was the happiest day of mine.

In the elevator I tried to think sad thoughts while my father continued to study my face. We heard Maeve crying before we saw her. My mother sat alongside her on a pew, with her arm around her shoulder.

'You go ahead,' I said, 'I need to go the bathroom.'

'Of course,' he said, 'this must be overwhelming.'

I nodded and left.

I stood at the washbasin and allowed the news of Léon's death to wash over me like the water rushing around the sink. I had never thought it possible, not to mention how it would feel. Amazing. Indescribable. Liberating beyond words. I imagined how different my life would be without Léon. No more cat and mouse games. No more psychotic mind games, or phone calls, or hotel room bookings, or holidays, or ultimatums, or threats.

No more. No more Léon. I said the words out loud — no more Léon — and breathed like a yogi mid-pose.

I phoned Alistair from a phone box, but his phone rang endlessly. I felt deflated. I wanted to share the best news of my life with someone who knew my secret. I wondered why he wasn't answering the phone. I tried a second time, but got no answer, so I returned to the chapel and attempted to hide my glee and relief from Maeve and my parents.

PART III

1992 - 1993

CHAPTER 24

After Léon died, everything changed. My parents divorced, and, unable to accept Jericho's will, but unwilling to fight it without Léon's help, my mother moved to Joburg to live with Maeve. My father buried himself deeper in work, leaving early and returning late, or not at all. Sea Breeze felt like a mausoleum on occasion; the ghosts of Jericho, Mohini, my mother, and Gunther haunting her corridors. After our brief flirtation at the Edward, Alistair raised the issue of age and made himself less available to me. I wasn't sure if he had ever had feelings for me, or whether he had been looking out for me like an older brother protects a sister. I knew that my feelings for him were not the sibling kind. Regardless, I had a whole year left on my matriculation dance card and he was fourteen years my senior. I decided to refocus my attention on more productive matters — like studying, learning to drive, and expanding my sailing experience by taking Jericho's yacht out every weekend.

I started Matric in 1992, and, unlike other academic years, I actually worked hard. The Spencer & Mason experience had cemented my interest in pursuing a Law Degree, and I was

determined to perfect my grades and keep my political shenan-
igans to a minimum. Fortunately for me (and my teachers), the
politics of apartheid was shifting, with the Referendum set for
March. The Referendum was an exercise, organised by the NP,
to take the temperature of the white population regarding the
changes initiated since Mandela's release and unbanning of the
ANC in 1990. Only whites over 18 were eligible to vote, so I
had to settle with witnessing my father's vote instead of casting
my own.

The voting queue snaked like an anaconda from the entrance
of the town hall across the field and out into the parking lot.
Groups of blacks had gathered to protest and could be heard
toyi toyi'ing over the crowds. My father emphasised his dis-
pleasure about voting. He said it was rigged; that the ANC and
de Klerk had already done the deal, and were only leading the
country on a merry little dance.

'Uncle Jericho said a similar thing before he died,' I said.

My father ignored what I'd said and continued talking. 'That
bloody de Klerk is going to sell us out. He's trying to convince
everyone that the government of the future will be bilateral,
but it won't, because the ANC are running the show. When the
majority vote *yes* to this Referendum, which will happen, they
will also be saying yes to a government run by terrorists. The
best we can do when the actual election rolls around, is to vote
locally, and give the IFP majority power of Natal. Buthelezi is
not a terrorist. And the world has turned a blind eye to the fact
that Mandela is.'

'Aren't all parties involved in the CODESA negotiations?' I
said.

'It's all a front, Ros. The real negotiations are going on between de Klerk and the ANC. You mark my words; the ANC

have already won the election.'

'Well, I hope you're wrong,' I said.

He shook his head. 'This vote will be followed by more violence.'

I felt frustrated that I couldn't vote. After all, I was months away from eighteen. Then again, it paled in comparison to the generation of blacks who had never been allowed to vote because of their skin colour. It made me sick. It was such moments when the reality of apartheid put the township violence and general uprising into perspective. The black majority were fighting four decades of oppression. The ANC and Mandela called themselves Freedom Fighters, while the whites called them Terrorists. It was all a matter of perspective. At least de Klerk was forcing the nation to finally act against apartheid instead of maintaining the status quo.

A sixty-eight percent majority voted yes to continue reforms and negotiations, with eighty-five percent of Durban voting yes. It brightened my outlook for a split second, but the Referendum only served to stir up more negative sentiment and high emotion. For one, the black population had not been allowed to vote. And second, reports persisted that de Klerk was negotiating solely with the ANC instead of including the other parties. The IFP were especially at odds with the arrangement.

My father's prediction of doom and gloom wasn't too far from the truth. First came the Boipatong Massacre in June that year. Forty-five township residents were attacked by armed men. The attackers were said to be members of the IFP, and because the IFP was the ANCs main rival, the ANC blamed the IFP and withdrew from the CODESA negotiations. Between news reports and my father's political knowledge, I started to see the bigger picture and understand how complex and volatile the whole situation was. My father told me about a military initiative called the Marion Operation. Started by the SADF during the Angolan War, its origins were said to trace back to the murder of Piet Retief in 1838 by the Zulu king Dingane. The murder led to an alliance between the Boers and the Zulus, after which Afrikaner security was said to be closely linked to Zulu security. Operation Marion became integral to the apartheid government's response to uprising during the 80s, where a Zulu militia was trained by the SADF Special Forces, the first of which came from the IFP. In relation to the CODESA negotiations, the ANC laid equal blame on the government and the IFP and reacted by withdrawing from negotiations, followed by a variety of organised protests.

One such protest occurred in the Ciskei's capital Bisho, where the ANC organised an occupation of Bisho to force the military leader, Gqoto, to resign. The occupation consisted of 80,000 ANC protestors, and ended in the Bisho Massacre, where 28 protestors were shot and killed by the Ciskei Defence Force.

The Bisho Massacre led to new negotiations between de Klerk and the ANC, and in September '92 they signed the *Record of Understanding* — an agreement that dealt with a constitutional assembly, interim government, and the granting of immunity to political prisoners. An agreement that my father predicted to be the beginning of the end.

In between the political manoeuvring, my father managed to do his own manoeuvring with Morris Construction. With Alistair's help, he assembled a board of executives and spearheaded an IPO to take Morris Construction public. With the company's strong financial history and stability, the offering was over-prescribed and the majority stockholders, being myself, made a small fortune. My father stayed true to his word and made me the majority shareholder. He organised a trust to protect my interests until such time as I finished studying and decided what I wanted to do. The whole thing seemed like a fairy tale to me. But if there was one thing that I'd learned, it was that fairy tales did not exist.

My matric year ended much like the CODESA negotiations. When my results arrived, I had narrowly missed the score required to gain entry into the LLB, due to my Afrikaans mark. As a result, I had to enrol in a Bachelor of Arts at Natal University. It wasn't the end of the world, but it required me to take a detour on the path to my chosen destination. I wasn't restricted to subjects, so I chose the subjects that were close to my heart — Politics, Literary Studies, Philosophy and Psychology — in the hopes that I would naturally excel.

CHAPTER 25

I started University in 1993; the year that South African Tertiary Institutions opened their doors to all races, in the lead up to apartheid's finale. My father was on edge, thinking the worst, saying that the Record of Understanding was really the Record of Misunderstanding for the oblivious majority. He harped on about Mandela, the terrorist, who was primed to be the next South African President, but who had maimed and killed hundreds of innocent people. Not to mention the possibility of a personal vendetta, considering how the apartheid government had subjected him to 27 years in prison. Given his hero-status to the black majority, who could expect him to have anything other than revenge on his mind?

I thought that my father was being overly pessimistic. I had been dreaming about the end of apartheid since the Wimpy Bar incident. It was time to redress the balance. The inequality had to end — whatever the consequences. And yes, there would surely be consequences. It was only natural. But, regardless of what I'd seen and experienced, I believed the cliché that good would conquer evil. Naïvety conditioned through religion, maybe, or maybe I wanted to believe it. The alternative — a civil war at worst — would be cataclysmic. What if the entire black population held strong to their white hatred and decided to crush us? What then? If I thought about it honestly, I couldn't blame them for thinking that way. I tried to imagine how I would feel if the tables had been turned. I wanted to believe that I could move beyond the past and see it as history, but then again, how could I possibly imagine what four decades of oppression felt like? I couldn't imagine it. Whatever I imagined would be tainted with the reality of my own privileged situation. My anti-apartheid sentiment had only been demonstrated via childish gestures. A far cry from Stompie, the activist. At face value, I was a white oppressor. The reality unnerved me, because I desperately wanted to erase those years of apartheid and start afresh. But wanting didn't make it so. Still, I held onto my optimism like a kite flying against the wind.

Due to record numbers, my Politics class convened in the largest auditorium lecture hall on campus. Of the hundreds present, I could count the white faces on two hands. I befriended a man named Paris during my first Politics lecture. I say man, because he was in his late twenties at least. His charisma attracted me like a magnet the second I saw him. Compared to the majority of African students, who either looked at me with contempt or not at all, Paris looked me in the eye — as if he could, and desired to, see beyond the colour of my skin. He was tall enough for me to ask how tall he was; six foot six. After the lecture he invited me for a coffee. If we hadn't known at first sight, then the conversation confirmed our mutual attraction. Like the ebony and ivory keys on a piano, we traversed every subject — taboo or otherwise — and discovered that we had many things in common.

He was a Drama and Literature Major, who aspired to be a playwright. He believed that characters on stage and paper could say and do things that people in the real world would be imprisoned or criticised for. Not that he didn't speak up in the real world, but rather that Art often made unpalatable ideas more palatable for a society that was governed by a totalitarian regime. Needless to say that our conversation outlived the coffee.

'Are you hungry?' he said.

'I could eat.'

'Wait here.'

He walked over to the canteen. My insides smiled and bristled as I watched him talking to another African student in the queue. Their public conversations were the antithesis of our subdued, anaemic interactions. They talked at full volume. As if life was a vinyl that could only be truly appreciated when plugged into an amplifier and turned way up. Paris returned with bunny chow — a half loaf of hollowed-out bread filled with curry. Eating it required one to throw out all western eating etiquette and get your hands dirty. It reminded me of Mohini, and how much my mother had despised the practice of eating with our hands.

'Can I ask you something personal, Ros?'

'Of course.'

'I've always wanted to ask a white person this question, but never had the chance.'

'Ask away,' I said.

'Was there a moment when you discovered apartheid and questioned it, or was it something you never thought about?'

I told Paris about the day in 1982 when I saw the *Whites Only* sign outside the Wimpy Bar and questioned my mother.

'What did she say?'

'She translated it into a rule that I must accept and obey.'

'And?'

'And, I refused to eat my food in protest.'

He wiped his hands, pushed his chair back and stood beside me. I looked up at him like I would the Umhlanga lighthouse.

'Stand up, Ros.'

I stood up and faced him. He held my face in his hands and said, 'I knew you were special.'

'I'm not special,' I said. 'I have spent my whole life criticising apartheid, but doing very little to change anything.'

'Tula,' he said, 'you knew right from wrong and you had the courage to speak up.'

'Fat lot of good it did.'

He kissed me, unexpectedly, and I reciprocated.

'Get a room, cousin.'

We parted lips.

'Ros, meet my cousin, Maleven,' said Paris.

'Hi Maleven.'

I held out my hand to shake his, but he grimaced and said, 'It's time to go, Paris.'

Paris hugged me and whispered in my ear, 'Don't mind my cousin, Ros. He hasn't learnt to forgive yet. I'll see you in Literature class tomorrow.'

'See you tomorrow,' I said.

I watched him walk away, feeling like a tourist in a foreign country.

From that day on, Paris and I spent time together in and out of varsity. I regularly played taxi, dropping him and Maleven at home after nights out. Neither of them lived at home as such.

They shared accommodation with a group of friends. Paris hailed from a township north of Durban called KwaMashu, while Maleven had grown up between homes — with his father in the Joburg township of Alexandra, and his mother in the inner city suburb of Hillbrow. After Maleven's parents broke up, his mother had conceived a child of mixed race and moved to Hillbrow to raise the coloured boy. During apartheid, multiracial and homosexual relationships were illegal, but not unheard of, and Hillbrow was known to be a progressive and subversive suburb that provided a hub for society's outcasts. When I learned about Maleven's background, I understood why he hated me. He would have experienced the worst of apartheid. A stepbrother considered illegal because of his mixed race parents, combined with the abject poverty of a township like Alex, as Paris called it. In all the conversations I had with Paris, I never once mentioned my own privileged situation. Knowing the reason behind Maleven's white hatred, I feared it would land me in trouble. Having my own car was privilege enough, and I thanked myself for insisting on a VW Polo as opposed to the BMW my parents wanted to buy me. Cell phones were another symbol of privilege and status. My parents insisted I get a cell given the dangers of driving alone. They were the only ones who knew I had one. I longed to belong to Paris's group of friends — aesthetically impossible, of course, philosophically impossible, perhaps, but I wanted to try.

From what Paris told me about his and Maleven's backgrounds, they were as different as the cities that birthed them. Paris, with a mind as expansive as the Indian Ocean, was the epitome of sunny Durban, while Maleven's immovable opinion on white-guilt epitomised the landlocked city of Joburg. To be fair, I did think that Maleven had a point. The difference between my and Maleven's Hillbrow was a case in point. I remember one of our annual trips to Maeve and Léon. I spent a Sunday with my father in central Joburg. In the morning, we shopped for jazz vinyls in basement-level music stores in Hillbrow, and met his friend from university for lunch at a trendy restaurant. Later, when dusk settled over the city, my father took me to the top of Carlton Centre to see Joburg from seven hundred feet up. Meanwhile, Maleven's mother lived in a perpetual state of fear because the apartheid government dictated who she could and couldn't love. While my father chose to visit Hillbrow for its variety of jazz records, Maleven's mother chose to live in Hillbrow because it was the only progressive, white-designated, suburb in Joburg that semi-accepted multi-racial relationships. In retrospect, there was undoubtedly such a thing as white-guilt, but I believed that it belonged to the generation who had established and accepted apartheid, not future generations who had never been given a choice either way.

In April '93 de Klerk and the ANC resumed talks in a new forum called the MultiParty Negotiating Forum (MPNF). However, with the NP and the ANC being the two main negotiating entities, not all parties were happy. The structure of the MPNF meant that the NP and ANC had to reach a bilateral consensus before bringing any issues to the rest of the Forum. For this reason, Buthelezi removed the IFP from the MPNF and formed COSAG (Concerned South African's Group).

The volatility of the different political groups and tribal factions made everyone antsy — especially Durban, with its large community of rivalling Zulus and Xhosas. Crime in and outside of townships increased, with necklacing becoming more prolific. Car theft and hijacking became so bad that Car Guards sprang up, and women driving alone after dark were given immunity to slow down, but not stop, at red robots. Car Guards generally comprised the unemployed and down-and-outs, and they tasked themselves with finding a parking space and/or guarding your parked car for a price. The economic realities of rising crime cemented the Insurance and Security Industries, and led to a steady stream of whites emigrating to places like New Zealand, Britain, and Australia. Race relations simmered in uncertainty for those who stayed behind. The whites wanted to forgive and forget, all the while knowing that the collective black population had the memory of an elephant.

CHAPTER 26

Paris surprised me with an invitation to a wedding feast at his mother's home in KwaMashu. The thought of entering a township sent shockwaves up my spine, and I stuttered a non-answer. He raised his eyebrow at me in disgust.

'Rosalinde. How are we supposed to mend fences if you live in fear of us?'

I didn't answer immediately. I knew he was right, but I had genuine fear in my heart at the thought of going anywhere near a township. Especially KwaMashu. Whenever my father mentioned KwaMashu, the mere inflection of those two words conjured the skull and crossbow symbol found on a bottle of poison. I may have been naïve in my desire to make amends, but I wasn't stupid. A white girl going to KwaMashu would be dumb and dangerous.

'Rosalinde,' Paris repeated. 'I promise that you'll be safe.'

'I don't know, Paris. Can I sleep on it and tell you tomorrow?'

'Sure, you sleep on it, Rosalinde. Like Sleeping Beauty.'

He walked away in a huff.

'Paris,' I called after him.

'What, Ros?'

'Who's getting married?'

'My sister,' he said.

'You have a sister?'

'Yebo.'

'What else are you hiding from me?' I said, trying to lighten the mood.

'I told my mother about you, and she's expecting you to come.'

'Okay,' I said in a moment of weakness.

'Really?' he said, smiling.

'Really.'

He linked his arm with mine and walked me to my next lecture.

'Will Maleven be there?' I said.

'Yebo, Ros.'

'He makes me very uncomfortable,' I said, sighing loudly.

'Has he said or done something to you, Ros? Tell me and I'll sort him out.'

'No, it's nothing concrete, Paris. It's more of an uneasy feeling. I sense an undercurrent of rage in him, and it scares me.'

'I agree that he's angry, Ros, but I think rage is a bit harsh. You probably need to give him time to get to know you like I do.'

'Promise not to leave me alone with him, that's all I ask.'

'I promise, Ros.'

When the day of the township wedding arrived, my nerves were strung as tight as guitar strings. I told my father that I was going to a friend's house for the day. I fetched Paris from his accommodation and he navigated me to KwaMashu. By the time we entered the township, my sense of foreboding had manifested in a raging headache, and I itched to turn around and go back home. I couldn't tell if it was my gut instinct or my white conditioning. I rationalised that it was likely to be the latter and tried to mask my thorny emotions with a rosy smile.

Sandy dirt lined the township streets, and an assortment of shacks and small brick houses were crammed together like the proverbial sardines. Rubbish littered the streets and grassy areas. Muddy puddles, caused by a lack of drainage and what smelled like sewerage, covered the streets in parts. Chickens, goats, and mongrel dogs ran loose. Barefooted children played soccer in the street, and women, with babies tied to their backs, went about their work. A group of men congregated to smoke, drink, and talk in a makeshift shebeen.

The shacks were constructed of assorted materials — scraps of wood, corrugated iron, breeze blocks, stolen billboard signs, number plates — and mostly roofed with rusted tin sheets that were held in place with bricks, tyres, tables, and rocks. Makeshift clothes lines hung in the tiny gaps between shacks, and car tyres were stacked like towers. The odd tree grew between patches of grassy areas, but sandy dirt predominated. Despite the poor conditions, the township was a colourful place.

When I climbed out of the car I couldn't help but dry retch at the smells that assaulted my senses. A combination of sewerage, raw meat, blood, boiled chicken — all intensified by the Durban humidity. On our arrival, Paris led me toward the kitchen to meet his mother, Dorothy. She was a typical African mama; heavy-set and jovial. I held out my hand to shake hers, but she pulled me toward her and squeezed. Her breasts felt like inflatable pillows and she smelled like the samp and beans that she stirred inside the army-size pot. Her motherly embrace settled my nerves and augmented my affection for Paris. She insisted I call her Dorothy and make myself at home. The bride-to-be was less welcoming. She looked me up and down when Paris introduced me and said something in Zulu before she rolled her eyes and walked away.

'What did she say?'

'She said that I couldn't afford your lobola,' said Paris.

'You mean how many cows it would take for you to marry me?'

'Yebo.' He hit his knee and laughed.

'Haha,' I said. 'Did your sister's fiancee pay a lobola?'

'Yebo,' he said, 'it's tradition.'

I rolled my eyes and shook my head.

Paris led me to an outdoor area, where the sun hung like a canopy and patches of grass sprouted at random amidst the loose dirt. The first thing I noticed was an Africander bull, tied to a lone tree with a rope that was too short to allow the bull to sit or lie down. It mooed loudly as if in discomfort and distress. My stomach knotted at the sight. Two African men sat in the tree with their legs draped over either side of the branches as if riding a horse. One held an assagei and the other held a large butcher's knife.

'Sawubona,' they both nodded in my direction.

'Yebo, sawubona,' I replied and smiled.

Paris led me to the seating; a semi-circle of breeze blocks that filled three quarters of the space. We sat in the front row, close to the bull, Maleven in the row behind us. Paris turned and gave Maleven the traditional African handshake — a standard handshake, followed by a handshake with interlocking of thumbs, and then pinkies. I said hello to him, but he stared at me, true to form, as if I was an official representative of the apartheid government. Minutes later, Dorothy joined us in the front row and sat adjacent to Paris.

'Is your dad here?' I whispered into Paris's ear.

'Yebo,' he said, pointing to a man in traditional clothing. 'He will lead the ceremony.'

The man, Paris's father —dressed in leopard skin neckpiece and headband, a skirt made from cow tails and animal skin, and a Zulu shield and spear in hand — took centre stage and addressed the audience in Zulu. Everyone clapped when he finished. Before I could think or speak, the man on the wall plunged the spear into the tip of the bull's head. He did this repeatedly. The bull's eyes widened, but it made no sound — as if it was paralysed from the head down. I made a move to stand up, but Paris pulled me down and whispered into my ear.

'Don't you dare. It would be considered highly disrespectful if you stood up and left.'

'I can't watch this,' I whispered back.

'Then look away,' he said.

I heard Maleven snicker behind me, and Dorothy leaned forward with her finger pressed against her lip to shush us.

'Sorry,' I muttered and stared ahead.

The other man had jumped down from the wall and cut the rope so that the bull fell to the ground. Then a handful of men went over to hold the bull steady as the one with the butcher's knife cut its throat painstakingly slowly. I wasn't sure if the knife was blunt, or the bull's neck and hide was particularly tough to cut through, but it took a long time to slice through.

'Why are its eyes still open?' I whispered to Paris.

'Because it's still alive,' he said.

'Oh my God,' I said, starting to hyperventilate.

When the blood flowed and spread toward the front row seats, my boiled egg and toast breakfast swelled like a whirlpool and before I could exercise any control I vomited over my feet. Paris grabbed my elbow and said something in Zulu to the crowd. I gave a final look back at the bull. The men were thrusting its neck up and down to drain the blood into a large silver pan that looked like the trays that gold diggers used to sift stones from the water. Its eyes were still open, and I vomited again — hating myself for doing nothing to stop the cruelty, and promising to never allow a morsel of meat past my mouth ever again.

'I can't believe you,' I said when we were inside and out of earshot.

'What?' he said, throwing up his hands in the air. 'What can't you believe?'

'You,' I said, 'This,' I waved my hand in the air. 'You should have warned me beforehand. I would have said no.'

'Maybe that's why I didn't warn you,' he said. 'Maybe you need a good dose of reality.'

'Reality?' I said.

'You're a hypocrite,' he said. 'Everything is so sanitised in your whitewashed world, Ros, including your food. You pick your neatly packaged steak off the supermarket shelf, never giving it another thought. Do you think your supermarket steak isn't slaughtered?'

'Of course I know it's slaughtered, Paris, I'm not a halfwit.'

'So why is this so different then?' he probed.

I sighed. 'Because I don't get a front row seat to its slaughter. I don't bear witness to its suffering and terror.'

He nodded his head as if vindicated.

'Don't nod your head, Paris. How can you watch an animal

suffer and eat it without guilt?'

'Are you saying that you're better than me because your slaughter happens behind closed doors, Ros?'

'I didn't say that.'

'Then explain yourself.'

'You and I come from different worlds, Paris. I don't need to explain that.'

His eyes narrowed and he leaned in close to my face. 'You think you're better than us.'

'No, I don't.'

'Yes, you do,' he said.

'Why did you bring me here?' I said. 'Are you testing me?'

'I'm trying to get to know you better, Ros, by inviting you into my world. Isn't that what you've been asking for?'

'Yes,' I said. 'But this…I'll never get used to living like this.'

'Living like this — what does that mean, Ros?'

'I refuse to say anymore on this subject. It's only going to end badly. I need to leave.'

'Spoken like a lawyer,' he said.

I walked toward the front door.

'If you leave now, you will disgrace me in front of my family.'

I turned around to face him. 'That's another thing that won't work between us, Paris. This whole African-male-sexist-bullshit. I'm not some subservient fucking woman.'

He started to speak, but I interrupted him.

'Before you play the racism/apartheid card, let me tell you that it has nothing to do with it. This is about my personal philosophy. I do not abide by patriarchy—be it black or white.'

'It's my culture and tradition, Ros.'

'Well then you know what? Your tradition and culture is no less fucked up than mine.'

I ran out of the door and clicked my alarm to unlock the car, but he caught a hold of me as I swung the door open.

'You know what I love about you, Ros?' he said.

My heart beat out of my chest like the drums that could now be heard from the courtyard. 'I'm guessing nothing,' I said.

The corner of his half-opened mouth curled, and he stared at me with a combination of contempt and lust. 'Drive safely, Ros,' he said. 'I'll tell my family that you're sick, and I'll see you at varsity next week.'

I got into my car, keeping my eyes on him the whole time, not believing that he would let me leave without incident. But he just stood there, and I watched him until he disappeared from my rear-view mirror. Apart from three goats crossing the street, and kids playing soccer, nothing stopped me from leaving the gates of KwaMashu, and relief flooded my body much like the relief that bull must have felt when death finally arrived.

CHAPTER 27

When I saw Paris at varsity the following week he apologised for being insensitive. I told him to forget about it, and in turn apologised for what I'd said. We shook hands and promised to move past it, until 10 April 1993, when Chris Hani, the leader of the Communist Party, and senior ANC leader, was assassinated outside his home in Boksburg by a right wing white male. Political simmering reached boiling point and riots broke out. My father insisted that I stay home from varsity the next day, especially my Politics class. He never used the word fuck in my presence, but he used it that night while we watched the news about Hani's assassination. Marches were announced for the following day and people were cautioned to avoid city centres, where violence had been, and was expected to continue to be, heightened.

I heeded my father's advice and skipped a day of varsity. We spent the day watching the news in despair. Angry looters trashed the city centres. Youth marches barricaded entries and exits with taxis, and blocked roads by burning tyres, throwing rocks and stones from overpasses and bridges. My instinct told me that Maleven was amongst the crowds that hurled abuse, but I had no idea what Paris was doing. A hopeful but naïve part of me balanced the future of racial harmony on the outcome of my relationship with Paris, and I worried that continuing political setbacks would spell the end.

The assassination caused such turmoil that Mandela gave a speech. And quite a speech it turned out to be; presidential, wise, and full of forgiveness. Much like his Rivonia speech, it filled me with hope, and I was obviously not alone, because every newspaper and channel played it on repeat until it gained the power of a subliminal message.

Tonight I am reaching out to every single South African, black and white, from the very depths of my being. A white man, full of prejudice and hate, came to our country and committed a deed so foul that our whole nation now teeters on the brink of disaster. A white woman, of Afrikaner origin, risked her life so that we may know, and bring to justice, this assassin. The cold-blooded murder of Chris Hani has sent shock waves throughout the country and the world. Now is the time for all South Africans to stand together against those who, from any quarter, wish to destroy what Chris Hani gave his life for – the freedom of all of us.

Soon after Mandela's speech, the government announced the official date for the first multi-racial democrat election; 27 April 1994. That announcement helped ease tensions off the boil and back onto simmer, and I started to pray every day for a miracle — the miracle of forgiveness in the heart of every South African.

I returned to varsity a week later, and promised my father that I would be careful. I lived to regret that decision. I only attended a Politics lecture that day. Well, half my lecture. The room broke out into a full-on riot. Paris grabbed my hand and led me to safety. When I got outside I realised that I'd left my bag under the seat. Paris went back to look for it, but it was gone. I had a sinking feeling and fled for my car, only to get there and find it stolen. I went straight to campus security to report it. Two men sat behind the reception desk. Both wore name badges. Clive had a belly the size of an oak wine barrel, and Rodney was as tall and lean as a bamboo stem.

'You'll need to report this to the police,' said Clive.

'They will give you a case number for your insurance company,' said Rodney.

'But it was stolen from this campus,' I said. 'Isn't that your job?'

'We don't stop people taking cars when they have the keys, Miss,' said Clive.

'It's pretty obvious that the person who stole your keys is familiar with your Car. How else would they match your keys to your car?' said Rodney.

'Are you a fucking tag team?'

'There's no need to be rude, Miss.'

I stared at both of them, and resisted the urge to unleash my anger before leaving. My mind drew conclusions that I didn't want to acknowledge, but how could I not? The answer stared me in the face. Paris and Maleven had seen me park my car that morning. Then again, Paris had been with me the whole time. Which left Maleven. My head drowned in a sea of wild speculation. I did not want to believe that Maleven had orchestrated the theft of my car, but more than that, I couldn't bear the thought that Paris had assisted his cousin and betrayed me. With the possibility of betrayal, came the probability that he had not forgiven me for the wedding incident. I cringed at my own naïvety.

My father's gut instinct about the car was red alert. He was like a dog after its first taste of blood, and nothing was going to stop him biting again. I pointed out that we could easily buy another car, but my father didn't care about the money. He saw a bigger picture. First the car, then a hijacking, then rape, then murder. He didn't want to send his only daughter out into an increasingly volatile world unprotected. With ongoing negotiations between de Klerk, Mandela, and the ANC, it was only a matter of time before the ANC gained power and the country began its inevitable decline and decay, like every other African country had decayed under their own corrupt rule. He urged me to get a gun, or take a self-defence class at minimum. I told him that I'd look into it, and I had every intention of doing so, but my hope kept me procrastinating longer than I should have allowed.

I kept Mandela's speech in mind when I confronted Paris about the stolen car. He smiled at me, touched my face and said, 'Don't worry, Ros, the insurance will cover it and you'll get a new car.' I hoped that his reaction would disprove my betrayal theory, but his flippant attitude only stoked my fury at being duped. I lied and told him that the insurance company were fighting the claim. I told him that there would be no new car, because I wasn't made of money.

His brown eyes darkened a shade and he said, 'What my people have been through is worse than a stolen car, Ros.'

'Don't try and guilt me with the weight of apartheid, Paris. I shouldn't have to pay the price for the generation that accepted whatever the government put on their plate.'

'Do you really believe that, Ros?'

'Believe what?'

'That you are not to blame?'

'Are you saying that I am to blame?'

'You're white. That's blame enough.'

'And you're black. The colour of our skin is not our choice, Paris. We're born with it. It's like fucking skin karma or something. After all the time we've spent together you still don't know me at all. I have hated apartheid my whole life. It thrilled me to sit amongst you that first day in Politics.'

'Ja, that's part of the problem, Ros. Do you really think that we don't see it?'

'See what?' I said, getting angry.

'See how you look at us. Like we're new little pets for you to play with. A cute puppy that you'll eventually get bored with.'

'This doesn't sound like you, Paris. This sounds like something Maleven would say. What has he been saying about me?'

'Only the truth,' he said.

'Bloody hell, Paris, what does that mean?'

'When you're ready to tell me the truth, Ros, you know where to find me.'

I raised my voice as he walked away from me. 'What truth, Paris? What are you talking about?'

He didn't look back and he didn't answer.

I stewed over our conversation for days. Were white children complicit in the crimes committed by previous generations? If that held true, then the situation was hopeless. The insurance didn't replace the car in the end, and we had to buy a new one. That meant different things to different people. Paris dismissed it as just a car. My father, on the other hand, viewed it as the inciting incident to a far bigger and uglier battle scene that was playing out under our noses. As for me, it was a blot on my record. A small but significant failure on my journey to racial equality and successful race relations. If my journey was a road, and my vehicle had already been stolen before I left the parking lot, then the future would likely be littered with potholes and detours. Still, with the first multiracial election to be held a year after Hani's death, I clung to the hope that an election date would bring more than a band-aid to a country bleeding from self-inflicted wounds.

CHAPTER 28

I saw Paris during Literature. We started a new text book —
Utopia, by Thomas More — which only served to amplify
the irony of our own situation.

'Utopia,' I said to Paris, 'wouldn't that be nice?'

'Utopia is a joke,' he said.

'As long as people like you are the denizens,' I said.

'There's more to it than that and you know it,' he said.

'Rubbish,' I said. 'People are the real problem. People and
their complexes, hang-ups, apathy, history, hatred, religion, and
predisposition for revenge. As long as people are in play, Utopia
is impossible. Case in point, South Africa.' I stopped to let him
get a word in, but he only smirked and changed the subject.

'How long are we going to keep each other at arm's length?'
he said.

'Don't put this on me, Paris. You're the one who conspired to
have my car stolen.'

'I never admitted to that,' he said.

'You smiled and mentioned insurance. Seemed cut and dried
to me.'

'We'll discuss this after the lecture,' he said.

I pulled a face and sank into my own thoughts. With too much water under the bridge of race relations, history was no different to a person with an ugly past, a volatile present, and a future destined for failure. I couldn't understand why they called it history. As long as it remained active in the hearts and minds of people, it breathed in the present, like a holocaust survivor.

After the lecture we found a quiet bench under a Tibouchina tree.

'Go ahead,' I said. 'I can't wait to hear this.'

He shook his head and said, 'Sarcasm, Ros, not a good start.'

'Just tell me the truth, Paris. I won't hold it against you.'

'The truth, Ros? You're really going to preach to me about the truth.'

'Okay, you need to explain this to me. What am I lying to you about, Paris?'

'Maleven told me about your family, Ros; one of the wealthiest in the country. You never thought it was important to tell me that?'

My face reddened and I felt the rush of blood to my head. 'Honestly, Paris, how could I explain my background to you without feeling the simultaneous need to justify it?'

'I have always been honest with you, Ros. I invited you into my world, into my family home. I didn't do it to make you feel guilty. I did it because I'm trying to love you.'

'I didn't tell you about my family, because I am trying to love you back,' I said.

'That makes no sense, Ros.'

'It does make sense if you think about it. Love is the easy part of this equation, Paris, don't you see. I love your face. I love your personality. I love your company. I love talking to you.'

'But,' he interjected.

'But, no matter how much I love you, I know that we will always be divided by the colour fence.'

'Apartheid is ending, Ros.'

'You know as well as I do that the philosophical divide will remain long after it is physically removed.'

'Ros,' he said, touching my face like he always did. 'I can get past this if you can. I just want you to be honest with me.'

'Honesty is a two-way street,' I said. 'Did Maleven steal my car? Did you help him steal my car?'

'Eish, Ros.' He stood up and shook his head. 'I don't know what's worse. That you think I would do that to you, or that someone in your position would care more about a car than a person's feelings?'

'This is not about a car, Paris, this is about being betrayed by someone I have romantic feelings for.'

'Romantic feelings, Ros? Is that why you keep me at arm's length? Is that why you pull away and make excuses every time I try to move beyond kissing?'

I covered my eyes with my hand and sighed. Sex was something I agonised over. I put my reticence down to my experience with Léon. The thought of intimacy with any male, except for Alistair, gave me pause. Though I had tried to break mental bonds with Alistair, the bonds of my heart remained steadfast.

'I have my reasons, Paris, but I can't talk about it yet.'

'More secrets, Ros,' he said. 'Is it because I'm black?'

I started to cry. I knew that the truth would dispel his doubts, but the fact that he assumed the worst made my heart sink.

'I cannot speak for Maleven, but I can tell you that I had

nothing to do with your stolen car. As for you and me; I'm not ready to give up yet, but I think you need time to think about what you really want.'

He kissed me on the crown of my head and left. I stayed on the bench, with my head in my hands, wondering if Paris and I were destined to the same fate as Sisyphus; constantly rolling that boulder up the hill, only to have it roll back down again. An eternity of punishment for the sins of our fathers.

We never discussed the stolen car again, and I tried to subdue any sentiment that made me question or distrust his intentions. Without being able to change it or prove a theory either way, I needed to get past it if I wanted to salvage the relationship. My feelings for Paris remained an indivisible equation. My only point of comparison was Alistair, who was safe, certain, and suitable in the eyes of my parents. Paris, on the other hand, was a wild card. I kept him a secret from my parents for fear of them going ballistic. Not to mention my fear of intimacy. Unless I told Paris about the rape, I knew that our romantic relationship was on a countdown to expiry.

CHAPTER 29

As the year inched to conclusion, Alistair inched into my mind. I used my end of year exams and entry into the LLB program as an excuse to phone him.

'Ros, you have no idea how good it is to hear your voice,' he said.

'Actually, I do; it's good to hear your voice too, Alistair.'

'To what do I owe the honour?'

'I wanted to say hello and talk about the LLB program next year. My end of year exams are coming up, and my marks to-date are great, but I will need a letter from someone in the legal industry to vouch for me. No pressure, but I'd love to nominate you?'

'Of course I'll write a letter for you, Ros.'

'You're amazing, thank you.'

'Do you want to meet for lunch sometime?' he said. 'I understand if you're too busy.'

'I'd love that,' I said.

'How about 12pm tomorrow at the Press Club?'

'Tomorrow is perfect.'

'See you then.'

'Bye Alistair.'

'Bye Ros.'

I hung up and felt my heart rise like a hot air balloon.

I had not planned to be fashionably late, but it helped me make an entrance. Alistair looked genuinely pleased to see me, and I felt the old spark flare when he kissed me on the cheek.

'Ros,' he said as we took our seats, 'you seem different.'

The waitress took our drink order and then left us alone to read the menu.

'Different, how?'

'More self-aware; like you're discovering who you are.'

'As usual, you're the first and only person to notice.'

He smiled at me. 'So, tell me what you've been doing.'

The waitress returned with our drinks and took our food order.

I filled him in on my varsity experience and the subjects I'd chosen. I told him about the African students, the visit to KwaMashu, and my stolen car. I forgot how cathartic it was to talk to Alistair, and before I could stop myself I told him about my relationship with Paris.

'Ros, I know you want to make amends. We all do, in our own way. But we can't change the past. The worst thing that we can do is allow blame and guilt to skew our good judgement and leave us vulnerable.'

'Uncle Jericho said a similar thing before he died,' I said.

I let him talk without interruption. I had deceived myself for the best part of a year, so his advice comforted me. I trusted and respected Alistair, in part because I knew that he had my best interests at heart.

'What should I do?' I said.

'It's not my place to tell you that, Ros. Paris sounds like a good guy, but his cousin gives me an uneasy feeling. Please promise to be careful.'

'I promise,' I said.

We stopped talking while the waitress placed our plates on the table.

'What is the political climate like on campus?' said Alistair.

'It feels like everyone is holding their breath until the election.'

'That's probably true for the whole country.'

'But, we remain hopeful,' I said.

He nodded. 'I hate to be cynical, Ros, but apartheid will never really be abolished. I mean sure, in a legal sense it will, but not in terms of government and governing.'

'How do you think it'll play out?' I said.

'South Africa will finally catch up to the rest of the Western world and admit its faults and failures in terms of racial inequality. Leading this philosophical ideology will be Nelson Mandela. Not to say that he is unworthy, but he has been groomed in a way by our government to carry the Olympic torch of a New South Africa. He is the long-suffering African male elder who was unfairly imprisoned for 27 years by the white supremacist South African government. You remember my investigator friend that I told you about?'

'Yes.'

'He has contacts high up in the government and he tells me that there is a deal being done — both within South Africa and with state figures of other Western countries.'

'What kind of deal?'

'Let's put it this way, Ros, certain people stand to make an

obscene amount of money. Certain people will indeed experience a reversal of fortune, but the rest of the country, and more
specifically those who are worse off now, will only suffer when
this deal is done. And it will be done. The world won't wait
for South Africa any longer. The government will change the
colour of its skin, but governing will only worsen. Corruption
will become the norm overnight. Infrastructure will begin its
inevitable decay the minute the ruling party switches to ANC.'

'My father keeps talking about a civil war,' I said.

'All the whites are talking about a civil war. It would be a
genuine concern and a high probability if it wasn't for this deal.'

'You mean Mandela and his cronies will be paid off and
given the chance to govern so long as they stem a civil war?'

'Exactly,' said Alistair, taking a sip of his orange juice.

'How long can they stem a civil war for?'

'As long as it takes. Anyway, they don't need a civil war to
cause havoc. A black middle class is sure to spring up, especially
when they introduce affirmative action, which is guaranteed.'

'I've been watching my father unravelling since the referendum.'

'Well, it's not surprising considering what happened in
Kenya.'

'He's told you about that?'

'Not the gory details, but he's given me the gist of it. Maybe
you should ask him. It might give you some insight into where
he's coming from.'

'My father is convinced that the redistribution of wealth will
be the basis of a civil war.'

'Well he's not wrong there. It probably is a matter of time.'

The waitress interrupted to take our empty plates and asked
if we wanted dessert.

'I'll have a coffee,' said Alistair.

'Make that two,' I said.

The waitress nodded and left us alone again.

'I've missed our talks, Alistair.'

'Me too, Ros.'

'What happened after Léon's and Maeve's anniversary dinner?' I said out of the blue.

'What do you mean?'

'I tried to phone you. I tried all day.'

'I wasn't at home, Ros.'

'Okay, you know what. I don't want to know, and it's none of my business right?'

'It's not what you think. My investigator friend told me about Léon's heart attack and we went out for some drinks. One drink turned into a blur and I don't remember much else until I woke up in his house the next afternoon.'

'I see,' I said.

'Ros?'

'Yes.'

'You were young and vulnerable, and it would have been inappropriate of me to act on my feelings.

'So you do have feelings for me?'

'You know I do.'

'No, I don't know, Alistair. That's why I'm asking. Any knowledge I have about your feelings are entirely in my imagination. They have been gleaned from moments, innuendo, and analysis on my part. They have never been confirmed by you at any time.'

He took my hand. 'I'm confirming it now. I have feelings for you. Strong feelings. But I'm also cognisant of the fact that you are fourteen years my junior, and I work closely with your father.'

I fell silent and looked away. For a split second I thought I'd seen Maleven on the street outside, but when I looked again he wasn't there. A figment of my imagination, no doubt. The waitress delivered our coffees. Alistair emptied a sachet of cremora into his cup and stirred.

'Say something, Ros.'

'I understand. But that was then, and I'm not in school anymore.'

'No, you're not.'

'Does that mean you're open to exploring a relationship at some stage?'

He raised his coffee cup like a champagne glass and clinked mine. 'A toast.'

'To what?'

'To us. No matter what happens or doesn't happen between us, may we always be friends. May we always be able to talk like this.'

'I'll drink to that.' I smiled and sipped my coffee.

CHAPTER 30

My father's veil between hatred and fear disintegrated after the Hani assassination and my car theft. He also talked incessantly about how much he missed Ouma. One evening at dinner, he suggested that we spend Christmas with her. I agreed enthusiastically.

My entry into the LLB program in 1994 depended on achieving A's for all of my subjects. In the six weeks before our trip, I distanced myself from Paris and approached my studies like a Tibetan Monk taking a vow of silence. On the one hand, I couldn't afford any distractions. On the other, my conversation with Alistair had triggered unexpected feelings. I eventually saw Paris at my Literary Studies exam.

'Aah, the prodigal daughter returns,' he said.

'Paris, I've been locked away with my books. It's now or never for the LLB.'

'Is that all you care about? Your LLB? What about me?'

'What about you?' I said without thinking how it would sound.

His brown eyes narrowed.

'That's not what I meant,' I said, reaching out to take his hand.

He retracted his hand as if mine was a mouse-trap.

'Can we talk about this after the exam?' I said.

'Sure, Ros, after the exam.'

We entered the air-conditioned exam hall together, and forked in opposite directions. I didn't try to catch his or anyone else's eye. I disappeared into my head and focused on retrieving the information I had stored there. Three hours later, I shook my aching hand, handed my exam book to the adjudicator, and dashed out into the fresh air and sunshine. Halfway home, I realised that I'd forgotten to wait for Paris.

My literature exam set the standard and I sailed through my other three exams. I had looked for Paris before the Politics exam, but due to the sheer size of the class, the exam participants were divided by name and seated in three different exam rooms. I put him out of my mind until the adjudicator collected my exam book, and raced out to catch him before he disappeared into the campus crowds.

'Paris,' I shouted his name and waved my arms to get his attention.

He spotted me and walked over.

'How did it go?' I said, trying to break the ice.

'Best one so far,' he said, 'you?'

'Good,' I said, nodding. 'Listen Paris, I wanted to talk to you about our last conversation.'

'So did I, Ros,' he said. 'I wanted to talk to you after our Lit exam, but you shot out of there so fast that I didn't have a chance.'

'Ja, sorry about that. Exam trance.'

'What did you want to say?' he said.

'I don't like how we left things.'

'I don't think you've missed me,' he said, examining me.

'Don't be silly, Paris. I've had my nose firmly in my studies. I'm serious about the LLB. I've already lost a year because of bloody Afrikaans. I don't want to lose another year.'

'So you keep saying. I don't see what that has to do with spending time with me. How can you turn it off and on?'

'What am I turning off and on?'

'Your feelings for me, Ros.'

'Can we talk about this somewhere else?' I said. 'I don't feel comfortable discussing our relationship with streams of students pushing past.'

'Lead the way,' he said, gesturing for me to walk ahead of him.

We walked in silence to the student cafeteria; the setting of our first conversation and kiss. I ordered a coffee and he ordered a coke. I picked a table away from people and we sat opposite each other.

'So,' I said. 'You obviously have a bone to pick with me. What is it?'

He narrowed his eyes, but said nothing.

'Come on Paris, don't give me the silent treatment.'

'I'm not giving you the silent treatment, Ros. I'm trying to work you out.'

'Well, you'll need more than an afternoon to do that,' I said, trying to make a joke.

He didn't laugh, but stared intently.

'You're making me feel uncomfortable,' I said, standing up. 'If you've got nothing to say then I might as well leave.'

'Sit down, Ros.'

I looked at him and pursed my lips, not wanting to stay. 'I'll only sit down if you promise to talk.'

He nodded. I sat down and met his gaze for the second time.

'I can't help but feel that you're pulling away from me, Ros, and I'm not ready to let you go.'

I couldn't help but frown at his choice of phrasing.

'You need to explain what you mean Paris, because that sounds like a threat.'

'I'm not threatening you, Ros. I'm trying to communicate my depth of feeling for you. I'm trying to communicate my perception that you don't feel the same way. Tell me I'm wrong.'

'You're reading way too much into things. I haven't seen you because I've been studying. You know this. Why are you making it about something else?'

'You haven't had time to see me, but you've had time to meet another man,' he said.

'What?' I said defensively.

'Maleven said he saw you, Ros, in a cafe with a white man in a suit.'

I wracked my brain for a second before I said, 'Oh, Alistair. He's my lawyer.'

'Wow, you have your own lawyer,' he said.

I silently admonished myself. 'Not that it's any of your business, Paris, but we were discussing the LLB program next year. I've worked at his law office previously and received advice about my studies and what direction to take.'

'Maleven said you two looked cosy.'

'Is Maleven spying on me?' I said.

'No, Ros. He passed by and couldn't help but notice you.'

'I think you should spend more time questioning Maleven's

motives than mine. He's got it in for me.'

'I've made you feel uncomfortable,' he said.

'Honestly, yes,' I said.

'I'm sorry,' he said, taking my wrist. 'Surely you can understand why I would jump to conclusions. We haven't communicated in months and then my cousin sees you having a cosy get together with another man.'

'I don't think your cousin just happened to see me, Paris. I think he followed me.'

'First he steals your car and now he's following you, Ros? You know how crazy that sounds, right?'

'You know what, Paris, I'm done.'

I stood up to leave, but he grabbed my wrist and begged me to give him another chance.

'I've ignored my instincts about Maleven because he's your cousin, but I can't ignore them anymore.'

'Okay, Ros, okay. I'll talk to Maleven and tell him to back off. Can we change the subject now and talk about the party?'

'What party?'

'A group from the Politics class have organised a dinner and after-party at a club in Durban. I hoped that you'd be my date.'

'Oh,' I said.

He cocked his head to one side and frowned at me. 'Ros, come on. I'm sorry about before. Don't I deserve a second chance?'

I thought to myself that I had already given him a second chance and doubted whether I wanted to give him a third. 'Where is it and when?' I said.

'Dinner is at Mykonos,' he said.

'Oh, yes, I know Mykonos. And the after-party?'

'At a club called Soul Groove.'

'I haven't heard of that,' I said.

'It's new,' he said.

'I'll come to dinner, but I'm not sure about the after-party.'

'That's all I ask,' he said.

I decided to go along with the charade until I could safely extricate myself from the situation. In truth, my intuition was screaming NO to the suggestion of dinner and a party, but I rationalised that there would be safety in numbers, and, if I got lucky, everyone would be drunk enough for me to slip away unnoticed. One final dinner needn't be the end of the world.

CHAPTER 31

Dinner at Mykonos was a loud affair, complete with plate throwing, an onslaught of shooters and cocktails, and an earful of bad karaoke singing. Over the course of the evening it surprised me to learn that hardly anyone knew about the extended party at Soul Groove. When I questioned Paris he said it was for intimate friends only. I squirmed at the word intimate and watched the clock like a prisoner counting the hours 'til release.

Soul Groove was located in Durban's seedy Point Road, but it was only after my ascent up the industrial aluminium stairs and walk across the threshold onto the red velvet carpet that I realised why I had never heard of it. The club was Blacks Only. Paris had used his connections to make an exception for me. For a second I was back in my bedroom bent over my desk, with Léon ramming into me, and my knees threatened to buckle. I heard Jericho's words echo from beyond the grave: *Your conviction will be an asset so long as it doesn't blind you to what's right in front of you.* My gut went into a spasm. It told me in no uncertain terms to turn around and leave. But I ignored

it. I told myself that it was my conditioning. That it was probably more to do with the fears that my father had instilled in me
over the years since Mandela's release. That there was nothing
to fear except fear itself.

'Ros, are you coming in or not?'

Paris's voice cut through my thoughts.

'Yes, of course,' I said.

'Give me your bag,' he said.

'Why?' I said, clutching it tighter.

'Ros, you've gotta get past this fear that all blacks are robbers
and rapists.'

'Paris!' I looked around self-consciously to see if anyone had
heard him, but they hadn't. The music was too loud. 'If you're
trying to make a joke and put me at ease, it's not working.'

He took my hand and led me to the bar. 'Hey, howzit,' he
shouted to the barman.

The barman held out his hand to Paris and they did the
African handshake.

'Can you keep this young lady's bag safe for me, brother?'

The barman nodded and smiled. I smiled and thanked him,
not wanting to cause a scene or insult my hosts. Paris led me
to the dance floor and didn't let me out of his sight for at least
five songs; Aretha Franklin, Michael Jackson, Tina Turner,
Bob Marley, The O'Jays…I started to relax and have fun, until
I caught sight of Maleven standing at the bar. He was watching me with a smirk on his face. My smile slowly disappeared,
like a sketch being erased from a magnetic drawing board, and
my instincts bucked like a mechanical bull. I held my breath
until I gasped from lack of oxygen. Paris clasped my wrists in
his hands, pulled me toward him, and tried to kiss me, but I
instinctively turned my face away.

'What's wrong with you, Ros? What just happened?'

I told a white lie and said that I'd left something in my car.

'Aikona, Ros.'

'Paris, please. Why are you making such a big deal about this?' I said, my stomach as tight as the stopper knot that Jericho had taught me whilst sailing.

He released my wrists and pushed me away from him. I looked over at Maleven. His smirk changed into a triumphant smile. As if he had been right all along. I asked the barman for my bag and made a beeline for the door with my head down. I said goodbye to the bouncers and surreptitiously watched my blind spots as I made my way safely down those industrial steps in my high heels. Relief washed over me as I reached my car. It was parked on the pavement alongside an alley and there was not a soul in sight. I rubbed my tight chest with my left hand and fumbled for my car keys with the right. The tension in my chest sank into my stomach when I realised that my car keys were missing.

'No, no, no, not again,' I said in panic. I looked around fearfully, but all was quiet. 'Calm down,' I said to myself, 'and breathe.' I inhaled and exhaled and then calmly searched through my bag a second time. A whining sound made me look up and listen. It sounded like an injured animal, and it was coming from the alley. Forgetting all about my keys, I approached the mouth of the alley and listened intently. It took a few seconds for my eyes to adjust to the darkness within the brick walls, but I couldn't make out the outline of an animal. As much as my instincts told me to run away, my conscience pushed me forward into the throat of the unknown. As I disappeared into the darkness, the brick walls came alive and surrounded me. The animal had been a ploy.

There were five men in total. I didn't recognise a single one. They closed shoulders and used their bodies to imprison me in a human circle. It was the kind of scenario that I had only experienced in nightmares and vicariously through film. I screamed and kicked and punched, refusing to give in without a fight, but they were much stronger than me. One of them put his hands over my mouth, which instantly triggered thoughts of Léon. I panicked. I lost control of my breath. Thoughts of Léon and Promise shot through my head, and a combination of mobilising anger and paralysing fear flooded my body. I bit down into the flesh of my attacker's hand until I tasted blood and heard him scream. He shoved me into the open arms of Maleven, who stood outside the circle. I saw the look in his eyes before I heard his words, and for the first time in my life I felt the weight of my own bones. Even my skin and internal organs knew — as if my brain had received a late warning for wild weather and was frantically sending signals, even though it was too late.

'Maleven, what's going on?' I said, desperately trying to buy time and sway him from whatever he planned to do.

'Do you think I'm stupid, Rosalinde?' he said, hitting me with the back of his hand, the sharp edge of his ring slicing my cheek.

'Why would you say that?' I said, stepping backwards.

'You can fool Paris, but not me.'

He nodded to his five partners in crime. Two of them grabbed my arms, while the other three grabbed my feet and pushed me to the ground, splaying my arms and legs.

'Maleven, please, let's talk about this. You and I have obviously gotten off on the wrong foot, and…'

'Don't try and sweet talk me, Rosalinde. I know all about your rich family and your big house. You made Paris feel guilty about your stupid little car, meanwhile you live in a fucking mansion with maids wiping your white arse.'

I swallowed and grimaced. I had no reasonable comeback, and I wasn't about to lie.

'You're right, Maleven. I come from a privileged family, but I'm not…'

'You're not a racist? Is that what you were going to say, Rosalinde?'

I swallowed again and shook my head, knowing in my gut that I was in deep trouble.

Maleven stood over my body, steadied my head with his foot, and urinated in my face. I tried to shake my head free in an attempt to avoid getting urine in my eyes, nose and mouth, but he only pressed down harder.

'You fucking white bitch,' he said. 'You think you're better than us.'

I closed my eyes and mouth and tried to breathe through my nose, but he aimed the flow at my nose, causing me to open my mouth and splutter.

'Maleven,' I pleaded, 'you're going to choke me.'

'You've had your day in the sun, Rosalinde, and now it's our turn.'

His friends cheered and he released his foot from my head. I tried to kick my hands and feet free again, but he wasn't having a bar of it. He pinned my head down a second time and invited his friends to follow his lead. Each took a turn to urinate in my face and on my body, while Maleven continued his diatribe against me and every other white South African.

When they finished urinating, the kicking began. As I twisted defensively from side to side, thoughts of my own naïvety filled me with anger and the fighter in me charged. I tried to stand up and fight back, but Maleven pushed me to the ground and sat on top of my pelvis, while the others held my legs and hands. He shoved his hand up my dress and ripped off my underwear, wrapped one hand around my throat and shouted someone's name. That someone handed him a sawn-off shotgun, which he rammed into my mouth. Then the sound of Maleven's zip, and the weight of his body on top of me as he thrust his rage and hatred inside of me. The violence was so indescribable, so beyond my bank of experience, that my mind intervened — having no choice but to leave my flimsy body, where so much damage was possible. Everything faded but for the white of Maleven's teeth and eyes—white flashes glimmered like a phantom in the darkness. My thoughts slipped away — how could something so bright be capable of such sadistic violence? The sounds — grunting, cursing, laughing, snorting, clapping, cheering — and smells — sweat, cigarettes, body odour, and semen — penetrated my defensive bubble in between the changeover from Maleven to his first, second, third, fourth, fifth friend.

After they'd all finished, Maleven returned. I think I closed my eyes. I can't be sure. All I know is that I could not look Maleven in the eyes while he continued to murder my insides with his aggression. Footsteps, at the mouth of the alley, electrified my body with panic that there were more coming. Enough panic to power my strength and strain my neck to lift my head up and look. The others were jeering and laughing, oblivious to anything around them, but when my eyes swam into focus, I saw Paris.

'Paris,' I said in a voice I didn't recognise. 'Paris, help me.'

Maleven shoved the shotgun into my mouth and said something in Xhosa to his friends. The taste of metal triggered my gag reflex and I tried to turn my head as I vomited.

'Give me the gun, Maleven, and let Ros go,' said Paris.

'This fucking white bitch has been lying to you all along. She comes from one of the richest families in the country. She is the reason our people have been oppressed, and she's made a fool of us all.'

'You already told me about Ros's family, cousin, and I understand why she never told me. Apartheid has not been one-sided. She never chose her family, and neither did we. Tell me cousin, what would you have done if the tables were turned? Ever since I've met Ros I've been asking myself that question.'

'This fucking bitch has put a spell on you, Paris.'

'Let her go, cousin, please. You don't want to make this worse than it already is.'

Maleven kicked me in the head and spat on me again, then aimed the shotgun at Paris's chest. 'She should be apologising to me!' he said, banging his chest like King Kong with his free hand. 'She is the oppressor.'

Paris stood so close to Maleven that their noses touched. 'This is not who I am, cousin. You hear me. This is not who I am.' He pounded his chest and shouted the last sentence repeatedly —'this is not who I am, this is not who I am, this is not who I am.'

Maleven raised his face to the sky and let out a primal bellow. Paris saw his chance and tried to get the shotgun away. They struggled like wrestlers for thirty seconds or more. The gunshot nearly deafened me. I saw Paris drop to his knees.

A gaping hole in his chest, with more shock on his face than pain. Maleven's friends scattered like buckshot. I thought I heard more gunshots. Adrenaline powered my body. I stood up and attacked Maleven from behind, jumping on his back and squeezing my arms around his neck like a choker. But his strength was superhuman compared to mine. He rammed my back into the brick wall and then threw me to the floor like a rag doll. Paris and I lay on the ground alongside each other. He was weeping and struggling to breathe.

I held Paris's hand as he uttered his final words, 'I'm sorry, Ros, I'm sorry. I love you.'

I shouted at Maleven. 'I always knew there was something wrong with you, Maleven, but Paris always stood up for you. He trusted you. He believed in you. And now you've gone and killed him because your hatred is bigger than your heart.'

Maleven stood over me, the hatred in his eyes palpable. I shuddered to think what he would do next. I looked away, not wanting his hatred to be the last thing I saw before I died. That's when I saw the silhouette of a white man at the entrance to the alley. He looked formidable with his crew-cut and goatie. I watched him pull out a gun, the length of his forearm, and purposefully attach a silencer onto the end of the muzzle. Without a word, he fired his weapon into the back of Maleven's head. Maleven fell on top of me. His head collided with my forehead, and the blow caused my eyelids to flicker and close. I felt woozy as his last breath tickled my ear and the heat of his blood soaked my neck. The smell of iron filled my nostrils. The shooter walked over to where I lay, picked up Maleven as if his body weighed little more than a pillow and threw him on the ground.

'Thank you,' I said, shaking and sobbing like a storm over

the Drakensberg Mountains.

'Shhhh,' he said, picking me up.

He carried me to his car and laid me on the back seat. My tears and adrenaline subsided, and exhaustion settled like cloud emptied of thunder and rain. My eyelids flickered and closed.

PART IV

1993 - 1994

CHAPTER 32

Hours later I woke up in a hospital bed. The stranger sat in a blue chair alongside me. He wore jeans and a black tee shirt, which revealed his tattooed arms and muscular frame. His arctic blue eyes looked distilled; a blue sky stripped of pastel.

'Thank you,' I said, reaching for his hand.

He took my hand and placed it back on the bed. 'What for?'

I searched his eyes and tried to decipher the meaning of his words.

'A detective will be here shortly,' he said. 'I've already given my statement. All you need to do is corroborate my side of the story.'

I opened my mouth to answer when a nurse came in, followed by a plain-clothed man with a notebook in his hand. The nurse checked the drip attached to my arm and adjusted the bed to an upright position.

'Is that comfortable?'

I nodded. 'Thank you…' I read her name badge, 'Bronwyn.'

'You're welcome, Rosalinde.'

'Can I talk to her now?' said the man.

'Rosalinde, this is a Detective. He would like to get a statement from you. Do you feel up to it?'

I nodded.

Bronwyn addressed the Detective. 'She's been through an ordeal. There is a high possibility of short-term memory loss due to concussion. She was in and out of consciousness on arrival and had severe lesions that had to be stitched immediately. We are still running tests and she is booked for an MRI in half an hour.'

'I have most of what I need from Mr Muller,' he said pointing to the stranger, 'so I won't be long.'

'I'll be at the nurses station if you need me,' said Bronwyn. She indicated to the buzzer alongside me.

'Thank you,' I said.

Bronwyn left the room and closed the door behind her.

'Evening Miss Wright, I'm Detective Jacobs.'

'Evening,' I said.

'I know you've had a rough night, but I need to ask you a few questions and verify Mr Muller's statement.'

'Okay,' I said.

'Mr Muller was walking to his car when he heard a shot from a nearby alley. He went to investigate and found a group of black men assaulting you.'

I grimaced at the memory of the attack.

'Mr Muller fired a warning shot into the air...'

I closed my eyes as Jacobs talked and covered my eyes with my hand. I didn't remember a shot being fired, or the stranger arriving before Maleven's friends scattered.

'On seeing Mr Muller,' Jacobs continued, 'the group of men panicked and fled the scene. Mr Muller was unable to chase them, because he was concerned for your life. When Mr Muller approached you, he noticed two other men lying dead alongside you. One had a fatal shot to the chest with a shotgun. The other had a fatal shot to the head with a hand gun. Both weapons were recovered at the scene. Neither were registered. Mr Muller drove you to the hospital, during which time you told him that you had accompanied the two dead men — fellow varsity students named…'

He double checked his notes.

'Paris and Maleven,' he said.

The muscles in my face slackened. My breathing became shallow. I looked at the stranger while Jacobs kept talking.

'You accompanied Paris and Maleven to a club called Soul Groove. You left the club on your own, but couldn't find your keys. That's when the five men attacked you and dragged you into the alley. When you didn't return to the club, Paris and Maleven came to look for you. Your attackers shot them. That's when Mr Muller intervened and rescued you.'

He finished speaking and looked at me. I swallowed and focused on the morphine drip instead of looking at Jacobs.

'Did you get a good look at the men who attacked you?' he said.

'It was a dark alley,' the stranger said on my behalf.

'Ja, of course,' said Jacobs. 'Just a few more details, and I'm finished. Do you have a last name for Paris and Maleven?'

I inhaled and exhaled through my nose. The lump in my throat ebbing like a king tide.

'Miss Wright,' said Jacobs, 'Not to diminish what you went through, tonight, but this sort of thing happens all the time in the new South Africa and we don't have much to go on. If you want to put this behind you right now, then help me close this case with the facts you and Mr Muller have provided. Paris and Maleven were shot by your attackers when they intervened in your attack. Mr Muller would have been shot had he not been armed himself. Other than the information that your attackers were black and there was five of them, it was too dark to get a decent description.'

I involuntarily inhaled five short breaths through my mouth and exhaled one long breath.

'If you give me the last names of Paris and Maleven,' Jacobs continued, 'I can inform their families and close the case. Meaning, there will be no loose ends and you can put this whole ordeal behind you.'

I swallowed. The lump in my throat gave way like an opening flood gate. Tears spilled through the filter of my lower lashes. 'My friend's name was Paris Mtembu,' I said, 'but I only know his cousin's first name. Paris's mother is Dorothy and she lives in KwaMashu.'

'Thank you, Miss Wright, that's all I need,' said Jacobs.

'Detective Jacobs,' I said.

'Ja?'

'Is there any way to leave my name out of this? I mean when you speak to Paris's family,' I said.

He looked at the stranger before he answered.

'If that's what you want, then I can do that,' he said.

'That's what I want,' I said.

Jacobs nodded. 'One more thing before I go, Miss Wright. Had you ever met Mr Muller before tonight?'

'No,' I said, 'never.'

'Baie goed,' he said. He stood up and held out his hand to me. 'Dankie, Miss Wright.'

I shook his hand and thanked him.

He gestured to the stranger and said, 'Mark, a word outside, my bru.'

As they left, the nurse entered.

'You okay, sweetie?' she said.

I nodded though I didn't mean it.

'Your father is on his way,' she said.

'Who contacted him?'

'Your friend, Mark.'

I frowned in confusion. A cluster of unanswered questions were forming in my head like stalactites in a cave.

'Are you on the pill?' said Bronwyn.

'I'm sorry, what?' I said.

'Birth control,' she said, 'are you taking any birth control?'

'No.'

'Okay, then I'll need you to take two of these pills.'

I didn't have to ask her what they were. They were the same pills that Alistair had given me after Léon had raped me.

Bronwyn proceeded to tell me about the six-month window period for the HIV test results, and the myriad other tests they were already running. I lay back in the bed and closed my eyes. My body shook like a building amidst an earthquake. Painful tremors reminded me about Maleven's violence. My mind, bloodied with paranoia.

Mark came back into the room and sat down next to me.

'Can you give us a minute alone?' he said to Bronwyn.

'She'll need to go for the MRI soon.'

'It'll only take a few minutes.'

She nodded and left.

'That's not how it happened,' I said. 'Maleven is a fucking rapist and murderer.'

'I know,' he said, 'I did it to protect us both.'

'I understand why you did it, but I don't have to like it.'

He laughed.

'What's so funny?'

'You,' he said. 'You're more angry about me lying than you are about me killing a man.'

I stared at him while I thought about it. 'I have no problem with what you did. I'm angry that Maleven will be seen as a hero.'

He leaned toward me and smoothed the frown on my forehead with his thumb. 'Rosalinde, if tonight was anything other than a random attack, which, believe me, happens all the time, there would be an investigation. By the end of it, your life and reputation would look like it had been dragged through the bush backward. I did it this way to keep it nice and clean for the cops and to protect you.'

'What about the other five?' I said, fighting a wave of nausea. 'What if they come back for revenge?'

'Listen to me,' he said smoothing my hair like a mother does to a distraught child. 'They're not coming back.'

'How can you be sure?'

He held my chin in his hand and made me look at him. 'Because, I took care of them.'

'Like you took care of Maleven?' I whispered.

He nodded.

'Who are you?' I said. 'How will I ever repay you?'

'Stick to our story, and promise to keep this secret between us. That's all I ask.'

'I give you my word.'

He extended his hand and I shook it.

'I'm late for work,' he said, standing up. 'Your father will be here soon.'

His abruptness threw me off balance and vulnerability nipped at me like frost bite. I felt strangely attached and dependent on him and I didn't want to part company.

'Will I see you again?' I said.

'I hope so,' he said, and then disappeared into the shadows of the hospital corridor, much as he had appeared at the mouth of that alley.

CHAPTER 33

In the days following my attack, I withdrew into a world where only two people existed; Mark and I. A world where I could hide, from Maleven and Paris, from my feelings, from the HIV results, and from my warring parents. I idolised Mark like some Marvel, caped crusader, and, day by day, the flames in my head and heart spread like a veldfire. I was only too happy to burn. Burning felt better than bleeding. Every time I thought of Paris, I saw myself soaking in a bathtub of blood. The blood, a symbol of my guilt. I would have drowned myself in guilt if it wasn't for Mark. Like Shiva the Destroyer, Mark had used his power to obliterate in order to prepare for a renewal. By saving me from future retaliation, he had given me a second chance to regenerate.

My mother returned to Sea Breeze for a few weeks, but her and my father only turned on each other like baby birds in a nest. One afternoon they knocked on my door.

'Ros, we want to talk about what happened.'

'I don't want to talk.'

They ignored me and sat on either side of my bed. Both

wanted to know more about this Paris person and why I had been at a blacks only nightclub. I looked from one to the other and rolled my eyes.

'He was in my Politics and Literature classes,' I said.

'Were you friendly with him?' said my father.

'Friendly, yes,' I said.

'How did you end up at a blacks only nightclub?' said my father.

'It was an end of year party, and I didn't know it was a blacks only club until I got inside. That's the long and short of it.'

'Did you have a relationship with this Paris person?' my mother whispered.

'God forbid I have a relationship with a black man,' I said with a raised voice.

'Okay, Ros, take it easy,' said my father. 'Marilyn, you're not helping.' He shot my mother a look and tried to change tack. 'Rosalinde, I think you should get a gun.'

'A gun?' My mother's voice was so loud that I imagined it hitting the bell of a carnival high striker. 'Are you fucking mad? She'll end up in jail for killing someone.'

'Can't you see how vulnerable she is?' said my father. 'Her attackers could come back, and if it's not them it'll be some other bloody kaffir.'

'Dad, can you please stop using that word. I know that I should embrace the term, considering what's happened, but I really can't. Saying it and hearing it only makes me feel worse. As for you, Mother, do you really think that I would randomly shoot people?'

'I didn't say that,' she said, 'but I know how hostile you can be.'

'Well, clearly I'm not nearly as bloody hostile as you think

I am,' I shouted. 'I was gang raped, mother.' I nearly said six against one and then checked myself. 'Five against one.' I flicked my fingers in her face like flash cards. 'Dad's right. It's a fucking shit hole out there and I need to be able to protect myself.'

'You need to forget about what happened and stay out of trouble,' my mother said.

'Are you serious?' I said. 'Not only are you suggesting that it's my fault, but you expect me to forget about it like it's no biggie? Are you fucking serious, mother?!'

'Stop swearing, Ros. You have no right to speak to me like that. Tell her, Wilstan.'

'Let's put Paris aside for a minute and consider the reality of our environment,' said my father. 'It's either kill or be killed.'

'Oh, don't be so bloody dramatic,' said my mother. 'Ros willingly put herself in a dangerous situation.'

'That's it,' I said. 'I'm not listening to any more of this bullshit. Thank you very much, mother. You are a fucking gem! If only you knew the danger you have put me in.'

'What's that supposed to mean?' she said.

I stood up and turned the door handle, planning to run out and slam the door behind me. But I was sick to death of harbouring secrets in order to spare my mother's feelings about her precious family. I turned around and stared them both down.

'Léon raped me,' I said, 'the night of Jericho's will-reading, but not before he harassed me for years before.'

The muscles in my father's face looked as if they'd suffered a stroke, and my mother pursed her lips. I was certain that I'd finally hit a major artery, that blood would spill, but I was wrong. She got off the bed and straightened her spine. With her chin raised and eyes meeting mine, she said, 'Whatever did or didn't happen, it is all in the past now.'

I narrowed my eyes and scrutinised her. The anger rising like flames in my throat. In a low voice, I hissed, 'Is that all you have to say?'

'What do you want me to say, Rosalinde?'

'Say you're sorry. Say you're partly to blame for continuously pushing me toward that fucking psychopath. Say something motherly. In fact, start acting more like a mother while you're at it. Mohini and Ouma have been more motherly than you have ever been.'

She slapped my already bruised face hard. I didn't retaliate.

'I won't apologise for anything. It's your fault that your father and I are divorced,' she said. 'It's all your fault. You ruined my life.'

I swallowed in vain. The tears flooded their gates, and I ran out of the room, slamming the door behind me.

My father found me in Mohini's abandoned room half an hour later. The scent of sandalwood still hung in the air, and the room was empty but for her single bed and altar. I shifted over for him to sit on the edge of the bed.

'Why didn't you tell me?' he said.

'I thought you would blame me.'

'Blame you? Why in God's name would I do that?'

'Because I blamed myself.'

'I've let you down, Ros. I'm supposed to protect you. I will never, ever, ever forgive myself.'

'It's okay, Dad.'

'No, it's not okay, Ros. There is nothing okay about this situation. First Léon rapes you under my own roof, and then you're brutally attacked. I have been so preoccupied with politics and work that I have neglected my only daughter. After promising to be a better parent than my own mother and father, I have turned out to be no bloody different.'

'Dad,' I said, patting his hand, 'I'm sorry that I never trusted you enough to tell you.'

'That's also my fault, Ros. You keep asking me about my childhood, and I keep putting you off.'

'Tell me now,' I said. 'If ever there was a time, surely this is it.'

He nodded and patted my hand. 'I grew up in Kenya,' he said.

'How come you never talk about it?' I said.

'I try to block it out, much like you will probably try to block out this trauma.'

I nodded and inhaled deeply.

'We lived in a small village that was situated at the edge of a forest and enclosed by sugarcane fields. Your oupa worked as a foreman in the mill. It wasn't much different to South Africa. Black labourers and white management. We grew our own food and kept chickens. I remember the first time your ouma asked me to help her with the chickens. I thought she meant feed them. I didn't realise she wanted me to help her slaughter one. She made me hold Speckles, face down, over the old tree stump and stretch her neck as far as it would go. Speckles screeched and clucked in distress. I started to cry. My mother called me a sissy boy and slammed the butcher knife down. I let go of Speckles in shock. Her headless body ran around the coop, spurting blood everywhere. My mother was furious with me and sent me to my room for the rest of the day.

'Ouma did that?' I said, trying to imagine her slaughtering a chicken.

'Yes,' he said. 'In hindsight I see that she was only trying to toughen me up, but it only made me hate her.'

'What happened after that?'

'After that episode I grew protective of nature. When my father went outside with his Twenty-Two Rifle to shoot the black-winged kites, that circled over the chicken coop, I would jump up and down, while waving my arms madly, and beg him not to shoot.'

'What did he do?'

'He struck me down with the back of his hand, and told me to be more like my brother.'

'How come I've never met your brother?'

'My brother and I are like chalk and cheese. I liked to read and he liked to hunt.'

'So what was this traumatic event?'

'We managed to co-exist with the Kukuyus and the Mau Mau without any violence for several years.'

My mother barged into the room.

'Great timing, mother,' I said, rolling my eyes.

'I've come to tell you that I'm leaving. It's obvious that I'm neither needed nor appreciated here.'

'You're unbelievable, Marilyn,' said my father. He stood up. 'We'll pick this up another time, Ros, I promise.'

I nodded and listened to his footsteps descend the stairs, before I curled into a foetal position on Mohini's bed.

CHAPTER 34

My mother flew to Joburg the following day and said goodbye to me as if she was the victim. My father took a month off work and drove me to Coetzeesdorp to recuperate and recover. Ouma acted like we had never spent a day apart and tried to soothe my pain with baked goods and bear hugs. Not that I had an appetite for food. I only wanted to write in my journal and cocoon myself like an ugly caterpillar. Ouma tried to tempt me outside with a visit to the public pool, or to help her prune the garden in the morning sun, or watch TV with her and my father at night, but I felt safer in solitary confinement.

My father let me be for the most part, but he insisted I accompany him to the Sunday morning service at the local Dutch Reform Church. It was a three minute walk at best, and my only exercise for the week. Like the Holy Trinity, the structure of the church consisted of three sections: the tower — complete with steeple and gothic-arched stained-glass windows; the body of the building, which held rows of pews and Holy Bibles; and the sacred altar and crucifix — flanked by secret wings from which God's messenger would appear and disappear.

Architecturally, the building was as beautiful as it was im-
posing; its bronze and camel coloured bricks casting a shadow
down the dirt road as we walked toward it, and its indigo roof
tiles closer to the heavenly sky than the tallest Karoo tree.
The clock, positioned beneath the eaves of the steeple and bell
tower, could be seen from my bedroom window — much like
the lighthouse at Sea Breeze, but far less reassuring. I made my
father promise that I could sit at the back and go home straight
afterwards. He agreed to the first part, but not the second. At
the end of the service, I locked myself in the toilet cubicle for
the post-service morning tea while my father milled about and
talked to the locals. On our walk home he asked me what I
thought about the sermon.

'For an intelligent person, I struggle to see how you believe
in something that is so obviously flawed.'

'My faith gave me great comfort after the worst event of my
life, Ros. Flawed or not, I was hoping that it could provide you
with the same sense of solace.'

'Religion is not the answer to my problems, Dad, and I don't
want to discuss it anymore. But I do want you to tell me about
this event.'

'It's not an easy tale to tell, Ros, and it won't be an easy tale
to hear given your current state of mind.'

'I'm not interested in some theoretic sermon that ends with
a hope and prayer, Dad, I need to hear something real. Something that literally broke the fabric of your life. A story that
ends with proof of life instead of some wishy-washy platitude.'

'Before we go back to Sea Breeze, I promise to tell you the
story.'

Alistair phoned me every day at midday. I appreciated that he cared enough to check on me, but we didn't stay on the line long. Conversation with me was awkward to put it nicely. A week in, he asked me if I'd received my exam results. I ignored his question and asked my own.

'Will you help me find the stranger who saved my life?'

Alistair went silent long enough for me to ask, 'Are you still there?'

'My investigator friend is out of the country on a private security detail, Ros. I'll organise it when he returns.'

I knew Alistair well enough to know that he was lying, but I didn't know why. I said nothing, but made a mental note to push the envelope again at a later date. He didn't phone the next day or the next, which only piqued my curiosity further.

On Saturday morning, Ouma knocked on my door.

'Come in,' I said.

She placed a cup of coffee and a homemade rusk on my bedside table and sat in the armchair next to my bed. 'Do you remember Piet Junior?' she said.

'The guardian of the pool,' I said.

She nodded. 'I'm delivering a batch of koeksusters to him today. Will you come with me?'

'I'd prefer to stay here,' I said.

'I know, Lindy, but he specifically asked for you and invited us for a cup of tea.'

When I didn't respond she said, 'When there is a power failure, do you go and look for candles and matches or do you sit in the dark and allow your fears to get the best of you?'

I frowned. 'Is this an analogy for my current state of affairs?' I said.

She nodded. 'It's time to go in search of candles.'

'I'm terrified to be around people,' I whispered.

'I know, my girl,' she said embracing me in a bear hug, 'but I'm right beside you.'

I buried my face in her chest and tried to control the lump in my throat that was getting harder and harder to swallow each day.

'It's okay to cry, Lindy.'

'I know, Ouma, but I'm afraid that I will break, like a dam without floodgates, or an earthquake beneath a fault line.'

'Broken cities and bridges can be rebuilt, Lindy, but a building without power will eventually become derelict and fall into a state of decay. If left too long it will be earmarked for demolition.'

'Shiva,' I said, thinking about my talks with Mohini.

'I don't know about that, Lindy.'

It occurred to me in that moment that while my father was religious, Ouma had never made any religious references.

'Why is Dad so hellbent on religion if you're not?'

'Your father witnessed a terrible thing in his youth. He needed reassurance after that. He turned to Christianity.'

'What about you?' I said. 'What did you turn to?'

'I learnt early on that the only dependable thing was me.'

'Can I stay with you when Dad leaves?' I said.

'You can stay as long as you like.'

'Okay,' I said. 'Can we go to Piet's another day?'

She patted my knee and nodded. 'Of course, Lindy.'

My father and I never did have our talk about his experience in

Kenya, because he cut his stay in Coetzeesdorp short. With the election date three months away and initiatives like Affirmative Action coming into play, tensions in the white business world were high, and Spencer & Mason pressured him to return. Weeks later, Alistair phoned with my exam results.

'I hope you don't mind, Ros, the first Semester starts in February, so it's not worth mailing it to you with the postal service being what it is these days.'

I had forgotten all about my exams and the LLB.

'Do you want me to open it for you?'

'Sure,' I said.

I heard him tear the envelope open, pull the letter out and unfold the paper. Part of me hoped that I had failed so that I would never have to return to the world outside of Coetzeesdorp ever again. But I had no such luck.

'It's all A's, Ros,' he said, expressing enough enthusiasm for the both of us.

'A's,' I said, sighing heavily.

'Ros, this is fantastic news.'

The good news didn't provide the pleasure that it would have previous to my attack. After the violence, a sort of ambition-apathy had emerged. Atrophy. Maleven's violence had scoured out who I thought I was and what I wanted to become, and replaced it with something strange. Something that changed on a daily and hourly basis. I could never be sure. My only mainstay emotion was relief that Mark had ripped Maleven from the spider web of my life. I had made a mistake with him. I had allowed the colour fence to colour my judgement. I had shown weakness to the enemy and the enemy had struck. I should have seen it coming, but my own misplaced guilt and blame had blinded me.

'Ros?'

'Ja, I'm here.'

'I thought that this would be good news, considering how studious you were leading up to your exams,' he said.

'Ja, I did work hard.'

'Ros, are you okay?'

'Ja, I'm fine. I don't feel as happy as I thought I would, that's all.'

'Is it because of the attack?' he said.

'I suppose. I don't know,' I said.

'The first semester starts in under a month.'

'I don't think I'll be starting.'

'But, Ros, you've worked so hard for this. It would be madness to give up...'

'Madness,' I interjected, 'is thinking that I could ever go back to the way I was.'

'Ros, it's completely understandable that you feel that way now, but you've got to get back on the horse, so to speak.'

'What do you know about what I need, Alistair? Have you ever been attacked, urinated on, raped, and beaten?'

I heard my laughter as if it belonged to someone else. I heard my voice rising and words flooding out, but I couldn't remember a word I'd said when I finally hung up the phone. Whatever I had said brought my ouma into the room with two blue pills in hand. She popped them onto my tongue, pressed a glass of water against my lips, and urged me to drink and swallow an ounce of sanity.

CHAPTER 35

I woke up a few hours later and told my ouma that I wanted to go for a walk.

'Are you sure that's a good idea?'

'I need some air, and I need to think,' I said.

She nodded and walked me to the door.

Ouma had talked about power failures and matches, and she was right. The attack had caused a metaphorical power failure in the house of my body and mind, but the truth is that I had not been without matches since the attack. Mark, my avenger, and Maleven's murder, was the only box of matches that I needed to light my way. The exam results had been the first whiff of wind capable of blowing out those matches. Probably because they spelled the end of my recuperation time. And although I knew that I could not live in isolation forever, the thought of returning to a campus full of memories of Paris made me feel like a tightly wound cotton reel on the verge of unravelling.

My father and Alistair were expecting me to return to the world in three weeks' time to start my LLB. They had given me time to recuperate. They had been understanding, but they didn't understand. They had no idea what I had experienced. They had no idea what fear sprung up inside my hollow insides when Alistair phoned me with those results. They might as well have been a flag waving me toward the finish line of a race that I was nowhere near completing. I had yet to round the corner of denial and compartmentalising. I didn't trust myself to balance on the tightrope of normality without falling. Worse than that, I think I wanted to fall.

I heard my name and stopped walking, but couldn't see anything through the cloud of dirt and dust that I had disturbed with my speed-walking. When it settled, I was standing outside a house made of dark brown brick walls. A wave of heat surged through my body, like a furnace prepped for cremation, as I relived the moment in that alley of eyes and white teeth. I started to hyperventilate as I felt the weight of Maleven on top of me, and the taste of metal in my mouth. I searched my surrounds for refuge — a tree, anything — but my body was paralysed with fear. I saw a man running toward me. My panic shifted into adrenaline and I ran like Zola Budd until I reached the pedestrian gate outside the church.

Whoever had called and ran toward me, had not followed. The street was empty. I looked up at the church, and felt the need to go inside. I wrapped my fingers around the brass looped door handles and twisted. The arched doors swung outward, and the stale, dusty air caught in my throat. My cough echoed and bounced off the stone walls. I closed the doors behind me, and walked between the aisles of wooden pews toward the altar where a statue of Christ on the cross hung on the wall behind the pulpit.

'It seems to me that you died in vain,' I said, straining my neck to look at the statue. 'The world is not a better place and we are certainly not better people.'

I sat on the pew and opened a bible. It fell to Psalm 23. I read aloud.

The Lord is my shepherd; I shall not want. He causes me to lie down in green pastures; He leads me beside still waters. He restores my soul; He leads me in paths of righteousness...Even when I walk in the valley of darkness, I will fear no evil for You are with me.

'What a load of bullshit,' I said. 'Where were you when Léon raped Promise and then me? Where were you when Maleven raped me? Where were you during apartheid? Where are you now? Seriously, Jesus. You say ask and you shall receive, well here I am asking, where the hell are you?!'

I heard the church door creak open, and turned to see my ouma and the man who I had run from. She had a look on her face that I wanted my mother to have after my attack; no judgement, only compassion.

'Lindy, my beautiful girl, this is Piet Junior. He told me you were in trouble.'

Piet smiled and said, 'I'm sorry if I scared you, Rosalinde.'

'That's okay,' I said, shaking my head. 'I'm not sure what happened.'

'I will give you ladies some privacy,' said Piet. 'Rosalinde, go well.'

'Dankie, Piet. Come by later for some koeksusters and tea,' said Ouma.

Ouma sat next to me on the pew and held out her hand. 'It's normal to have frightening flashbacks after a trauma,' she said.

I nodded.

'Perhaps it's time to talk about what happened.'

I nodded again.

She embraced me in that same bear hug, and I finally broke down and sobbed.

'I know this attack is the reason you're here, Lindy, but I feel that there is more you're not telling me.'

I nodded through my tears.

'Let me help you, Lindy. I have kept secrets my whole life, but they have only served to poison me. Don't make the same mistakes I did Lindy, please. If I am allowed to do one extraordinary thing in my life, then please let it be helping my beloved granddaughter through a dark passage.'

I nodded, knowing that I needed to grab onto my ouma's offer like a lifeline.

'What do you say we get out of this dusty old church and go home? I'll make you a cup of tea and we can talk,' she said.

The warmth of my ouma's strong grip guided me out of the church, and onto the dusty road, where the cloudless Karoo sky stretched over us like a blank canvas.

CHAPTER 36

Like ladies attending a Japanese tea ceremony, Ouma and I shared secrets between sips of steaming Rooibos. I told her about Léon, Promise, and my relationship with Paris. And although I didn't talk about the attack, or expose Mark's secret, it did feel as though I'd managed to stop the unravelling, or at least slow it down. Compared to my ouma's story, mine seemed far less permanent.

Ouma had been married and widowed twice. She had met both husbands during World War II, where she was stationed as a nurse in Malta. Her first husband, Henrik, died in the line of fire, and my oupa had been injured in the same battle. His injuries had kept him in my ouma's care for a month or more, and they had fallen in love. After the war drew to a close in 1945, they moved back to South Africa. But the effects of war rapidly took their toll on my oupa, whose drinking moved from coping mechanism to full-blown escapism. He struggled to hold down a job and became increasingly violent with my ouma. In 1949, they moved to Kenya. Ouma was pregnant with my father, and hoped that a quiet, country life would benefit them. My oupa had got a job in the Mill and the dust of their lives had settled for nearly a decade when violence had struck again. That was the day she fled Kenya with her two sons and left her husband behind.

After their neighbour's brutal murder, Ouma had put the two boys into the car and shouted at her husband to join them. He refused to leave. With his eyes glazed over, he began mumbling about fighting his last fight, and his destiny to protect his family. She yanked his elbow and begged him to get in the car, but he told her that he couldn't survive in the world after the things he'd seen and done during the war. My ouma left her husband standing in the garden with a rifle in his hand and reversed the car to turn away from the wave of Mau Mau that were approaching like high tide. She never saw him again, and insisted that my father fill in the remaining details when he was ready to tell his side of the story.

I phoned Alistair later that afternoon to apologise. His secretary answered the phone and connected me straight away.

'Ros, thank God. Are you okay?'

'Yes, I'm okay,' I assured him. 'I phoned to apologise.'

'You don't need to apologise, Ros. I should apologise for pushing you.'

'No, that's not true, Alistair. I shouldn't have taken it out on you. I don't want you to worry.'

'It's okay, Ros. I can't imagine what you're going through, and I apologise if I ever gave the impression that I did. I guess I feel responsible and I'm trying to overcompensate.'

'Responsible for what?'

'The attack. I should never have let you go to that bloody dinner. I thought that you would be safe.'

He seemed to be concealing something. 'Alistair, is there something you're not telling me?'

The line went quiet and I thought that I'd lost the connection. 'Alistair, are you there?'

'I'm here, Ros. The man who saved you.'

'Mark?' I said.

'Yes.'

'What about him?'

'I sent him to watch over you that night.'

'Your investigator friend?'

'Yes.'

'The investigator friend who helped you win Jericho's business and watch over me at the Edward that night?'

'Yes, Ros. One and the same.'

'Oh my God.'

'Don't be angry with me Ros. I was only looking out for you.'

'I'm not angry with you, Alistair.'

'You're not?'

'How could I be angry? You saved my life. Well, Mark saved my life, but only because of you.'

'Well, he wouldn't have needed to save you if he had done his job properly.'

'What do you mean?'

'He was supposed to intervene before you went to the club.'

'Did you ask him about it?'

'He wouldn't say, and I haven't spoken to him since. I blame him.'

'Alistair, why didn't you tell me this before?'

'You had enough on your plate, Ros. Besides, I thought you'd be angry with me for interfering.'

'Honestly, Alistair. if there is one thing I'm certain about in this life, it's that you have always had my best interests at heart. It's the one thing I love you for unconditionally.'

It sounded like he was crying.

'Alistair, are you okay?'

'When I heard about your attack I felt like someone had thrown me off the top of Table Mountain. I would never have forgiven myself if Mark had not gotten there in time.'

I sighed heavily. 'It's okay, Alistair. I never gave any thought to how this attack impacted the people around me. Least of all you. You've always been a rock in my life, and I've leaned on you thoughtlessly.'

'I love you, Ros. I've always loved you.'

I was speechless; totally unprepared for a love confession. If he had said it at the Edward, or during our lunch at the Press Club, I would have swooned, but that moment had passed. The mysterious stranger, foretold by the fortune cookie, had materialised, and he was all I could think about.

'Can I meet him?' I said, insensitively changing the subject.

'Who?'

'Mark.'

'I'm not sure that's a good idea, Ros.'

'Why not? He saved my life. To be honest, he's the only thread holding my sanity together. I want to thank him for saving my life. Surely you can understand?'

'Yes, of course I understand. I, um. I hadn't, um.'

'You don't want me to meet him?'

'It's not that I don't want you to meet him, Ros. He's not the sort of character I want to introduce into your life.'

'Well it's too late for that, Alistair. You've already introduced him into my life indirectly.'

He fell silent and I realised that I hadn't acknowledged his love confession.

'Listen, Ros, I have to go. We'll talk about this tomorrow.'

'Alistair, please don't go. I wasn't expecting you to confess your feelings for me, and I cannot think about romance right now. Every time I think about sex, I think about violence. I'm plagued by nightmares and insomnia. I'm not sure how long it's going to take me to heal, and I can't expect you to wait.'

'I'm willing to wait for you, Ros.'

'You may be willing, but you shouldn't. I'm damaged goods for the foreseeable future.'

'Don't say that Ros. You need more time, that's all.'

'Time, yes. Time is the answer to everything, isn't it?'

He didn't respond.

'Alistair?'

'Yes, Ros.'

'If you can organise a meeting with Mark then I will find a way to enrol in Semester one.'

'You don't need to negotiate with me Ros, and you don't need to enrol on my account. It's your life and your career.'

He hung up before I could speak. When I called back seconds later, Mariette said he was unavailable. I slumped into the armchair and sighed.

CHAPTER 37

Alistair phoned back a few days later to tell me that Mark didn't have time to babysit my whims. I felt deflated. Silly. Worse than the time Léon had died and Alistair hadn't answered his phone. I told Alistair that he hadn't tried hard enough, that he didn't care about me. I asked him why he was threatened by my request to meet Mark. He told me that he'd speak to me when I was in a more reasonable mood. I told him to go to hell. He hung up.

Alistair; we seemed to be destined for a relationship defined by limbo. When I ran hot, he ran cold. When he ran hot, I ran cold. My father once told me that the dynamics of the Agulhas current was called Retroflection; the movement of an ocean current that doubles back on itself. That's what Alistair and I were like. Repeatedly meeting in the middle, only to double back and retreat into our own bodies of water. But there was more to that equation than retroflection. Alistair had always been a safe bet; my guardian who watched from the wings and waited. But he had waited too long. My experience with Paris and Mark had turned me into a risk taker. My exposure to danger and violence had only served to heighten my appetite for adventure.

For months I had fantasised about Mark. Especially his parting words: I hope I'll see you again. I held onto those words. Wrote them into my comic story. My fantasy world where we were destined to meet and be together. All of which had been reinforced when Alistair revealed my hero's true identity. He wasn't a figment of my imagination; a superhero I had conjured during my darkest hour. He was real, and Alistair's revelation had filled the gap in my subplot, and made a meeting both possible and likely. So, when Alistair called and delivered his message, he might as well have crumpled up my comic book story, doused it in petrol and set it alight.

I asked Ouma if I could use her car. She looked alarmed and wanted to know why. I told her that I needed a change of scenery. The public pool.

'But there's a pool right here, Lindy.'

'I know, Ouma.' I took her hands in mine and tried to explain. 'There's things that I need to sort through.' I tapped my head as if it was a Rubik's cube on its way to being solved.

'I understand my girl, I do, but I worry. Why don't you let me drive you?'

'No, Ouma. I need to do this on my own.' I looked around for something to convince her. 'Here,' I said, holding out my pinky to her. 'I pinky swear that I will not harm myself.'

She wrapped her pinky around mine and squeezed.

'I pinky swear that I will be back in a few hours. I pinky swear,' I said squeezing, 'I pinky swear.'

'Okay, Lindy. You can use my car. But, please, be careful.'

I nodded my agreement and hugged her tightly. She unhooked her car keys from the key holder on the wall and placed them in my open palm.

'I'll see you in a few hours,' I said.

The road to the pool was deserted, so I drove with the window down and stuck my arm into the oncoming breeze. It felt good to be free and isolated. Not a soul in sight. As I drove, I wondered if I'd ever be able to return to a room of crowded people, to shopping centres, or varsity. The thought of returning to my old life made my stomach somersault.

The pool was also deserted. I laid my towel on a deck chair and then climbed the ladders to the diving boards. I stopped at the middle level and walked out onto the board. As I stood there, I had a vision of Jericho. Like my earlier fantasy, I saw Cabo das Tormentas in the middle of the ocean, with Jericho sinking beneath it; down, down, down into the darkness of the ocean's heart. I thought about what it could mean. Perhaps he had felt my sense of personal nihilism after the death of his wife and son. Perhaps, that day, something inside him changed or died. Or maybe it didn't die. Maybe he murdered it in order to survive the grief.

We weren't dissimilar, Jericho and I. I had done the same to survive Léon's violence. I had turned my life into a living balance sheet, and learned to master the art of double entry. In public, I compartmentalised my emotions to the point of not having any at all. In private, I dragged myself to the edge of my own darkness and admitted that there was no light at the end of tunnel. The accountants had it right after all; it was all about balance.

I drew my arms up over my head and dived into the cool water. Again and again, I swam to the side, climbed up the ladder, and dived, until my knees wobbled and forced me to rest on the deck chair. I fell asleep and dreamed of Paris. I was young and he was grown. We stood outside the Wimpy Bar and watched the old African man shuffle past. Paris held a mirror to my face and told me to look at my own racial hypocrisy before he smashed the glass into my face.

I woke up crying and touched my face to check for blood. So vivid it had been. I pulled the towel over my head and curled into a foetal position. Paris wasn't wrong. I wanted redemption for my role in apartheid, but the damage had been done, and that damned colour fence — doomed to stay and never fall — would never be disassembled in our hearts and minds.

I threw the towel off and climbed back up the ladder to the top diving board. The question that repeated like a musical refrain was how much guilt and blame did I carry as a white South African? Enough to keep me in my country of birth despite the approaching slaughter? Did I deserve slaughter? I bounced on the board, catapulted myself into the air, and landed feet first into the cold water.

When I got back to Ouma's house, I hugged her for a long time.

'Alistair phoned when you were out,' she said.

'What did he want?'

'He wants you to phone him back.'

'Okay,' I said.

'Why don't you have a bath after your phone call and then we can talk at dinner?'

I nodded and yawned. 'Okay,' I said. 'I'd like that.'

I headed straight to the room to phone Alistair.

'Ros?'

'Yes.'

'About before.'

'Before you say anything, Alistair, let me say that I'm sorry. I didn't mean what I said.'

'I'm sorry too,' he said. 'Truce?'

'Truce,' I said.

CHAPTER 38

Three months after my attack, I returned home to a dramatically different Sea Breeze, and a father who was convinced that the country was on the fast-track to civil war. He had installed a state of the art security system, complete with surveillance cameras, panic buttons, and alarm keypads on virtually every door in the house. He had also taken ownership of Jericho's study and transformed it into a type of war room. Along with the monitors for the myriad cameras, he had taken to cutting out newspaper clippings of grisly murders, armed robberies, car hijackings, township necklacing, muti murders, farm murders, and every other kind of violent crime that had spiked and grown commonplace in the new South Africa.

While the international media told the age-old good-conquers-evil story where everyone lived happily ever after in the rosy, rainbow nation, my father's clippings told the real story. They told of a land under siege. A country of natural beauty, but whose cities were becoming literal rubbish tips. A country of spectacular wildlife that was buckling under pressure from poachers. A country whose infrastructure was headed for decay thanks to government corruption and ineptitude. A country of unimaginable violence, where a clash of cultures was eternally doomed to a living hell of their own making.

A few nights after I returned to Sea Breeze, my father told me the story of his Kenyan childhood. He was ten years old, living next door to his childhood sweetheart, Rebecca. Rebecca came from a family of five — eight if you included the unborn foetus, the Siamese cat, Simmy, and German Shepherd dog, Constantine. One Friday, Rebecca and her brothers were absent from school, so when home-time arrived my father rushed to her house (under the guise of homework) to say hello and spend time with his love. He knew something was amiss when he saw the gate and front door wide open. He ran up the steps and into the house, not realising that the wooden floors were soaked with blood, and slipped. Unable to stand without slipping, he crawled to the lounge room where he discovered the first grisly scene. Rebecca's father lay on the floor face down, hacked to pieces. Constantine lay in two pieces at his side, tongue hanging out of his mouth. My father's adrenaline pumped, but nausea immobilised him. He vomited uncontrollably over the bodies and then moved as fast as he could to the bedrooms. The boys had been hacked in the kitchen, having tried to defend their family as they both held knives in their hands. The master bedroom came last. There, on the bed, lay Rebecca's mother — splayed, hands tied above her head with wire from the vegetable garden, her throat slit and pregnant stomach cut open. Another round of vomiting ensued and panic seized his imagination as he continued his search for Rebecca. There was no sign of her in the house, so he headed outside to the back yard. What he witnessed there, he would never manage to clean or erase from his memory no matter how hard he tried.

The Mau Mau held a crucifix — constructed from two twigs and fixed with wire from the fence that protected the family vegetable garden. On the crucifix was Simmy, the Siamese cat; wire tied around her waist, arms and legs so that she looked like Jesus on the cross. Rebecca lay naked and bloody at their feet while they sang their victory.

When they saw my father, he bolted for the fence, where he and Rebecca had cut a hole the previous summer, and ran faster than he thought possible. The houses were semi-rural, with large land tracts between houses, so there was a fair distance between his house and the neighbours. Once inside, he shouted to his mother and father, telling them what had happened and warning them that the Mau Mau were in pursuit. His father loaded his shotgun and ordered his wife and two sons to get into the car and never return. They didn't want to leave him, but he was adamant. He would not let those kaffirs get away with it. He would fight them. He would not allow them to destroy his family's home. My father told his father that he was outnumbered. That a shotgun would not be enough. His father kissed his forehead and told him to take care of his mother and brother. He pressed his nose against the glass of the car window, as his mother accelerated away from the scene, and watched his father, shotgun in hand, face the mob of Mau Mau who approached like a storm from the other direction.

A piece of him died that day. A big piece. He, his brother, and his mother travelled for five weeks along the Great North Road, in a Hillman Minx. They had no money, so Ouma would stop and pick fruit from trees along the way and whatever else she could get her hands on. She would drive all day, and at night they would find a hotel and park in the garage so they could rest. They followed the Great North Road from Kenya, through Tanganyika, into Northern Rhodesia, then across the Zambezi River by bridge at Chirundeu, until they finally reached the South African border crossing at Beitbridge, and crossed the Limpopo River into the Transvaal. It was a harrowing journey that my father never forgot, and an experience that formed the basis for his acceptance of apartheid.

Once in South Africa, Ouma sent my father to a strict Afrikaans boarding school. She was unable to cope with the demands of a ten-year old child who had questions about what he had witnessed, and grief over losing a father. He hadn't been able to understand why his father stayed behind.

At school, he was singled out for being English and bullied by the Afrikaans boys, who were holding ancestral grudges of their ancestors from the days of the Boer War, when Great Britain defeated the two Boer Republics. The older boys had done everything from throwing ice cold water over him while he slept in his dormitory bed, to ambushing him in the communal showers to piss on him and beat him. He said that he had cried for weeks on end when he first arrived, and might not have survived if it weren't for an English teacher, Miss Mason, who had taken him under her wing and supplied him with a never ending pile of books.

He didn't see his mother for a year — she didn't have enough money to travel — and when she did finally visit he hid in the garden. He heard her and the teachers calling and calling for hours, but he never moved a muscle, and went so far as to sleep outside overnight, thinking that his mother would leave. But when he woke in the morning she was waiting for him, and she was furious. She told him to get in the car, but he flat out refused and said he wanted to stay at school. She eventually left without him. That day, their already broken relationship suffered further damage, and they never spoke about it again.

After that first year, he had learnt to speak Afrikaans fluently and stemmed the bullying tide by confronting the ring-leader, Hansie, one afternoon during rugby practice. Hansie had tripped him up, causing my father to sprain his ankle, and my father had charged him like a bull and landed a right hook. He broke Hansie's nose and told him in no uncertain terms that if the bullying continued, he would have to nurse more than a broken nose. Hansie and the other boys never touched him again. And while he survived those years at school, he developed a deep-seated hatred for the Boers, and never forgave his mother for sending him to that place.

CHAPTER 39

The 27th of April 1994 was a typical autumn day in Durban; the African sun unblinking in its warmth. I hoped that it was a good omen considering the historical significance of the date — South Africa's first Multiracial Election.

I sat outside with my cup of coffee and thought of Mohini. A woman, older than my mother, who had never been allowed to vote until this day. I wondered if her feelings were similar to mine. The election that I had been waiting for since my awakening outside the Wimpy held mixed emotions. On the one hand, it marked an historical day that would undoubtedly end apartheid and lay the first step to racial equality. On the other hand, it was tainted. Everyone knew that the ANC would win by a landslide. And therein lay the dilemma. As if the country had not suffered enough through four decades of apartheid. Now it was poised to suffer through four decades of reverse apartheid, corruption, and increasing violence. It was bittersweet.

Regardless, my father and I set out early to stand in line and cast our vote. We had both discussed it and decided to vote for the IFP. Although de Klerk had laid the stepping stones to end apartheid, I couldn't bring myself to vote for the NP, who had also been responsible for apartheid all along. An ANC vote was out of the question. As civilised as Mandela had been after his release, and through the negotiations, it was also obvious that he had been pre-picked as the figurehead. He had been integral in cementing the ANC's position and stronghold both within South Africa and overseas. Maybe it was because I had lived my whole life in Durban, the Zulu heartland, but I had more of an affinity with the Zulus than the Xhosas. So, with the mainly Zulu IFP, and majority Xhosa ANC, it was a foregone conclusion to vote for the IFP. I knew that my vote would have minimal impact on the outcome, but it was my right and my responsibility to at least try.

We voted at the same town hall where my father had cast his Referendum vote. Only this time, there were not queues of whites, but queues upon queues of blacks, coloureds, and Indians too. It did make the corners of my heart smile. Whatever the outcome, the historic vote would mark the end of apartheid and the beginning of a new era.

We queued for several hours, and made a day of it. There were braais dotted around the field, cooking and selling boerewors rolls. Johnny Clegg and Savuka played over the loud speaker — *we are the scatterlings of Africa*. I thought back to that day at the Wimpy. The day my life had changed. It was dizzying to think about how much had transpired and changed since that little girl in the Wimpy Bar had protested apartheid by refusing to eat her food. Amazing, to be queuing on this historic day, about to vote for the first time in my life, in the first multiracial election. It was also amazing to think how the relationships in my life had evolved since then. The one with my mother had suffered and never recovered. My father, on the other hand, had gradually invited me into his confidence, which in turn provided meaningful context I hadn't understood as a child.

'Johnny Clegg fought against apartheid,' said my father. 'He was arrested at 15 for breaking the curfew law and congregating with other races.'

'I know,' I said. 'Another reason why apartheid was so reprehensible. The fact that the government censored and punished artists, musicians, intellectuals, and writers proves that it was in fact a totalitarian regime for everyone. That is why, in my opinion at least, we have to vote against it. It has to end.'

'You're right,' he nodded. 'When people hear the word apartheid, they only tend to think about the racial discrimination and forget that the government oppressed freedom of speech for all.'

'I always think I should have done more,' I said.

'Ros, take it from your father, you did more than most people. There were times when I couldn't believe your audacity.' He laughed a little and patted my shoulder. 'Stop being so hard on yourself, okay?'

'Okay,' I said.

I'm searching for the spirit of the great heart, sang Johnny Clegg. The upbeat, nostalgic music kept everyone's spirits high as each and every person stepped closer to casting their vote. When we finally stepped inside the air-conditioned town hall, I couldn't hold back the tears. My father held my hand and hugged me tightly. He didn't need to say anything. I knew that he understood. I knew that he felt the same way, in his own way. He had never been for apartheid — not really. He had done little to oppose it, certainly, but so had the white majority.

It was time to forgive him. It was time to forgive everyone and move forward with a renewed sense of hope and optimism. We owed our country that at least. I marked the cross next to the IFP and held that piece of voting card for a long time before I slotted it into the box; half praying, half covering it with my intention. I desperately wanted this day to mark the beginning of change. The beginning of a new dawn. The end of violence. The end of hatred. The end of blame and guilt. 'Please,' I said in my head, 'please, let us all forgive and forget from this day forth.'

The ANC won in a landslide vote, as expected. In the days that followed the election, news reports told of how the ANC had employed all kinds of tactics to win votes — stories of money and food bribes, as well as tricking uneducated and illiterate blacks to tick the ANC box instead of IFP. But still, I held onto my prayer and renewed it in the days that followed, hoping against hope for a miracle.

CHAPTER 40

My ouma called me with marvellous news. She'd reconsidered her priorities after our time together, and decided to accept my Uncle William's long-standing offer to sell her house and live with him on his farm in Umlaas; eighteen kilometres from Pietermaritzburg, and about seventy kilometres from Umhlanga.

'I would like you and your dad to come for lunch a month from Sunday,' she said.

'Does Dad know that you've moved?' I said.

'No, not yet. I know how he feels about his brother.'

'Ja, say no more. I'll speak to him and smooth things over.'

'Thank you, Lindy.'

I wrote down her address and phone number and promised to confirm once I'd spoken to my father.

My father didn't need much convincing. After spending time in Coetzeesdorp after my attack, he was keen to make amends with his mother. His brother was another story. All I knew about my uncle William had been gleaned from conversations I'd had with Ouma and my father. Unlike my mother and Maeve, William and my father were mortal enemies and polar opposites. William had always chosen to speak Afrikaans, while my father spoke English. William collected guns, my father collected books. William had dropped out of school in Standard eight whereas my father had a Master's Degree.

On the drive to Umlaas, my father warned me to be on my best behaviour.

'Whatever you do, don't stir up trouble by mentioning the ills of apartheid, okay?'

'As if I would do that.'

'You say that now, but you don't know my brother. Trust me, he will rub you up the wrong way.'

'He can't be that bad, can he?'

'No, you're right. He's worse.'

I held up my two fingers in a scout's honour type of gesture, but my father's raised eyebrows told me that he was unconvinced.

We pulled into the dirt driveway that led to the farmhouse and parked the car alongside a barn made from corrugated iron.

I pointed to a man walking toward us. 'Is that him?'

My father nodded and muttered, 'He obviously hasn't changed a bit.'

In addition to different characters and personalities, they looked to come from different parents. William had a thick crop of blonde hair and eyes the colour of Eugene Terre'blanche. Judging from his strut, hip-holstered-gun, and rugged, sun-weathered skin, he looked to have a lot more in common with the AWB's leader than his eyes. He greeted my father in Afrikaans and nodded at me. My manners and upbringing told me to approach and embrace him, but his body language told me otherwise. Instead I said hello and left it at that. My father and I followed William toward the double storey farmhouse. It had a wraparound balcony and that junky farm look — rusted tractors and farm machinery that nature was in the process of reclaiming, as though farm labour and maintaining aesthetics were too much effort. Knee-high grass grew in patches. Spider webs glinted in the sunlight. When we reached the house, the verandah proved to be another dumping ground. Old sofas, that were no longer suitable for indoors, had been dumped and claimed by the two staffies — Jock and Lucy — who greeted us with excited barks and yelps. I thought of Gunther and smiled. A yellow fly strip, full of dead flies, dangled above the door as we entered, and the same fly strips hung inside the house too. We found Ouma in the kitchen stooped over the aga, turning the roasted potatoes with tongs. William grunted something about our arrival and then disappeared back outside.

'A man of many words,' I said, struggling to swallow my sarcasm.

My father shot a look at me and Ouma squeezed me until my breath began to constrict.

'I'm making lots of veggies and Yorkshire puddings for Lindy, and roast beef for you,' she said, pinching my father's cheek.

She told us that lunch would be ready in an hour and offered us a drink in the meantime. My father chatted to Ouma while she cooked and I excused myself to go to the bathroom. I wandered out to the lounge and opened the sliding door to go outside. Rows of vegetables went for miles into the distance — lettuces or cabbages by the looks of them. I went to take a closer look when I heard shouting to my left. William was standing in front of a group of African workers, swearing in Afrikaans and waving his hands like an air traffic controller about to lose a plane.

'Is everything alright?' I said, approaching them.

He swung around and stared at me with his Terre'blanche eyes. 'Mind your own business,' he said.

'What do you grow?' I said, trying to distract him from his verbal lambasting. 'Is it agriculture only?'

'Gaan kak,' he muttered, then turned back to the workers.

The three African men, or better described as teenagers, looked as if they were getting a telling off by their father. Judging by their hung heads and quivering knees, it would be fair to assume that they both feared and loathed their boss. I wondered if my Uncle had lost his sanity. The end of apartheid had ushered in a new norm; aggressive land seizure and killing of white farmers. It had become commonplace for farm workers to fight back, or, at a minimum give information to those with an outside agenda. Just because my uncle had not been a victim yet, did not mean that it was not in his destiny. Rumours of a white genocide agenda being levelled against white farmers were rife. My father believed it to be much more than a rumour. There was solid evidence to support it. Farm murders were also the most violent and personal. The women were always raped, tortured and murdered, while the men were forced to watch. Then the men were tortured and murdered — burned or hacked to pieces with machetes and pangas.

Given the increase in crime since apartheid had been abolished, I thought it madness for a white farmer to continue to treat his or her workers like slaves. They may have been uneducated, but they weren't stupid. They weren't immune to unjust treatment. I felt a pang of concern for my ouma as I watched my uncle with his macho, aggressive stance and attitude, along with his refusal to speak English. Perhaps it had not been a good idea to sell her safe little house in the middle of nowhere to come and help her ungrateful, racist son.

William had turned his back on me again and resumed the verbal assault on his workers. I weighed up the pros and cons of walking away or engaging him. My father had explicitly told me to keep my mouth shut and not antagonise my uncle, but his reckless behaviour was putting Ouma at risk. When William slapped one of the workers with a backhand and told the other two to 'voetsak', I stepped in.

'Do you have a death wish or something?'

He approached me like a matador would a bull, and, for the first time that day, he spoke to me in English. 'Who do you think you are?'

'An intelligent person who can see the writing on the wall.'

'Let me tell you something, girlie,' he said, thrusting his face into mine, 'the minute you show weakness those kaffirs will go for the jugular.'

'Yes, I'm aware of that. I myself have shown weakness and had my jugular exposed, but this is a different situation. You're antagonising and bullying them. Isn't that going to make it worse? What if they gang up together and attack you in the middle of the night? What then? Your mother is at risk too.'

He glared at me as if he couldn't quite believe my nerve. He wrapped his fingers around the butt of his gun and said, 'I can look after my mother.'

'I wouldn't be so sure,' I said. 'It takes more than one macho man and a gun to fight off a group of blood-thirsty attackers.'

He thrust his head forward in an effort to intimidate me. 'You're just like your father.'

'I'll take that as a compliment, and see you at lunch,' I said, turning my back on him to avoid any further confrontation.

We managed to get through lunch without any arguments. William wasn't much of a conversationalist, and he excused himself the minute he cleared his plate.

'I have some deliveries to make,' said William.

'Want some company?' said my father.

'Suit yourself.'

'What are you delivering?' I said.

He ignored me and went into the kitchen. I heard him dump his plate and cutlery in the sink.

Ouma spoke for him. 'We have a bit of a co-op with the neighbouring farms. I bake a range of steak pies, using meat from Henry's and Daisy's farm, and chicken pies, using meat from Deon's and Bonnie's poultry farm. We sell them at the truckstop down the road and split the profits. I also supply the shop with koeksusters and melk terts.'

'And we sell our vegetables at Heidis farm stall,' said William returning to the dining room. It'll take me about two hours, Wilstan.'

'We're in no rush,' said my father. 'I'm sure Ros and Mâ would like some time to talk.

William nodded and headed towards the door.

'I've made apple pie with fresh apples from Stan's and Peggy's orchard, Wilstan. You can have it when you get back.'

'Look forward to it,' he said. 'See you in a few hours.'

Ouma and I talked while she washed the dishes and I dried. She had soapy, steaming water in the left sink and clean water in the right. With her sleeves rolled up, she methodically washed and rinsed each dish before placing it in the rack for me to dry and stack.

'How have you been coping?' she said.

'I've been okay,' I said. 'I'm still avoiding social situations and people in general, but I'm making progress.'

'I'm happy to hear that, Lindy.'

'I'm more concerned about Dad. He finally told me about what happened in Kenya.'

'That must have been difficult for him.'

'Ja, it was difficult for me too. I can't get the scene out of my head.'

She nodded. 'You have to find a way, Lindy.'

'It's not that easy. Dad has plastered Jericho's office with newspaper cuttings of all the horrific crimes that are taking place. I'm concerned about him, to be honest. This political conflict is causing him a lot of internal strife. He isn't sleeping well, and he has lost interest in work too.'

'Your dad will be fine, Lindy. He has survived many hardships.'

'I'm worried about you too.' I told her about the incident I'd witnessed earlier with William and the workers.

'William is strict with those young workers, like a father is strict with his sons. If he was too soft, they would resort to laziness and quite easily become little tsotsi's.'

'I don't know, Ouma. This is not the old days. Aren't you concerned about becoming a farm murder statistic?'

She shook her head. 'No, Lindy, William can look after us.'

I sighed. 'Well, promise me you'll be careful.'

'I promise, Lindy.'

Ouma served tea and apple pie in the sunroom when William and my father returned. William didn't hang around, saying that a farmer's work is never done. I couldn't understand how siblings could be so different — having none of my own — one

Afrikaans, and the other English; one dark haired, the other blond; one, a lawyer, the other a farmer. It was a mystery.

'I don't think it's safe to stay here,' my father said out of the blue.

Ouma and I looked at him.

'My brother is going to get you both killed.'

'What happened when you two were out?' Ouma said.

'Nothing happened, Mâ. He's not adapting to the new South Africa. He still talks, thinks, and behaves like the bloody Boers I went to school with.'

Ouma dropped her head at the mention of school.

'He walks around with that gun like a wild west sheriff.'

'I hoped that your sibling rivalry was behind you,' she said.

'This has nothing to do with sibling rivalry, Mâ. I never worried about you when you lived in Coetzeesdorp. It is one of the few places in this God-forsaken country that is relatively safe. Farms have become targets. You're sitting ducks.'

'We have a community, Wilstan, and we take turns to patrol at night.'

'You should know better than anyone else that these kaffirs are brazen enough to strike at any hour of the day.'

I sighed loudly. 'Dad, can we not do this now, please?'

'I'm sorry, Ros, but this whole country is living in denial.'

'What would you have me do, Wilstan?' said Ouma.

'Come and live with us at Sea Breeze.'

Ouma shook her head vehemently.

'Why is that such a terrible idea?' I said defensively.

'Sea Breeze is your mother's house,' she said. 'I don't belong in such a fancy place, and I won't discuss it any longer.'

She stood up and went to the kitchen.

'This is my childhood all over again,' said my father, following her. 'You sent me off to boarding school and only visited once a bloody year, but you didn't do the same to William.'

'William was younger than you, Wilstan.'

I stood at the kitchen door, wanting to intervene but knowing that I should stay out of it.

'That's bullshit! When are you going to admit that you love him more than me?'

Ouma's nostrils flared as she faced my father. 'I sent you to boarding school because you were the smartest person I ever knew, goddamnit.' She pointed her finger at him. 'You were the one with potential. You were the one who belonged in the white-collar world, not me and not your brother. I had to let you go so that you could become who you are today.'

My father pulled out a stool from the kitchen table and sat down. 'You abandoned me, Mâ. In a place where I was hated and bullied for being English.'

I swallowed the lump in my throat.

Ouma sat next to him and put her hand over his. 'What do you want me to say, Wilstan? What can I possibly say to make up for what I did?'

'I don't want you to say anything, Mâ. I want you to stop being so stubborn and consider the fact that Ros and I might need you more than William does.'

'Okay,' she said, 'I will think about it.'

He rolled his eyes and sighed.

'I promise,' she said, squeezing his hand.

'I'll build you a granny flat, Mâ, with your own garden. And you can still bake, and visit William whenever you want. I can't live through another Kenya.'

Ouma met my anxious gaze. 'Why don't we start with a visit,' she said, putting her hand on my father's shoulder.

'That'll be amazing,' I said, taking a seat on the other side of my father.

'Sooner than later,' he said.

'I promise,' she said.

On the drive home, my father raised the subject of immigration.

'I used to dream about leaving all the time when I was a child,' I said, 'but when the end of apartheid became a reality, I wanted to stay.'

'Apartheid is over, Ros. It's time to prepare for the aftermath.'

I stared out of the window. We were passing a sheep farm in Camperdown.

'Do you know about the Judas sheep?' he said.

'No.'

'It's the sheep that they train to lead all the others to slaughter.'

I grimaced.

'Hendrik Verwoerd was the first Judas sheep that led us into apartheid, and de Klerk is the second Judas who is leading us all to slaughter. We will have to make a choice at some stage, Ros — to stay or leave.'

'Where would we go?'

'When you have money, you can go anywhere, Ros, but I've been researching options since your attack, and I've narrowed it down to New Zealand or Australia. They're both safe places with natural beauty.'

'What about Ouma and Mom?'

'You heard Ouma earlier. She can't even agree to a visit. As for your mother, she refuses to leave Maeve.'

I didn't reply. We had passed the sheep farm, and were driving past agricultural land populated with dams.

'I'm thinking about your future, Ros. I don't want you to live in fear. I want you to be safe and happy. Most people are incapable of leaving because they prioritise material wealth and status. Women have grown accustomed to having maids to do their cooking, cleaning and child-rearing. Men have their powerful jobs and contacts. But you and I both know that those things pale in comparison to peace of mind and quality of life.'

'I'm willing to consider it,' I said.

'That's all I ask.'

CHAPTER 41

Six months to the day of my attack, I received a call from my doctor.

'Your HIV results are negative,' he said.

'Thank you,' I said, exhaling so deeply that my body felt emptied of breath.

'But,' he said.

I inhaled.

'Perhaps it's better if you come in.'

'No, just tell me,' I said. 'The wait for these results has been excruciating enough.'

'I understand,' he said. 'Well, Rosalinde, as you know, we have run a series of tests over the last six months — mostly for STDs.'

'Can you cut to the chase,' I said, struggling to breathe.

'Rosalinde, I'm afraid that there's a high chance that you won't be able to conceive in the future. The internal injuries you sustained...'

I put the phone down, unable to hear anymore, pretending not to hear the last part of the conversation. I phoned my father immediately to tell him that the HIV results were negative. He sounded so relieved, so happy, that I omitted the bad news. He suggested that we celebrate at the Oyster Box for dinner after he got home from work. I said goodbye to him and then booked a table for dinner.

I stood in the hallway. The phone rang. My chest constricted.

'Hello,' I said.

'Rosalinde, I'm not sure what happened. We got cut off,' said the doctor.

'We didn't get cut off,' I said. 'I couldn't...' I stopped mid-sentence.

'I understand, Rosalinde. This is why I wanted you to come in. I'm not saying that it's impossible to conceive; miracles happen every day...'

'The odds are stacked against me,' I interjected.

'Your attack was brutal, Rosalinde.'

I swallowed, trying not to think about it.

'If you haven't already, I'd like to suggest some counselling,' he said. 'I'm writing a referral right now. Her name is Hannah van Rensburg. She's a Psychologist who specialises in sexual trauma. Have you got a pen?'

'No,' I said. 'Hold on a sec.'

'Her number is...'

I wrote it down, thanked him and said goodbye. Then I stuffed the number inside my wallet along with all of the other business cards I had no use for. I wanted to forget; not dig it all up again and relive the horror. I went upstairs and put on my cozzie. Swimming always cleared my head. I grabbed my book and went down to the pool. Our resident family of vervet monkeys had the same idea. The mothers were attached to their young, while the rest of the pack preened one another in the umbrella thorn tree.

I plunged into the cool water and swam freestyle, tumble-turning at the end of every lap, until fatigue stopped me. I shimmied onto the lilo, closed my eyes, and invited the sun to warm up my chilly thoughts.

I must have dozed off, because I woke up startled when I heard the monkeys screaming. I sat up too quickly and fell into the cold water. I couldn't see the umbrella tree from the pool, so I swam to the edge, jumped out, grabbed my towel and exited the pool area.

Two male monkeys, with their long teeth exposed, circled each other. Round and round so many times that I started to feel dizzy. From what I could tell, one was a rogue; not belonging to the family that inhabited our garden. At first I thought that he was merely threatening the females and their young, but it became clear that he was challenging the existing male. The younger monkeys jumped from branch to branch, screaming and squawking, while the females clutched their babies tightly. I had often fed bananas to the monkeys over the years, but I had never noticed the size of their teeth. They looked ferocious; their teeth appearing too long to fit into their mouths. I wasn't sure what to do. It was too dangerous to intervene. I ran inside and grabbed a stainless steel pot with a lid and then ran back outside with the intention of banging the lid against the pot in the hopes of scaring the rogue away. But it was too little, too late. The opposing male stood over a baby. His mouth was covered in blood, and the lifeless baby lay on the floor. I banged the lid anyway, and rushed toward him while shouting and swearing. He ran off in the direction of the yellowwood plantation and disappeared. The mother approached her baby. Prodded it with her hands. The monkey family had stopped screaming. All was deadly quiet. The mother dipped her finger in the blood and dragged it down her cheek.

I'm not sure what happened next; the shock of unprovoked violence, the news about my inability to conceive. Whatever it was, it triggered a series of flashbacks…Léon grunting behind a naked Promise. Me bent over the desk naked and helpless. The ferocity in Maleven's eyes. The excruciating pain of the sawn-off shotgun ripping my insides. The glint of white teeth. The bang of Mark's gun firing. The smell of iron. The heat of Paris's blood. I shut my eyes, willed my head not to explode, dropped the pot and collapsed on the grass.

When I came to, I lay there and sobbed, momentarily oblivious to my surroundings, and forgetting about the monkeys metres away from me. An urgent tapping on my head brought me back to reality. I lifted my head slowly to see the mother of the dead baby staring into my face, her cheek marked with a bloody tear. She reached out to me and patted my head. I sat upright and looked into her eyes.

'I'm sorry about your baby,' I said, gently holding out my hand to her.

She patted my hand three times and then ran back to sit with her dead baby. I stayed in the same position until the sun had moved across the ocean and began its descent. When the light sky dimmed, the mother picked up her baby, and the troop of vervets disappeared into the yellowwood forest that sheltered them every night.

When they were no longer in sight, I went inside and ran a deep, hot bath. I soaked for hours, continuing to top it up with hot water when it grew cold. My head was a stormy sky crowded with heavy clouds, each rubbing against the next causing massive amounts of friction. Thoughts of Maleven and what he did to me. Thoughts of the vervets and their dead baby. Thoughts of my future prospects. Thoughts of how exposure to violence was like a slow-release tablet. You never knew when the real effect of violence would trigger and knock you down. In most cases you never knew that it would hit. Like the toss of a coin, you had a fifty-fifty chance. It all depended on the level of violence that you had experienced, and your individual immunity. I was building an immunity to violence, learning to desensitise myself, but it was an artificial immunisation, and I always ran the danger of that one violent encounter that would push me over the edge.

The incident with the vervets had revealed the violent blueprint of Africa. It wasn't just humans capable of violence and cruelty, it abounded in nature too; lions chased impala across the savanna, sank their sharp claws into exposed throats, pulled them down and ate their prey alive. No wonder African humans were so wild and primal. They were not far removed from the heartbeat of their land. The question that I needed to ask myself was how did I fit into that landscape? What if I beat the odds and miraculously conceived a child at some future date? Wouldn't it be irresponsible to expose her or him to such a violent place? Maybe my father had a point. This constant exposure to violence would eventually take its toll.

PART V

1994 - 1995

CHAPTER 42

I tried to put a positive spin on my future by focusing on the HIV results, combined with the knowledge that Ouma was within driving distance. I made three phone calls —to Natal varsity; an acquaintance; and Alistair.

I arranged to return to the LLB program in Semester 2, which gave me four weeks to acclimatise back into a life of crowds and strangers. I decided that a baptism by fire was my best approach, so I called Liezl —a girl I met during my first Psychology lecture. She sat next to me and left early, because she had a waitressing shift at Spur Steak Ranch. Before she left, we swapped numbers so that I could give her my notes before the next lecture. Leaving early and skipping lectures became a habit for Liezl during the semester, so I felt comfortable enough to call her and arrange a night out.

She answered with a mouthful of gossip. 'Did you hear about Paris?'

'No,' I said cautiously. My rape had never been made public, thanks to Mark. 'I've been away this semester. What about him?'

'Oh. My. God.' She said each word as if they were statements in themselves. 'Him and his cousin were shot and killed outside a nightclub.' She took her first breath since speaking. 'Hey, weren't you and Paris an item?' she said.

'Oh my God,' I said, addressing her first sentence and ignoring the last, 'I've been staying with my grandmother for months in the Karoo so I'm totally out of the loop.'

'Jislaaik yong, tell me about it,' she said. 'Is your gran okay?'

'Ja, she's fine.' I managed to steer Liezl back onto the subject of a night out and she happily suggested that I meet her and a group of waitressing friends at the local Sports Café. Two things about her invitation put my mind at ease. One, it was a week night. And, two, the venue was an unusual combination of restaurant, bar and club, located on the top floor of a shopping centre. It would be safer than a nightclub, less dodgy than a bar, and more lively than a restaurant.

When I finished speaking to Liezl, I called Alistair. He was ecstatic about my news; the HIV results, my return to varsity, and my readiness to plunge back into life. He suggested we meet for lunch. I suggested dinner, and he surprised me with a 'yes, what about Saturday night?'

'I'd love to,' I said, feeling satisfied with the outcome of all my calls.

When Thursday night arrived, I changed my outfit ten times or more. My dresses and skirts were too tight or too short. They would only serve to attract unwanted male attention. I settled on black bootleg jeans, platform shoes, and a long sleeve black shirt.

I met Liezl at the club. She was standing in line and waved

me over. Once the awkward introductions with her waitressing pals was over I slinked against the glass bricks and observed my surroundings like a surreptitious owl in a tree. The politics of night clubs hadn't changed since my absence from the world. I only spotted whites queuing and filtering in and out of the club. A tall man exited the club and stopped to talk to the bouncers. My pulse took flight like an owl swooping a mouse on the ground, and I dropped my head in panic.

'Ros,' said Liezl gripping my elbow.

I lifted my head. There he was. The stranger. My avenger. Mark.

'Wrighty,' he said, calling me by my surname and smiling at me like an old friend he hadn't seen for years. 'What are you doing here?'

'I thought it high time I rejoin the world,' I said, faking confidence.

'Do you mind,' he said to my friend, 'if I steal her from you for a few hours?'

She looked at me for guidance, and I gave a slight nod.

'Of course not,' she said, 'I'm meeting a bunch of friends inside.'

He slipped his arm through mine and ushered Liezl and I past the queue like VIPs. My mind raced. I had fantasised about the moment I would meet him, but never entertained the reality. I half expected him to not recognize me, or, worse, to completely ignore me, considering Alistair's feedback. I also expected him to feel uncomfortable, given the circumstances of our first and last encounter. But none of those anxieties or hallucinations came close to fact. I felt the strength of his arms, smelled his cologne, closed my eyes and felt safe.

We found a quiet booth in the corner and sat opposite one

another. He reached across the table, and I placed my palms over his.

'How are you?' he said. He seemed to look into my eyes and see me in a way I had stopped seeing myself; desirable, undamaged, and full of potential.

'I'm much better, thanks.' My voice broke with nervous energy.

'I hoped to see you again. In better circumstances.'

'Really?' I said. I felt shy and tongue-tied. 'Alistair gave me the impression that you didn't want to meet me.'

'Now it's my turn to look surprised,' he said.

I frowned.

'I haven't spoken to Alistair since the night of your attack.'

A waitress interrupted our moment to take a drink order. She spoke directly to Mark as if she had known him for years, as if she had been intimate with him. A pang of jealousy nudged me in the ribs.

'We're not staying,' he said.

She pouted and said, 'oh,' before she walked away.

He took my hand and pulled me out of my seat. 'Let's get out of here.'

'I, um.' His ice blue eyes pulled me in like a window draws a visitor to the vista it frames. My stomach lurched like it did when I took the elevator to the top of Carlton Tower as a child, and I could have sworn that the volume of my heartbeat increased to such a degree that the whole club could hear it.

He didn't wait for an answer, and I didn't resist when he led me outside to the car park where his motorbike was parked.

'What about my car?' I said stupidly.

'I'll drop you back here later.'

'I've never been on a bike before.'

'A virgin,' he said and smiled. 'You'll never forget your first.' He winked and handed me a helmet. Wrap your arms around my waist, and don't let go'.

'Where are you taking me,' I said.

'My place.'

He revved the throttle and my belly purred in unison with the Ducati engine. His virgin comment struck a nerve and occupied my mind more than the thrill of the ride. I wasn't a virgin. I had Léon and Maleven to thank for that. But, from a consensual point of view, I was a virgin, and if I was reading Mark's signals correctly then I was about to experience my first consensual sexual encounter. Both of which thrilled and terrified me. Considering my sexual experiences were associated with violence and shame, I worried that I would only disappoint an experienced lover like Mark. I also worried that my body would cringe when touched. Not because of Mark, but because it possessed its own memory of sex. Every foreign fingerprint on my skin belonged to trespassers.

We drove to a house in Berea and parked on the curb outside. At the pedestrian gate, he punched in a code, the buzzer sounded, and the gate clicked open. I'm not sure what I had expected, but it wasn't what I found. It was an older house, situated on the ridge, with expansive views of Durban City and harbour. It had been renovated simply and elegantly. The soft, romantic lighting accentuated the polished wooden floors, whitewashed walls, and sparse pieces of retro artwork. It all seemed rather feminine, cultured, and at odds with Mark himself.

'Is this your house?' I said.

He smiled knowingly and said, 'Want a drink?'

'Yes, please.'

'Wine, beer, coffee?'

'I'll have whatever you're having.'

'Ja, this is my house, but my ex did the décor.'

'Oh, right,' I said, feeling embarrassed.

He told me to make myself comfortable while he poured the drinks. I sat down on the white chaise longue and tried to mine conversation topics while I waited.

'Rum and coke,' he said, handing me the heavy glass.

'Thank you.'

He pressed play on the stereo and unleashed the sounds of UB40 before he sat down next to me. I must have looked uncomfortable, poised on the edge of the seat, because he told me to sit back and relax. I did as I was told and sipped while I thought of something to say.

His face turned serious and he said, 'So, Wrighty, how are you, really?'

I lowered my eyes and swirled the ice in my drink. 'I'm getting there,' I said, nodding, 'the HIV results were clear – thank God.'

He took my hand and raised it to his lips. 'That is good news. I can't help but feel responsible.'

I shook my head. 'Don't be silly. It's nobody's fault except my own.'

He took my glass and set it down on the table. 'It's not your fault.'

'Why didn't you want to meet me?' I blurted out.

'What?'

'I told Alistair that I wanted to meet you.'

'And?'

'He said you weren't interested.'

Mark smiled as if he knew something I didn't. 'Alistair never mentioned it to me.'

My expression must have clouded, because he said, 'Don't be angry with Alistair. He's only trying to protect you.'

'It's not his decision,' I said.

'I'm curious, why did you want to meet me?'

'Honestly,' I said, looking into his eyes with a confidence that I did not feel, 'I have thought about you every second of every day since you saved me. I have fantasised about you like a child fantasises about becoming a superhero. If I had any real idea about love and relationships, I would say that I love you.'

'You weren't kidding when you said honestly,' he said.

I shrugged. 'What have I got to lose at this point?'

He put his arms around my waist and drew me to him. At the same time, *Can't Help Falling In Love* started playing. Before I could speak, he kissed me, gently at first, teasing and drawing me in, then the urgency increased as I kissed him back. His tongue was cold from the ice and he tasted like rum. Nothing about that first kiss was awkward. Whatever memory of touch my body held onto, it differentiated between trespassers and Mark. He lifted me off the sofa, carried me to the bedroom and lay me down on the bed. 'Are you okay with this?'

I pulled him toward me to kiss my answer.

He undressed me slowly, first taking off my shoes, shirt, then jeans, until my underwear remained.

He studied me and smiled. 'You are fucking gorgeous.' Then he drew me toward him again and kissed me, unclasping my bra and removing my underwear, setting off tiny explosions of pleasure inside me. He rolled me onto my front and told me to place my hands under my hips. He dragged his lips from the tip of my neck to the base of my spine and I shivered as goose bumps travelled like dominoes across my skin. He brushed a handful of my hair away from my neck and kissed the sensitive skin behind my ear lobe. I shivered again and felt the anxiety leave my body as I exhaled deeply and sighed. He lowered his body over mine. I could feel the skin of his torso press into my back. The weight of his chest against my shoulder blades. He turned me over and used his fingers to guide his penis inside me. I writhed and moaned beneath his warm body, and surrendered to his desire like a shoreline embracing high tide.

We must have fallen asleep in each other's arms, because I woke with a jump when Mark's hand pounded into my chest. I jolted upright to find him still asleep, but highly agitated and talking. I couldn't make out any words, though they grew louder and angrier. When he started tossing from side to side, I jumped out of bed and pulled my underwear on. I stood and watched him, transfixed, unsure of what to do, undecided if I should wake him up or leave him to wake on his own.

I didn't have to wait long, because he woke himself up with a jolt. He looked disorientated, and stared at me like I was a stranger for several seconds, before he snapped out of it and lay back in bed with a huge sigh.

'It's okay, Wrighty,' he said, 'nightmares.'

'Nightmares?'

'Ja, remnants from my time in Angola.' He held out his hand and patted the bed. 'Come and sit next to me.'

I pulled the sheet up over our laps. I didn't know what to say, so I kissed his hand and pressed it against my cheek. 'Do you want to talk about it?' I said quietly, not wanting to push or to intrude on his private moment.

'I was a Koevoet reckie in the Angolan Bush War during the 80's. We saw and did a lot of bad shit! The memories are trapped,' he said tapping the side of his head with his index finger.

'Tell me more,' I said.

'You don't wanna know,' he said dismissively.

'Actually, I do.'

He studied me for a minute. 'You might regret sleeping with me when you hear the story,' he said.

'I doubt it,' I said. 'Plus, I'm not easily shocked.'

He leaned into me and studied my eyes intently. I stared back. Neither of us blinked or looked away.

'There's something about you, Wrighty. I can't put my finger on it. Like I've known you my whole life.'

I swallowed. 'I know what you mean.'

He bent down to reach for something under the bed. 'A picture is worth a thousand words,' he said, putting a box in my lap.

'Photos of the war?' I said.

'Ja,' he nodded.

I put my hand over his. 'Before you show me, can you assume that I know nothing about the Angolan War?'

'You want background?'

'Yes, please,' I nodded.

He removed the lid and took out a pile of photos. 'Well, I'll tell you what we were told. We were fighting against communism. South Africa was trying to keep hold of South West African interests and the commies were trying to gain a stronghold by helping the natives gain independence. We were up against SWAPO — South West Africa People's Organisation — and their military wing PLAN — People's Liberation Army Namibia.'

He took out the first photo. It depicted a dirt road that

reminded me of the Karoo with its scorched plains and tufts of sand-coloured grass. Bloated dead bodies scattered the roadside, and heavily armed soldiers, in camo gear, stood alongside an armoured vehicle.

'I belonged to a paramilitary unit called *Koevoet*.'

'Koevoet?'

'Meaning "Crowbar".'

'Why crowbar?'

'Probably something to do with the way we tracked and extracted SWAPO terrorists.'

'Terrorists being the dead bodies?'

He nodded. 'Had enough yet?'

'No, keep going.'

'We were organised into platoons and patrolled in MRAPs.'

'What's an MRAP?'

'Mine-Resistant Ambush Protected. Basically, an armoured vehicle. You probably know it as a Casspir or a Wolf.'

'Ja, I've heard my father talk about Casspirs.'

He tucked my hair behind my ear and continued. 'SWAPO were usually on foot, so we moved around a lot to track them. We spent one week in the bush and one at camp. When we were in the bush, we roughed it and ate whatever we could confiscate or kill.'

I gritted my teeth at the thought. 'Why are the bodies so bloated?' I said.

'Because they were left to rot in the heat and drought. Sometimes we would collect the dead bodies and dump them in villages.'

My stomach muscles contracted at the thought of living amongst rotting bodies 'Why dump them?'

'Intimidation,' he said. 'Keep going?'

I nodded.

The second photo was worse. Two reckies, as Mark called them, held and wore their human trophies. One held the head of his victim. Another wore a makeshift chain threaded with ears. Mark called it common practice. I thought it macabre. The third photo showed a Casspir parked opposite a tree. It looked like the kind of tree where you'd find a sleeping leopard, but instead it had dead bodies tied to, and hanging from, its branches.

'Why the brutality?' I said.

'Don't forget that these were terrorists, Wrighty. Armed with RPG Missiles, AK47s, grenades, landmines, and God knows what else. They weren't innocent. Both sides were fighting to survive. We worked on a bounty system.'

'Like a mercenary?'

'Ja. We were paid for kills, prisoners, and seizing equipment. We killed on a grand scale, Wrighty. After a while killing became its own high. I have never come close to that amount of adrenaline before or after Koevoet.'

'Shit,' I said.

He watched me hesitantly as I flicked through more photos.

'Who is this?' I said, pointing to a photo of a fellow Koevoet soldier. He had a half-smile, and pointed his gun at the camera.

'That's Luke. He committed suicide when we got back home. He was like our little brother. The sensitive one. He couldn't harden himself like the rest of us did. War and killing killed him.'

'I'm sorry,' I said.

He squeezed my hand 'Wanna keep going?'

I nodded.

He talked me through the rest of the photos and offered an

explanation for the brutality depicted in each.

'Tell me something,' I said.

'Shoot.'

'Were SWAPO essentially fighting against apartheid?'

He looked at me for a long time before answering. 'Essentially, yes.'

I rubbed my eyes and face. 'Apartheid strikes again,' I said sarcastically.

'Still want to talk to me?' he said.

'Of course,' I said patting his hand. 'I won't deny that I feel nauseous now, but I understand that it was a war zone. In the absence of firsthand experience, who am I to judge?'

He searched my eyes for several seconds before he said, 'You're going to make it impossible for me to not fall in love with you.'

I smiled wryly and blushed. I already knew that my heart was plummeting like a skydiver, despite his brutal war stories.

'I want you to have these,' he said. He took out his dog tags from his reckie days and put them around my neck.

'Oh no, I can't,' I said. 'These must be worth gold bullion in sentiment.'

'Exactly,' he said. 'I want you to keep them for a while. It'll be my way of staying close to you all the time.'

I swallowed. Overwhelmed. 'You're sure?' I said.

'I'm sure,' he said. He pushed the photos and the box onto the floor before he climbed on top of me, and we melted into each other for the second time.

He wanted me to stay, but I told him that my father would worry if I didn't make an appearance soon. In truth, I didn't want to leave. Being with him was comfortable and familiar, but

I had no experience with lovers or relationships. Judging by his female admirer at the club, I couldn't rule out the possibility that I was one of many conquests. The thought of being duped made my stomach lurch and I scolded myself for being so quick to give him more of myself than I had ever given anyone else. I placed the dog tags back in the box underneath the pile of photos without telling him.

He drove me back to my car and kissed me goodbye. I kissed him back, but with less fervour and abandon than earlier.

He pushed a business card into my palm and said, 'Call me.'

I nodded, and he waited while I unlocked my car door and got in safely. I waved and he drove away. My heart sank a little. I wasn't ready to leave him, wasn't ready to say goodbye, but didn't know how to show him that without making myself completely vulnerable. I thought back to the night at the Edward and the fortune cookie message: *A Stranger will turn your life upside down*. Mark definitely had the power to turn my life upside down. I felt it in my gut. I clutched the business card like it was his hand and drove home.

CHAPTER 43

I met Alistair for dinner at Porcini; a family owned Italian restaurant in Umhlanga Rocks. I was apprehensive and annoyed. Apprehensive, because of my meeting and hook-up with Mark. Annoyed, because Alistair had lied to me about having a conversation with Mark. I tried to bear in mind that Alistair had always been my rock; grounded, stable, and solid. Whereas Mark was whitewater, and I might as well have been a pebble. Mark was my superhero. Alistair was the person behind the suit. In truth, I wanted them both for different reasons. But I knew that was unlikely.

We ordered a couple of starters to share and told the waitress we would order the mains later.

'I need to tell you something,' I said.

He frowned. 'Sounds serious.'

'I went out with a varsity friend during the week and bumped into Mark.'

Alistair's eyes narrowed ever so slightly.

'We spoke for a long time.'

Alistair nodded.

'Aren't you going to say something?' I said.

'What do you want me to say, Ros?'

'Say you never had a conversation with him about me.'

'That would be redundant it seems.'

'Oh, come on, Alistair. Don't be lawyerish with me.'

'Sorry, Ros, but I've nothing to say on the subject. I was trying to protect you.'

'Protect me from the person who saved my life?'

'Mark may seem like a caped crusader from your vantage, but he's also a dangerous womaniser.'

I straightened my spine when he said the word womaniser. 'Well, maybe he hasn't met the right woman yet,' I said.

Alistair laughed and shook his head.

'What's so funny?'

'You are one of the most intelligent women I have ever met, and I did not expect that cliché to come out of your mouth.'

I wanted to make a smart comment, but drew a blank. He had simultaneously complimented and insulted me, and I wasn't sure where I was going with my line of questioning anyway.

'Okay, let's drop it,' I said.

'Actually, I've lost my appetite.' He stood up to leave.

'Alistair,' I said, touching his arm, 'don't.'

'I'm not interested in going anywhere Mark's gone.' He stood up and threw money on the table for the bill.

My face burned with humiliation, and I made a beeline to the bathroom before the onslaught of tears overpowered me. I splashed water on my face. Breathed in and out. Then took five more minutes to compose myself, before I walked out into the restaurant with a confidence I did not feel. Alistair was waiting outside for me.

'Go fuck yourself, Alistair.'

'Ros,' he said, catching my elbow as I brushed past him. 'I'm sorry.'

'You can still go fuck yourself.'

I tried to pull away, but he pulled me back toward him and took my face in his hands. 'Ros, I was lashing out. The thought of you with Mark kills me. He's not good for you. He doesn't deserve you.'

'But, I'm not with Mark.'

'You are. I can see it in your eyes, and hear it in your voice when you talk about him, when you say his name.'

My cheeks burned again and I looked away. 'Alistair,' I said, 'you need to understand that Mark saved my life. I have intense feelings for him.'

'I do understand, Ros. But, what you don't realise is that he was also partly responsible.'

I frowned. 'He said the same thing. What the hell am I missing?'

'I don't want to discuss this in a public place, Ros. Will you come home with me so we can talk in private?'

I hadn't been to Alistair's place in all the years I had known him, and I was curious to say the least. 'Okay.'

We drove in partial silence to his house in Essenwood Road. I don't know why, but I had always imagined him living in a minimalist flat. He had always been a lawyer first and foremost to me, and I hadn't considered his life outside of work.

He led me inside, across polished wooden floors, and told me to take a seat while he found a bottle of wine. The décor was African-themed with an earthy colour scheme. I sat on the weathered brown leather sofa in the lounge and surveyed the room. A variety of animal prints hung on the white walls;

a leopard draped over the branch of a thorny tree, a male lion standing on a hill while surveying a plain of wildebeest.

'White or red?' said Alistair.

'Red, please.'

'Good choice.'

He poured the wine into two crystal glasses, handed me one, and sat next to me.

'So,' he said, 'that night.'

'You said Mark was partially responsible.'

He nodded. 'You know that I asked Mark to look out for you that night.'

'Yes, I know all about that.'

'Have you ever asked yourself why he didn't intervene sooner and stop them from...' he trailed off.

'Raping me,' I finished. 'It's okay, Alistair, you can say it. I'm not going to fall apart.'

'Sorry, Ros.'

'Did you ask Mark about it?'

'I did. He gave me some bullshit excuse about getting temporarily distracted.'

'And you don't believe him?'

'No, I don't. And I haven't spoken to him since.'

I took his hand. 'Alistair, we all want to blame someone for that night, but it's nobody's fault.'

Alistair nodded, took my wine glass, and kissed me. With Mark's memory swirling around my head and heart, I thought about pulling away, but the old flame of my love for Alistair flared up and licked my insides.

'I don't want to talk about Mark anymore,' he said. 'I've got something to show you upstairs.'

'Alistair,' I said, 'I don't want to keep anything from you. The other night with Mark...'

He put his finger over my lips and said, 'shhh, you don't owe me an explanation, Ros. Going forward, I won't hold you back from seeing Mark, but I'm also not giving you up without a fight.'

I swallowed and nodded.

He led me up three flights of stairs and led me into his study. I noticed the floor to ceiling window first, followed by the most spectacular view of Durban City with its night lights and the harbour beyond. A built in bookcase lined one wall of the room, a green velvet ottoman on the other. He let go of my hand and removed the white sheet that covered a telescope positioned in front of the window.

'I planned to show you this after dinner,' he said, drawing me close to him.

The excitement in his voice gave me goose bumps.
He positioned his eye over the telescope lens and adjusted the focus several times until he found his target. 'Come,' he said.

I positioned my eye over the lens and waited for his instruction.

'Tonight, you can see a constellation Leo, known as the Lion.

'No way,' I said, smiling. 'As in my star sign.'

He kissed the back of my neck and then explained what I was looking at.

'Okay, so you're looking for an upside down question mark called the Sickle.'

'Yes, I see it.'

'Right, that is Leo's head and mane,' he said. 'At the base of the question mark is a star called Regulus, aka little king.'

'Aha, yes, I see it.'

'Once you have those points of reference, the rest of Leo's body, legs, and tail extend to the East.'

'Oh my gosh, I can see it. That's amazing.' I turned to face him. 'You are amazing.'

'After everything you've been through, Ros, I'm just happy to see you smile.'

He was so different to Mark. I melted.

'Now,' he said, 'how about we make up for that dinner?'

'Yes, please, I'm ravenous.'

He took me to Legends, a late night restaurant in Musgrave, and we stayed until the early hours of the morning talking like old friends.

CHAPTER 44

After my evening with Alistair, my heart swung like a pendulum; Mark at one end, Alistair the other. Unsure of where I stood with Mark, I decided not to call him. If he was interested, then he knew how to contact me. After eight days of playing a childish game of he-loves-me-he-loves-me-not, he eventually made contact.

'Wrighty, you forgot something the other night?'

I wracked my brain before I said, 'what?'

'What are you doing tomorrow?'

'Um, I have lectures from 8 to 12.'

'Good, meet me at Circus Circus for lunch.'

'Okay,' I said, but he had already hung up.

Circus Circus was a newly opened cafe in Musgrave Centre; the latest place to be seen.

'Wrighty,' he said, kissing me on the cheek. 'Where've you been hiding?

'I wasn't sure...' I started to say. He stopped me mid-sentence by putting his finger over my lips and led me inside toward a table away from people.

'Did I give you the impression that our night together was a one-night stand?' he said.

'No. I. Well, I didn't know what to think. For all I know this is your standard operating procedure.'

'We shared an incredibly intimate night, don't you think?'

'Ja, I thought so too, but I'm not as experienced as you are, and I wasn't sure what your intentions were.'

'Is that why you left in such a hurry the other morning?' he said, smirking.

'It all happened so quickly. I wasn't planning to run into you and I certainly wasn't expecting to end up in bed with you. Honestly, I don't do that kind of thing normally.'

'I know you don't, Wrighty.'

I bowed my head and covered my forehead with my hand.

'I've done a lot of bad shit, but I'm not so cruel as to mess with your heart. Especially after what you've been through.' He took my hand away from my forehead and said, 'I'm sorry I wasn't there for you. I'm sorry that someone as beautiful as you has had such a shitty time.' He put his fingers under my chin and raised my face to meet his eyes. 'And I don't mean external beauty, although that goes without saying. I'm talking about your heart and your nature. You're as fierce as a lion on the outside and tender as a sparrow on the inside. But not many people can see that.'

'But you do,' I said.

He nodded and then reached across the table to kiss me. 'What do you say we get outta here?'

I nodded and smiled.

We drove back to his place, and I left all thoughts of Alistair in the rear-view mirror. Mark didn't need to reassure me like the first time. I made the first move by pressing my lips against his and kissing him with an urgency I had not experienced before. I had a desperate need for him to make love to me. I wasn't sure if it was lust or love. Whatever it was, he intoxicated me.

Later, our limbs tangled like ivy, a soft breeze filtering through the open window, he repeated his offer of the dog tags. I recognised the gesture second time around and accepted without hesitation.

'Can I ask you something?' I said.

'Shoot,' he said.

'Interesting choice of words,' I said, 'are you a mind reader as well a caped crusader?' I laughed and kissed him.

'You want a gun, Wrighty?'

'See,' I said, 'mind reader.'

'You're going back to varsity soon and you want to be able to protect yourself.'

'Ja,' I said, nodding. 'Can you help me?'

'If you want it to be legal, your dad will have to sign a consent form because you're under twenty one. If not, I've got plenty for you to choose from.'

He got off the bed and walked over to the closet. I couldn't help but admire him. He had started bodybuilding in his late teens and hadn't stopped. His body, lifestyle, tattoos, and war wounds were the antithesis of Alistair's suit, tie, and legal ethics. Mark was the only person who understood and embraced my dark side. As much as I loved and respected Alistair, I had a deep, insatiable need for Mark's renegade nature.

The closet had a fake panel on top. He removed it and brought a sleek black gun over to the bed.

'How does that feel?'

'Light.' I turned it over and examined it. 'Is this a Glock?'

'A woman who knows her guns. You couldn't get sexier if you tried,' he said, kissing me.

'Not to ruin the mood,' I said, pressing my fingers against his lips, but my dad will happily sign a consent form.'

He smiled. 'You haven't ruined the mood. Now that we've got that out of the way, come here.' He slipped his hand beneath the curve of my lower back and pulled me under him. I wrapped my legs around his waist and surrendered.

CHAPTER 45

I returned to varsity a few weeks later in an ethical pickle. Technically, I loved two men, but I knew full well that there would never be a situation where I'd get to keep them both. So, I threw myself into my studies and played a little hard to get by agreeing to weekly dates.

Alistair understood and encouraged me to focus on my studies, but Mark was not satisfied with breadcrumbs. We made plans to see a Steven Segal movie one Wednesday night, and were driving back to his place when he pulled over on the side of the motorway.

'What's going on?' I said.

'I want you to move in with me.'

'Move in with you? Why?'

'One, I don't see you enough, and two, it's the next logical conclusion.'

'Are you serious?'

'I'm serious,' he said, looking at me expectantly.

'Move in together?' I repeated, rather redundantly. 'I... er...I....' I stopped mid-sentence.

'What's there to think about Wrighty? I thought you'd be over the moon?'

'So did I,' I said insensitively. 'I mean, I am amazed that you're asking me, but I don't think I can…' My voice trailed off behind my thoughts. I found myself slap bang in the passenger seat of my own fantasy, and yet something stopped me from saying yes to Mark's proposal.

'Fucking unbelievable,' he said.

His voice pulled me out of my mental paralysis and I blushed, then attempted to backtrack and make an excuse, but he didn't care. He started the car, and slipped in a CD; Foreigner's *Cold As Ice*. The scathing lyrics only served to deepen my regret as we sped along the motorway and I envisioned our relationship skidding off the road. When we drove into the driveway at Sea Breeze, Mark reached across me and said goodbye as he opened my door. I asked him to hear me out, but he shook his head and assured me we were done talking.

You know that desire to turn back the clock and do something differently? Well, that desire grew and grew every second of every day after that night. I replayed the scenario ad nauseam and questioned what the hell had come over me. I certainly wasn't responsible; I had been a train heading for destination Mark when the control room suddenly forced me onto another track. A bizarre moment that I wished I could do over again. But I couldn't. I had said the words, and delivered them without ambiguity. And therein lay the problem. I decided to attempt another round of damage control and visited the club where he worked.

When he saw me he looked both relieved and slightly annoyed.

'Hi,' I said smiling, unsure whether to hug him, kiss him, or do nothing. He didn't make a move either way, so I did nothing.

'Wrighty,' he said raising his eyebrows in surprise. 'Where have you been hiding?'

'How are you?' I said, ignoring his comment and frowning with disapproval at this coldness.

'I'm great. How are you?'

'Can we please go somewhere and talk?'

'What's there to talk about?'

'You're making this really difficult. I want a chance to explain what I meant. It didn't come out right...' I said trailing off.

'I think you made yourself crystal clear. In fact, you were so clear that I made a decision of my own.'

'What decision?' I said.

'My ex moved back in with me, so you don't have to worry about feeling pressured or whatever the hell you're feeling,' he said.

I stared in disbelief. 'Is that it then? We have one misunderstanding and it's over? If that's the extent of your feelings for me then I'm glad I said no.'

'Don't be so dramatic, Wrighty. I'm not planning to stop seeing you.'

'What the fuck are you on about?' I said, getting angrier by the second.

'I gave you the choice and you turned me down. I have my needs. I would have preferred it to be you, but hey, that's life. It doesn't need to change our relationship.'

'I'm not interested in sharing you with your ex. I mean, what the fuck?'

'God, you're sexy when you get all worked up.'

'Oh fuck you! I can't believe we're standing here having this conversation.'

He tried to kiss me, but I backed away. 'You know what? I've been beating myself up about saying no to you, but now I see that it was fate intervening and saving me from a god-awful mistake.'

He raised his eyebrows in surprise. Before he could make a comeback, I turned my back on him and stomped to my car. Once inside, I hit the central lock and crumpled in the driver's seat.

A knock on the window brought me face to face with him.

'Open the door, Wrighty.'

Against my better judgment, and with no trace of the protective voice in sight, I ignored what my head screamed at me and followed my broken, but hopeful heart. I unlocked the passenger door and he climbed into the car. I could smell his cologne and had the urge to bury my face in his chest. I half expected him to take it all back and admit that it was all a big mistake. But, he didn't. Instead he pulled me up onto his lap, so that I straddled him. He held my head in his hands and pulled me toward him so that he could kiss me.

'I won't deny that my body craves your touch, but I'm not interested in being your mistress,' I said.

'You broke my heart, Wrighty, and I won't let you do it again.'

I climbed off him and sat back in the driver's seat. 'I didn't mean to break your heart, and I would take it back in an instant if you let me, but I won't be your mistress. End of story.'

'Then I guess we'll see how long we last as friends,' he said.

When he got out of the car I banged my head against the

steering wheel. Of all the scenarios I had played in my head, that wasn't one of them.

CHAPTER 46

A listair invited me to dinner at his place. He had important news that he wanted to deliver in person. Intrigued,
and reluctant to be the recipient of any more surprises, I asked
him for a hint, but he wouldn't say. He greeted me at the door
with a kiss, and I followed him into the kitchen and sat on a
bar stool. He handed me a gift and poured me a glass of my
favourite red wine; Mulderbosch Faithful Hound. I wasn't sure
if it was the flavour of the wine or the story behind it, but it
remained a firm favourite regardless. Faithful Hound was a dog
whose master abandoned him outside a cottage on the Mulderbosch farm. Living up to its reputation for being loyal to
the end, the dog waited, faithfully, for three years outside that
cottage, but his master never returned and the dog passed away.
The picture on the label — reminiscent of a George Stubbs
painting — depicted a melancholy Pointer dog, and told the
story without words.

'Can I open the gift?' I said, while Alistair stirred the creamy
mushroom sauce on the stove-top.

He nodded and smiled. 'I can't wait to see your expression.'

I raised my eyebrows and slipped my finger beneath the first, second, then third strip of sellotape. 'How did you find this?' I said, pulling out the Nina Simone CD. 'I went to every single record shop in Durban to look for this and nobody stocked it.'

'I phoned a store in Hillbrow. They had one copy and posted it to me.'

I shook my head. 'You're amazing. I don't deserve you.'

'Nonsense,' he said, turning the stove-top off and coming to sit next to me.

'Thank you,' I said, hugging him.

'No need to thank me. Your smile is enough.'

'Can I play it now?'

'Of course. Are you ready to eat?'

'Ja, I'm starving.'

While I slipped the CD into the hifi, Alistair dished up the food. The dining room table was candlelit and dressed with a crystal vase of long-stemmed red roses. He had cooked creamy mushroom pasta, topped with truffle oil, and served with a side salad of rocket and parmesan. Alistair saved his news until after dinner, so that we could catch up on this and that. After dinner, he made us Amarula Coffees and we drank them in the lounge.

'So,' he said, shifting in his seat, 'I have some news.'

'I know, I've been trying to guess what it is since you told me.' I chuckled.

He put his coffee down on the table and turned serious. 'Spencer & Mason have offered me a six month secondment with a firm in London.'

'Wow,' I said, putting my coffee down on the table. 'That is fantastic news, Alz.' I opened my arms and moved over to hug him. 'When do you leave?'

'In a week, if I accept it.'

314

'Why wouldn't you accept it?'

'Honestly? You, Ros. The thought of leaving you for six months is…' he sighed, 'giving me serious pause.'

'It's only six months, right?'

He nodded.

'And it's an opportunity, right?'

He nodded again.

'I'm not going anywhere, Alz, and I know how much your work means to you, so it's a no-brainer in my opinion.'

'Are you still seeing Mark?' he said out of the blue.

'No. Mark and I are just friends.'

'Be honest with me, Ros. I need to know.'

'I am being honest,' I said. 'I did see him a number of times, but it's over now.'

'Why, what happened?'

'It's like you said. Serial womaniser.'

He sighed and looked away. 'I can't be second place, Ros.'

'You're not second place, Alistair. I have never denied my feelings for Mark, but you are not second place.'

'Then marry me,' he said.

'What?'

'Marry me, Ros. The thought of being without you or losing you is driving me crazy.' He pulled out a velvet box from his pocket and got down on one knee.

My chest constricted. I bent over to try and catch my breath.

'Ros, are you okay?'

'Ja,' I said, between sharp breaths, my chest feels tight. I dug my knuckles under my breast to show him where it hurt.

'I'm taking you to the doctor.'

'No, I'll be fine.'

He ignored me and led me to the car.

Three hours later he dropped me at home. The doctor called it a panic attack, and Alistair didn't seem overjoyed by the prospect.

'Not a good sign,' he said. 'I proposed and you had a panic attack.'

'Alistair, I'm sorry, I don't know what happened. I'm sure it's unrelated.'

'I'm fairly sure it's not, Ros.'

He turned to leave.

'Alistair? Will I see you before you go to London?'

'Probably not, Ros. I have a lot to organise before then. I'll call you in a few weeks.'

I sighed heavily and watched him walk to his car. As he drove away, I felt the tight fist reach around my heart a second time that night.

My gun licence was approved weeks later, and Mark accompanied me to take possession of my Glock. Its carbon frame felt cool inside my warm palm. To celebrate, he took me to the shooting range and gave me my first lesson.

'Are you sure you haven't fired a gun before?' he said, studying the target.

I shook my head. 'I'm sure.'

'Remind me to stay on your good side.'

He was impressed, and I liked to impress him. I notched an imaginary point under my name.

My firearm education continued for months. He taught me everything I needed to know about guns and shooting, including the law. He warned me that a gun was a serious responsibility. If I ever drew it, it would only be to protect myself. If I ever shot anyone, it would be in self-defence.

'You don't shoot to wound,' he said. 'You shoot to kill. You don't want any hostile witnesses left behind.'

I nodded. It wasn't difficult to imagine, with the memory of Maleven never far away.

The final element of training involved a series of shooting tests — in and out of the shooting range — followed by a speed test whereby I had to disassemble and reassemble the gun in under sixty-seconds. When I passed both tests he gave me a graduation present — a hollow point bullet. It was illegal to shoot, but it was the poetry of the bullet world. Its hollowed centre was designed to spin and travel faster, before entering and shredding the designated target. He also extended an invitation to accompany him on a trip to the Skeleton Coast. He warned me that we would 'be going bush' — making fires on the beach, camping, driving long distances in a 4x4, eating baked beans and whatever else presented itself along the way. Given how I'd hurt him with my rejection, and considering it was a fascinating place that few people rarely got the opportunity to see, I saw my chance to atone and said yes.

'Why isn't your girlfriend going with you?' I said.

'She wouldn't last a day.'

I nodded. 'Okay, and when your friends ask who I am?'

'I've already told them I'm bringing my flossie.'

'Haha, that's not funny.'

'We won't have time for that anyway. Well, except when you're freezing cold and you want to share my sleeping bag with me.'

'Note to self, buy an arctic sleeping bag.'

He punched me affectionately on the shoulder, shook his

head and laughed. 'You crack me up, Wrighty.'
'Seriously, thanks for asking me. I cannot wait!'

CHAPTER 47

We flew from Durban to Windhoek on an early morning flight and were picked up by Mark's friend, Jake, in a white Land Rover. Mark got into the passenger seat and I sat in the back.

Jake and Mark did the African handshake, and both said, 'Howzit my bru.'

'Jake, this is Wrighty,' said Mark.

'But you can call me Ros,' I said, leaning forward to shake his hand.

Jake laughed. 'If he calls you by your last name, you're officially one of us.'

'As long as he doesn't call me flossie.'

Mark let Jake in on the joke and Jake roared with laughter.

Jake looked at me in the rear-view mirror. 'So, tell me, Ros, have you been to the Coast before?'

I shook my head. 'No, but I've always wanted to see it. Do you live in Namibia, Jake?'

'Ja, I've lived here since our Koevoet days.'

'I imagine it would have been hard to assimilate when you

came back?'

Jake nodded. 'Not all of us are as tough as this guy.' He patted Mark on the shoulder.

Mark threw his head back and laughed.

'How did you two meet?' said Jake.

'I'll let Mark answer that one,' I said.

'Wrighty was attacked by a group of k...'

'Angry black men,' I interjected.

'They were gonna kill her.'

'Fuck,' said Jake.

'I intervened.'

'He saved my life,' I said.

Mark changed the subject. 'Wrighty recently got a Glock, she's a fucking good shot too.'

Jake looked at me in the rear-view mirror and winked. 'I can see why he likes you.'

I smiled and tried to steer the subject in another direction. 'Tell me a bit about the trip,' I said, 'where do we go from here?'

Jake handed me an old map of the Namibian Homelands. The homeland regions were marked in salmon-pink and the rest of the map was sepia, with coffee stains and creases from being folded in dozens of different ways over the years.

'We drive to Swakopmund from here. It's about three hundred and fifty K's. We'll be meeting some of the other guys there. From there we take the C34 coastal salt road and drive through Hentiesbaai and then the Cape Cross Seal Colony until we reach the Ugab Gate, which is basically the entrance to the Skeleton Coast. That's our main meeting point. From there, we go bush.' He laughed and winked at me in the rear view mirror.

'Do you guys do this every year?'

'Without fail,' said Jake, 'But this is the first time Mark has brought someone along.'

'Really?'

He nodded. 'In fact, we've never had a woman join us.'

'To what do I owe the honour?'

'You're not like other women,' said Mark.

'I'll take that as a compliment and say no more.'

They both laughed and then fell into an easy conversation of catch-up. I relaxed into my seat, and opened my window to breathe in the hot, dry air. Like the Karoo, the scenery started out as an endless horizon of dry scrub savannah and then, as if crossing some invisible border or portal, we passed through pure desert and sand dunes reminiscent of ancient Egyptian pyramids. When the Land Rover passed the 'Welcome to Swakopmund' sign, the landscape changed again into a seaside village.

Jake parked in the centre of town and took Mark to buy supplies and meet up with his friends. I opted to stretch my legs and explore the history of the town. Swakopmund — German for 'mouth of the Swakop' — was once a primary harbour for German South-West Africa. The colonial seaside town still had its European architectural gems, such as the tower of Woermann Haus, built in 1906 and later used as a library. Not to mention the candy-striped lighthouse. It also had a unique climate. Surrounded by the Namib desert on three sides, and the cold Atlantic to the west, the region received less than 20mm of rainfall a year. The cold Benguela current supplied moisture in the form of fog for approximately 180 days a year. That fog created a major hazard for ships and was responsible for the many wrecks scattered along the coast, but it also provided moisture for the flora and fauna.

I met Mark and Jake at the car an hour later. Jake was letting air out of the tyres.

'Tyre problems?' I said.

Jake shook his head. 'I'm letting out a little pressure for the loose gravel, sand, and salt on the road ahead.'

I nodded. 'You learn something new every day.'

We set off to the Ugab Gate. On the way, we passed the Swakopmund saltworks — a collection of salt ponds — and much later, the Cape Cross Seal Colony. The stench of fish blew into the car long before we caught sight of the glint of wet seal coats sprawled across rocks and diving into the tempestuous waves. We reached the Ugab Gate by late afternoon. The double gates were flanked by long, arching whale bones, and skull and cross bone signs, made from galvanised steel, were nailed in the centre of each gate. The concrete wall on either side of the gate was decorated with stones, and a variety of bones — including a giant whale skull. We met the rest of Mark's friends and drove in a convoy along the sandy road. It was getting dark by the time we reached the campsite, so the guys organised the tents and made a fire. After a meal of baked beans, heated over the fire, and bread, I mostly listened while the guys caught up on each other's news.

By the time I reached our tent, the chilly wind, blowing off the sea, had set into my bones. Mark zipped up the tent and set up the camping light in the corner. Too cold to get undressed, I kicked my shoes off and pulled the sleeping bag up around my ears. I finally started to warm up when Mark got into his sleeping bag and spooned me from behind.

'Glad you came?' he said.

'Ja,' I said, my teeth still chattering a bit. 'Although I'm surprised you asked me.'

'I'm sorry about that night in the car,' he said.

I sighed. 'I'm the one who should be apologising. I still don't know what came over me.'

'It's probably for the best.'

'Why?'

'Because I'm not good for you, Wrighty.'

'I'll be the judge of that.'

He wrapped his arms around me and drew me in tight. 'You and I have very different futures ahead of us, Wrighty, but that doesn't mean we can't enjoy each other now.'

He kissed my neck. I closed my eyes and thought about all the reasons I should pull away. Instead, I turned over and kissed him like it was the last time I would ever kiss him. We made love like it was our last meal, the sound of hostile waves thrashing themselves against the rusted ruins of ghost ships outside our tent.

I woke up early, before anyone else, brushed my teeth with ice cold water and went for a walk. The fog was thick, but the further I walked, I glimpsed patches of sky and sea — indistinguishable from one another in many ways, like a shade of silver without the light, or the underbelly of a grey whale. Aside from the whip of wind striking the foamy sea crests, and the sound of crashing waves, the beach was eerily quiet. I walked until I saw my first wreck. The rusted ship hull looked like a bison that had fallen and decomposed in the salt water and white sand. It felt corrosive against the skin of my finger, and I tried to imagine what it would be like to be a sailor wrecked in this bleak wilderness of fog and strange light. A little way beyond the wreckage, I came across a watery grave of bleached whale bones. I guessed they were whales from the sheer size of them.

As wide as elephant tusks, and a similar shade of ivory. Gigantic skulls, with hollowed out eye sockets, and mouths that once made ocean music, but now made an altogether different sound while exposed to the wind. I sat amongst the bones for a while and watched the ocean as it churned, thinking that Africa was the most wild and devastatingly beautiful place that I would ever have the privilege of knowing.

That evening, around the fire, I asked a question.

'How did this tradition start?'

They all looked at Mark.

'Sorry,' I said, waving my hand, 'I didn't mean to pry.'

Mark swigged his beer. 'My father committed suicide soon after I came back from Koevoet.'

'Shit,' I said, not knowing what else to say.

He raised his eyebrows and nodded. 'Ja, it was shit.'

'You don't need to talk about it,' I said. 'I'm sorry for bringing it up.'

'It's okay, Wrighty. My mother got sick with leukaemia while I was away. She died before I could say goodbye. My father just couldn't get past it.'

'That is devastating,' I said, 'I'm so sorry.'

'The guys suggested we come here and scatter their ashes amongst all the other bones that wash up on these shores.'

'We've come here every year since,' said Jake.

Mark held up his beer. 'Cheers.'

They all said cheers in unison and then broke off into individual conversations. I slipped away when nobody was looking, and went back to the tent. The more Mark revealed himself to me, the more I felt drawn to him, and the more conflicted I felt about Alistair. The Skeleton Coast was a perfect metaphor for my relationship with Mark; I never wanted to leave, but I knew that I would eventually have to, because as thrilling and beautifully wild as it was, it was also bleak and inhospitable.

Mark unzipped the tent door and peered inside. 'I didn't see you leave.'

'I didn't want to make a fuss.'

'You okay?'

I nodded. 'I'm sorry about your parents.'

He shook his head. 'It's ancient history, Wrighty. Don't worry about it.'

'I love you,' I said, surprising myself.

He narrowed his eyes and sighed. 'I know you do, but it's not enough.'

'Why not?'

'I told you last night. We have different futures ahead of us.'

'So, you and I are allowed to share moments together but not a life?'

'Something like that.'

'Why did you bring me here?'

'Because I love you. Because I can't get enough of you. Because I know we're getting closer to going our separate ways, and I want to make memories with you before it's too late.'

'It sounds like you're counting down to something. What am I missing?'

He sighed. 'Come and sit with me. There's something I need to tell you.'

I kneeled opposite him and held his hands. 'What is it?'

'I'm involved in the drug business, Wrighty.'

'Define involved?' I said, frowning.

'I'm the head of a drug syndicate.'

I swallowed and shook my head. 'Why?'

'Money, Wrighty.'

I raised my eyebrows. 'I know you better than that, Mark. It can't just be about money.'

'You're right. I'm sick of hustling, Wrighty, and I'm not getting any younger.'

'What about the ethical side of the equation? What about kids, and desperate prostitutes, and pregnant women? I mean, for God's sake, have you thought about any of that?'

'My dealers don't sell to kids.'

'Oh come on, Mark, be serious. You can't guarantee that.'

'I told you love wasn't enough.'

'Love has nothing to do with this. What's your exit strategy?'

'Get in and get out quick.'

'I think that'll be easier in theory than in practice.'

'Meaning?'

'Our first night together, you compared Koevoet to a drug. A high you could never top. This could be your way of topping that high.'

He smiled wryly and shook his head. 'How do you do that?'

I didn't answer him. Instead, I leaned toward him and pressed my cheek against his. 'Your stubble is so reassuring,' I said, closing my eyes.

'Wrighty, you deserve more than I can give you. One day in the future, you will want a husband and child, and I can't give you that.'

'I can't have children.'

He pulled away and frowned.

'A vestige of my attack.'

'Fuck. Why didn't you tell me?'

'I haven't told anyone.'

'Did the doc tell you it was unlikely or impossible?'

'Unlikely.'

He nodded. 'Alistair loves you, and I know you love him. He will be better for you in the long run.'

'Shhhh,' I said, kissing him, 'I don't wanna talk about this anymore.'

Later, after we'd made love, and he'd fallen asleep beside me, I cried. Like the fog that swallowed the ocean and sky outside, so did my dilemma over Mark swallow me. My God, I loved Alistair, but Mark was like a ghost with unfinished business; a lover from another lifetime that would haunt me forever. At times, my love for Mark felt bigger than me — the size of whale skeletons that littered the shore. Big enough for me to lose my compass, lose my way, lose my self. There were moments where I would have dropped every moral fibre in my body to be with him. There were moments when I would have compromised everything in exchange for his love. And the worst thing is that he knew it. He knew it and he wouldn't let me. I felt devastated. Lost. Sick. Like a teenager who thinks she can live on love instead of food. That's what Mark was to me, and, perhaps, if he had been ten years younger, it might have been the same for him. But he knew better. If Koevoet had been his drug, then he was surely mine.

CHAPTER 48

A few weeks later, on my drive home from varsity one afternoon, I was mobbed by a group of street kids while stopped at a red robot. One of the older boys stuck a knife through the crack of my open window and tried to open my locked door, while the others literally threw themselves on the windshield, the bonnet, and surrounded the car. Some sniffed and sucked on their plastic glue cartons, while the others banged on the windows, tried to open the locked doors, and shouted. It seemed to happen in slow motion and double speed. I pulled my gun out from between my thighs (where I kept it when driving, lest hijackers struck from nowhere), and used the barrel to push the tip of the knife out of the window, and threatened to shoot every last one of them. Fortunately, the mob dispersed and I accelerated away, thanking God that I had central locking and a gun.

My experience turned out to be a prelude to something more disturbing. An internal alarm sounded when I arrived at Sea Breeze and saw my father's car parked in the driveway. He usually left before I woke up and returned after eight. I found him sitting at the kitchen table with a bottle of Macallan in his hand.

'What's happened?' I said, standing in the doorway. 'Is it Mom?'

He shook his head and swigged the whiskey.

'Has something happened to you?' I said, feeling increasingly anxious.

'It's Ouma,' he said. 'Goddamned kaffirs!' He slammed his fist down and I jumped.

'What?' I said. 'What has happened?' I sat down and touched his fist. 'Dad,' I said, 'speak to me.'

'My girl, I hoped that I would never have to tell you what I'm about to tell you.' He put the bottle down and dropped his forehead into his hands. 'They attacked the farm.'

My stomach clenched, as if it were clairvoyant.

'Ouma was raped, stabbed sixty-one times, and then set alight.'

My lip quivered uncontrollably and I screeched a 'What?!' before my vision blurred and his words sounded like a tape recording whose tempo had been slowed right down.

'They tied up your uncle and tortured him for two days. And then they hacked him to pieces with a machete. A neighbour found them. He identified the bodies and has given information…

'Stop,' I said, holding up my hand. 'Please, stop talking. I need a minute to process this.'

He stopped talking and stood up. 'I'm sorry, Ros.'

I stood up to leave.

'Where are you going?'

'To my room. I need some space.'

I lay on my bed and cried. I cried for my ouma, for me, for my father, for my country. I cried and cried until my crying turned to hysterical laughter. I pinched myself in case I was lost in a bizarre dream world. The red welt confirmed that I wasn't dreaming, but South Africa was becoming the closest thing to a living nightmare. How long could we all sustain this repeated violence? How much loss could we each endure before we cracked under the pressure? I couldn't speak for anyone else, but I was tipping the scales of my personal quota. I couldn't justify it anymore. Maybe my father was right to want to flee. At the end of the day, if we stayed in South Africa, we might well become another statistic of random, but probable violence. Rather abandon your roots, history, and life, than remain in a country where your karmic debt would never be paid.

I rang Alistair in London to tell him the news. He offered to come back for me, but I declined and told him to stay put. He reluctantly agreed and promised to phone every day. He also promised to visit in 6 weeks.

I hung up and phoned my mother next. She hadn't heard about my ouma's murder, but had no intention of returning home for the funeral. When I confronted her, she said that it had been no secret that she and Ouma hated each other, and that it would be hypocritical if she suddenly started to care after her death. I couldn't believe the words that were coming out of her mouth. We argued worse than we ever had. She said that I might as well have been someone else's daughter, because I had always been a stranger, and that leaving was the best decision she had ever made. Her words stung like a cluster of blue bottles. But in a funny, awful way, she was right. I felt the same way. She might as well have been someone else's mother. My father and I were more alike. I had grown to realise that after my attack.

I organised Ouma's funeral, because my father was incapable. After her murder, he took an extended leave of absence from work and practically locked himself in Jericho's study day and night. He didn't say much, and when he did talk, it always involved the Kenyan murders of his childhood, and the latest grisly story of local murders and hijackings.

On the morning of Ouma's funeral, I found him in the library, unshowered and unshaven.

'Dad, it's Ouma's funeral today. You need to get ready.'

He waved a book at me. 'When I talked about war at Brenthurst Gardens and told you to go with the flow, you were too young to understand.'

I took the book from him. It was Alan Paton's famous novel, *Cry, the Beloved Country.* 'This is still one of my favourite books,' I said. 'And what's that line?' I flicked through the pages until I found the highlighted line that had troubled me so much when I read it the first time at school.

I have one great fear in my heart — that one day, when they are turned to loving, they will find that we are turned to hating.

'Prophetic,' said my father.

'Sadly, yes.'

'Did you know that the apartheid government withdrew Paton's passport in 1960 because he had been outspoken about apartheid in his travels overseas?'

I nodded. 'Yes, I knew that. Is that what you meant by going with the flow?'

He nodded.

'When you spoke to me at Brenthurst Gardens, I was angry with you and mom — everyone, actually. I couldn't accept your acceptance of apartheid. And, while I will admit that I was naïve to the complexities, I still maintain that apartheid was an atrocity.'

He nodded. 'I don't deny that apartheid was unjust, Ros. Of course it was. But like you say, Africa is complex. In essence, apartheid has made it impossible for the majority of whites and blacks to co-exist, because one group has been conditioned by western education while the other has retained its tribal tradition.'

'I have to admit, this post-apartheid spiral into senseless violence is a bitter pill to swallow. On the one hand, I can understand the hatred. I often try to put myself in their shoes and ask how I would react if the tables were turned.'

'You have no reason to feel guilty,' he said.

'Don't I?' I said.

'No, you don't.'

I raised my eyebrows in doubt.

'Maybe I do, Ros. After all, I never fought. I never spoke up like you did. I accepted it, and used my own terrible experience to justify it.'

He looked like a room that was previously furnished, but now stood vacant. It worried me, but I didn't know what it meant exactly.

'Dad, don't be so hard on yourself. What you experienced in Kenya has scarred you for life.'

He embraced me tightly and said, 'Promise me something, Ros.'

'What?' I said.

'Promise me that if anything happens to me, you'll leave this God-forsaken place.' He released me and held me at arm's length. 'Promise me,' he repeated.

'I promise,' I said. 'But, nothing is going to happen to you, okay?'

He nodded unconvincingly and went upstairs to get dressed.

The funeral was small. Less than twenty people. We held it at a local cemetery surrounded by mahogany trees and rolling hills. Most of my ouma's friends lived in Coetzeesdorp and had apologised in advance for not being able to travel. My Uncle had no friends to speak of. The local farmers in the surrounding area turned up to offer their condolences, and they were the only ones to stay and talk after the service.

My ouma's neighbours, Stan and Peggy, who had supplied Ouma with the fruit for her sweet pies and pastries, had offered to host the after-service at their farmhouse. We travelled in a convoy, along the dirt road for several kilometres and then up a hill. The house and grounds were completely different to that of William's. Set on 80 acres of manicured gardens and rolling lawns, the sprawling homestead, with its thatched roof and terracotta walls, was stylish and immaculate. Once parked, we followed the others up the driveway and past the stables to the entrance. Stan greeted us at the door and led us through the hallway, then parlour, and dining room — all spaces revealing the thatch between exposed beams, and polished parquet floors — before exiting through french doors to the outside deck area.

'Peggy is organising the food,' said Stan, 'make yourselves at home and I'll be out in a minute with some drinks.'

We thanked him and found seats around the rectangular wooden table. I sat myself where I could see the view. The property was elevated, and boasted views of fields, rolling hills, fruit trees, and dams in the distance. More immediately, were views of a pool and tennis court.

Stan and two black maid's brought out trays with tea, coffee, and alcohol, and placed them in the middle of the table. Peggy, and another two maids, followed seconds later with trays of food; strawberry and cream sponge cakes, cheese and biscuits, fresh fruit, mini meat pies, vegetable curry puffs and samosas, as well as sandwiches with egg mayonnaise on one plate and cucumber cream cheese on another.

'Help yourselves,' said Peggy.

Everyone grabbed a plate and picked their food.

Peggy sat next to me and patted my hand. 'I was so fond of your ouma, Ros.'

'Thank you, Peggy. When I visited her for lunch last time, she baked an apple pie with apples from your orchard.'

'Ag, ja, she made everyone so happy with her baking.'

The two couples who had supplied Ouma with meat for her pies nodded in agreement.

'William kept to himself before your ouma arrived,' said Peggy.

'I only met him once,' I said, 'I don't think he was very social.'

'He wasn't too bad once you got to know him,' said Stan.

A lull fell over the table for a few seconds while people ate and sipped their drinks. I leaned over conspiratorially to Peggy and told her about what I'd seen the afternoon we'd visited the farm. 'Do you think the workers were involved?' I said.

'Ag no,' said Peggy, 'it's these other tsotsi's that pay the workers for information about the comings and goings of the farmers. They are targeting all farmers, Ros.'

'Aren't you concerned about your safety?' I said.

'Of course,' she said wringing her hands, 'but our money is wrapped up in this property and the market is terrible at the moment because of the murder sprees.'

'My father keeps talking about emigration. Would you leave if you could?'

'Ag, I don't know Ros. Our whole lives are here and we're probably too old to emigrate. But someone your age should definitely think about it. There will be no opportunities for the next generation.'

'Have you got children, Peggy?'

'Ja, they're all grown up now. I worry about my grandchildren. They are the ones who will suffer the most.'

'Where do they live?'

'My son lives in a small, quiet place in the Cape called Kommetjie. There isn't much trouble there, so I don't worry about him too much. My daughter and her husband live in Sandton.'

'My ouma lived in the Karoo, in a tiny dorp called Coetzeesdorp. It was so safe and quiet. I wish she had never left.'

Peggy held my hand and sighed. 'I'm sorry, my darling. I'm so sorry.'

A few minutes later, I stood up to pour a cup of tea. My father seemed in his element talking to the men about the farm murders that were taking place around the country. He knew as much as the locals, thanks to his wall of newspaper cuttings. He was like a chameleon. So easily did he slip from his stuffy lawyer's suit to a down-to-earth everyman. Before Uncle Jericho died and my mother left, I'd only seen glimpses of that side of him. I wondered if he was more comfortable on the other side of wealth, having been raised there to begin with. The old person I knew as Dad seemed to be unravelling and becoming someone altogether different.

As I sat there and listened to them rattling off story after story, and name after name of brutal murders and torture, I realised how desensitised I was becoming to events that should have made me cringe or cry. The longer I stayed in South Africa, the more my immunity to violence increased. Every time I saw or heard about more violence I received another shot of immunity. I was becoming inured to the point of the psychopathic. Murder, rape, and torture were fast becoming words in a dictionary; barren of any emotion. There were still goings-on that shook my foundations, like the growing number of muti murders. Hundreds, if not thousands of babies, kidnapped on behalf of sangomas, only to be mutilated and left for dead so that the witchdoctor could make his concoctions. Those stories turned my knees to jelly, and pushed me to work harder at desensitising myself. Then there were the babies and girls being raped by grown men with HIV. All because they believed that a virgin would cure them of Aids. A westernised person could not possibly understand this mentality, rife in the new South Africa, because, frankly, it would be exempt from their experience. I couldn't stomach the stories my father pasted on his wall. The barbarism. The unimaginable and unnecessary violence. Stories that the rest of the world never heard. But, like everyone else, I wanted to believe that the country was travelling on a dark stretch of highway, and that we would eventually see the cliched light at the end of the tunnel.

On the drive home I urged my father to stop immersing himself in grisly stories. He nodded while looking absentmindedly out of the passenger window, mumbling about something that I couldn't quite make out.

CHAPTER 49

Four weeks later, I was sitting in the Sea Breeze library working on an assignment when Alistair called from London. Once the pleasantries were out of the way, he got straight to the point.

'Ros, I've heard some work rumours about your father.'

'What kind of rumours?'

'Spencer & Mason are planning to fire him due to his long leave of absence. I suggest he goes back as soon as possible and convinces them that he's fit to return.'

'That's not going to be possible.'

'Why not?'

'Because he's not fit to return. His state of mind is rapidly deteriorating and he refuses to seek help. I don't know what to do.'

'Shit. I had no idea it was so bad.'

'Any suggestions as to what I can do to help him?'

'Why don't you take him away for a few days. Somewhere peaceful like the Drakensberg.'

'That's not a bad idea.'

'I have my moments.' He laughed.

'How is London?'

'It's a lot safer. I didn't realise how much stress we're living under until I left.'

'You are planning to come back, are you?'

'Why, do you miss me?'

'Of course I miss you, Alistair. Do you really need to ask?'

'I'll be finishing up a couple of weeks ahead of schedule, so I'll be back by the end of next week.'

'I can't wait to see you.'

'Ditto, Ros. In the meantime, try and get your father's mind off the doom and gloom. I know this place in Kamberg called Glengarry. I used to go with my parents when I was younger. It's in a beautiful, quiet spot, and there are walking tracks and a dam for fishing. It's in the phone book. Look it up.'

'That sounds perfect. Thanks, Alistair.'

'If you need anything before I get back, call me, okay?'

'Okay, thank you.'

'See you next week.'

'Bye, Alistair.'

I hung up feeling infinitely better. Alistair always had that effect on me.

I found a travel guide in the Sea Breeze library and looked up Kamberg. It was situated alongside the Mooi River, in the foothills of the Ukhahlamba Drakensberg Park, and boasted the highest concentration of bushman rock art. Several trout dams attracted anglers all year round, and there were a large number of nature trails for amblers and hikers. I looked up the number for Glengarry and booked a chalet for the weekend.

We were greeted by Revell, the Owner, and his two dogs; Reagan, a black Labrador, and Midge, a Corgi. Revell had rugged, tanned skin, and wore khaki shorts with long white socks and camel-coloured Caterpillar boots. The reception was located in the main house — a double-storey with thatched roof, and enclosed with a spectacular English garden.

'Beautiful garden,' I said.

'My wife, Rose, has a green finger. She spends every waking hour in this garden. In twenty years these young beeches, birches, maples and dogwoods will be a sight to behold.'

'It's already a sight to behold,' said my father.

'Follow me,' said Revell. 'As you can see, the chalets are within walking distance to the main house, so if you need anything, don't be shy.'

We followed him and the dogs along the dirt track to the first chalet. Like a miniature version of the main house, it had a thatched roof and cottagey windows. Revell unlocked the door and showed us around the two bedroom, self-contained unit. The main bedroom had a double bed and the second had four bunk beds. The lounge had double french doors that opened out onto a patio that overlooked the Little Mooi River and mountains in the distance. I liked its rustic charm, and hoped that it was exactly what my father needed.

'There's also a golf course, walking tracks, tyre swing (down at the caravan park), and two dams for fishing —Windmill Dam and Plum Dam.' He pointed across the river and said, 'If you follow the trail that leads to Plum Dam, you'll find a grove of plum trees. You're welcome to go plum-picking if you're so inclined.'

'Thanks Revell,' we both said in unison.

My father walked back with Revell and his dogs to get the car. I sat outside on the patio and admired the view. To the right of the chalet, a grassy hill protected the property from strong winds. Straight ahead, I could have been in the Scottish highlands, with rows of trees and the flat-top mountain reflecting in the glassy dam water.

My father returned a few minutes later, and joined me outside.

'Revell said that it storms most afternoons. It usually knocks out the power for an hour or two, but it is spectacular to sit and watch,' he said.

'Sounds amazing,' I said. 'Alistair said that he came here often with his parents.'

'How is Alistair?'

'He's doing well. He said he's finishing earlier than expected in London and will be home next week.'

'Did he mention my absence from work?'

I chewed my lip, as I weighed up the pros and cons of telling him.

'You don't have to protect me, Ros. I know how Spencer & Mason operate. I'm surprised they haven't fired me already.'

'Okay, yes, Alistair did mention that he had heard rumours. He suggested that you go back before they can make their move.'

'I'm not going back, Ros.'

'Do you mean not now, or not ever?'

'Not ever.'

'Dad, I'm worried about you. You need to talk to me.'

'How about we go for a walk, and I'll try and explain it on the way.'

'Okay,' I nodded.

We put on our walking shoes, locked the door, and headed down the hill toward the river.

'I can't keep pretending that it's business as usual, Ros.'

I nodded. 'Can I just say one thing?' I said. 'You're probably suffering from depression. It's not surprising after everything that has happened. You and Mom getting divorced, my attack, your Kenyan memories, Ouma and William. It's a ridiculous amount of trauma for any person to sustain.'

'It's no more trauma than you've sustained. How do you cope?'

I chewed my lip and looked at my feet.

'Tell me, Ros, I need to know.'

'I think it has something to do with apartheid and Léon.'

My father closed his eyes and rubbed his forehead.

'I didn't tell you that during the Christmas of '88, when we visited Brenthurst Gardens, I found Léon raping Promise in a hidden jail cell beneath his house.'

'What?'

I nodded. 'I confronted him and he said he would spare Promise if I took her place.'

'Good God, it just gets worse.'

I sighed. 'I'm not telling you this to make you feel worse, Dad. I'm trying to tell you that I had to keep a lot of secrets in order to survive. In the years following that visit, I thought about suicide all the time. But each day, I would wake up and manage to get through another day.'

'How?'

'I learnt to compartmentalise for the most part, but the thing that really got me through was comparison.'

'Comparison? What do you mean?'

'I kept comparing my situation to people like Promise, and Stompie, Mohini, Gladys and Philemon. No matter what happened to me, they would always be worse off.'

He shook his head and said, 'I imagine that there are moments in a parent's life when they realise that their child is better than they could ever hope to be. This is one of those moments.'

'I am not better than you, Dad. But I do want to help you, and I don't know how. Tell me how to help you, please.'

'Have you heard the Leonardo da Vinci quote about three types of people?'

I shook my head and said, 'Remind me.'

'*There are three classes of people: Those who see, those who see when they are shown, those who do not see.*'

'You're referring to Africa in general,' I said.

'Yes, Ros. The place is doomed. I know that you see the writing on the wall, but, like most of the population, you don't want to face reality.'

'Okay, then let's get serious about the immigration applications and start the ball rolling.'

He kept talking, as if I hadn't said anything. 'Do you know what I saw the other day, Ros?'

'What did you see, Dad?'

We reached the river bank and veered left toward a little wooden bridge.

'I read an article in The Highway Mail that turned my blood cold. I didn't want to believe it, so I drove down there to check it out. A Sangoma has set up a shop in a little shopping arcade and is offering money for body parts.'

'What?' I said, stopping in the middle of the bridge and putting my hand over my mouth in shock.

He nodded and stood alongside me with his hands on the rope rail. 'Three hundred rand for a nose. Fifty rand for a finger.'

I shook my head, not wanting to picture it, but failing miserably.

'There were queues of people, Ros. Poor bloody kaffirs who have no food, no hope of employment, no bloody better off with the ANC in power. Mothers, grandparents, and children.'

I started to cry, then sob, causing the bridge to wobble. 'Dad,' I said, 'you have to stop.'

'Stop what?'

'Stop talking about this stuff, stop immersing yourself in it. When I hear stories like this I literally don't know what to do with myself. I feel sick to my core, I feel angry. It makes me violent. No wonder you're depressed. This stuff is insane.' I pulled a tissue from my pocket and blew my nose.

'Exactly, Ros. This fucking continent is insane. Conrad didn't call it the heart of darkness for nothing.'

'So, what's the answer?' I said, looking down at the water rushing beneath our feet.

'The answer is to leave, Ros. Because it's never going to change.'

I nodded and sighed loudly. 'Let's keep walking. I think I can see the plum trees over there.'

He nodded and followed behind me. We didn't talk until we reached the trees. I tried to put his story out of my mind and focus on the beautiful nature that surrounded us. Yellow, and red, bishop birds flew in and out of bushes and trees, like butterflies, and the distant sound of baaing sheep could be heard over the rushing river. I paused as we reached a mass of bramble. On closer inspection, it was full of plump blackberries. 'Want one?' I said, passing him a blackberry. He nodded and popped it in his mouth.

'Do you think you'll ever love a country as much as you do this one?' I said.

'There are plenty of beautiful countries, Ros.'

'I know there are. But they don't hold your childhood memories, and hopes and dreams. They don't hold your nightmares and fears.'

'A blank canvas. Isn't that a good thing?'

'I'm not saying it's not.'

'You're not ready to leave yet.'

I shook my head. 'I will leave at some stage, Dad, but no, I don't think I'm ready to leave yet.'

He nodded. 'Shall we keep walking?'

'But that doesn't mean you can't leave in the meantime,' I said.

'I won't leave without you, Ros.'

We walked in silence to the grove of plum trees. The only sounds were sweet birdsong and the persistent sighs of the breeze as it skated along the river bank and through the cluster of plum trees. We walked to the dam and sat on the grass to watch the clouds cast shadows over the escarpment. When the breeze paused or died down for longer than a minute, you could see the reflection of the mountain on the water's surface.

'What are you planning to do about work, Dad?'

'I've taken leave, Ros. If they decide to fire me in that period, then so be it.'

'And what if they don't fire you. Will you go back at the end of your leave?'

He shook his head. 'I told you, Ros. I'm done.'

'Dad,' I said, putting my arm through his, 'tell me what I can do to help. Please.'

'I don't need the money, Ros. What does it matter?'

'I'm not concerned about money, Dad. I'm concerned about your state of mind. You seem to be losing interest in everything except these awful stories.'

'When is Alistair back?' he said, changing the subject.

'The end of next week.'

'Good, invite him for dinner. I'd like to see him.'

'Great,' I said, feeling slightly more hopeful than I had seconds before.

'When are you two going to get together?' he said, out of the blue.

'It's complicated,' I said.

'It's complicated, or you're complicating it?'

'Maybe a bit of both.'

'Take my advice. Uncomplicate it. You and Alistair are good together.'

'Like you and Mom were good together?' I said without thinking. 'Sorry, Dad, I didn't mean it like that.'

'It's okay, Ros. Your mom and I were never really a good fit. She fell in love with the person she wanted me to be, and I fell in love with the woman I thought she would become. Neither of us were to blame. It's what happens when you're young and infatuated.'

'Alistair and I are definitely past infatuation stage.'

'I know, and that's a good thing. Your feelings for each other run deeper than infatuation, and that is the basis of lasting love.'

I sighed and put my head on his shoulder. 'Shall we start walking back? It's getting a little chilly.'

We stood up and dusted the grass off of ourselves.

'Ros?'

'Yes, dad.'

'Thanks for bringing me here this weekend. I needed a change of scenery, and it's good to spend some quality time with you.'

347

'You're welcome, Dad,' I said, giving him a hug.

On the walk back we stopped at the blackberry brambles and he told me about the etymology of Mooirivier; meaning 'pretty river' in Afrikaans; Mpofana, meaning little eland, in Zulu; and Mpafana, meaning 'wild mulberry tree'.

'How do you know all this stuff?' I said.

'When I was at school, surrounded by Dutchmen who hated me, I knew that the only way to get ahead would be to know more than anyone else did. That's why I spent so much time reading books and studying.'

'Can you tell me more on the walk back?'

'Of course.'

We were hungry when we got back from our walk, so I made some cheese and tomato sandwiches and put the kettle on for tea. We sat outside on the patio and watched the weather shift into a storm. Revell drove past in his bakkie and stopped to give us a pile of logs for a wood fire.

'The temperature drops at night,' he said, 'a fire will warm the place up.'

'Thanks, Revell.'

'Are you guys sorted for dinner?' he said. 'I can recommend a few places to eat out.'

I wrote down the names on the off chance that we went out, and thanked him.

'Shout if you need anything else. Otherwise, I'll see you in the morning with fresh milk.'

'Thanks, Revell. See you tomorrow.'

'I'm going to jump in the shower before the storm knocks out the electricity,' I said to my father.

'Okay, I'll start the fire,' he said.

By the time I dressed, and sat down in the lounge, the crackling fire had warmed the room up. My father was writing in a journal.

'What are you writing?'

'I've been writing my memories down since Ouma died.'

'For a book?'

'For you, Ros. One day when I'm gone, I don't want the stories and secrets of my life to die with me like they died with Ouma.'

'Ouma told me a few stories.'

'She did?'

'Ja, when I stayed in Coetzeesdorp. I had a bit of a meltdown after you left, and I promised to tell her my secrets if she told me a few of hers.'

I told him what Ouma had told me. He nodded and made notes as I talked, and interjected from time to time to add details from his own memories.

'What's keeping you here, Ros?' he said unexpectedly.

'Are you referring to our talk earlier today?' I said.

He nodded. 'Is it Alistair, your studies, something else?'

'It's difficult to explain,' I said.

'Try,' he said. 'I need to understand.'

I sighed and stood up to stoke the fire. When I sat back down, I said, 'It's difficult for me to picture a future for myself.'

He frowned. 'Do you mean here or somewhere else?'

I didn't want to tell him, because I feared it would be the proverbial nail in the coffin. But he wasn't going to let it go, and I owed him the truth. I swallowed. 'There's something I haven't told you, Dad.'

'What is it, Ros?'

'The test results after my attack.'

'Oh my God, you're not...'

'No,' I cut him off, 'the results were all negative. But the doctor found something else. Before I tell you, promise not to go off the deep end,' I said.

'Tell me.'

I wrung my hands together and squirmed in my seat. 'The doctor said it's unlikely that I'll ever be able to conceive.'

For a minute, the only sounds were thunder and the crackling fire. I watched his face change — like a chalkboard that had been wiped clean — and immediately regretted telling him. He was physically in the room, yet he seemed ghost-like — frail enough to disappear like a wisp of smoke, and tormented enough to haunt the space.

'Dad, say something.'

'I'm going to lie down, Ros. I'll talk to you in the morning.'

I stood up. 'Dad, I'm sorry that I didn't tell you. I hoped that it would reverse itself one day, or turn out to be a mistake.'

He went into the room and closed the door behind him. I sat on the sofa and stared into the fire, wishing that I could take my words back and burn them to a crisp.

I slept on the bottom bunk, fitfully. Each time I started to drift off, thunder struck and lightning flashes lit the room. When the sandman eventually claimed me, I had a nightmare about my father. He paddled a blue canoe into the middle of Plum Dam during an electric storm. I stood on the bank and begged him to come back in before he got struck. But he just shook his head and said that if I didn't have a future, then neither did he. I dived into the water and swam with my eyes closed until it felt like I'd swum a mile, but when I looked up and around, the canoe and my father had disappeared.

When I woke up, I rushed out and knocked on my father's door. He didn't reply. I opened the door. The bed hadn't been slept in, and he wasn't there. I pulled my walking shoes on and grabbed a jacket, then ran outside to look for him. The car was missing. I bent over and breathed like an asthmatic.

'Everything okay, Ros?'

I looked up to see Revell holding a bottle of fresh milk.

'My dad,' I said. 'I can't find him.'

'Oh, he went out to get you some breakfast. He wanted to surprise you.'

'Oh,' I said. 'Crisis averted, then.'

He laughed and handed me the milk. 'I'll catch you later, Ros.'

'Thanks, Revell,' I said, taking the milk and smiling weakly.

I went inside and had a hot shower. He wasn't back by the time I finished, so I made a cup of coffee and drank it outside on the patio. He arrived twenty minutes later with takeaway cartons.

'Dad, I was worried when I couldn't find you this morning.'

'Sorry,' he said, kissing me on the cheek, 'I figured you'd be hungry as we didn't have dinner last night.'

I set the table while he unpacked the scrambled eggs, hash browns, bacon for himself, grilled tomatoes, mushrooms, and toast.

'Dad, about last night.'

'I'm sorry, Ros.'

'You don't need to apologise, Dad. I shouldn't have kept it from you.'

He shook his head. 'I'm not talking about that.'

I looked at him and waited for him to continue.

'I'm sorry that I didn't leave sooner. I'm sorry that I have subjected you to this place. I've been selfish.'

'Dad, please don't say that. I'm fine, honestly.'

'One day you will realise that you don't belong here, Ros. None of us do. Because the sad reality is that we are not Africans. Even though we, and generations before us, were born and raised here, we are not Africans.'

'You make it all seem so hopeless.'

'It is hopeless, Ros. As long as our skin is white, we will always be seen as the enemy. And as long as the ANC has a stronghold, they will perpetually be seeking revenge.'

I nodded, sat down, and dished up some food. I didn't have the inclination to agree or disagree. His pessimism had morphed from barbel to whale, and I could feel its force sucking me in like plankton.

'Dad, can we try to remember why we came here this weekend and forget about politics and crime while we're here?'

'Sure, Ros.'

I smiled and sighed. 'Thank you. I'm enjoying spending quality time with you.'

He waved his right hand as if to say, 'say no more.'

CHAPTER 50

Days later, I woke up in the middle of the night. I heard a loud bang and reached under my pillow to grab my gun. It wasn't there. Instead, I found an envelope. I turned the bedside lamp on and saw my name written in my father's handwriting. I knew before I knew. I dropped the envelope and ran straight to the study. My father sat in Jericho's chair, his head hanging backwards, my gun still in his hand. Blood spattered on the wall behind him. I screamed his name in vain and ran to check his pulse. But he was gone. I dropped to the floor. Put my head in between my knees and screamed until I got dizzy from a lack of breath.

I'm not sure how long I stayed in that position, blaming myself, crying and begging my father to come back. Praying for God to return him. When I eventually resurfaced to reality, I phoned Mark. He answered with an attitude; as if I'd interrupted a business meeting. I cut him off before he could reprimand me.

'I'm in my father's study. He's committed suicide with my gun. I..'

He stopped me mid-sentence.

'I'll be right there, Wrighty. Don't touch anything.'

He hung up. I stood there with the receiver in my hand — looking at it — unsure of what to do and how to do it. I felt like there were roots growing out of my feet and into the ground. Roots that immobilised me. Roots that would need to be dug out and lifted by force. I felt myself disappearing into the branches of my mind. Branches, heavy with leaves of truth that I had tried to repress. Paris, Maleven, Mark, Léon; numerous leaves waited patiently for me to pick them off the tree and turn them over in my palm to study them. Acknowledge them. Confront them. Stop running. Stop pretending that I was fine, that I was strong enough to absorb the hate and dissolve the pain. And now my father. My father had gone and done something so drastic, so final, so absolute, so undoable. Immune to time. Time was usually the answer to everything. Time would not fix this. Time would not heal. Time was a powerless ally this time around.

Mark's image on the monitor from the gate and his persistent buzzing snapped me out of my daze. I was still clutching the phone receiver. I buzzed him in and met him at the entrance. He held me, and my roots melted like ice in sunshine. I collapsed into his arms and told him that I wanted to close my eyes and never open them again.

'You're in shock, Wrighty. You need to sit down.'

He led me into the lounge, sat me down on the sofa, and poured me a glass of Macallan from the silver tray on the sideboard. Then he sat next to me and phoned the police.

'You'll need to give a statement when they get here,' he said. 'They'll probably ask to see your gun licence. Did your dad leave a note?'

I nodded. 'I dropped it in my room.'

'I'll go and get it. Where is your licence? I'll get that too.'

'It's in my bag, in my room.'

'Okay, sit tight, I'll be back in a sec.'

I put the drink down and shut my eyes tightly. I couldn't get the image of my dead father out of my head. I thought of all the calls I'd have to make, and felt weary. My mother would find a way to blame me. Spencer & Mason probably wouldn't give a shit. Alistair would get on the first plane to be by my side.

Mark returned and sat next to me. 'I found the letter.'

The buzzer sounded.

'I'll get it,' said Mark. 'You stay here. I'll handle everything, okay?'

I nodded.

He left the room. I leaned toward the coffee table to take a sip of Macallan, and then sat back with the envelope in my lap and stared at it. I heard footsteps on the wooden floors and voices moving toward me.

'Evening, Miss Wright, I'm Captain Botha, and this is Lieutenant Strydom. We'll need to take a statement and then cordon off the room where you found your father.'

I dropped my head and started to cry.

'Do you have somewhere to stay for a few days?'

'I'm not leaving,' I said. 'Do whatever you need to do tonight and tomorrow, but I'm not leaving Sea Breeze.'

'I'll stay with her until you clear the scene,' said Mark.

'Is that a letter from the deceased?' said Botha.

'Yes, it was under my pillow.'

'I know this is difficult, Miss Wright, but we will need to take a look at that.'

I clutched the letter and looked at Mark. 'I haven't read it yet,' I whispered.

Mark addressed the two men. 'Can we have a word outside?'

They nodded and followed him out into the hall. I tuned out, hoping they would both vanish into thin air. Mark returned a few minutes later — on his own.

'They'll be here for a few more hours taking photos etcetera. I told them you'd give them a copy of the letter if there was any doubt about it being a suicide. But it won't come to that. It's an open-closed case.'

'Thank you,' I said, reaching for his hand.

'Do you want me to call anyone?'

I shook my head. 'I need to do it.'

He nodded. 'I think it's best if I stay with you for a few days.'

'I won't argue with that.'

'Okay.' He kissed me on the forehead. 'I'm going to keep an eye on everything. Call me if you need anything.'

I nodded and looked at the envelope.

To my darling daughter, Rosalinde:

From the day you were conceived, I struggled to do right by you. Raising a child is an enormous responsibility in any country, but raising a child in Africa is fraught with peril. Africa, that eternal battlefield of good versus evil. My cradle and my grave.

You always knew right from wrong, even when your parents and Jericho tried to teach you the opposite. You knew. Even after your attack, you still wanted to believe, still wanted to forgive and forget.

My child, I hoped and prayed that South Africa would not follow in the footsteps of Kenya, but when it did, so did the shadow of my childhood nightmares, followed by the inevitable unravelling of my fabricated self. I can tell you this, because I know you will understand, it took the violent attack of my own daughter to finally sit up and see your strength. And for that, I am truly sorry. For that I can never ask forgiveness. A father's only job is to protect his child, and I failed. I failed. I failed.

You know, Ros, when I left Kenya with my nose pressed up against the window, I couldn't understand why my father chose to stay and face certain death. Years later, I still didn't understand. It was only after your revelation at Glengarry that the answer arrived. When you told me that you cannot conceive, I knew what I had to do. I knew that I could not stand by idly while Africa stole everything from you.

Like my father, who failed at fatherhood, I am following in his footsteps and sacrificing myself for your future. I know you. You will want to stay and fight. You will hold onto hope as long as you can. But, there is no hope here, Ros. I want you to promise me something. Call it my dying wish. Once I'm cremated, I request that you keep my remains until you leave South Africa for good. Only then, when you have officially left, and have settled in a new country, only then do I want you to scatter my ashes.

And one final thing, Ros. Alistair loves you. Very much. I know it. I can see it. Don't play this waiting game too long — the only thing keeping you two apart is your infatuation with Mark. I know that he saved your life, and you formed a strong bond with him, but he is like a drug to you. When he lets you in, you're high, and when he pushes you away, you're down. I know you know this. I'm simply *reminding you to stop ignoring it and move on with your life. You have to think about your future now, and there is no future with Mark.*

Take care, my darling. I'm sorry.

Your loving father, Wilstan.

I couldn't see through my tears. Couldn't calm the hammer of my heart against my chest. Couldn't admit that I had not seen some version of this coming. But, suicide. I had honestly never anticipated suicide. I took it hard. I blamed myself. I should have seen it coming. I should have done more. I should have helped him, reached out to him. I shouldn't have waited like a child to be told. My father was gone and I had done nothing to stop him.

CHAPTER 51

My mother returned to Sea Breeze the day before my father's funeral. As expected, she immersed herself in the drama of it all — as if she was the lead actress in a Shakespearean tragedy. The first words out of her mouth, as she stepped into the entrance hall, were not, *I'm sorry, Ros*. No. Instead she blamed me.

'It's all your fault,' she said. 'You manipulated him into getting you a gun. The same gun that I was against. The same gun that I predicted would end in tragedy. And now it has. Except it's a bigger tragedy than anyone imagined. Your father, my husband, is dead, and it could have been prevented.'

'You mean your ex-husband,' I said. 'The same ex-husband that you abandoned and never thought to contact. Is that the husband we're talking about?'

'You have no right to speak to me like that, Ros.'

'Oh, I think I do,' I said, nodding my head angrily. 'If you gave two shits about Dad, you would have known that he has been suffering from depression since my attack.'

'There's the crux of it,' she said. 'Your attack. You. You. You.

All the misery comes back to you.'

'My God,' I said, taking two steps back, 'why do you hate me so much?'

'I lost my mother, Ros, and not a day goes by that I don't miss and need her. I thought that you would fill the void that she left, but you never did. I thought you would need me, like I needed my mother, but you never did. You've never needed anything from me. All you've ever done is argue with me and remind me how I don't measure up to your impossible standards.'

She swirled around like a cyclone and sunk into an armchair, as if her vortex of power had suddenly dissipated.

'I'm sorry,' I said.

She eyed me as if I'd blasphemed.

'Is it okay if I sit next to you?' I said.

She frowned and said, 'Suit yourself.'

'Have you read the book L'Etranger, by Albert Camus?' I said.

'Nga, you see, this is what I'm talking about. You know I haven't, Ros. I don't read all that intellectual stuff that you and your father love so much.'

'Listen, Mom, I'm not trying to belittle you, I'm trying to give you an analogy for our relationship.'

She rolled her eyes and shook her head.

'L'Etranger,' I said, was translated into English as *The Outsider*. It's about a man called Mersault, who learns that his mother has died.'

She looked at me out of the corner of her eye and pursed her lips.

'At his mother's funeral, he acts indifferently — smoking and drinking in front of her coffin, and not knowing (or seeming to care) when she died or why. Later in the book, he murders a man and stands trial. In the end, he is convicted —not so much for what he's done, but rather for his indifference about his mother's death.'

'And what is that supposed to mean, Ros?'

'I have identified with Mersault most of my life. If you died, and I was asked to give a speech at your funeral, like I am for Dad, I would be hard pressed to say anything, because, the truth is, you've always been a stranger to me.'

'Why must you always be so cryptic, Ros? What is your point?'

'My point is that I would like to mend fences and change that. My point is that we cannot build on the past, because it's broken and we are both like Mersault in our indifference. Maybe you're right when you say that we have never needed each other, and never will, but we have to decide right now if we want to start over again, or if we just go our separate ways and never look back.'

'There's something I need to tell you,' she said.

I looked at her expectantly.

'Maeve and I are emigrating to Australia next month.'

'When were you planning to tell me?'

'Honestly, Ros, I wasn't.'

'I see,' I said, standing up and pressing the creases out of my skirt.

She stood up too and said, 'Ros?'

'Yes, Mother?'

'I'm sorry that I can't give you what you want.'

'All Dad wanted was to leave,' I said. 'If you had told him you might have given him some hope.'

She shrugged and left the room.

The funeral only made me feel worse. Not because I had to say goodbye, but because hardly anyone else felt the need to. Apart from Alistair, Mohini, and Mark, none of my father's work colleagues or friends paid their respects. From the whispers I'd heard, everyone thought him a coward for taking his own life. I disagreed; my father wasn't a coward. He had committed a selfless act for his child.

My mother didn't greet Mohini. So great was her pride, or lacking were her manners — I wasn't sure which. I stood at Mohini's side the entire time, while my mother stood with Maeve — my father's ghost between us.

After the service, Mohini and I caught up over a cup of tea. She had met a widowed man named Vijay, who had five children of his own, along with several grandchildren. They had met while bringing their respective pets to the vet; Vijay's family tabby cat had been bitten by a stray dog, and Gunther had lost half his body weight in a few weeks. While they waited to be seen by the vet, they had fallen into easy conversation and realised they had much in common. Mohini saw the vet first, and received devastating news. Gunther's body was riddled with cancer, and he was euthanised the same day. Fortunately, Vijay had supported and comforted her.

She and Vijay had set everyone's tongues wagging when they had moved in together, unmarried, months after their first meeting. She smiled broadly whenever she mentioned his name, and her happiness made me happy. If anyone in the world deserved to be blessed and content, it was Mo. She said that Vijay's children had welcomed her with open arms as a surrogate mother and grandmother. Not having children had always been her greatest regret. But raising me had made up for it.

Then she turned serious and asked about my father. I told her about his slow unravelling after my ouma's murder, but omitted the part about my attack. I didn't want to turn my father's funeral into a pity party about myself. She offered to stay the night, but I told her to go home to Vijay.

Alistair offered to stay the night. I told him I wanted to be alone. He looked hurt and offended. I didn't care. I wanted to lock myself in a castle and raise the moat. Alistair told me that I shouldn't make any decisions while emotional. I nodded and gave him my cheek when he tried to kiss me goodbye. It wasn't his fault. He wasn't the enemy — I knew that logically, but my heart was going in another direction. I only wanted Mark. Not because I needed him to comfort me, but because I wanted to share space with someone who had as many broken pieces as me.

I called his cell and told him I needed him. When he arrived, I asked him to take me upstairs. He said he would, eventually. He shifted in his seat at the kitchen table and pulled a small plastic bag of white pills from his pocket.

'Take one,' he said, placing it in my palm.

I turned it over to inspect it — an image of a dove was embedded in the centre. 'Is this what I think it is?'

He pushed a glass of water toward me. 'Do you trust me?'

'You know I do.'

'Good,' he said. 'I'll take one too.' He popped two pills in his mouth and sipped from my glass of water. 'Your turn,' he said.

I followed his lead. 'How long does it take to work?' I said.

'Half an hour, give or take,' he said.

I nodded and sighed. 'How did you deal with your father's suicide?'

'Badly.'

'Tell me.'

'Drink, drugs, women.'

'Did you blame yourself?'

'When it comes to suicide, it's impossible not to, Wrighty.'

I nodded. 'That's true.'

'It's not your fault, Wrighty.'

'I think it was. When I took him to Glengarry recently, I told him that I couldn't conceive.' I shook my head and shivered at the memory. 'His expression gave me chills, and I knew that I should never have told him.'

'Wrighty, when someone commits suicide, you can find a hundred different reasons to blame yourself — things you said, things you didn't say. But at the end of the day, your dad made his own choice.'

I took his hand and kissed the back of his palm. 'Thank you for being here.'

He leaned in and kissed my neck. 'What do you see in me, Wrighty?'

'I see you,' I said, touching his chest with my hand. 'I see the person that you try so hard to camouflage behind your badass veneer.'

'It's not all veneer.'

'I'm well aware of that. But I see that more as a product of your life to date. It's something that's been manufactured.'

He took my face in his hands and kissed me. 'Your brain

drives me crazy.'

'Ha,' I said, 'that makes two of us.'

I felt a wave of heat surge my body, followed by the red hot glow of passion. 'I feel hot,' I said, 'is it the dove?'

He nodded.

I took his hand and led him upstairs to the bedroom. Within seconds we were naked, on the bed, kissing. The little white dove lived up to its name. Like a bird released, my prison of thoughts broke free, and a sense of euphoria took their place. Uninhibited. Unadulterated joy. Mark and I. The way it could have been in a parallel life.

When I walked out of the ensuite I thought I was hallucinating. Mark and Alistair were wrestling and punching each other like a couple of teenagers. I pulled on a pair of shorts and tee shirt, and tried to break them up, but got knocked over in the scuffle. In desperation, I threw a glass of water at them. It snapped them out of the moment long enough for me to get in between them.

'Alistair, what are you doing here?'

'I was concerned about you, Ros. I didn't want you to be alone. When you didn't answer the door, I came in to check on you and found fucking Mark in your bed.'

'I can't do this right now,' I said.

'Why not?' said Alistair.

'Because I'm high.'

Alistair narrowed his eyes at me and then swung another punch at Mark. 'It's not enough for her to get attacked on your watch, now you must ply her with drugs too,' said Alistair mid-punch.

In desperation, I threw another glass of water at them.

'Stop!' I shouted. 'Please, stop.'

'We're going to talk about this whether you like it or not, Ros,' said Alistair.

'Fine,' I said, 'but not here, and not now.'

Alistair nodded and put his hands in his pockets.

'Tomorrow,' said Mark. 'I'll call you in the morning to arrange.'

'No way,' I said. 'I know how difficult it is to get hold of you.' I thought about it for a minute and said, 'lunch at Picken Chicken.'

'Picken Chicken,' said Mark, laughing. 'Talk about a blast from the past.'

'Ha ha,' I said.

Mark started walking toward the door.

'Where are you going?' I said.

'Home,' he said. 'I thought you were giving me my marching orders.'

'Ha ha, again,' I said. 'You're both sleeping here tonight. There's enough spare rooms to host an army.'

'No,' said Alistair. 'I'm fine to drive.'

'No you're not,' I said. 'I insist. You're staying here tonight, and tomorrow we are going to talk about this over lunch.'

'At Picken Chicken,' Mark said, laughing.

'Oh, ha ha, Mark. Really,' I said, it's not that fucking funny.'

Alistair threw up his hands.

I led them both to spare rooms and then returned to my own, but I was so wired and so hot that I couldn't dream of sleeping. I put my cozzie on and swam lap after lap after lap, until the first crack of sunlight appeared.

CHAPTER 52

Picken Chicken was a beachfront diner, located at Addington Beach, that served hamburgers and diner-style food. I chose it because it reminded me of my father; he loved swimming in the ocean, but Umhlanga was better suited to surfers than swimmers, so he would swim at Addington Beach on weekends he didn't work. When I accompanied him, we would have a burger at Picken Chicken after our swim. Besides my father, there was something constant about Picken Chicken that had not changed in years; with the sea metres away, the windows were permanently covered in a film of sea salt, and they still served their burgers and fries in a red plastic basket, with the chips in the bottom and the burger sitting on top. Back in its day, Picken Chicken had been a popular lunch destination, but by the mid 90s, Addington had grown increasingly dangerous and it sat empty most week days, which made it the perfect setting for our discussion.

Mark and Alistair ordered hamburgers and cokes. I ordered a toasted cheese and tomato sandwich. I told Mark to un-chamber the round in his gun and flick the safety on. I had grown accustomed to his idiosyncrasies; one of which was to always have a bullet chambered and the safety off.

'That won't be necessary,' he said.

The Indian waiter delivered the baskets of food and asked if we needed anything else. We said no and waited until he had disappeared through the kitchen swing door.

'Is someone gonna speak?' I said.

'He has some explaining to do,' said Alistair, his eyes trained on Mark like a sharp shooter.

'I thought that Wrighty was in the clear when she got to her car, so I walked back to my car, which was parked around the corner. That's when Alistair phoned for an update.'

'And?' said Alistair.

'And when I drove past and saw Wrighty's car, I knew something was wrong. I parked next to her car and heard her screams when I opened the door. I found her in the alley with Maleven on top of her.'

'Wait,' said Alistair, 'I'm confused. Maleven, as in Paris's cousin?'

I nodded.

'Didn't Maleven try to help you, Ros?'

The silence stretched like an elastic band.

'Ros? Tell me what really happened.'

I looked at Mark for guidance, or permission. Mark and I had led everyone to believe that I had been raped by random strangers, and that Maleven and Paris had died trying to help me. Was it really in our best interest to tell Alistair, the lawyer, that Mark had killed all six of my attackers and that I had helped him cover it up?

'Ros?' Alistair repeated.

'It wasn't a random attack,' I said. 'When I left the club,

368

Maleven and his friends followed me. They gang-raped me and murdered Paris when he tried to help.' I swallowed and felt my insides cringe at the memory. 'Mark shot and killed Maleven and his five friends.'

Alistair turned to Mark and said, 'You executed them and involved Ros in a police cover up?'

'For fuck's sake, Alistair, take off your fucking lawyer hat for a second and consider the bigger picture.'

'What's the bigger picture, Mark?'

'Those kaffirs were going to murder her,' he said pointing at me. 'All six of them.' He held up his hand to reiterate the number six. 'But not before they all took turns raping her with a fucking sawn-off shotgun in her mouth.'

Alistair looked like someone had lit a fuse inside of him and it was slowly burning its way toward an explosion.

'I don't fucking get you, Alistair. What happened to the guy I knew? The one before the lawyer? Don't act all fucking shocked and surprised. You've also killed people in the line of duty.'

I shifted in my seat and eyed them both with caution.

When Alistair eventually stopped glaring at Mark, he turned to look at me. 'You're studying to be a lawyer, Ros. How can you be okay with this?'

'Excuse me?' I said. 'Okay with what exactly?'

'Okay with Mark murdering six people on your behalf, tampering with evidence, and getting a corrupt policeman to help cover it up?'

'You're kidding, right?'

Alistair's serious face told me otherwise.

'You're un-fucking-believable,' said Mark.

'No, you're fucking unbelievable,' said Alistair standing up and sticking his finger in Mark's face. 'You may have saved her life in the short-term, but you have jeopardised it in the long-term. You fucked up, my friend, and I'm not going to let you get away with it.'

He started to walk away.

'It's as much your fault as it is mine,' said Mark.

When Alistair didn't turn around, Mark hit below the belt.

'You let Ros down twice, Alistair. First with Léon, and then with Maleven.'

He hit his mark. Alistair swivelled round in rage and charged at Mark. By the time Alistair reached the table, Mark had already pulled his gun. Alistair stepped up to Mark and positioned the barrel against his own chest. The waiter waltzed out of the kitchen swing door at the same time.

'Get out of here,' he shouted, 'or I'll call the police.'

Mark's and Alistair's eyes were trained on each other. I apologised profusely to the waiter and assured him that we would leave immediately. Then I persuaded Mark and Alistair to take their face-off outside. I followed them up the stairs and out into the parking lot, where I told Mark to leave so I could talk to Alistair alone. I didn't consider Mark a problem. Alistair's legal ethics were another story. Mark agreed and told me to call him later. Alistair was less gracious, and I had to block him each time he attempted to lash out at Mark.

When Mark left, Alistair refused to look me in the eye. I wasn't sure what to say or how to make it right. I started beating myself up in my head as to why I had ever believed that Alistair would have understood. He eventually agreed to talk to me in his car. I tried the sympathy route first. Reminded him what Maleven had done to me. What the others had done and were going to do. But his eyes had that lawyer glaze; beyond emotion and deep in the well of legal ethics.

'Why don't you stop hiding behind the law, Alistair, and admit why you're really angry?' I said.

'What?' He said, as if in a daze.

'You heard me. Admit that the law has fuck all to do with it.'

He narrowed his eyes at me, but said nothing.

'You're jealous. Mark was there for me. You weren't. And now you're taking it out on him and me.'

'You don't know what you're talking about, Ros.'

'I think I do.'

'Think what you want,' he said. 'I can't condone murder. End of story.'

He made a move to get out of the car, but I grabbed his arm and pulled him back toward me.

'Please, Alistair. Stop for a minute and think about this. Think about me. Whatever you do to Mark, you do to me too.'

'I need time to think about this.'

I softened toward him and said, 'Alistair, please try to understand this from my perspective. Mark saved my life, and my sanity.'

Alistair cocked his head. 'Sanity?'

'Yes,' I said, seeing a window of opportunity to convince him. 'If Mark had let Maleven go I would never have been able to move on. I couldn't change what happened, but at least I didn't have to worry about him seeking revenge. It gave me peace of mind that I otherwise wouldn't have had.'

'Listen to me, Ros. I don't condone what happened to you. It was horrific. Now that I know the full story I don't know how you've survived. I'm not angry that they're dead. I'm angry that Mark took the law into his own hands. Like he always does. No matter the collateral damage. No matter the ramifications.'

I sighed, sensing something else. 'He did something when you two were in the army together?'

'Not something, Ros. Many things. There are soldiers and then there are mercenaries.'

'Like it or not, that mercenary saved my life, Alistair.'

'I know you feel indebted to him, Ros, but please don't think that he did this out of the kindness of his heart.'

I frowned in confusion.

'Mark always has an ulterior motive.'

'Perhaps this is the exception to the rule.'

Alistair's eyes swelled with tears. 'It all makes sense now.'

'What makes sense?'

'Why you and I have continuously passed like ships in the night, but never come together. I thought that I was losing you to lust or something else. I had no idea about the bond that you two must actually share given what you went through together.'

I understood what he was saying and reached out for his hand. 'Alistair, I do love…'

He placed a finger over my lips before I could finish. 'Don't, Ros.'

'Don't what?' I said. 'Don't say that you were my first love. Don't say that I've loved you a long time and always will. Yes, the bond with Mark is strong, but that is not enough to form a proper relationship.'

He looked at me for a long time. A look I couldn't quite read.

'You turned to him last night, not me,' he said.

'Mark's father committed suicide,' I said, 'and he was there for me the night my father died.'

'You don't need to explain yourself, Ros. All I know is this: if I lit a match between you two, there would be an explosion.

You share a chemistry with him that you have never shared with me, and I cannot share you with him. I just can't.'

He leaned across me and opened the door for me to get out.

'Alistair,' I said in a last ditch attempt.

'Don't worry about the secret, Ros. It's safe with me. I give you my word. But you and I are over.'

'Alistair.'

'Please, Ros, just go.'

I got out of the car and had barely closed the door when he drove away.

I dialled Mark's number.

'Speak to me,' he said.

'The secret is safe, but Alistair wants nothing to do with me.'

'Alistair is angry because he loves you, Wrighty. He'll come around.'

'He won't come around. Not as long as you and I are together.'

'But we're not together, Wrighty.'

'How can you turn it on and off like that?'

'I'm not turning it on and off, Wrighty. I'm a realist. And the reality is that your future is in upholding the law, and mine is in breaking it.'

'You're really going to continue with this drug thing?'

'Ja.'

'Well then I hope you stick to your original plan and get out before it's too late.'

'I can't make any promises, Wrighty.'

'So that's it?'

'Wrighty, I will always have a soft spot for you, and I am always here for you, but it's time to think about your future and move on without me.'

'What if I can't?'

'I'm not giving you a choice.'

I hung up before he heard me choke on my tears.

I withdrew into a type of she-cave in the days that followed. I spent countless hours pondering my feelings, my actions, my past and my future. My feelings for Mark, and thoughts about his involvement in the drug business, oscillated. In weak moments, I didn't care, and in stronger moments, I couldn't accept it. Mark was going to keep pushing me away, which made me question my willingness to overlook his faults. If he was not willing to do the same for me, then why was I wasting my time? The question of love versus lust continued to rotate like a revolving door in my head, along with Alistair's theory. Had violence been the catalyst for love? It certainly went a long way to explain my obsession.

When I finally emerged, I was resolute in my decision to leave Alistair and Mark to their own devices and focus on my own future. I had a law degree to complete and a decision to make about leaving South Africa for good.

CHAPTER 53

After my final phone call to Mark, I bit the bullet and distanced myself. I would have respected Alistair's request to leave him alone, had I not fired Spencer & Mason, given how they'd treated my father after his suicide, and moved the business to Schmidt & Blackstock. But my decision had consequences. Alistair was fired for losing Spencer's & Mason's biggest account, and rumours of a hostile takeover at Morris Construction quickly surfaced. When I called an emergency meeting with the board they admitted that a representative of the original co-founder, Henry Malvern of Malvern Bros., had approached them with offers to vote in favour of a takeover. Call it karma, call it kismet, but I saw it as an opportunity to extract myself from a business that I would never have chosen for myself.

Before I made my move, I phoned Alistair.

'Ros,' he said.

'Hi Alistair, long time no speak, how the hell are you?'

'Not bad,' he said, 'considering you cost me my position at Spencer & Mason.'

'So it's true then. You actually hold me responsible for that?'

'Why did you screw me, Ros? I promised to keep your secret. Why did you sell me out?'

'I didn't sell you out, Alistair. I fired Spencer & Mason after the way they treated my father. It had nothing to do with you.'

'You didn't so much as consult me first, Ros. You could have given me that at least.'

'Excuse me, Alistair, but aren't you the one who said that you never wanted to see or hear from me again?'

'I meant personally, Ros. I didn't know you were going to destroy my fucking career.'

'Look, I have no interest in arguing, but I do have an idea that might help us both.'

'As long as it doesn't involve Mark fucking Muller, I'm all ears.'

'It doesn't involve Mark. I haven't seen Mark since our meltdown at Picken Chicken.'

'You expect me to believe that?' he said.

'Alistair, I don't expect anything from you. After all you've done for me over the years, I want to do something for you. Do you want to hear my idea or not?'

'You've got my attention,' he said.

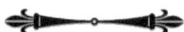

I met with Henry Malvern in his Sandton office at nine am on a Monday morning. He shook my hand and bowed his head like a Japanese gentleman. 'Miss Wright,' he said, 'please have a seat.'

'Thank you,' I said. 'Please call me Rosalinde.'

He sat behind his glass desk, pressed the intercom on his phone and asked his secretary, Linda, to bring a tray of coffee. I noticed an old picture of Jericho and Henry on the wall.

'Did you hang that up for my benefit?' I said.

He smiled wryly and shook his head. 'No, Rosalinde. I was always fond of Jericho, but he was a difficult man. After his wife died he grew as adversarial as a lawyer and treated his friends and family like strangers. We had a fall out and went our separate ways.'

'You never came to his funeral,' I said.

'No, I didn't. Perhaps I should have. It felt hypocritical given our last conversation.'

'It ended badly?' I said.

'You could say that,' he said.

'Jericho and I never saw eye to eye until the months before he died. Now that he's gone I see how misunderstood he was and how he did everything to provide for his family. Especially me.'

Linda placed the tray with coffee and Romany Creams on the desk and closed the door behind her.

'I'm going to get to the point,' I said. 'There's no need for a hostile takeover, because I'm not interested in retaining controlling interest. But I need to do right by Jericho. I'm here to negotiate a deal that we can both live with.'

'You remind me of him,' he said. 'Direct and formidable, but fair.'

The phone on Henry's desk buzzed. 'I told you to hold my calls, Linda.'

'It's not a call, Mr Malvern, it's another party asking to join Miss Wright.'

Henry looked at me for an explanation.

'Direct, formidable, fair, and loyal,' I said, 'which is why I need to include Alistair Steadman in any deal I make today.'

'Send Mr Steadman in, Linda.'

He picked up the silver pot and poured coffee for three.
'Let's get down to business,' he said.

PART VI

1998
3 YEARS LATER

CHAPTER 54

Henry Malvern, Alistair, and I negotiated a deal that we could all live with. I agreed to sell my controlling interest in Morris Construction, on the condition that Jericho's name was retained. Malvern agreed, and the rebranded company became Morris Malvern Group. But the added bonus, and cherry of our negotiation, was securing Morris Malvern Group as the first and biggest client for our new law firm — Steadman & Wright. My gesture went a long way in atoning with Alistair, but we agreed to keep our relationship professional.

In the three years that followed, I gave Alistair carte blanche to run the law firm while I continued studying my Law Degree. I also kept my promise and stayed away from Mark — not that he seemed to notice. In what seemed like a parallel world, he single-handedly built a drug empire with roots in Durban and tentacles beyond. I knew that much due to the frequent newspaper articles about his criminal misdeeds. In the three years that I was studying, he conquered the drug territory in Joburg, thanks to his connections with the Hell's Angels gang, and then every city and province with the exception of Cape

Town. Drugs in the Cape Province had long been run by Jamaicans, and they were not so easily bought or intimidated. Stories about the Jamaican drug lords were no less brutal than those involving the Colombian and Mexican drug cartels. The papers called Mark *White Mamba*, due to his ability to thrive in a post-apartheid world and dodge numerous assassination attempts. How long his reign of terror would last, remained to be seen, because the Police Force, facing constant scrutiny about racism in its ranks, initiated a standalone investigative unit known as *Black Mamba*. From what I could glean from newspaper articles, the unit was headed by a young and ambitious agent named Inspector Patel. He was of Indian descent and had ample experience with various Law Enforcement Agencies including the London Metropolitan Police and Interpol. When asked for a comment on his new position and his approach to the White Mamba, he said:

The best way to hunt a snake, is to become a snake. This individual has long reaped the benefits of operating beyond the arm of the law, but no drug lord is untouchable forever. My unit has been given every power to flush out police corruption and cut off the head of organised crime.

I won't deny that I missed Mark terribly. The experience that brought us together would always be an invisible thread between us; a powerful thread that would bind us until death. But, watching him turn into a monster from the sidelines made it easier to quell my indomitable desire for the man who saved my life and stole my heart.

I decided early on to specialise in Criminal Law. Not because I enjoyed it, but rather due to my insatiable need for justice. I had a vendetta against people like Maleven and Léon. People who didn't care about who they hurt. Sadistic, violent misogynists who deserved to be punished for the crimes they doled out to their victims. Besides, the writing on the Rainbow Nation's wall was undeniable; not only was there a palpable absence of a rainbow stretching over our country, there was no sign of one on the horizon. Home invaders, hijackings, farm murders, and random acts of violent crime continued to spike, and, like Darwin's evolution theory, we adapted by imprisoning ourselves in our own homes in order to survive. The exterior of Sea Breeze became defaced; the knee-high wall, overlooking the Indian Ocean and lighthouse — that I once dangled my legs over as a child — was fortified into an eight foot concrete wall, topped with electrified barbed wire, and pinned with closed circuit television cameras. Oftentimes, when I was restless and lonely during the twilight hours, I would press my body against the cool wall and listen to the crashing waves. My daily walks on the beach became less frequent; not because I didn't want to, but because a walk on the beach required a level of personal security. Since apartheid had ended, the beaches had become a hotspot for crime, and litter was a monumental problem. Discarded *glue* containers, used condoms, junk food wrappers, and human faeces were commonplace. It wasn't unusual for the tide to wash up everything from plastic bottles to rusted car engines. With crime so rife, it was by no means safe to walk along the beach, so I only did it every so often, and only if I had my gun. On the occasions that I did walk, I took a bag with me and filled it up with litter before I reached the lighthouse. I walked close to the shoreline, where the sand was wet and easier to run on if necessary. I pitied the tourists who believed the tourism ad campaigns. They were not immune. One of the first post-apartheid news stories involved a German tourist who naïvely ventured to Durban beachfront for New Year's celebrations. He was stabbed and left for dead in the children's paddling pool.

In my three years of study, I had no interest in socialising or romance and lived like a hermit. I attended lectures during the week and studied at home in the Sea Breeze library. On weekends I continued Mohini's Pippal tree tradition, and sailed Jericho's yacht. Soon after Alistair and I established Steadman & Wright, Alistair met a woman called Hannah. After their three month anniversary, Hannah insisted on meeting Alistair's business partner. I agreed to have dinner with them, because I owed Alistair that much, but I didn't relish the prospect of seeing him happy in love with another woman.

We booked a table at the Oyster Box Hotel. Hannah arrived late. While Alistair and I waited, I quizzed him. He took out a business card from his wallet and handed it to me. I took one look at it—Hannah van Rensburg PhD, Specialty: Sexual Trauma—and recognised her to be the same Hannah van Rensburg that my Doctor had referred me to after my attack. Fortunately, neither Hannah nor Alistair knew that, because I'd never followed through. I gave the card back to Alistair.

'She is certainly accomplished,' I said, feeling more than a pinch of jealousy.

'She is,' he said. 'She is dedicated to her work.'

'Sounds like you're smitten,' I said.

'This isn't difficult for you, is it Ros?'

I shook my head and sipped my water.

'You know, Ros, it wouldn't hurt you to see someone like Hannah.'

'Meaning?'

'Meaning you have no social life. Other than your lectures and the odd work function for Spencer & Mason, you don't exactly participate in the world.'

'How would you know what I do in my personal time, Alistair?'

'Don't get defensive, Ros. I'm not the enemy.'

'You haven't told her about my past have you?'

'Of course not, but the more she talks about her work, the more I think about you.'

I didn't have a chance to reply, because Hannah appeared. As if a cloud had hand-delivered her from the sky to our table.

'I'm sorry I'm late, darling.' Hannah kissed Alistair's cheek before she sat down between us. She smelled like strawberries and vanilla, and spoke in a deliberate and hypnotic fashion. Her smooth, honey-coloured hair sat shorter on the nape of her neck and longer around her face. She extended her hand to me and said, 'I've heard so much about you, Rosalinde. It's a pleasure to finally meet you.'

I shook her hand like a man at a hostile board meeting.

She laughed without opening her mouth. 'Your hand shake tells me a lot about you,' she said.

'Well, it's a good thing we're here to have dinner and not psychoanalyse each other,' I said, 'because your hand shake tells me a lot about you too.'

'Ladies,' said Alistair.

Hannah laughed and patted Alistair's hand. 'It's okay, darling. Rosalinde is absolutely right. Sometimes I forget that I'm not at work.'

I forced a smile, and opened the menu. While Alistair and Hannah discussed which dishes they would share, I decided to use Hannah's work as a distraction to avoid talking about my personal history. If my first impression was correct, Hannah's theories about trauma would be as neat as her appearance, but I doubted that she fully grasped the messy reality behind them. I imagined her slow, hypnotic voice weighing in on Rosalinde Wright, the patient: *She has, what is termed in the psychology community as, a history of unprocessed trauma.*

'Ros?'

Alistair's voice brought me back to the moment.

'Yes?' I said.

'Are you ready to order?'

'Yes, ready.'

He gestured to the waitress, who took our order and said, 'I'll be back with your drinks shortly.'

I turned to Hannah and said, 'I hope we didn't get off on the wrong foot, I would love to hear more about your work.'

Her face lit up like the chandelier above us and off she went. 'The hot topic is a condition called Post Traumatic Stress Disorder,' she said. 'PTSD for short. The disorder was initially associated with soldiers returning from war zones, but new studies suggest that any lay person who has experienced a traumatic event could in fact suffer from PTSD.'

'That's fascinating,' I said. 'What are the symptoms of this PTSD?'

'The most common are violent nightmares, panic attacks, mood swings, and insomnia,' she said.

If Alistair had been able to nudge me with his elbow or kick me under the table without attracting attention he would have, instead he caught my eye and raised his eyebrows.

I nodded and said, 'I knew an ex-soldier who suffered from violent nightmares.'

Alistair glared at me.

'Oh?' said Hannah, leaning forward conspiratorially.

'But I'm more interested in the lay-person theory,' I said, steering her in another direction.

'It is fascinating and ground-breaking,' she said.

'If you think about it,' I said, 'the whole of South Africa might be suffering from PTSD in the near future, if not already.'

She sat back in her chair and scrutinised me for a moment. 'You know, Ros, I hadn't actually thought about that,' she said.

'Who knows what the psychological repercussions will be for children in say twenty years time.'

She nodded. 'Hmm, yes, the research isn't there yet, Ros, but that would make a fascinating study.'

The waitress interrupted with our drinks.

The rest of the night was a breeze; Hannah expounded her PTSD theories and I took mental notes for my own purposes. At the end of the night, Hannah suggested that we turn the dinner into a monthly tradition. I agreed for Alistair's sake, but I never did relate to Hannah on a deeper level.

CHAPTER 55

When I graduated at the end of 1997, the only sentiment I had for my chosen profession was abject cynicism. In a country that was top heavy with violent crime, overcrowded prisons, and no death penalty, the system perpetually failed to punish violent offenders and provide justice to the most aggrieved victims. I started my Articles in early 1998 alongside a fellow graduate named Jabulani — Jabu for short. His charisma and grace reminded me so much of Paris, and I struggled on a daily basis with guilt over Paris's premature death. If he'd survived, he would have been a successful playwright and actor. I used his unnecessary murder to fuel my professional drive as well as my decision to stay in South Africa, and fight the good fight, a little longer. Jabu and I worked under the wing of a criminal lawyer called David Dunstan. I specifically chose David because he was one of the few high-profile lawyers who took on pro bono cases for the Department of Public Prosecution.

Among our myriad cases, Jabu and I were assigned to three high-profile DPP cases. The first was a home invasion; two black males broke and entered the home of a white family and proceeded to stab and kill the father, rape and murder the mother, and then drown the seven-year old son in a bath of hot water. The second case involved the kidnapping, rape and near death of a four-year old black child. Kidnapped from her grandmother's home, she was dragged into a bush, raped, beaten, and hung from a tree with the threads of her pink blanket. How she survived was a miracle. The case upset me so much that I contacted an immigration consultant about my options. He said I could get a wealth-based visa anywhere I chose, but advised that I should complete my studies before I make any big decisions, because I had Steadman & Wright to consider. I begrudgingly agreed — not wanting an impulsive decision to jeopardise Alistair's career a second time — and decided to reassess after I passed the admissions exam. The third case was assigned mid-year. It involved a drug-related murder of a high-ranking police official from the Murder and Robbery Unit. The words drug-related, followed by Murder and Robbery conjured thoughts of Mark, but the victim's name — Jacobs —set off goosebumps up and down my arms.

I stayed at work after everyone had gone home to read the case notes. From my cubicle, the city of Durban was lit up and beautiful, but beyond the safety of my high rise window violence fuelled by hatred and fear pervaded. It was getting harder to stare the truth in the face and turn a blind eye. I opened the legal folder and read from cover to cover. The DPP had been building a case for years, but the recent involvement of Inspector Patel and his Black Mamba unit had moved the case beyond an armful of unproven theories and into a body of crimes that could be proven. The notes detailed Mark's operation. He paid government officials and diplomats to clear drug shipments through customs, and had key members of the SAPS to warn him about, and quash, any investigations involving him and his operation. He used homeless black children as his drug-runners, which was both clever and cruel. Street kids were the most aggrieved in the new South Africa. Their ages varied, but they were as young as three and old as fourteen. Street kids were seen, by the white public, as a nuisance and a threat, because they would loiter at traffic lights and mob stationary cars in an attempt to solicit money. They were generally addicted to "glue" —a substance that they would ingest or inhale via an empty plastic bottle. Glue was popular because it was cheap and masked the symptoms of hunger and cold — two harsh realities a street child faced on a daily basis. Street kids generally moved in groups because they were vulnerable on their own and were often victims of random acts of violence, sexual predators, and organised crime. The thought of Mark selling drugs was bad enough; to see that he had exploited children tipped the scales. But the DPP had a bullet of justice, much like the hollow point that Mark gave me, to hit its target and cause collateral damage as it ricocheted. The Black Mamba unit had a police informant on their side — a street kid called Lucky. One of Mark's top earners, and his most trusted runner, Lucky's territory was Point Road, with the majority of his business originating from two nightclubs — a rave club known as 330, and a blacks-only club known as Soul Groove.

Hannah had explained how a word or sound or smell could trigger flashbacks in a person with PTSD, and this reference to Soul Groove was my trigger. An instantaneous return to the smells, sounds, and buried memories from that nightmare of a night. I suddenly felt vulnerable and fearful; angry with myself for staying late. I retrieved my gun from the safe and called

Alistair. I lied and said I had car trouble. While I waited for him to arrive, I read the rest of the report. The final gun in the DPPs arsenal was the murder of Jacobs; Murder and Robbery Unit's top honcho. The same Jacobs who had taken my statement in the hospital after my attack. Following a complex money trail, the Black Mamba unit had identified Mark as the main conspirator behind Jacobs' murder. Jacobs had been lured to a Durban nightclub to receive a pay-off for information, as was the protocol. He was shot execution style, in the back of the head, before he got out of his car. The why was as simple as it was cliched. It was believed that Jacobs had become greedy and planned a coup. Mark had struck first.

I closed the file and crossed my arms. I wanted to lay my forehead on the desk and sob, but crying was not the answer. To cry was to admit defeat. To cry was to drown in the sea of hopelessness that grew more expansive each day. Crying didn't change a damn thing. I had chosen to study Law so that I had an option other than crying. Since the day Mark had saved my life, he had been my anti-hero, and I had found it relatively easy to turn a blind eye to his ever-growing list of wrongdoings because I felt indebted to him. But, as I processed what I'd read in the case notes, I realised that the time had come for me to draw a line between justifiable and unconscionable deeds. If selling drugs had not warranted that invisible line, then surely the exploitation of homeless children did. I felt a surge of purpose and trepidation. Mark on one side of the law, me on the other. He was no different to apartheid. His reign of ethical wrong-doing was out of control, and he needed to be stopped.

CHAPTER 56

When I received Henry Malvern's invitation to his eightieth birthday bash at Sun City, I sighed at the prospect of seeing Alistair and Hannah together in a romantic setting. Unfortunately, declining was not an option, and neither was finding a suitable plus one. Until my feelings for Mark and Alistair were resolved, I would likely remain single for the foreseeable future. Alistair and I were to meet at Virginia Airport, where Henry's private jet would be waiting. It stirred up old memories. I hadn't been to Virginia since Alistair and I flew to the legal hearing during my first week at Spencer & Mason.

On the morning of our departure, Alistair arrived alone.

'I think you forgot something,' I said with a chuckle.

'Hannah's not coming, Ros.'

'Why not?'

'Because I didn't ask her.'

'Say what?'

'I told her it was a work function.'

'Okay, spill the beans, what's going on?'

'Nothing's going on, Ros, I just want to relax this weekend.'

'And you can't relax with Hannah?'

'Ros, can we enjoy the weekend please?'

'Well I know my weekend just got better.'

He shot me an ambivalent look — half warning me to stop, and half welcoming me to continue. I decided to strike a balance and leave it alone until he mentioned it again. We talked about my graduation and work at the DPP during the flight.

'Do you plan to practice Criminal Law when you finish your Articles?' he said.

'I'm not sure yet. The criminal cases can be brutal on me emotionally, but the opportunity to punish these monsters is a sweet reward. One thing's for sure, I'll be ready to make a decision one way or the other when I finish my Articles at the end of the year.'

'How can you be so sure?'

'A case I'm working on.'

'Anything I can help you with?'

'You know I can't discuss it, Alistair.'

'I know. That's not what I meant. I'm always here for moral support. You are fully capable of convincing the world around you that you are as strong as iron, but the world doesn't know why your defences are so strong. I do. I know your true nature and your heart, Ros. I know what you've been through and I've watched you harden yourself over the years in order to maintain your sanity.'

'Alistair, how do I love thee, let me count the ways.'

'Don't joke, Ros, I'm serious.'

'I know you're serious, Alz, and I'm not joking. I probably wouldn't have gone back to varsity if you hadn't pushed me. All these years that I've isolated myself you have always been there in the wings. The truth is that I appreciate and love you more than you will ever know.'

The pilot announced our descent and reminded us to fasten our seat belts. The weekend weather forecast was sunny and warm. I sat back in the white leather seat and sipped my champagne. I was always so damned serious and uptight. I wanted the weekend to be different. I wanted to relax and enjoy myself with my best friend. No Hannah or Mark between us. Just like the good old days.

Sun City, a luxury resort and casino in Bophuthatswana, was born from the imagination of Sol Kerzner, a business magnate. The project began in 1979 with the main hotel, international 18-hole golf course, and resort-style pools. By 1994, the resort had grown to include the Cascades Hotel, The Cabanas, and The Palace of the Lost City. The Palace was inspired by an African legend of a Kingdom in the heart of the jungle that was destroyed by an earthquake. The legend told of a nomadic tribe that built a lavish palace for their royal leaders in the bowl of an extinct volcano. Years later, an earthquake shook the crater and destroyed the city. The royals were whisked to safety on the backs of kudus, but the city ruins were eventually consumed by the surrounding jungle. The Palace at Sun City recreated this legend by setting the resort on an extinct volcanic site among the Pilanesberg Mountains and on the edge of a Game Reserve. Like the legend, a jungle was recreated — complete with rainforest canopy and home to nearly two hundred bird species. Like a movie set for Jurassic Park, the grounds were populated with mammoth statues of elephants, lions and kudu. The Palace itself had echoes of the Taj Mahal with its turquoise copper domes and turrets as well as the myriad water features to be found both inside and out of the palace.

Henry Malvern's party and guests were accommodated in the magnificent Lost City. Alistair and I had adjoining rooms that overlooked the gardens and swimming pool. An itinerary for the weekend was hand-delivered by a staff member shortly after we arrived;. a cocktail party on Friday evening, the main event on Saturday evening, and a final brunch on Sunday. Other than those times, Alistair and I were free to do what we pleased. We spent a few hours in the casino and then went for a walk to the wave pool — a manmade beach with mechanised waves and white beach sand — but didn't stay long as it was heaving with families and kids. We visited reception for entertainment options, who suggested a movie at the Imax theatre.

'Do you know what movies are showing?' said Alistair.

'Blue Planet, and The Serengeti,' she said. 'Here is a brochure with session times and information.'

'Thanks,' said Alistair.

'You're welcome,' she said. 'The hotel provides a free minibus which will take you to the entertainment centre.'

'Thank you,' we both said in unison.

Outside, a mini-bus arrived almost immediately, and whisked us off to the entertainment centre. The Imax had session times around the clock, so we spent a bit of time exploring the complex. It had everything from Bingo to slot machines, restaurants and movie theatres, as well as a video arcade for kids.

'I have not played video games in yonks,' I said.

'Me neither,' he said. 'What are your favourites?'

'Battlestar Galactica, Ms Pacman, Tetris, Space Invaders… take your pick,' I said.

'Wanna play?'

'Yesssss!'

Alistair laughed. 'Come on then.'

An hour later we'd had our fun and headed upstairs to watch *Africa: The Serengeti*. We loved the Imax experience so much that we watched *Blue Planet* as well. By the time we'd finished, we were peckish, so we hopped back onto a mini-bus and returned to the Lost City.

We found a quiet spot in the hotel lounge and ordered coffee and cake. The oversized armchairs could easily seat two and were reminiscent of oriental bird cages. It was impossible not to relax.

Alistair leaned back and sighed. 'I had a lot of fun today, Ros.'

'Me too,' I said, 'I haven't had that much fun since nineteen voetsak!'

Alistair burst out laughing. '19voetsak! I haven't heard that saying since 19voetsak.'

We both laughed.

'What's going on with you and Hannah?' I said.

'We broke up before I left,' he said.

'Proper break-up or cooling off period?' I said.

'Proper break-up.'

I sipped my coffee and lifted a teaspoon of chocolate cake to my lips. 'Why?'

'Do you want the honest answer?'

'Always,' I said.

'Because I'm still in love with you.'

A cake crumb went down the wrong way and I coughed like a smoker to clear my throat. Alistair jumped up to pat my back and handed me a glass of water. When I had composed myself

Alistair was sitting next to me with his hand on my thigh.

'I thought we were past tense?' I said.

'Do you want us to be past tense?' he said.

I shook my head.

He gestured to the waiter and put the food on his tab. 'Come,' he said.

I held his hand and followed him to the elevator. I hadn't considered that Alistair still had feelings for me. I thought his love was long lost, like the Lost City, after our personal earthquake that left our relationship in ruins.

In the elevator, I took his face in my hands and pressed my cheek against his. 'My heart is beating faster than I can breathe,' I whispered in his ear.

I've always been a gentleman around you, Ros. I used to think that was a good thing, but now I'm not so sure.'

'I won't disagree,' I said. 'I've both appreciated and cursed your impenetrable decorum.'

The elevator pinged and the doors opened to our floor. Alistair led me to his room and pushed me onto the king size bed. I ripped his buttoned shirt open and clawed at his jeans like a woman possessed. He pulled a condom out of his pocket.

'I like a man who comes prepared,' I said laughing.

He kissed and bit my lip. I wrapped my legs around his waist, guided him inside me, dragged my nails down his back. He arched his back and moaned. Bolts of electricity surged my body. He pulled out and went down on me. My eyelashes flickered like a candle in the rain and I abandoned myself to Alistair's tongue and fingers. It was almost spiritual. I trusted him like nobody else. I don't know why I waited so long. I don't know why I sabotaged our time together. Perhaps this was why. I was afraid of the real thing. I was afraid of letting someone love me properly. The way I deserved to be loved.

We drank champagne in a bubble bath in preparation for the cocktail party at seven. My cheeks were still flushed from love-making and I couldn't stop smiling.

'We should probably talk about what just happened,' said Alistair.

'You're not having regrets, are you?'

'No,' he said, flicking bubbles at me.

'Good,' I said, 'just checking.'

'I have never stopped loving you, Ros.'

'Even when you were angry with me,' I said.

'Especially then, Ros.'

'What happened with Hannah?'

'Long story short, Hannah isn't you.'

'Why didn't you tell me, Alistair, give me an inkling or something?'

'Because I thought you were hung up on Mark, and you've never given me any signals.'

'I'm not hung up on Mark. Not anymore.'

'You sure about that?'

'I'm sure.'

He put his glass down and leaned in to kiss me. I kissed him back and whispered I love you in his ear.

'I love you back,' he said. 'I have always loved you.'

I wore an ankle-length, open-backed, body-hugging black sequinned dress with a plunging neckline for Henry's black-tie-party on Saturday night. If I didn't have Alistair by my side, I wouldn't have worn it. I was standing in the bathroom with a hair straightener in my hand when Alistair walked in. He kissed the back of my neck. I smiled and felt my shoulders relax.

I switched the straightener off at the wall socket and placed it on the marble bench top.

Slipping my fingers beneath his lapels, I said, 'You look handsome in a tux, Mr Steadman.'

'And you are more breathtaking than ever,' he said kissing me.

'Any chance we can stay in this room forever?' I said, smiling.

'Maybe not in this room,' he said, 'but we do have a chance at forever.'

I smiled and raised my eyebrows. 'What are you up to?'

'Close your eyes,' he said.

'Okay.'

He took my hand and slipped something cold onto my ring finger. I opened my eyes. A platinum band with a white stone. Not a diamond. This was milky white.

'Is this a moonstone?' I said, bringing it up to my face to inspect.

'Yes. What do you get a woman who is against blood diamonds?'

'Alistair,' I said, swallowing back happy tears. 'You are the most thoughtful man I have ever met.'

'And you are the only woman for me,' he said. He got down on one knee, as was the custom, and kissed my hand. 'Marry me, Ros. Be mine forever.'

I held his face in my hands and pulled him close. 'Yes,' I said, 'yes, a hundred times.'

The party took place in a private room that had jungle print wallpaper and an array of glittering chandeliers hanging from the ceiling. The bar was equipped with every drink under the sun and waiters passed around canapés. All in all, it was a blur of colourful people and vibrant music, because my mind was occupied with Alistair. My fiancé. He told Henry at some stage, who swooped in to congratulate me.

'Your news is the best birthday present of the night,' he said.

I hugged him and said, 'Happy birthday, Henry.'

'Thank you my dearest. Your father and Jericho would be very proud of you.'

Alistair nodded in agreement, and I did my best to swallow the lump in my throat.

We left the party in the early hours of the morning.

'Are you tired?' I said, when we reached the room.

'Not a bit.'

'Fancy taking a walk to the pool and getting some fresh air?'

'Sounds good,' he said. 'Give me a sec to get out of this tux.'

'Oh, God, yes,' I said, stripping off the dress and grabbing a pair of jeans.

The night air was cool and quiet. The palace looked even more regal lit up. We lay on poolside loungers that were scarce during the day thanks to families and kids.

I squeezed his hand and said, 'There's something I need to tell you.'

'Sounds serious.'

I swivelled my feet to the floor and sat up to face him. 'There's no easy way to say this, so I'll just say it.'

He sat up and faced me. 'Okay.'

'I can't have children,' I said. 'A vestige of my attack.'

He got off his chair and hugged me. 'Ros, my darling, I'm so sorry.'

'I understand if you don't want to marry me,' I said.

'Not marry you, Ros? Why on earth would I...'

'You're a lot older than me, Alistair, and I imagine you've entertained the idea about having children at some stage.'

'Honestly, yes, I've thought about it. If I'm even more honest I'll admit that I broke up with Hannah because I couldn't envision a future in which I would ever want to have children with her.'

'There you go,' I said.

'Let me finish, Ros.'

I nodded.

'While I would love to have a child with you, I'm not marrying you for children. I'm marrying you because I miss you when you're not around, and dream of ways to keep you close when we're apart.'

I started to cry. 'I have spent the last three years convincing myself that I am destined to be alone and lonely.'

'That's not your destiny, my darling. Besides, there is more than one way to have a child. If we ever reach that point. Okay?'

'Okay,' I nodded.

'I love you, Ros, and everything is going to be fine, I promise.'

CHAPTER 57

Six weeks later, on a Thursday evening, I was leaving the doctor's office and heading to Alistair's when David called an emergency meeting.

'The case against Mark has come to a head,' said David. 'There's been chatter on the street, and we suspect Mark is aware of Lucky's informant status. Inspector Patel is bringing Lucky in to get a recorded testimony before they take him into protective custody.'

'What can I do?' I said.

'Prepare for an all-nighter, Ros. I need you to sit with Lucky and handhold him.'

'I'll be there shortly,' I said.

At the office, I followed David to a meeting room at the end of the passage. The table was laden with food — biltong, samosas, pizza, Kentucky chicken with mash and gravy, soft drinks, and donuts. Everything a hungry street kid could ask for.

'Inspector Patel is bringing Lucky in himself, and he's not taking any chances.' He pointed to the windows. 'You'll notice that we've closed the blinds. Inspector Patel is prepared for all eventualities. This Mark Muller is as brazen as he is violent. Don't let Lucky out of your sight.'

'I understand, David. I won't let you down.'

'If we can pull this off, your career will know no limits.'

'David, do you mind me asking why you chose me and not Jabu? I would think him a better fit.'

'Lucky has never had a mother.'

I instinctively touched my belly.

'If his story is correct,' David continued, 'his mother died in childbirth and he was raised by his uncle for the first four years of his life. That should have been the worst of the story, but it's not. His uncle passed him around to strangers for money until his bad deeds caught up with him and he was brutally murdered. Lucky ran away and somehow managed to survive on his own. He's been on the street ever since.'

'Four years old,' I said, trying not to cry. 'How is that even possible?'

'Sad truth is that there are hundreds of Lucky's on the street, Ros. We declare war on drugs and racism in this country, but the greatest threat is poverty. You and I are among the fortunate few. That's why I take these pro bono cases.'

'I know, David. It's why I chose to do my Articles with you, and I appreciate the opportunity.'

'I can rely on you to think on your feet, Ros, that's why I chose you for this situation.' He closed the door behind him and left me to ponder my bizarre predicament.

Inspector Patel spoke with a cockney accent.

'Miss Wright,' he said with an outstretched hand.

I stood up and shook his hand. 'Inspector Patel.'

He was in his early thirties and his clean-shaven skin was the colour of cardamon. He smelled like mint and lemon.

'This is Lucky,' he said.

A boy with ripped pants and dirty vest stepped forward and held out his hand.

'Hi Lucky, my name is Rosalinde, but you can call me Ros.'

He shook my hand. 'My name is Lucky and you can call me Lucky,' he laughed.

I smiled at him and said, 'I hope you're hungry, because if you're not I'll have to eat all of this food myself.'

He walked past me and sat down. 'You can have the donuts,' he said grabbing the bucket of chicken.

I turned on the TV and showed him how to channel surf then spoke to Inspector Patel in the corridor.

'He really is just a child,' I said.

He nodded. 'Hard to believe that someone could be cold enough to exploit his situation.'

'Yes,' I said, my thoughts of Mark souring by the second.

'This situation escalated without warning,' said Patel. 'I need you to stay with him and reassure him while we set up a video to record his testimony. Anything he says to you can be used in our investigation, so if he feels comfortable talking then let him.'

'Okay,' I said.

'Don't let him out of your sight,' Patel reiterated.

'I won't,' I said.

He walked toward the conference room.

'Inspector?' I called out.

'Yes, Miss Wright?'

'Could we get Lucky some clean clothes?'

'Someone is handling that,' he said.

I nodded.

I joined Lucky at the table and watched him wolf down the chicken, mash and gravy. David's words tied up my thoughts. When this night was over I would use my money to do something good for these street kids. Instead of fearing and pointing guns at them, I would find a way to love them like the parents they never had. Starting with food, shelter, and safety.

'You look like you're far away Miss Ros,' said Lucky.

I smiled at being called Miss Ros. 'Sorry, Lucky, I have a habit of thinking too much.'

'Do you have a habit of being sad too?' he said.

'Sad?' I repeated.

'Ja, Miss Ros, I can see the sadness underneath your smile.'

I picked up a donut and took a bite. Something to stop myself from crying. 'Your situation makes me sad, Lucky.'

'Don't worry about me, Miss Ros, I've never seen so much food in my whole life. Can I take some for my friends?'

Every time he said something, the lump in my throat got bigger. 'I will make sure that your friends get plenty of food, Lucky. Is there a place where I can find them?'

'We don't have a house, Miss Ros.'

'I know, Lucky. But is there a place where you meet up or go to often?'

'You mean my territory, Miss Ros?'

'Your territory,' I repeated. 'Is that where you met Mark?'

He dropped the drumstick and looked at me. 'You're a nice lady, Miss Ros, but Mister Mark is not a nice man. I don't want you to get hurt.'

I inhaled and exhaled through my nostrils. It was sobering to hear a child refer to the man I had once been intimate with as a monster. 'Lucky, if you help the Inspector, Mr Mark will not hurt me or you.'

'Mr Mark has lots of friends, Miss Ros.'

'If you are scared of Mr Mark, then why are you helping the Inspector, Lucky?'

'That's easy, Miss Ros. Mr Mark shot my friend, Jack, in the head.'

'What? Why?'

'Mr Mark told us that he knew someone was talking to Inspector Patel.'

'Did Jack talk to Inspector Patel?'

'No, Miss Ros. Mr Mark did it to scare us.'

'Lucky, does Inspector Patel know about Jack?'

'No, Miss Ros. They don't care about my friend. They care about putting Mr Mark in jail. I'm telling you because you're a nice lady and I don't want you to get hurt like Jack.'

'Lucky, one last question. When did Mr Mark shoot Jack?'

'Last night, Miss Ros. That's why it's not safe for you to visit my friends.'

My heart rate spiked and my breathing grew shallow. 'Lucky, aren't you scared that Mr Mark will hurt you?'

'No, Miss Ros. I will never live as long as you. If Mr Mark doesn't shoot me, another tsotsi will.'

To hear a child talking about his death as if it was a dentist appointment rattled the cage of my soul.

'I will do everything in my power to keep you safe and put Mr Mark in jail,' I said touching his arm.

'Can I have the chocolate donut?' said Lucky.

'Of course,' I said, passing him the donut.

He stuffed half of it into his mouth at once. 'I've only seen a TV through the shop window,' he said flicking the channels and stopping on a Tom & Jerry cartoon.

When the time came for Lucky and Inspector Patel to leave for the safe house, Lucky begged me to go with.

'It's too dangerous, Ros,' said David.

'He's right,' said Inspector Patel.

'I have a Glock, and I know how to use it.'

'Nice,' said Patel.

'Jesus, Ros, really?' said David.

'I don't know why you're surprised, David, have you met the new South Africa?'

Lucky burst out laughing and said, Miss Ros is right, this place is a fucking nagmerrie. Eish.'

Lucky shook his head and we couldn't help but laugh.

'Okay, look,' I said, 'do I need permission to go Inspector Patel?'

'No, as long as you're aware of the danger, you don't need permission.'

'Ros, I strongly advise...'

'I know, David, and I appreciate it. But I'd like to do this.'

'Okay,' said Patel, 'that's settled.'

We left the office at 3 am on Friday morning.

'Ros, I'll see you back here at 10 am,' said David, 'we have a lot of work to do.'

'Okay,' I said.

I phoned Alistair, before I got into the lift, to tell him I wouldn't be coming over. He sounded disappointed, but cheered up when I suggested we get together on Friday evening. When the lift door opened, there were three unmarked cars —

black Mercedes with tinted windows — waiting in the basement parking lot. Lucky, Patel, and I were in the middle car.

'Today was my first time to drive in a car,' said Lucky.

Patel and I exchanged glances, neither knowing how to respond. I patted Lucky's knee.

'Where are we going?' said Lucky.

'Inspector Patel is not allowed to tell us, Lucky, but we are travelling inland, away from the city.'

Patel held out his hand to me and said, 'Enough of this Inspector Patel stuff, please call me Dinesh.'

'Only if you call me Ros,' I said, shaking his hand.

'Tell me, Ros, I'm intrigued, what made you get a gun?'

'Let's just say I've been on the receiving end of violent crime.'

He nodded. 'I heard stories before I got here, but I never believed it until I saw it for myself.'

'What's it like in the UK?' I said.

'Put it this way,' he said, 'the police don't carry guns.'

'No way,' I said.

'Are you taking me to the UK?' said Lucky.

'No, Lucky, the UK is the country where I grew up. It's a long plane trip to get there.'

Lucky nodded.

Outside the window, I noticed that we were on Fields Hill and said, 'Have you seen the Comrades Marathon? They run from Durban to Pietermaritzburg. This hill is a famous part of the route.'

'My colleagues insisted that I watch it soon after I arrived,' he said.

'It's a bit of an institution,' I said. 'My dad used to take me to Hillcrest every year to watch the race. We would leave early in the morning with a flask of tea and sandwiches. Fond memories.'

'Is your dad dead, Miss Ros?'

I squeezed his hand. 'Yes, Lucky.'

We all fell silent for several minutes. I felt stupid and insensitive for bringing up my dead father, considering Lucky had spent most of his life as a homeless orphan.

Lucky pointed to the bridge ahead as we approached the turn-off for the Kloof gorge. 'Look, Miss Ros.'

I leaned forward and ducked my head to see beyond the driver's windshield. The streetlights on the bridge revealed a man dressed in black gear and helmet.

'Oh shit,' I said. 'Dinesh, are you seeing this?'

The man on the bridge launched an RPG at the car in front, and we swerved to avoid rear-ending the inferno.

'Go, go, go,' Dinesh shouted.

Our driver accelerated and sped beneath the bridge and out the other side. I grabbed my gun and told Lucky to stay close to me. He was watching the bridge from the rear-view window.

'Miss Ros, there are motorbikes behind us.'

'Shit,' I said.

The burst of sustained automatic gunfire drowned out Dinesh's radio for help, and I watched as the car behind us rammed into the bridge column right after it was peppered in bullets.

'It's only us left,' I said to Dinesh. I tapped the driver's shoulder and said, 'turn off your lights and accelerate past the next two exits. We're heading towards a dark stretch of road. If we can make it that far, we might have a chance.' Lucky buried his head in my lap.

'You heard the lady, drive, dammit!' said Dinesh.

The driver did as he was told. I could feel Lucky's heartbeat racing against my thigh and I tried to soothe him by patting his head. Silence reigned down inside the car as we sped past the first, then second exit. The sound of gunfire was followed by tyres popping. Time slowed down to the nanosecond as the car flipped nose-first, landed upside down, and spun round and round like a merry-go-round. When the sound of screeching metal ceased, I fumbled for the seat belt and tried to blink my eyes back into focus.

'Lucky,' I said, shaking his shoulder, 'you okay?'

'I'm okay, Miss Ros,' he said lifting his head and looking around in a daze.

'Oh, thank God,' I said.

'Dinesh,' I said, leaning forward to shake him. 'Dinesh.'

A motorbike headlight illuminated the car from outside, revealing the bullets that riddled the driver's body, and the blood that covered Dinesh's face.

'Get out of the car.'

I froze when I heard the voice.

'That's Mr Mark,' Lucky said, his voice catching in his throat.

'I know,' I said, 'I'm going to talk to him.'

Lucky clutched my shirt. 'No, Miss Ros, he will hurt you.'

'Lucky, I know Mr Mark from a long time ago, and you need to trust me, okay?'

He nodded. His face didn't show fear, but a resignation borne of the streets.

'Here,' I said, putting my gun into his hand. 'If I fail and he tries to hurt you, shoot him. Okay?'

'Okay, Miss Ros,' he nodded.

The door was jammed, so I kicked the glass out of the window and climbed out.'

Mark and I came face to face. He signalled the other motorbikes to leave, and levelled his forty five at me.

'What the hell are you doing here, Wrighty?'

'I'm here to protect Lucky.'

'It's too late for that.'

I shook my head. 'No, it's not.'

'I can't let the kid testify against me.'

'Mark, listen to me, if you let Lucky go, I will personally hand you the DPPs case so you can beat it.'

'I don't give a shit about their case, Wrighty, the only thing that hurts me is Lucky's testimony.'

'Then I'll convince him not to testify.'

He threw his head back and laughed. 'How?'

'By adopting him,' I said, surprising myself.

'Are you fucking serious?'

'Yes, I'm fucking serious. Before I was thrust into a room with a homeless child, whom my ex-lover is exploiting, the doctor confirmed that I'm six weeks pregnant.'

'I thought it was impossible to conceive.'

'It was.'

Mark shook his head and sighed.

'No child should be subjected to what Lucky has endured,' I said. 'I have the means to help him, and show him that he really is lucky. Please, I'm begging you. Let me help him, and you.'

Mark sighed and shook his head. 'You have no idea what Lucky is capable of.'

'I had no idea what you were capable of either, but I'm giving you a second chance.'

Lucky climbed out of the window, my gun in his hand. Mark took aim. Distant sirens screamed out into the night.

'Lucky,' I said approaching him, 'Lucky, put the gun down.'

He shook his head and aimed the gun at Mark. 'No, Miss

Ros.' Mark fired first. The bullet hit Lucky between the eyes. Blood spattered my face. I dropped to my knees and let out a piercing scream.

'I'm sorry, Wrighty.' He walked over to Lucky and retrieved the gun. 'Here,' he said handing it to me.'

'Do you have any idea what you've done?' I said, taking the gun.

'Killed the DPPs case.'

'No,' I shook my head, 'you've just turned me into the DPPs witness.'

'You won't testify against me.'

'Won't I?'

'No, you won't, because I have evidence from the night you were attacked.'

'What evidence?'

'Your clothing.'

'What?' My shoulders slackened and I bent my head like a priest.

'It doesn't look good that you're the only survivor tonight,' he said. 'If I have proof that you colluded with me after your attack, then I can sure as hell prove that you colluded with me tonight.'

'It's not looking good for me regardless,' I said.

'It'll be fine. Use the blow to your head to feign memory loss when the ambulance arrives, then take a few days off work, and go home.'

'I don't have a blow to my head,' I said.

He swung the base of his gun at my temple and knocked me off my feet. 'You do now.'

I watched him straddle his motorbike and lower the helmet over his head.

'I'll meet you at Sea Breeze next week to discuss how we're gonna handle this,' he said. 'Until then, you remember nothing.'

He revved the engine and sped off. The sirens were getting closer. I wiped the blood from my head and climbed back into the car to check on Dinesh. I sighed with relief. He was unconscious, but he had a pulse.

CHAPTER 58

When I saw Alistair parked in the driveway at Sea Breeze, my heart swelled at the thought of delivering my good news, and shrank at the prospect of telling him about Mark. I opened the gate remotely and watched the monitors until he had reached the garages and the gates had closed. The motion detectors kicked in and the exterior lights switched on when I opened the back door and he got out of his car.

'I hope you're hungry,' he said, unloading grocery bags from his boot.

'As long as you're cooking,' I said, and hugged him hello.

'What the hell happened to your head?' he said, touching the plaster.

'Long story short, I was part of the convoy with Lucky and we were ambushed.'

'Jesus, Ros, and you're only telling me now?'

'Sorry,' I said and started to cry.

'Come on, let's go inside.'

'What's for dinner?' I said.

'Porcini mushroom risotto.'

415

'Oh my God, I am so hungry,' I said.

'Do you want to tell me now or over dinner?' he said.

'Over dinner, please. Speaking of which, can I help?'

'No, I want you to go upstairs and soak in a hot bath.'

'Two hands are better than one,' I said. 'Let me help you prep at least?'

'You're not giving me a choice, are you?'

'Nope,' I said, laughing.

When I left him in the kitchen, the smell of sizzling garlic and the sound of Nina Simone followed me up the spiral staircase. While I waited for the bath to fill, I watched the lighthouse beam make its revolution. The lighthouse in Umhlanga, and those around the country, were the only buildings in South Africa that hadn't undergone security modifications. They contained no material value for thieves to steal, or people to murder, and were therefore immune to the threat of damage or invasion. My lighthouse was the same one from my childhood. My constant. It still possessed the power to mesmerise and comfort. My literal light in the dark.

In the bathroom, I turned off the taps, tested the water, and added a few drops of lavender oil before I sank in. The night's events replayed in my head: Mark, shooting Lucky, then threatening to expose my secret; my unborn miracle. I suddenly felt a deep fatigue setting into my bones, as well as a yearning for love and safety, and a reprieve from being on constant alert. A return to the days when we worried about bombs in public places, instead of restless nights with guns under pillows and ears trained to hear the faintest sign of violent home invasions. A break from looking over my shoulder. An iota of normality. In that moment, I craved it like a pregnant woman craves ice cream. I wondered if Alistair felt the same — did he dream about leaving the Cape of Storms, or did he belong to the camp of eternal hope? In truth, I had no idea. While Alistair didn't share my level of cynicism, he knew the situation would worsen before it improved. How long was he willing to wait? I had my answer, but I wasn't so sure about his.

I must have laid on the bed after my bath and fallen asleep, because I woke up as the sun was rising. I thought of Mohini and felt sentimental. I left Alistair asleep and went in search of the key to Mohini's deserted room. The smell of incense still hung in the air. I thought of the night when I had watched Mohini unravel her bun. The moment when I had really seen her for the first time. A woman. A beautiful, gentle woman with a story of her own. A book judged by its cover. A book that nobody ever picked up to read.

I thought of an incense stick and its slow burning. I thought about how similar life was. Each experience and year bringing us closer to the end. The past, a pile of ash in the incense holder of life. How many experiences and years did Alistair and I have left? Was that number slashed the longer we stayed in Africa? I already knew the answer to that question. I didn't want to push my luck. The longer I stayed in Africa, the more I blew and agitated that burning incense stick. I wanted to extend the burn as long as possible. Extend the time between burning and ash.

Tears flooded my eyes, like a pool in torrential rain, as the urgency to leave it all behind swelled. First, the ethical burden of apartheid. Then, the psychological struggle of facing our own mortality on a daily basis. The struggle that my father had committed suicide to save me from. Death's voice echoed on every street. Its stench clung to the air like the incense in Mohini's room. It was a spirit with unfinished business. It would never end.

I fell asleep on Mohini's bed and dreamed about Ouma. She wasn't on the farm; the last place I had seen her. She was at her old house in Coetzeesdorp. The place where she was supposed to end her days in peace and tranquillity — not ending up raped, stabbed, and burnt to death. She kneeled on the edge of the strawberry patch, removing weed sprouts and relocating ladybirds. The cloudless Karoo sky accentuated the glowing African sun, and she hummed a tune that I vaguely recollected from childhood. She saw me, smiled and waved, then handed me a strawberry and said, 'Everything will be okay, my little Lindy.'

I treated Alistair to breakfast at the Oyster Box Hotel. It was an overcast day. The only way you could distinguish the chalky grey sky from the lighthouse was the splash of red paint beneath its light room. The choppy ocean looked as restless as I felt. I ordered scrambled eggs and orange juice. Alistair ordered the big breakfast. I told him the story about the Pippal tree and my Saturday tradition, which had changed since that first time with Mohini.

'I tie red ribbons for Jericho, my father, and Ouma. In recent years I have asked the tree to undo the damage that Maleven did and bless me with a child one day in the future.' I dropped my head and laughed. 'Silly, I know.'

Alistair placed his hand over mine. 'It's not silly at all.'

418

'There's something I need to tell you,' I said. 'Please don't be angry that I didn't tell you straight after it happened.'

'What is it?'

'Not here,' I said. 'Come with me to the Pippal tree after breakfast, and I will explain everything.'

Back at Sea Breeze, Alistair and I took a slow walk to the Pippal tree. We stopped at the umbrella thorn tree to give the vervets a bunch of old bananas, then headed into the yellow-wood forest. On gloomy days, the forest was darker than usual and the birds more animated. As we walked, I recounted the story; Lucky and Inspector Patel, the convoy, Mark.

Alistair stopped walking at the mere mention of Mark's name.

'You saw Mark?'

'Yes.'

'Why didn't you tell me?'

'With the exception of Patel and I, Mark killed everyone in that convoy and then said he had evidence from the night of my attack.'

'What evidence?'

'My clothing,' I said.

The colour of Alistair's face matched the sky. His expression grew stormy. 'He kept your clothing all these years as leverage to use against you in the future.'

'Apparently.'

'What happened next?'

'He hit me with his gun and told me to feign memory loss until he visits me next week to sort it out.'

Alistair went quiet while he processed the information; a deep frown forming between his eyebrows, his brain ticking

419

like a grandfather clock. I noticed that the birds had stopped chattering and chirping. A bolt of lightning tore through the canvas of the sky, lighting up the forest for a split second, followed by a raucous rumble. As if the sky had hunger pains. The sound of rain drops splashing on leaves lasted all of ten seconds before the rain turned into diagonal sheets and then hail stones.

'We'll have to do the Pippal tree later,' said Alistair.'

He grabbed my hand and we ran back toward the house. We were drenched before we reached the umbrella tree.

'Let's go to the pool house,' I said, steering Alistair left.

I punched the number into the keypad to unlock the door. The space smelt musty. I flicked the light switch, but the power was out.

'I'll check the mains box,' said Alistair.

'No, don't,' I said and pulled him toward me. 'There's something else.'

'What is it?'

'I'm pregnant.'

He wore an expression I couldn't decipher, or hadn't seen before. 'I thought…'

'So did I, but the doctor confirmed it. We are six weeks pregnant.'

'Oh my God, Ros.'

He picked me up and swirled me around like a ballerina in Swan Lake. I smiled in spite of everything. He put me down and kissed my belly. I pulled him in close and kissed him with an unbridled urgency. We made love on the handwoven white rug, embroidered with a gold and turquoise dragonfly; a mirror image of the one that adorned the floor of the pool.

Afterwards, as I lay with my head on his chest and my legs entwined with his, I said, 'I thought you'd be angry with me about Mark.'

'I am angry,' he said, 'but not with you. He's out of control and it has to end.'

'I have a plan,' I said, 'but it is extreme and there will be consequences for both of us.'

'I'm listening,' he said.

CHAPTER 59

David Dunstan spun in his executive chair and stared out of the window. Alistair and I waited for him to speak.

'You understand that you'll be ending your career before it begins, Rosalinde,' he said. His back still turned to us.

'I do,' I said.

'You also understand that if you follow through with testifying against Mark Muller, the story about your rape and cover-up will go public.'

'Yes,' I said.

'Not to mention what Mark will do to you if we prosecute him successfully.' He swivelled around to face us. 'You understand that he has connections everywhere. Including this office. You will always have a target on your back.'

'If I stay in South Africa,' I said.

He considered my statement before he replied. 'You're willing to sacrifice everything, Ros? Your career, your family name, your law practice, your home?'

'Yes,' I said. 'Obviously, I would need time to get my affairs in order. Steadman & Wright. Sea Breeze. Visas.'

'I will need time too, Ros. Given what transpired with Lucky and Inspector Patel.'

'How is Inspector Patel?' I interjected.

'He's in critical condition. As soon as he is cleared, he's going back to the UK.'

I nodded.

'I have no idea who I can trust in and out of this office,' David continued. 'I'll have to handle everything myself. We're looking at a couple of months at least.'

'I can help you with the legal work, David,' said Alistair.

'Thanks, Alistair. I'll organise a press conference to say that the case cannot be prosecuted without a key witness. It's not a lie, and it'll buy us some time.'

'What do I do in the meantime?' I said. 'Mark is coming to Sea Breeze this afternoon.'

'I could use it as an opportunity,' said David. 'I'll show him your signed affidavit detailing everything that's happened, and make it clear that the case hinges on your decision to testify against him — which you don't want to.'

'Like a restraining order,' I said.

He nodded. 'It's basically a legal document pointing to Mark as the main suspect should anything happen to you.'

I looked at Alistair. He nodded his approval. I felt a pang of guilt at the thought of betraying Mark, but couldn't think of another way out. 'Okay,' I said.

When Mark arrived at Sea Breeze on Monday afternoon, the sun sparkled like a glitter ball and surfers dotted the horizon. Had it been a scene from a movie, the sky would have been monochromatic, the rain so heavy you could barely see your hand in front of your face. We sat in the kitchen. I cradled a cup of rooibos tea with a slice of lemon.

'Sorry about the head,' he said, reaching out to touch the plaster.

'Don't touch me,' I said, leaning back in my chair.

'You weren't supposed to be part of the convoy, Wrighty.'

'And what if I was part of the convoy? Would you have done anything different?'

'What does it matter?'

'It matters to me.'

'Why were you there?'

'Lucky asked me to go with him.'

'You were fond of him. I was too.'

'You don't murder people you're fond of, Mark.'

'I looked after Lucky for many years, Wrighty. Not in the conventional way, but I gave him an opportunity to earn money instead of beg for it.'

'You think that exploiting a homeless orphan is akin to opportunity?'

He shook his head and tapped the table with his knuckles. 'Wrighty, Wrighty, Wrighty,' he said.

'What?'

'Miss High and Mighty. It's always been so easy for you to point fingers and judge from the luxury of your ivory tower.'

I lost my composure and kicked the leg of his chair. 'That is fucking bullshit,' I said. 'You deserve to be judged. You're a fully grown man who chose a life of violent crime for financial gain, only to discover that the source of your greed had nothing to do with money and everything to do with the high that you've been trying to recreate since your Koevoet days.'

'You have no idea what it's like out there.'

'I was gang-raped, my ouma was murdered, and I witnessed you murder a seven year old child who is running drugs for you because he has no food and no home. I know exactly what it's like out there.'

He leaned forward and narrowed his eyes. 'Do you have any idea how many homeless kids are out there? Don't answer, I'll tell you. There are thousands. And tell me this, Wrighty, what kind of future do you think they have in this country? Don't answer, I'll tell you. They have no fucking future. And you know why? Because Nelson fucking Mandela and his ANC cronies have lined their pockets and sold out their own kind. There may not be apartheid anymore, but those kaffirs are worse off than they've ever been.'

I put my hands over my ears and shook my head.

'Oh, come on Wrighty, don't tell me that you still have a problem with that word?'

Post-apartheid, the use of that word, kaffir, was no less prevalent, but, unlike apartheid days, when it was used derogatorily, the context had changed. After the rise in violent crime, blacks had been at the forefront of every story of rape, torture, and murder, and the ignorant hatred associated with the word had been usurped by legitimate fear. *Kaffir*. A verbal defence for acts beyond justification or comprehension.

'Yes, I still have a problem with that word because it's a huge generalisation. I know plenty of Africans who are good, decent people.'

'The educated ones, maybe,' he said.

'Lucky wasn't fucking educated, Mark, and he was a good person trying to survive in a shit hole of a world with people like you.'

'When I tell you that I was the best thing that Lucky had, I fucking mean it. Tell me, Wrighty, would you rather have him exploited by paedophiles or running drugs for me?'

'Neither,' I said.

'That's because you want to live in an ideal world, Wrighty, and there is no such thing in Africa.'

'I could have improved Lucky's life, if you'd given me the chance.'

He shook his head and laughed. 'You mean adoption?'

I nodded.

'And what about all the other Lucky's you come across in your career, Wrighty? Because there'll be more than you can keep count of, trust me. You have to be ruthless to be a criminal lawyer, and you have to be ruthless to survive this strain of African madness.'

I chewed my lip and willed the tears to stay put.

'And while you are tough, you don't have a ruthless bone in your body.'

'That's right, she doesn't,' said Alistair, walking into the room.

Mark pushed his chair back and stood up. 'This has nothing to do with you,' he said.

'I should have done something to stop you when I had the chance,' said Alistair. 'But I didn't, out of respect for Ros and what she went through.'

'Don't kid yourself, Alistair, you did nothing because you're weak.'

Alistair smiled. 'You might not want to bait me when you hear what I have to tell you.'

'Give it your best shot,' said Mark.

'I met with David Dunstan this morning and told him

everything,' I said.

Mark stared at me and frowned. 'What do you mean by everything?' he said.

'She means everything,' said Alistair. 'The attack and subsequent cover-up, the ambush, you shooting Lucky and trying to implicate Ros in the whole sordid affair.'

'She wouldn't,' he said to Alistair. 'You wouldn't,' he said to me.'

'I did,' I said.

'To what end, Wrighty?'

'To neutralise you, and to put an end to this secret that you're wielding against me to get away with murder.'

'You expect me to believe that you've ended your career before it even begins?'

I took my tea and walked over to the kitchen window. The Indian Ocean glistened beyond the wall that was originally built for aesthetics, but had since been fortified for security. 'When I was eight years old,' I said, 'there was a sign outside the Wimpy Bar that said "Net Blankes." I asked my mother what it meant, and she told me that apartheid was a rule that I had to obey.' I shook my head at the memory. 'So, I refused to eat my food in protest, because I knew it was inherently wrong.' I turned around and faced them. 'Now, nearly two decades later, I realise how naïve I was. But, while I have learnt that the situation is much more complicated than right and wrong, and there are a thousand shades of colour between black and white, I also realise that I'm still the same little girl who wants to live in a world where right and wrong is uncomplicated.' I sighed. 'And Mark is right when he says I'm not ruthless enough to survive Africa. And Alistair is right when he says I have locked myself away at Sea Breeze for the last three years, hoping and praying that things will get better — rationalising the violence and scrutinising the concept of white guilt, as if I deserved what Maleven did to me. But when you say that I'm insane for ending my career before it begins, I see it another way. I look at how ruthless you've become to survive in this place, and I think that you are the one who is insane.'

David Dunstan walked into the kitchen with two uniformed officers behind him. 'Mark Muller, I am here to advise you that Rosalinde Wright gave testimony against you this morning. This is a signed affidavit detailing what she told me.'

Mark took the affidavit and scanned through it. 'This is not a basis for an arrest.'

'No, but it is the basis for a new case against you, should Rosalinde become a key witness.'

'Wrighty won't testify against me.'

'If any harm comes to Rosalinde, this affidavit implicates you as the key suspect,' said David.

Mark ignored him and addressed me. 'You know that I would never do anything to hurt you, Wrighty.'

'You've already hurt her,' said Alistair, 'and I'm not going to let you do it again.'

'You're not hearing me, Alistair. Do you really think that I'm the only one affected if Wrighty testifies against me? I'll answer that for you. I'm not. There are powerful people who stand to lose a lot of money if my operation is exposed and I go down. If you let Wrighty testify against me, you're signing her death warrant. Not by me, but by the people I'm in business with.'

Alistair shook his head and sat down. 'Fuck you, Mark. Fuck you.'

'We can protect you, Rosalinde,' said David.

'No, they can't, Wrighty. Don't listen to them.'

'Get him out of here,' said Alistair, 'before I do something I regret.'

The two policemen escorted Mark outside, and David sat opposite me.

'He's trying to scare you, Ros.'

'What if he's not?' I said. 'Is it worth finding out?'

Alistair stood up. 'Can we have a word in the other room, David?'

David nodded. They left the kitchen and went into the next room. I snuck to the door to listen. Alistair spoke first.

'I know, Ros. She will never be able to betray him when it comes to the crunch. She feels indebted to him for saving her life.'

'What do you suggest?' said David.

'You and I need to put our heads together. Find a way to take Mark down without Ros's testimony.'

I headed for the front door, hoping to catch Mark before he left. The policemen were flanking his car as he climbed in. I told them that David needed them inside.

Mark narrowed his eyes at me. 'I'm not trying to scare you, Wrighty. It's the God's honest truth.'

'I know,' I said. 'But Alistair isn't going to let this go, and the case isn't going away — with or without me.'

'How do you know that?'

'We can't talk now. I need you to drive around the block a couple of times, and come back here in twenty minutes.'

'What about Alistair?'

'I will talk to him.'

I watched him drive away, and walked into Alistair at the front door.

'After everything he's done, you still have feelings for him.'

I shook my head. 'That's not true.'

'He knows how to manipulate you, Ros. Why can't you see that?'

'He's not manipulating me, Alistair.'

'Yes, he is. I know you, Ros, I can see it in your face.'

I put my hand on his arm and whispered in his ear. 'Alistair, you need to trust me. I have an idea.'

He frowned at me, but nodded his agreement.

'Here comes David,' I said.

'Ros, Alistair, I think we all need some time to decompress and think about the best way forward.'

'Good idea,' I said.

Alistair thanked David and shook his hand.

'Don't mention it. I'll be in touch.'

Inside, I told Alistair that Mark was coming back.

'Tell me you're joking, Ros?'

'Hear me out, Alistair, I have a plan.'

I gave Alistair a quick overview of what I was thinking.

'Are you insane? He'll never go for that.'

'I think he will.'

'Okay, Ros, here's the thing. Maybe I don't want him to go for it. Maybe I want to see him pay for his crimes instead of getting away with them. The thing I don't understand, is why you are so intent on helping him?'

'I know you hate him, Alistair. But you heard what he said. I will end up being a target if this case goes forward.'

Alistair held my arms. 'No, Ros, not if we find another way.'

'There is no other way, Alistair. The damage has been done. He's in this mess and he's dragged us in whether we like it or not. This is the only way out.'

'Are you getting cold feet, Ros?'

'What? No! I love you, Alistair. I love you and I want to marry you. I'm doing this because we have a child on the way and I don't want this hanging over our heads. I'm doing this because I'm sick of having Mark come between us, and because I still feel indebted to him for saving my life, and I want to pay it off once and for all so I, scrap that, we, can move forward.'

'Sweetheart, you don't owe him. I wish you could see that.'

'I'm loyal to the death. You know this about me.'

He nodded and wrapped his arms around me. 'I know. I know.'

The intercom buzzed.

'He's here,' I said.

He kissed me and said, 'Good luck convincing him.'

'Where are you going?'

'Upstairs. Unlike you, I can't bear to look at him.'

I nodded. He turned to leave. 'Alistair?'

'Yes.'

'I love you with all my heart.'

He smiled and nodded.

I woke up the next morning with a head full of ideas and a belly full of optimism. Outside on the verandah, accompanied by the soundtrack of waves and squawking seagulls, Alistair brought a silver rack of wholewheat toast and two glasses of orange juice. While we talked about our plans, we wrote a to-do list.

'My first port of call is to the immigration consultant, followed by Henry Malvern. Oh, and I need to call Mohini,' I said as I scribbled down names of people to call.

'You're forgetting the most important thing,' said Alistair.

'What's that,' I said, looking up and biting a slice of my toast.

'Tying the knot,' he said.

I leaned back and smiled.

'Are you happy for me to organise it?' he said.

'Absolutely,' I said. 'Just promise me it'll be small.'

'Scout's honour,' he said, holding up his right hand.

I phoned my immigration consultant first and told him my plans, followed by a discussion with Henry Malvern, who wanted to talk about my proposition in person at his office in Joburg the following week. My last call was to Mohini. Vijay answered and made small talk before she came to the phone. Her voice was as comforting as a hot bath and my smile, then tears, could not be contained.

'Lindy?' she said.

'Yes.'

'Oh, Lindy, I'm so happy to hear your voice.'

I asked her if she would accompany me to Joburg the following week. Leaving on Saturday morning.

'Joburg?' she said.

'I have a few surprises up my sleeve,' I said. 'Please, say yes.'

She agreed. I felt happier than I had for a long time.

CHAPTER 60

Mohini and I landed at Joburg airport on a Saturday morning, and drove to Pretoria in a rental car.

'I'm intrigued, Lindy. What is in Pretoria?' said Mohini.

'You'll have to wait and see,' I said.

We arrived an hour and a half later, having taken a few wrong turns along the way. Once I'd parked the car, I blindfolded Mohini with an orange ribbon and led her to her first surprise.

'Okay, Mo, open your eyes,' I said.

I removed the ribbon from her eyes and she blinked.

'Oh my,' she said, 'are those heart-shaped leaves?'

'Ja,' I said. 'This place is called Wonderboom Grove. It is a dense area of fig trees that are over a thousand years old, and the Wonderboom is the oldest sacred fig tree in South Africa.'

'Why have I never heard of this magical place,' she said, rubbing a leaf between her thumb and index finger.

'Well, it's only fair that I get to teach you at least one thing in this lifetime.' I laughed and hugged her shoulders.

The tree was a marvel. Or rather, the trees. For it wasn't a single tree, but a whole family of trees that had grown from a single seed.

'I especially chose Saturday,' I said, placing the orange ribbon in her hand, 'so Lakshmi should be here somewhere,' I winked.

'Lindy, my girl, you are an angel.'

'Speaking of Lakshmi and ribbons,' I said, 'I have some news of my own.'

We wondered through the grove as we talked. I told her that I had continued her Saturday tradition.

'Do you think that the Pippal tree at Sea Breeze will eventually grow to the size of the Wonderboom?' I said.

'As long as you're looking after it,' she said.

'Or you.' I nudged her elbow conspiratorially.

'Lindy, what are you up to?'

We stopped walking and found a place to sit between the mammoth above-ground roots. Moving from the sunshine into the shade made me shiver.

'Okay,' I said. 'I am up to something, but I can't tell you that part just yet. And before I can tell you my good news I have to tell you a bad story from my past.'

'Is this the story you promised to tell me when I left Sea Breeze?' she said.

'No, this happened in my first year of varsity.'

She nodded, and I began the story of Paris and Maleven. The attack and my reasons for keeping it quiet.

She held both of my hands in hers. 'I wish you'd told me, Lindy.'

'I'm sorry for shutting you out, Mo, but...'

'But nothing,' she interjected, 'the only reason you shut people out is because you think you are a burden. Which is fine for strangers and acquaintances, Lindy, but I practically raised you. What did I ever do to make you think you were a burden to me?'

I dropped my head and started to cry, because I knew she was right. She patted my back like a mother pats an infant.

'You need to stop all this secrecy, Lindy, and tell me everything that's happened. I was never able to have children, but for a long time it didn't matter because you were as close to a child as I could come.'

My tears turned to sobs as she spoke.

'Let me share some wisdom of my own, Lindy. While it's noble to put others before yourself on occasion, it is unhealthy to make a habit of it. Believe me when I tell you that you are not a burden to me. The only burden is the one you've been carrying around all these years.'

I sat up and composed myself. 'You're right,' I nodded. 'You, of all people, deserved to know. And I kept it from you because I didn't want to burden you. So, here goes. Léon raped me in my room the night that Alistair came to read Jericho's will.'

She closed her eyes and clutched my knee.

'It started years before,' I continued. 'I caught him raping his maid's daughter at their house in Joburg. He said he would let her go if I took her place. I was so angry and guilty about apartheid at the time that I agreed. Nothing else happened during that trip, but when we returned to Sea Breeze the harassment calls and visits started. I finally plucked up the courage to tell Jericho the night he died. Later on, Alistair revealed that Jericho had suspected, but he died before he had the chance to take action. After Léon raped me, Alistair and I were going to confront him. Fortunately, death intervened and saved me the ordeal.'

'Lindy.' She shook her head and put her hand over her

mouth.

'There's more,' I said. 'Six months after the attack by Maleven, the doctor told me that I would probably never be able to conceive.'

'Lindy, no,' she said, tears flowing down her cheeks and splashing onto our joined hands.

I swallowed back my emotion and nodded. 'I was so preoccupied at the time with surviving the trauma of my attack that it didn't sink in straight away. But, as the years have passed and I've gotten stronger, the prospect of being childless has weighed on me, considering I have lost all of my family already.'

She hugged me, like Ouma.

'But,' I said, disentangling myself so I could face her, 'just when you think that life is moving in one direction, it boomerangs.'

I took two red ribbons from the hand basket and gave her one, then stood up to tie a ribbon around a twisted branch.

'The last few years, I have been tying red ribbons on the Pippal tree and asking for a child.'

Mohini tied her ribbon at the base of a leaf while I spoke.

'I'm not sure what I expected to happen, or if I expected anything to happen, but it became a ritual that soothed and comforted me. A ritual that yielded a seed of hope.'

'To be human is to be vulnerable, Lindy. Sometimes rituals and faith help us feel a little less so.'

I nodded and continued. 'Two amazing things have happened this year. Alistair and I got engaged...'

'Oh, Lindy.' Mohini threw her hands in the air.'

'And,' I stretched the word out like a drum roll, 'I'm pregnant.'

Mohini cupped my face in her hands and kissed my forehead. 'Lindy, my special girl. You deserve to be showered in blessings after everything you've been through.'

She hugged me for the longest time.

'What do you say we tie some ribbons and give thanks to Lakshmi?' she said.

'I'd like that.'

'Lindy,' she said holding me back.

'Yes, Mo?'

'Lesser people would have fallen apart. Thank you for trusting me.'

I nodded.

'Thank you for calling me on my bullshit.' I laughed and blew my nose.

Before Mohini and I flew out of Joburg on Monday, I met with Henry Malvern in his Sandton office.

'Thanks for meeting me on such short notice, Henry.'

'Please, take a seat.' He gestured for me to sit on the sofa.

Linda placed a silver tray of tea and biscuits on the glass table and closed the door behind her.

'I'm about to tell you a personal story that I have managed to keep secret since it happened five years ago, Henry.'

Henry closed his eyes and bowed his head as I told him about the attack. He shook his head and said, 'My God, Ros,' when I told him about how Mark saved me and then covered it up later. When I told him about my decision to testify against Mark, he moved to the desk to dial his oldest lawyer-friend.

'Henry,' I walked over to his desk and put the phone down. 'It's okay. Alistair and I have run through every possibility and angle, and while this decision involves risk and loss, it is the only decision that will remove Mark's leverage over me.'

'But my dear, he sounds like the type of man who will seek revenge.'

'He is, and he may, which is one of the reasons why Alistair and I plan to leave South Africa for good.'

'You've a strength I wasn't aware of, Ros. To still carry yourself with so much humility after what you've been through says a great deal about your character.'

'If Madiba has taught our nation anything, it is that humility is a superpower,' I said, trying to make light of everything.

'Nobody could have blamed him if he had chosen the path of retribution,' he said. 'If only the majority would follow suit.'

'I won't argue with that,' I said.

We sat down and continued our talk on the sofa.

'What about Steadman & Wright, Sea Breeze?'

'Alistair is handling Steadman & Wright, I am handling Sea Breeze.'

'What do you need me to do, my dear Ros?'

I told him about my plans. He agreed that Morris Malvern Group would head the construction and fund my project as one of their charitable projects.

'Do you plan to call it Sea Breeze after the work has been done?'

'Actually, I've been thinking about naming it after Jericho.'

'Something like Jericho House?' he said.

I shook my head. 'Do you know what Jericho means?'

'Something biblical, no doubt,' he smiled.

'That's what I assumed too,' I said. 'But, no, it actually means Moon City.'

'Moon City,' he repeated and nodded his head in approval.

'Considering our country has become a place of perpetual nightfall, the reference to the moon is like a light in the dark.'

He touched his nose and winked. 'That's your name,' he said. 'Jericho would be proud of you.'

'Thank you, Henry. I appreciate you saying that.'

'Have you set up a trust for the day to day running?'

'Yes, I'm calling it "The Lucky Foundation".'

'You really are leaving a Legacy.'

'I hope so.'

'If you need anything else, Ros, anything at all, I'm here for you day and night.'

'Thanks, Henry. You've become a father figure to me, and I owe you a lot.'

'I think of you as a daughter, too, Ros.'

I left his office with a sense of relief.

CHAPTER 61

Mohini and I sat at the kitchen table at Sea Breeze. The greying streaks around her temples glinted silver in the sunlight that streamed through the window.

'I've got something important to tell you, and something even more important to ask you,' I said.

'Your meeting with Mr Malvern?' she said.

'Yes, and no,' I said. 'The long and short of it is that I'm leaving South Africa.'

'Leaving?' said Mohini.

'Yes.'

'For a holiday?'

'No, for good.'

I stopped talking and let it sink in. Emotions flickered across her face like clouds moving over the Drakensberg escarpment.

'Why?' She said eventually. 'I thought everything was finally falling into place?'

'It is. It was. Now that I'm pregnant, I cannot ignore and deny the horrendous violence that goes on everyday. I will not bring a child into this chaos.'

'You have to put your child first,' she said, her eyes moist.

'Yes, Mo.' I reached for her hand.

'Will you keep Sea Breeze?'

'That's what I met with Henry Malvern about, and that's what I need to discuss with you, but before we do, I have a favour to ask.'

'Anything,' she said.

I stood up and opened the cupboard. 'I am craving your vegetable biryani so badly!'

We both laughed.

'The pregnancy cravings have started,' she said.

'I paid a special visit to the Plaza to get the right spices,' I said.

She turned serious then. 'Promise that you'll stay in touch and send me photos after you leave.'

'I promise, Mo.'

She stood up and embraced me. A long, maternal embrace that compensated for all our lost years.

A few hours later, the delicate fragrance of biryani wafted through the house, awakening childhood memories as it drifted. Recreating our ritual, I unearthed the turquoise mat and white bowls from the yellowwood kist, where I stored my Mohini-memories, and laid it out on the shag carpet in the lounge. Mohini joined me on the floor, spooned the steaming biryani into our bowls, and we ate with our hands. My youth, my innocence, my hope was all brought to life with that aroma, that flavour, that ritual.

Afterwards, we sat outside on the verandah with a glass pitcher of icy water between us.

'I want to leave a better legacy than my ancestors,' I said, 'and children are the future of this country. The night I met Lucky, the homeless boy who was going to testify against Mark, was the night I found out I was pregnant. Lucky spoke of death like you and I speak of going to the shop to buy a loaf of bread. It broke my heart, Mo. I wanted to adopt him then and there, take him home with me and mother him until he felt loved and safe. Mark murdered him hours later. I made a promise that night to use my privilege and money to make a difference and leave a lasting legacy.'

'I'm intrigued now. What is this legacy you are planning to leave?'

'I want to divide Sea Breeze into two lots,' I said. 'One lot will be a refuge and counselling centre for homeless children, the other will be a home for you, Vijay, and the kids.'

'But I can't afford to buy Sea Breeze, Lindy.'

'You don't need to afford it, Mo. I am gifting it to you. The refuge centre will be built from scratch, and Henry Malvern has agreed to bankroll the project under the charitable arm of Morris Malvern Group. The main house, yellowwood plantation, Pippal tree, and swimming pool will be yours. For safety reasons and privacy, the two properties will be completely separate.'

'Lindy, I don't know what to say.'

'Say yes. Please. You and Vijay and all the kids can fill Sea Breeze will love and make it a happy home.'

She bowed her head for several seconds and when she lifted it her eyes were moist.

'I tell you what,' I said. 'Why don't I give you some time to phone Vijay and talk it through.'

She nodded. 'Is this really what you want to do, Lindy?'

'Yes,' I nodded. 'I've never been more certain about anything in my life.'

'What if you decide to come back?'

'I'm not coming back, Mo. I can assure you.'

She found me half an hour later with my feet dangling over the edge of the pool. The water glistened and dragonflies hovered like tiny helicopters above the surface. She sat down next to me. I looked at her expectantly.

'I've spoken to Vijay.'

I nodded.

'He says that it's my decision. He will support me either way.'

'Good man you've got there,' I said with a wink.

'Lindy,' she sighed. 'I don't know if I can do this.'

'Tell me why,' I said.

She shook her head and patted my knee. 'Let me try to explain,' she said. She looked at the sky as she inhaled. 'Sea Breeze was my home for twenty-two years. But it wasn't ever really mine. It belonged to someone else. I was a visitor. A servant.'

I opened my mouth to speak, but she stopped me.

'Please, Lindy. Don't say anything. Just listen.'

'Okay,' I said.

'This proposal of yours has made me realise something. I feel unworthy. Like I don't belong in a place like this. I am a simple person with simple needs. All of this grandeur and status makes me uncomfortable. Do you understand?'

'Yes, Mo, I understand. Can I say something now?'

'Yes, of course.'

'You have spent much of your life in service to others. You are a natural giver. Apartheid or not, your career would have had service at its centre. Do you agree?'

She nodded.

'Right,' I said, squeezing her hand. Would you agree that you have taught me a lot of things?'

'I hope so,' she said.

'Take it from me, Mo, you have taught me a lot. One such thing is to give and receive with equal humility. You have given to me my whole life. Selflessly. Wouldn't you agree that the true joy of giving is to witness the receiver's pleasure in receiving?'

'Yes,' she nodded and smiled. 'I can see where you're going with this.'

I smiled and softened my eyes. 'Please, Mo, allow me to give back to you. For all the years you have taken care of me. For all the lessons you have taught me. For all of the wisdom you have imparted. Please, accept this parting gift from me.'

She looked into my eyes for several moments before she nodded.

'Does that mean you'll accept my offer?'

'Yes, Lindy.'

'Thank you,' I said. 'You have made my heart very happy.'

We hugged for a long time. A bittersweet hug of love and sadness. The type of hug that said time was running out. The type of hug that united two women who were once divided by the colour fence.

I said a prayer for Mohini as she walked to her car. I prayed for her protection. To never let her become a statistic of violence. To live out her days in well-deserved peace.

CHAPTER 62

Alistair and I married a month later in the Drakensberg Mountains. Although, with eleven official languages in the new South Africa, it was also known as Ukhahlamba, meaning Barrier of Spears, in Zulu. It would always be the Drakensberg to me, and it would always remind me of the last trip I took with my father. The escarpment stretched over a thousand kilometres, with the highest peak tipping eleven thousand feet. The mountains were home to five hundred sandstone caves that contained thousands of works of art by the San People.

Alistair stayed true to his word and kept the guest list small — the most important being Mohini, Vijay and the kids, Henry Malvern, and Alistair's parents. The ceremony took place on a Saturday afternoon in the garden. Vijay's daughters and Mohini wore traditional Indian saris. Each had a different colour. Turquoise, royal blue, pink, orange, and green. All were finished with gold trim. Vijay and the boys wore traditional jodhpuri suits. Alistair wore a black tux and I wore a bohemian wedding dress made of ivory silk chiffon, with a deep V neckline and beaded lace bodice. I wore a matching moonstone pendant that matched my engagement ring.

Because I didn't want any religious overtones, Alistair organised for a female celebrant, by the name of Debbie, to perform the ceremony. She was a jovial woman who embraced the fact that Mohini would be giving me away in the absence of my father. Alistair's parents added an extra layer of support and warmth to the day. Both, at different times during the celebrations, told me how much Alistair had talked about me over the years. Both said how happy they were that we were tying the knot. Neither wanted us to leave South Africa, but both understood why we had to.

After the ceremony, when people were dishing up plates of food, talking, and dancing, Alistair and I found a quiet bench near the river. A gaggle of white geese waddled along the bank, and a family of vervet monkeys primped and preened each other in the branches of a sweet thorn tree. Dramatic mountain peaks cradled our garden valley like protective mothers, and the only sound for miles was the distant echo of the falls and the sweet chatter of yellow bishops and laughing doves.

I rested my head on Alistair's shoulder and sighed. 'Pity we can't have the beauty without the brutality,' I said.

'Having second thoughts?'

'No, feeling sentimental. We take so much for granted, and only realise it when time begins to run out.'

'I know what you mean. I've been thinking about my career, and how much of my life it has consumed. I'm looking forward to starting over again.'

'Reinventing ourselves,' I said.

'It's not going to be easy if we go somewhere like the UK or US.'

'I've been thinking about that,' I said.

'And?'

'The thought of going to another Anglo-Saxon country and getting back into the rat race is not appealing.'

He turned to face me and smiled. 'You have something in mind.'

I smiled and nodded. 'Jericho wanted me to travel the world, and he left me his yacht. What's stopping us from sailing into the sunset and staying in France, or Italy, or Greece for the next few years?'

'Portugal, Spain...' he said.

'Exactly.'

'What about the baby?'

'The baby can be born anywhere,' I said, 'and I've been thinking about what kind of childhood I'd want her or him to have.'

'Bohemian, like your dress.'

'Yes,' I said, 'something like that.'

'I love you, Rosalinde Wright Steadman,' he said and kissed me.

CHAPTER 63

I organised to meet Mark at the Kloof gorge — a quiet place where nobody would recognise us. When I arrived, he was sitting on a ledge that jutted out over the canyon. An African crowned eagle glided, circled, then swooped down toward a bush and rose seconds later with a small animal in its powerful talons. A group of vervet monkeys shouted noisily from a nearby tree.

'Do you mind if we sit over here?' I said, sitting on a large, flat boulder.

He shook his head and joined me.

'Is everything prepared?' I said.

He nodded. 'Ja, tomorrow is the big day.'

I reached into my pocket and pulled out the dog tags that he had given me years before. 'I found these when I was packing. I'm sorry I didn't give them back sooner.'

'I want you to keep them.'

'Why?'

'Because I want you to remember the old Mark — the Mark who saved your life, the Mark who tried to love you, the Mark who made love to you on the Skeleton Coast.'

I sighed and took his hand. 'Honestly, you will always be that Mark to me.'

'When are you and Alistair leaving?'

'Soon. I have a few loose ends to tie up.'

'Such as?'

'Lucky,' I said. 'I spent time with him in the office before we left for the safe house.'

Mark rubbed his face and sighed.

'He ate KFC and donuts and watched Tom and Jerry cartoons on TV like a man on death row having his last meal, but he was only seven years old.'

'Are you trying to make me feel guilty, Wrighty?'

'Do you feel guilty?'

'Feeling in my business equals weakness.'

'Well, I have feelings,' I said, 'and while I can't change the politics that caused Lucky's situation, I can change the outcome of those like him.'

'What are you planning?'

'I am building a refuge centre for homeless kids. Morris Malvern is paying for the construction, and I've set up a trust, called The Lucky Foundation, to keep it afloat.'

'For the record, I am sorry about Lucky. If he had stayed in the car, this would have ended very differently.'

'Ja, I know.'

'Our story is ending the way it was supposed to, Wrighty. You deserve someone like Alistair, and you're going to make an amazing mother.'

'What about you? This is not how I wanted your story to end.'

'You were right. The drug business only leads down one

road — more money than I can spend and an early death.'

'Do you have plans?'

'I'm meeting Jake and a few of the crew in Dubai. I don't think I can stop fighting, Wrighty. It's in my blood.'

I sighed and put my head on his shoulder. 'I will miss you.'

'Ditto, Wrighty.'

CHAPTER 64

The phone woke me up. The clock read 4 am.

'Ros, it's David Dunstan. I'm sorry to call at this hour.'

'David,' I said, nudging Alistair and turning on the bedside lamp.

'It's Mark. He was involved in a shoot out near the Ushaka Marine World. Several witnesses saw him flee the scene in a vehicle, but he didn't get far.'

'What happened?'

'His vehicle was burning by the time police found it. The body of a man, matching Mark's description, was inside the vehicle and badly burnt.'

'Oh my God.'

'You might want to turn on the TV. It's all over the news.'

'Where does this leave the case?'

'It's over, Ros. Perhaps it is better this way.'

'Yes, perhaps it is.'

I said goodbye and hung up.

'Is it done?' said Alistair.

I sighed loudly. 'Ja, it's done.'

Alistair shook his head. 'I still don't know how you convinced him to fake his own death.'

'Best to not speak of it again.'

'Hmmm.'

'I need a hot drink. Want one?'

'Please. I'll be down in a few minutes.'

'Okay.'

I lined the coffee machine with filter paper and put the kettle on for my herbal tea. The phone rang.

'Hello?'

'Rosalinde Wright?'

'Speaking.'

'I am phoning on behalf of Mr Mark Muller.'

'Sorry, who am I speaking with?'

'It is better if I remain anonymous, Miss Wright. In the event of Mr Muller's death, he instructed me to pay a sizeable donation to the Lucky Foundation. He said that you would understand.'

'How sizeable?'

'Thirty million rand.'

I held the phone to my chest and swallowed.

'Miss Wright? Are you still there?'

'Yes, I'm still here.'

'I will need the bank details.'

'Of course. Um, can you hold on while I get them?'

'Yes, Miss Wright.'

I found the details and relayed them.

'Thank you, Miss Wright, and goodbye.'

'Thank you,' I said and hung up.

Alistair came in and kissed me on the cheek. 'Was that David again?'

I shook my head and blinked. 'No, it wasn't David.'

He scrutinised me for a second. 'Who was it?'

'A gift from beyond the grave.'

With the bones of our plans taking shape, Alistair suggested that we spend the rest of the day like tourists. We snapped photos of all the sights and scenes we both held dear. An ice-cream at Addington Beach. A cable-car ride at Durban beachfront. Photographs of Picken Chicken, the Edward Hotel, and Valley of a Thousand Hills. A slow drive past the white cottage-style house in Glenwood, where Alistair had grown up, and the sports field where he'd scored his first soccer goal. A walk around Natal University campus, where we'd both studied law and graduated. In the afternoon, we visited my Morris ancestors. Jericho's grave lay in the shade of a Natal mahogany. And, like its relatives in Hill Street, it was chocka-block with Indian mynas; the colonisers of the bird world. My Morris ancestors had a lot in common with those mynas. They had come to the Cape of Storms and conquered, but they had never truly respected it, and failed to turn it into the Cape of Good Hope. They had left a legacy of Empire, and it was up to me to leave a different kind.

I dusted Jericho's grave, and laid a bouquet of white arum lillies on the grey marble tombstone.

'Goodbye Uncle Jericho,' I said out loud. 'Your name won't be forgotten.'

CHAPTER 65

Alistair and I set sail on a Saturday morning. The sun sparkled like a cut diamond. The sky, unblemished by clouds, was brilliant blue. A turquoise dragonfly skimmed the Indian Ocean and alighted on the silver railing where I stood hand in hand with Alistair. I thought of Sea Breeze and shed a tear.

Alistair hugged me reassuringly. 'Did you know that the dragonfly is considered to be an agent of change and a symbol of self-realisation?'

'I do now,' I said, laughing through my tears.

'How about a hot drink?' he said

'Please,' I nodded.

He kissed my forehead and went below deck. I went to the bow of the ship and focused on goodbyes. I said goodbye to the lighthouse that had never really protected me, but had been my eternal constant. I said goodbye to the wild coastline that held so many memories, and promised to tell her stories — good and bad. I promised to never forget. I promised to never look back, to never return. From the moment that I had heard those words, whites only, no blacks allowed, Africa had begun to wage her war on me. She had battled for my soul and nearly won.

As the shoreline disappeared, the wind picked up and the white sails flapped their response. The bow of the yacht dipped and rose through the swells, spraying cool seawater as it went. A pod of dolphins appeared from the belly of the ocean, taking turns to dive and speed alongside the yacht. The sight and mere presence of dolphins filled me with hopeful tears. Friends of the ocean coming to guide me safely away from the place my ancestors had conquered. The place that could have been the Cape of Good Hope, but now was destined to stay the Cape of Storms.

Later, when we sailed into open water, the dolphins disappeared back into the depths, and I let the tears flow. I cried for all of the things I'd lost, and all of the things I had yet to gain. I cried for my beautiful country. Beautiful Africa. Knowing that I'd be hard pressed to find another place more breathtaking or bewitching or wretched.

I patted the urn containing my father's ashes and said, 'Dad. Ouma. Your deaths will not be in vain.'

Alistair patted my belly and said, 'your father and ouma would be proud of you, and this life that we have created is worth more than everything we have left behind.'

Dear Mo,

I hope this letter finds you well.

We weren't sailing very long before I started suffering from the worst morning sickness. Well, to be honest, I have no idea why they call it morning sickness, because I was nauseous twenty four seven. The rough seas didn't help, and I couldn't take any medication. We hired a crew to sail Cabo for us, and Alistair and I flew to Greece.

As I write to you now, I am sitting at a writing desk overlooking the aquamarine water of Hydra — a remote island with no vehicle access, but plenty of berths for yachts. It is absolutely exquisite, and I have never felt so relaxed in my entire life. Alistair says it's like my wedding dress — bohemian and care free. There are lots of artists and writers here, and I am taking a creative writing course with a local writer. I've mostly been writing poetry — in truth it's been like a tap that I can't turn off — and he says I have potential. Hmmm.

Alistair is well. He keeps talking about how clean and safe the island is. We are talking about going to France next. We want to buy a house and prepare a space for the baby. We are keeping the gender a surprise.

It's probably best to save your letters until we have a permanent address. I will keep you posted.

Hugs and kisses,

Lindy xoxo

Dear Mo,

We are finally in France, and my morning sickness is a distant memory. My due date is the 13th April 1999.

Alistair and I have bought a house in Vaucluse — a region in the South of France. It reminds me of a Mediterranean version of Sea Breeze, and it is the perfect place to settle.

Alistair and I are brushing up on our high school French, and Alistair is taking steps to convert his law qualifications so that he can practice again.

The next time I write, I'll be a mother. Send my love to Vijay and the kids, and send letters soon!

À bientôt,

Lindy xoxo

Dear Mo,

It's a girl!!!

Nina Bel Steadman was born on her due date — 13 April 1999 at 13h00 — and weighed 6 pounds and 2 ounces .

Named after Nina Simone, and Bel, which is a Sanskrit word meaning 'sacred wood of the Apple tree'. Wait for it, there's a story behind that.

We have this beautiful tree in our garden, with thorns and fragrant flowers. It reminded me of Africa and Sea Breeze and made me homesick. I asked the neighbour if he knew what it was. Turns out that the previous owners were a couple — an Indian woman and her French husband. She planted the tree because it reminded her of her childhood home in Kerala. Anyway, it is a Bel tree — wood apple — and it is a sacred tree associated with Shiva. All parts of the tree are said to cure human ailments.

Of course, I thought of you and the Pippal Tree.

Nina is a very peaceful baby. She eats and sleeps and smiles a lot. Alistair is smitten! I would love for you and Vijay to come and visit.

Look forward to hearing your news, Mo.

All the love,

Lindy, Alistair, and Nina xoxo

P.S: I'll be tying ribbons every Saturday until you visit!

THE END

READ ON FOR A LETTER
FROM THE AUTHOR, A
THANK YOU NOTE FROM
THE AUTHOR, AND READING
GROUP QUESTIONS.

December 2019

Dear Reader,

I thought of Durban Rickshaws and Tuk Tuks mid school run this morning, and I wondered how on earth I'd forgotten to include them in my novel? I suspect I will have many of those moments now that it's published. In retrospect, this tricky aspect of memory and lost history that has been the most difficult part of writing Cape of Storms.

> *"The infrastructure of my world began to decay when I collided with apartheid during the summer of 1982."*

I chose this metaphor of decaying infrastructure in the opening sentence, because South Africa has literally undergone a process of decay since I left. If you compare a picture of Durban from say the beginning of the millennium to current day you will notice that, apart from the world cup building initiative, the architectural landscape is relatively unchanged, and the literal infrastructure (roads, water pipes and power grids) is so degraded that it is beyond repair. For example, the country now faces a daily schedule of load-shedding (a forced power cut for long periods of time, because the system has not been maintained or upgraded since the end of apartheid in 1994). The reason? A corrupt government who is more concerned with lining its pockets and retaining its power base by keeping the masses uneducated and poverty-stricken. A far cry from Mandela's impassioned inauguration speech in 1994:

> *"Out of the experience of extraordinary human disaster that lasted too long, must be born a society of which all humanity will be*

proud. Our daily deeds as ordinary South Africans must produce an actual South African reality that will reinforce humanity's belief in justice, strengthen its confidence in the nobility of the human soul and sustain all our hopes for glorious life for all."

REDACTING HISTORY, WHILE HISTORY REPEATS ITSELF

Like the opening of my novel, South Africa's historical landscape has undergone a similar process of decay in the two decades since I left. I have watched it happen in real time while I have quietly and diligently worked on this novel. For instance, when the internet made research more accessible, my research got a lot harder because street names from the apartheid era had been changed and any negative news from the post-apartheid era was either filtered or censored entirely for international audiences in order to preserve the rainbow nation vision that Mandela alluded to in his speech. A vision that never came to pass—not for the 5 years when Mandela was president and not in the 20 years since his successors have retained power. With the majority of South Africa's news coverage being censored internationally, much of the world remains blissfully unaware of the reverse racism, pervasive poverty, and violent crime that keeps South Africa in the literal dark and continues to push the country to the brink of disaster.

LEGACY AND LETTING GO

When I first finished Cape of Storms in November 2016, my editor suggested that the conclusion was too harsh and hopeless, and I argued that harsh and hopeless was entirely the point. But in the months I spent thinking about his comment, I realised that the ending was a product of my personal anger over the demise of my cherished motherland. At some point of the writing process, I realised that although I had spent the first 23 years of my life in South Africa, I would eventually have to come to grips with the fact that my South Africa would one day be little more than a memory. And so I pressed on with Cape of Storms, documenting the horrific and honouring the beautiful things that I will forever miss and dream of touching/tasting/seeing/smelling/hearing one last time. I pressed on knowing that it would be more than a work of fiction, more than just a novel; it would ultimately be a testament to a portion of my life, and a sacred memory that is slowly but surely decaying. A life that I was forced to leave behind as suddenly and violently as any political uprising. The memory of a life that I want to share with my children, who were born in Australia, and whose reality is very different to my upbringing in South Africa.

Cape of Storms is dedicated to my motherland, but it belongs to all South Africans (in residence and in exile) who love(d) their country as much I do(did) and who genuinely wanted freedom, equality, and racial harmony for all—a society of which all humanity could be proud.

Bianca Bowers

ACKNOWLEDGEMENTS

I am deeply thankful to the following:
My editor, Richard Gibney, who I have counted on to provide
honest and constructive feedback during my endless rounds
of revisions and rewrites over the last two years. Your valuable suggestions have resulted in a more balanced and tighter
narrative. My husband, who thought up the title and found
the opening quote by Thomas Pringle. My late father, Errol
Bowers, whose real-life childhood trauma inspired the Kenyan
storyline in Cape of Storms, as well as his knowledge of South
African history. Natalie Riviere, a valued reader and friend,
for providing helpful feedback. The beta readers who received
Advanced Reading Copies and reported back on typos and
formatting issues. All the South Africans who filled in forgotten details over the years, especially Mr Lindeque, who remembered that the trees in Hill Street were Natal mahoganies.
The countless books, websites, and people that I've consulted to
ensure that the historical events are as accurate as possible.

CREDITS

I gratefully acknowledge the following sources:
Cape of Storms, by Thomas Pringle
Rivonia Trial Speech, by Nelson Mandela
Cry, The Beloved Country, by Alan Paton
Chris Hani Speech, by Nelson Mandela
Scatterlings of Africa, by Johnny Clegg and Savuka
Historic Lighthouse Plaque, at Cape Point, South Africa
Great Heart, by Johnny Clegg and Savuka
Three classes of people quote, by Leonardo da Vinci

ABOUT THE AUTHOR

Bianca Bowers is an independent poet, novelist, publisher and editor who is currently based in Australia. In addition to authoring several books, Bianca has a B.A. in English and Film/TV/Media Studies and her poems have appeared in print anthologies, online journals and a trailer for a short film.

Among her published works, BUTTERFLY VOYAGE, was an Amazon #1 New Release.

Bianca's second novel, Three Hearts, is planned for release in May 2021.

To stay updated on Bianca's projects, please subscribe via her website:
https://biancabowers.com/contact-bianca/subscribe/

To connect with Bianca online, you can find her on the following platforms:

Instagram: @BiancaBowers_Author

Twitter: @BiancaBowers_BB

Amazon: https://amazon.com/author/biancabowers

Goodreads: https://www.goodreads.com/BiancaBowersAuthor

To hire Bianca as an editor:

Direct: https://biancabowers.com/poetry-editing-and-critique-services/

Fiverr: https://www.fiverr.com/biancabowers

OTHER BOOKS BY BIANCA BOWERS

Butterfly Voyage (Paperfields Press, 2018)
Pressed Flowers (Paperfields Press, 2017)
Love Is A Song She Sang From A Cage (Paperfields Press, 2016)
Passage (Paperfields Press, 2015)
Death and Life (Paperfields Press, 2014)

GENERAL READING GROUP QUESTIONS

+ What was your initial reaction to the book? Did it hook you immediately, or take some time to get into?

+ What was your favourite quote/passage?

+ Which characters did you like best? Which did you like least?

+ How credible/believable did you find the narrator to be? Did you feel like you got the 'true' story?

+ How did the characters change throughout the story? How did your opinion of them change?

+ Did the book change your opinion or perspective about anything? Do you feel different now than you did before you read it?

+ If the book were being adapted into a movie, who would you want to see play what parts?

CRITICAL QUESTIONS

• What do you think are the main themes of the novel?

•What impact does apartheid have on the lives of the main characters?

• What did you think about 8-yr old Rosalinde's reaction when she collides with apartheid outside the Wimpy Bar? How might you have reacted?

• Do you think that Rosalinde's opinion to apartheid and race relations changes over the course of the novel? If so, how, and what are your thoughts about it?

• What impact does the end of apartheid have on the lives of the main characters?

• How did the setting impact the story?

• Did you gain a new perspective about South Africa after reading this book? If so, explain.

• Did the book feel real to you?

• Are there any characters you'd like to deliver a lecture to? If so, who? What would you say?

• How does Rosalinde's relationship with her father change during the course of the novel?

♦ What do you think about Wilstan's final decision?

♦ Which romantic partner did you want Rosalinde to pick? Do you think she made the right choice, and if so, why?

♦ Do you agree with Rosalinde's decision to leave South Africa? If you were in her position, what might you have done?

A NOTE FROM THE AUTHOR

Dear Reader,

As an independent author and publisher, I want to personally thank you for supporting my work.

You might not realise this, but the publishing landscape has undergone significant changes over the last decade:

1. Books now live and die by the amount of reviews they receive.

2. Traditional publishers have the upper hand when it comes to quantity of reviews, because they pay for reviews from outlets like Kirkus (who charge $425 for a single review). This means that independent publishers are even more reliant on the goodwill of readers to leave a rating and/or a few words about the book.

3. Reviews are no longer the task of journalists, nor are they the complicated book reviews we learnt how to write at school. Reviews are now generally reader-generated, and the more simple and honest they are, the better.

So, if you enjoyed this book and wish to help it reach a larger audience, then please consider leaving a brief review on Amazon, Goodreads, or the online store from which you purchased this copy.

Quick links to the main review sites are:

Amazon https://amazon.com/author/biancabowers
Goodreads https://www.goodreads.com/BiancaBowersAuthor

To stay in touch, please subscribe to my newsletter for updates as well as a free PDF version of my poetry book, Pressed Flowers:
www.biancabowers.com/contact-subscribe

Thank you,

Bianca xo

www.ingramcontent.com/pod-product-compliance
Lightning Source LLC
Chambersburg PA
CBHW020001120726
47903CB00004B/1080